A Bruce Hardin Mystery

Stolen Lives

Body in a Trash Bag

BILL HANKINS

The Demons of Draiocht is the third installment to
The Captain of Nemain's Revenge series.

This book is intended for mature audiences.
These characters are morally grey.

It contains some sensitive elements such as violence, torture
scenes, implication of sexual assault and child abuse, profanity,
abuse, slave trade, sexual explicit scenes, death, suicidal thoughts,
and race related discrimination.

PRONUNCIATION GUIDE FOR MAP

Samsara: sam-SAHraw
Kheli: KHEE-lih
Carriwitchet: karr-e-wIHtch-eht
Brettania: brit-AY-ni-ah
Koi No Yokan: koy-noh-YOE-khahn
Draiocht: drah-ou-SHET
Keraunos: kAIRa-ounohs
Toska: TUH-skah
Sumerian: suh-mAIR-ian

ANOIA
SUMERIAN SEA
NERII CASCADES
ATLAS
DEAD MAN'S WASTES
QUARAFA
RUINS OF OLD KALON
SAMSARA
CARRIWITCHET ISLES

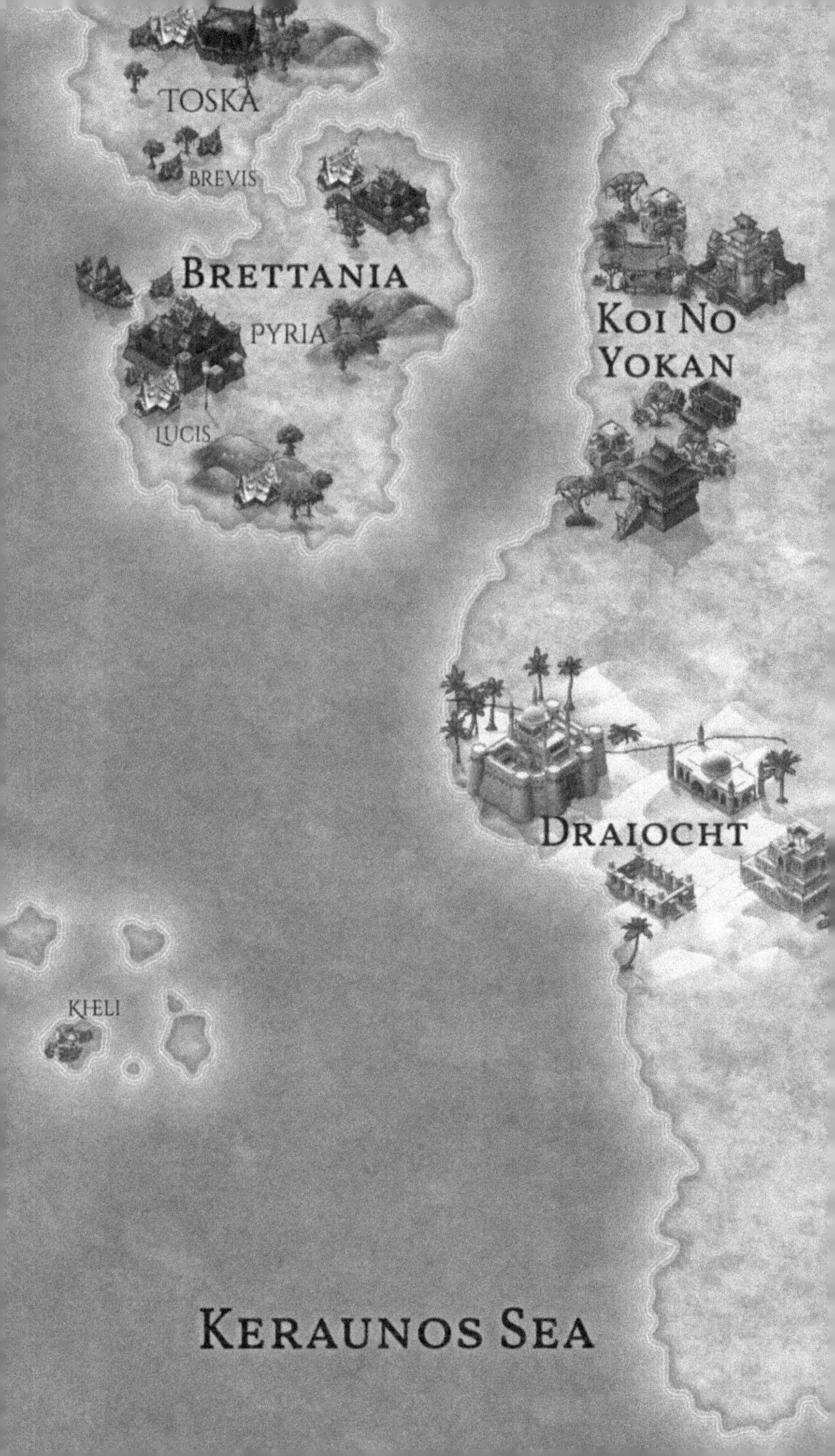

TOSKA
BREVIS
BRETTANIA
PYRIA
LUCIS
KOI NO YOKAN
DRAIOCHT
KHELI
KERAUNOS SEA

MCKENZIE A HATTON

Editing by Rachel Ohm (www.rachelo300.wixsite.com/website/work)

Cover Design by Maria Spada (www.mariaspada.com)

Scene Art by Hanna @sovana.art

❀ Created with Vellum

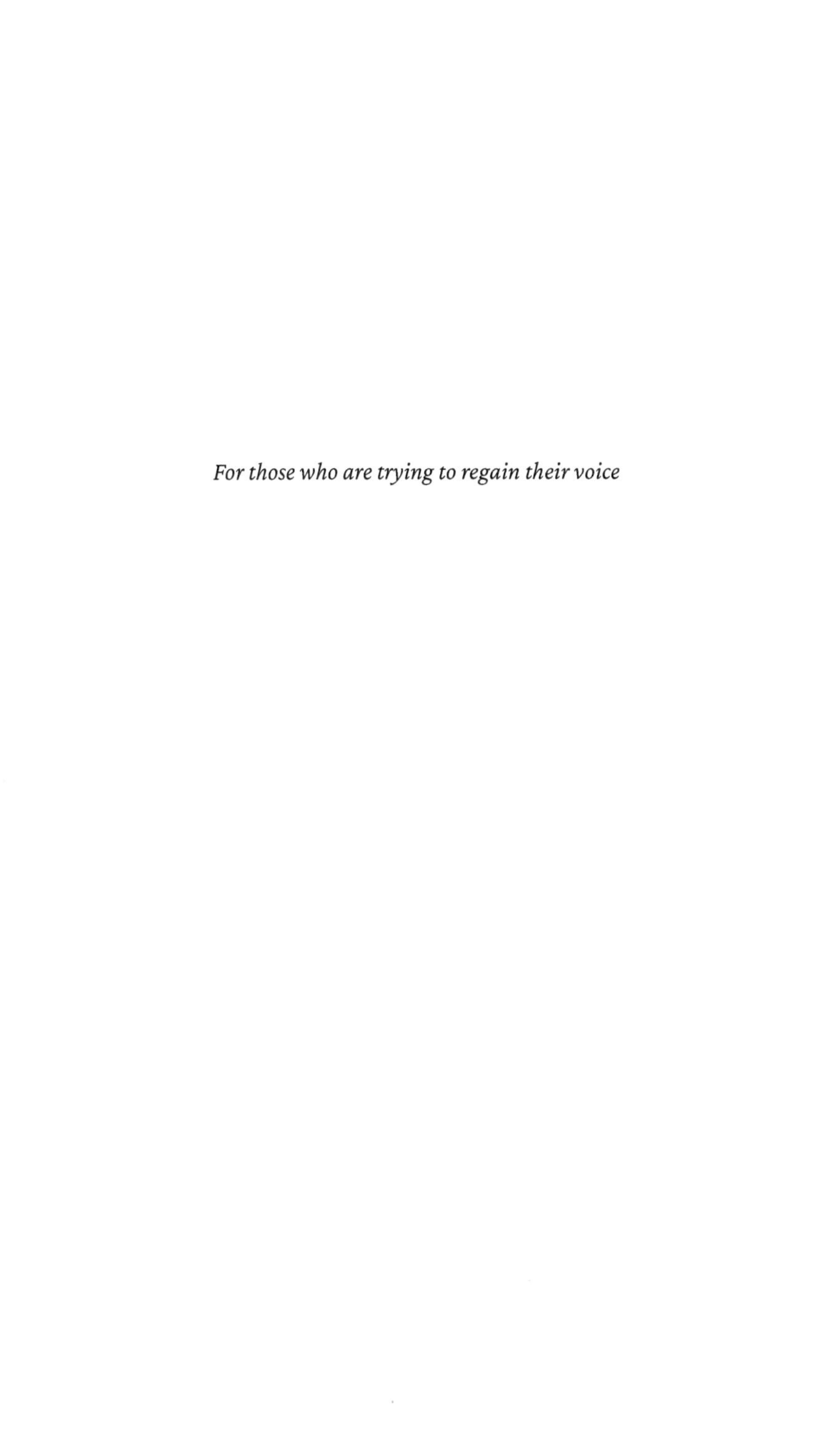

For those who are trying to regain their voice

Part One

RED

BIRD & BEAST

"Once upon a time, centuries before you were born, my sweet," her mother started a story Kendall had begged for. The first of many. This one she called the bird and the beast.

Kendall snuggled into her mother's side, the hearth warming them as snow blanketed the balcony outside.

"There lived a girl born with wings and she learned to fly." Kendall's heart swelled at the thought of flying, the wonder of it bringing her untethered joy. "Her people believed her to be the daughter of Rán, since only the sun god could create a creature that would travel to the heavens. Her people loved her. They worshiped the very ground she walked on. Foreigners came by boat, by cart, by horseback, all to see her fly above them. They brought gifts, jewels, animals, clothing, all to honor her as the daughter of Rán."

Kendall's brows drew together, confusion making her little mind spin. "But we worship Davina and the other two goddesses. Who is Rán?"

Her mother smiled sadly. "An old god. He ruled long ago, even before the winged girl was born, but her people didn't know that. They still believed their old gods watched over them."

Kendall's heart ached with sympathy for the winged girl's people. How did they not know? But before Kendall voiced her question, her mother continued the story.

"Though loved by everyone, many desired her. Her claim to the throne threatened men of great stature, to rule as the gods commanded, but they found a way around it. A man with scars across his arms, marks for every kill he'd made in the hunt and in battle, convinced her to marry him. He wished to control her influence over the people, ruling over them through her, but she was too young to understand such things."

Kendall perked up. "How old was she? Was she like me?"

Her mother chuckled. "Not quite, dear one. She was thirteen, but not yet of age to be married, so the scarred man had to wait until she was old enough."

Kendall's nose scrunched. "He sounds like he's old."

"He was, but he was charming enough to win her over. But while he waited, she flew through the skies as often as she could. Until one day she found a boy alone in the desert. He was her age and very skinny. She coaxed him out of the hovel he lived in, caring for him. Soon, she took him to her city. The boy was infatuated with her, following her wherever she went. The scarred man did not like the boy since he saw the child as a future threat to his plans. So, he ordered his men to kill the boy."

Kendall gasped, but didn't dare to disrupt the story further.

"But the boy had a secret. When he was threatened, he changed into a monstrous beast, too strong for any man to slay. He cut down the men trying to kill him and ran away. He didn't want the winged girl to see him like that. When she couldn't find him, she ran to his hovel to see him still in his beastly form, licking his wounds. One man had stabbed him in the shoulder. The winged girl ran to his aid, collecting supplies to help, then returned to him. He relaxed at her touch, letting her mend his wounds and feeling comfortable enough to shift back into a boy."

Kendall snuggled in closer to her mother.

"The winged girl understood she couldn't bring him back to the city again, so instead she visited him, bringing him food and clothing when possible. They grew to be best friends."

She looked up at her mother, feeling the warmth of such a thought. A best friend. Her cousin was a bit like that, but she was a girl and couldn't turn into a beast.

"Then what happened?"

"Well, the years went on and eventually their friendship grew into more, but as she grew closer to marrying age, the scarred man grew impatient, forcing the priests' hands and allowing her to marry before the law permitted."

Kendall didn't quite understand why, but sadness spread across her mind. It was as if she could feel adults trying to take her childhood away from her too soon. That empathy bled into her bones until a tear fell from the corner of her eye.

"But when the boy heard of this, he refused to allow it to happen."

Relief flooded her chest.

"He ran into the city in his beastly form, searching for the winged girl. He tried to convince her to come with him, to run away, but she refused, knowing what the scarred man would do to her people if she left. The boy tried to kill the scarred man instead, but he failed. Too many of his men were in the way. So, the boy ran, but he didn't realize his presence inspired the people, thinking the beast was an omen from their gods. The citizens turned on the scarred man, rising and ransacking his home."

Kendall bit at her nails nervously as she pictured all the destruction and chaos.

"But the scarred man raged, unleashing his fury on the winged girl, determining he no longer required her. The rioting distracted him long enough for her to escape, flying into the desert in search of the boy. She found him, but the scarred man had followed her, bringing an army with him. The boy tried to defend himself and the girl, but there were too many of them. The boy perished in the desert and the girl was shot down from the sky."

Kendall's heart dropped, the tears flowing freely now. The story resonated in her heart and soul, as if she felt her own body falling to the ground.

"You see why I did not tell you this story sooner, my sweet?"

She didn't understand. All the stories her mother told her before had happy endings. Why tell her this one?

"Do not fear for the winged girl and her beastly boy. They will be reunited in the next story."

Hope eased her chest, making her look up at her mother. "They come back?"

"Many times. I will tell you about each one."

Kendall wiped at her tears with the back of her sleeve. "Do they all end that way?"

Her mother leaned over her, kissing her forehead gently. "We shall see."

CHAPTER 1

WE'RE ALL MAD HERE

ROSE

Quiet, child.

Rose Davenport had spent most of her life with a gag around her mouth.

You wouldn't want to cause harm, would you?

Her mouth was used to the dryness, the thirst that came with having cloth between her teeth for hours.

After all, you're the reason your mother is dead.

Her tears had dried. Spent since they stuffed her in a dusty hold they called a cell. The ropes around her wrists and ankles burned with the extended use, causing red irritation to build up on her skin. Tendrils of gold fell into her face from the failing braid. Although, the gag they wrapped around her head did its part to keep her hair back, too.

Before she could think to sing away from the man three times her size, he had a hand clamped over her mouth. If she had time to struggle, she might have kicked him in the trousers and ran as fast as her legs would take her.

But he transported them directly to her captors. The two men were more than prepared to deal with her. They didn't even speak to her. One had a stoic, unreadable face, the other wore a smile of poison, as if her capture was the single most important thing to happen to him.

Maybe it was.

Rose didn't know why she was here, wherever here was.

There was sand, and lots of it. The air was drier than she had ever felt before, stealing the moisture from her pores.

Be useful, child. Get him to tell me the truth.

Rose clamped her eyes shut against the memory, her father's requests that grew into demands over the course of three years. Shutting her eyes only made things worse. Her father's voice filled her head on a good day. On a bad day, all the voices in her head would join her father's voice.

A pair of boots crossed her vision, stopping just before her knees, yet they didn't disrupt the sand at all. The boots were old, worn, and covered in blood. Rose's eyes trailed up the creature before her. Tight fitting black clothing. Olive skin. A long sword strapped to her back. Intricately braided hair. Brown, striking eyes with wrinkles at the corners from the extended use of glaring.

Isabeya.

Rose really was going mad.

"Get up." Isabeya's bitter tone held no sympathy for Rose's situation, no remorse for her tears.

She stared up at the voice in her head that was — real.

She couldn't speak, not with the gag in her mouth. She couldn't even speak in her mind anymore; the difference between her own thoughts and that of her past lives felt jumbled and uncertain.

Isabeya knew this, yet she glared.

"I didn't tell you to speak. Get. Up."

She wasn't real. The warrior queen was a ringing in her ear, not a flesh and blood person who could do something to her. Why would she get up, anyway? What could she do? Her ankles were bound, she would only fall again. Even if she could stand, what would be the point?

Hum at the door until it opened? She'd tried that. Several times.

Rose lowered her eyes, accepting her fate. She'd die in this hell and get reborn into another one. It seemed to be her entire existence. Denied happiness in life. Denied peace in death. What could she do?

That boot kicked against her bare feet.

Shock tumbled from Rose as her eyes refocused on the scowling queen. Isabeya lifted her chin, staring down at Rose.

"Get. Up."

Fine. If this mad hallucination needed to see her try, what else did she have to lose?

With a grunt, she lifted her back off the brick wall, moving to raise herself on bound feet. The voice in her head could be helpful for once and cut her bonds.

Isabeya noticed her motion, but she lifted a fingerless, leather gloved hand. "Not on your feet, songbird."

Songbird.

A pang of longing shot through her. James. Her phantom. Her pirate and thief that stole her heart. She had parted from him too soon. Isabeya knew what she was doing, reminding her of all the things she still had to live for.

Or someone—James.

But if Isabeya didn't want her on her feet, what did she want?

As if the queen could understand her thoughts, she crossed her arms and looked at the ceiling. There, a hole let the beating sun in. It was easily thirty feet from the prison floor, too far for anyone to reach.

A dove chose that moment to coo softly as it descended through the hole into the cavernous sand pit below.

A memory hit her. She flew above the officers and townspeople alike, removing her influence from the men and shattering the Minister's control over them.

But she had tried to summon those wings again. They wouldn't come. The voice those belonged to was too distant, hiding from everything.

Rose shook her head, curling in on herself.

Isabeya leaned down to look into Rose's eyes. The woman's stature was small, easily five feet in shadow to Rose's five foot six. But it didn't matter. Isabeya could face Jon and look down on him.

"Soldiers don't sit and wait for someone to rescue them. You have the means. Get. Up." Isabeya's eyes flashed green for a moment, showing her impatience.

Rose slammed her eyes shut, searching inside herself for the scared little girl, or trying to expel the hallucination before her. She did not know.

But the queen's voice didn't go anywhere. "Find her. Make her listen."

Rose reached deep into her mind, tunneling into the faucets that never see the light of day. In one, a shivery creature was curled up, every bit of her dark skin on display. She hugged her legs close to her body, her wings spread out behind her. Unlike the white feathers Rose remembered, her wings were brown like a robin.

The girl looked up at her, no older than fourteen, dirty and terrified. She didn't look to Rose in fear, nor comfort. She just was. They were each other.

A fresh tear rolled down Rose's face. The voices' stories weren't all clear to her, but she understood one thing: they existed in her mind at the ages they died. She had rarely faced this one before.

Rose never even learned her name. She wished she did now as she examined the dirt on her. It wasn't just mud, but also blood, cuts and bruising marred her skin as well.

She died like this?

"What's your name?" Rose said softly, so as not to scare her.

"Skye," she breathed, her voice trembling. She was so very young.

Rose reached out, instinct driving her to place a hand on the girl's knee in comfort. "What happened to you, Skye?"

Skye flinched, her wings bowing, hugging close to her body to shield her. Her head shook, refusing to speak about whatever horrors she endured.

That pair of boots stopped next to her. Isabeya glared over at them with stony features. "Kill her."

"Wha—"

Skye shivered under the attention, folding in on herself even further.

"Kill her? Why? She's a part of me, just as you are."

Isabeya lifted her chin, regret filling her eyes. "You'll kill us all, eventually."

Rose stood, straightening her spine, but before she could respond, another figure came from behind her. Her skin was warm and her hair wavy, but a solemn look of sadness painted her beautiful face.

"It is the only way this stops."

Rose noticed a slight orange aura to the woman. Looking back at Isabeya, there was a similar aura in green, and Skye was red. But unlike the others, Skye's aura bled around her and flickered like it was too weak to exist.

"The only way what stops?"

"The pain." This was a different voice, but it sounded stricken, as if plagued by smoke and time.

Rose turned to see a lithe woman with hair as red as blood. Her frame was athletic like Isabeya's, but she was much taller, with a sort of determination set in the hardness of her jaw. But that wasn't what Rose noticed first.

A fire had burned away half her forehead, one cheek, and the underside of her jaw, leaving melted flesh clinging to her face.

"Scarlett," Rose whispered. She knew the woman even if she hadn't seen her face yet. She had tormented Rose with dark thoughts. Thoughts of rage, flames, fury, and vengeance.

The women all stood around her now, but it was Isabeya, standing shorter than all the rest, who spoke. "You must kill us one by one. Otherwise, it will happen to you too. If we die, you are no longer cursed."

"But you're all already dead. You're just voices in my head. Echoes of my past lives. How can I kill you?"

"Because we are you," the woman with the orange aura spoke softly, dotingly like a mother.

Lani. That was her name.

"Defeat us, and you can use the power we have."

"Defeat you? How can I—"

"By defeating yourself," Isabeya chimed in, crouching to the huddled winged figure. She watched Skye intently, caressing her jaw. Skye leaned into the touch as if starved for affection. Isabeya's gaze found Rose, capturing her there. "Skye is your fear. Your worry for your safety and well-being. You have no need of it because death is unattainable for you, yet she is still here."

"Death is unattainable? What about you? If I kill you all, that sounds like death."

Isabeya rose again. "Not for us."

"When you kill us," Scarlett stated, "we will not die."

Rose's brow crashed down on her face, confused by the ramblings of the voices in her head. Perhaps she really had gone mad.

Not perhaps. She had.

Lani's hand came to Rose's chest, resting on her heart. They felt real enough, as if she wasn't in her head at all.

"We will become a part of you. Not a voice, but a memory. You will see everything we have seen like it was once your own life. Because it was. We are all you. We've only been — shattered."

Rose drove her fingers through her hair, but she didn't feel the tug. This was all in her head. Still, she wanted to rip her hair out to prove she wasn't dreaming.

"I'm sorry." Isabeya caught her attention again. "I'm so sorry. But it will hurt."

"But it is the only way the pain will stop. Otherwise, you will die, and we will be reborn in a new body until one of us is strong enough to finish the job."

A sob crawled up Rose's throat. It was too much. Why must she even do this?

A slamming door jolted Rose from her mind and all her counterparts.

"Awake or meditating?" A graveled male voice had her focusing on the silhouette before her. "I can never tell with these people. It's crazy the amount of people who meditate here. Although for you, I can see the usefulness of such a feat." He crouched before her. His dark hair and stubble reminded her of James. His voice was lighter, as if assuming friendship before he earned it.

But his eyes were dark. Black, really. Pools of unending darkness that swallowed the surrounding light. He grinned, his teeth on display were whiter than anyone truly could have.

"How are the voices in your head doing?" He laughed, crouching before her. "I'm sorry. If you would have asked me a few centuries ago that I'd be asking someone that question, I wouldn't have believed you." He spread his arms out. "But here we are."

Rose narrowed her eyes at the man.

"Apologies, manners." He pulled down the gag around her mouth, letting it dangle around her throat. "I'm Colt. At least, that's what people here call me. If you were to ask certain underground parties, they would call me Astaroth, but that's another story. I'm here because of you." He clapped his hands together, pointing them at Rose, then leaned over, putting a fingertip to her temple. "More specifically, what's inside here. Those little voices of yours are going to set me free."

Isabeya appeared beside him, standing over him with a glare that could cut glass. "He's a demon. He's here to kill us."

Colt's attention followed Rose's sight line, looking straight through Isabeya. "Oh, she's here, isn't she?"

Rose's panicked eyes traveled back to Colt. Could he sense her?

He smiled, but it didn't reach his eyes. He inched closer, whispering, "I know she doesn't like me. Hell, all your past lives are probably warning you about me right now. However, I think if we work together, this could be a beautiful partnership."

Yellow flames flickered into her vision, nearly blinding her. *He's lying. He wants us dead.*

Rose wondered how far she could get into a song before he attacked her. One of those mind-bending ones she used on the officers would do, but he was too close to risk it. But — restraining him first might do the trick.

"You see, if you can get that winged creature inside you under control, we could get this show on the road. Once you've mastered them all, we'll all be free."

Rose hummed quickly, vines finding some kind of purchase in the sand to reach for him. An answering note hummed from his own throat, wilting the vines before they ever touched his skin.

Rose's eyes widened in surprise, jolting away from him as he laughed.

"Did you think you were the only one? Song is an art, not some divine ability only you possess, little birdy." He sniffed. "But I'll forgive you this once. After all, would you really be the Phoenix if you didn't try to escape at least once?"

Rose's hands shook, the trembling hitting her core and disorienting her. Red washed over her vision. No one had ever been as powerful as her. James came the closest, but she defeated him on a primal level. This was a threat she didn't know what to do with.

Would he kill her?

Once he gets what he wants from us, he will.

She felt the trembling in her breath. It had been a while since she felt Skye's fear so viscerally. It was all-consuming, not letting her breathe.

"I see you need some time to come to terms with your new reality," Colt said, putting his hands on his knees and rising to his feet. "But you'll accept it. You have no choice. If you refuse, I'll just ask the next version of you. And on and on, until one of you pulls through. Then you can finally be free..."

The sinister way he said the word "free" made her believe that freedom was only permanent death. That's what he was offering her. She could feel the way his words were all twisted up.

She would kill her past lives in her mind, and he would kill her.

He put his hands in his pockets and strode out the door. "You'll see things my way, birdy. Once my colleague gets his hands on your mind, you'll be begging for my offer. Then the actual work can begin."

The door slammed behind him, and she could feel the shock of it through her entire body.

CHAPTER 2
WARNED ROYALTY
PHANTOM

Phantom's head hit the ship deck, shooting pain running all the way down his spine.

"Get up," Wilson bit out like he did the last dozen times Phantom fell on his ass.

Frustration gnawed at him as he used his legs to propel himself up, swinging the staff in his hands. He was rusty with the bloody thing; a fact Wilson hadn't failed to remind him of.

"If you had practiced, you would not fall."

Of course, the implication was that Wilson would still best him no matter what he did. If he should ever need someone to humble him, Wilson would be first in line.

Anger bubbled with the frustration, making his vision focus on Wilson. He needed one good shot. He had the strength and speed to do so, even if Wilson liked to use it against him. Still, he believed he needed to beat Wilson once.

He charged; staff raised to strike.

Wilson's staff moved more quickly, diverting his energy to the stairs. Phantom rolled down the steps on his ship, landing on his feet like a falling cat, one knee on the ground. He expected the rolling laughter of his crew, but if they noticed his tumble, they did not let on.

The devils were smarter than to be caught in their captain's ire right now. All but Wilson.

"Never lose your staff," he scolded, picking up the ribbed wood from the top steps where Phantom had dropped it. "You think your enemy will allow you to pick it up again?"

Phantom glared at his *kyoshi*. Teacher, being the closest translation, though he liked to think it meant 'pain in the ass'.

"I expect I would put a bullet in his head before it got that far," he grumbled, but not soft enough for Wilson not to hear it.

Wilson pointed the staff down at him. *"Geeuleun bèn rén!"* Phantom had come to find out this insult to mean 'lazy fool', although apparently in Yokan it was more offensive.

He'd been called it several times since he asked Wilson to train him again. To Phantom's approval, many devils took on lessons from the cook as well. He had his hands full, but Phantom didn't hear him swear at his other students so much. No, that delight was for the captain alone.

Phantom stood, spreading his arms out. "Teach me fire stance."

Wilson's eyes narrowed. They'd had this conversation multiple times. It was the one style of *kata* Wilson refused to teach. He believed the old cook had no intention of teaching him something so lethal. Though he could hardly understand what was so dangerous about it.

"Give me one good reason you won't teach it to me."

Wilson tossed the staff in his direction, and Phantom caught it with ease. Then his *kyoshi* was stomping down the steps. "You are foolish and inane. You do not think before you strike and distract easily. I would not choose you even if I only need a dog to guard my home."

What were you just thinking about humility?

Sam's comments proved unhelpful.

Wilson stopped just before he reached Phantom, standing a step above him. "But it is not my choice, boy." Irritation rose like tingling along his flesh. *"Jigoku kata* is not something I can teach." He poked Phantom in the forehead. "It is something known. When you are ready, you will know." Phantom nearly rolled his eyes as the man brushed past. "Ey ah." That meant the lesson was over.

Wilson's cryptic answers remained the last thing Phantom needed right now. He needed to know Rose was safe.

It's been nearly two weeks since he had seen her.

Letters came from Samsara on the feet of crows, detailing their troubles and Sebastian's requests for them to return. But Samsara's hardships were the least of his concerns. Not until he had a whole and healthy songbird back in his arms would he consider their problems.

He stopped responding after admitting the truth. Samsara was marked for death. Get everyone out. Now the responsibility fell to Sebastian.

Robin jumped down onto the deck from the mast, crouched on all fours like a primate.

"Captain? Or is it the captain right now? Is someone else there?"

Phantom let out a frustrated breath at Robin's incessant questions. Ever since he told the devils everything, they inquired constantly. Occasionally, he even let Sam speak to them instead. Sam was growing quite fond of this devil; of his monkey-like antics and peppering questions.

"Is it Sam? Oh, oh oh, I wanted to ask more about Kalon. Is it true you slayed a dozen necromites with your bare hands?"

Phantom pinned a glare on Robin. "It's still me, boy. Shouldn't you be in the crow's nest?"

Robin's face instantly paled at his captain's sharp tone. "I'm sorry, Captain. Just came down for a meal."

Anxiety soured his stomach, thinking about not having a pair of eyes on the horizon. Gritting his teeth, Phantom stepped close to the boy, looking down at him. "You don't leave your post. Is that understood? Wilson will bring up your meals from now on."

Robin straightened. "Aye aye, Captain." Then he turned to climb back up the mast. A glance at Wilson told Phantom that he heard the exchange. He grumbled a bit before wrapping up bread and dried meats to bring up to the boy.

Green assaulted his vision. *You could have been nicer.*

Phantom ignored the comment. "What exactly are you telling the boy?" He didn't even try to whisper. The crew understood he wasn't truly talking to himself. "A dozen necromites with your bare hands? I didn't think you exaggerated your stories."

He especially likes the story of when I wrestled a thunder tiger.

A rare smirk left his lips. "Now I *know* you're lying." He nicked two apples from a nearby barrel before climbing the steps to the quarterdeck. "Thunder tigers are your greatest fear." He took a bite of one apple, offering the other to Earhart, who stood at the helm.

Second greatest fear. Isabeya has firmly declared the first spot as hers.

The thought of Isabeya brought thoughts of Rose, taking away what little joy he had in the conversation.

Phantom looked to the East where the shore lapped against the endless sand dunes to the North and towering stone walls to the South.

The Draiocht watch would not let them dock. It was no longer a bustling country with beautiful cities. Nemain had arrived here too. Necromites were crawling all over the sandy countryside. Any survivors were secluded into a walled off, heavily guarded citadel. An improved sea wall and watchful sentinels blocked the docks, denying entry to unauthorized people.

They had taken a page from Brettania's approach to the apocalypse, and with Phantom's last appearance on their shores, they weren't willing to allow red sails to get anywhere near them.

Phantom was unimpressed with the delay it would cause them. But Rose existed within that citadel. He knew it; he could feel Davina pulling on him to get there. To save her. If only the Goddess of Fate's meddling was this useful all the time.

Phantom looked through his scope to see a small ship with white sails. It had been some time since the devils had raided a ship, and he was itching for violence.

"Sir, why this ship?" Earhart's value resided in many things but witnessing those little details that meant everything was not one of them.

Phantom handed the scope to his first mate. "Take a close look at the name."

Earhart squinted through the scope. "It looks like a pictograph of the sun."

"Exactly. What do the Draiocht people worship?"

"Many gods, really, if Kazeboon is to be believed."

Phantom's voice turned deeper. "But one above them all. Rán, the sun god. And who could claim the king of gods as their own?"

Earhart's blank expression annoyed Phantom.

"Royals. That ship belongs to the royal family."

Earhart's mouth curved into a sinister grin. Finally, he was catching on. "They wouldn't dare turn away a royal ship."

"Ready the men."

Earhart nodded, turning to the crew and spouting orders as fast as the crew could take them.

***

They approached the ill-prepared ship, the sailor's grim faces already peppering the deck as they scrambled for some way to protect themselves.

Serena screeched overhead, flying before them and letting her blue flames lick at the sailor's heads. Phantom whistled, calling her back to his side. She often disappeared now, hunting on her own, or exploring nearby, but she didn't wander too far in the open ocean.

Would that be different once they were on dry land?

Her talons dug into his shoulder as she landed on him, roaring back at the fisherman.

Subtle, as always, Draven remarked. The counterpart that felt of smoke and shadows, yet also bright orange sunsets, had cursed Phantom with his presence. The bitter man plagued his thoughts since the absence of Maahes. A heavy pressure on his chest weighing heavily with each interaction.

"You would know."

"Pardon?" Earhart asked at his side, perking up with his captain's voice.

"Nothing."

Earhart's frown was there, then gone in the next moment. Phantom was grateful for the dismissal of his foul mood. It would only worsen things to mention it.

Lara's concerned brow came into his view. He didn't have time to drop her anywhere, even if she wanted that, but her insistence on helping them find Rose was both endearing and infuriating. What could she do to help?

Her hands moved frantically. "Let me come. I can help." She spoke the words as she signed them, remaining polite to nearby devils. Though it was clear, it had been some time since she'd had to use her voice.

Phantom drew in a breath, wishing anyone could help her, but the devils didn't understand her. "No. If anything happens to you, Rose will kill me." Phantom spoke as he signed as well, just in case he got something wrong, and she needed to read his lips. He cared very little for his crew's understanding of the conversation.

Lara's glare pierced him as her foot stomped at her side. His chest flickered with amusement at the adorable gesture. A sensation he stifled before it could show on his face. He didn't deserve to experience such things. Rose's safety came first.

"She is my friend, too. I want to help."

He locked on to her dark eyes, his hands moving. "I need you here when I get her back. She'll need you."

Her lips pursed, but she argued no further. He used his fingers to gesture to Tick. The silent one came quickly, understanding Phantom's command, wrapping a hand around her arm but giving her a sympathetic look. The ease with which the two communicated without words surprised him.

She relented, letting him lead her to the captain's quarters, which she shared with Sophia. Phantom couldn't be there without thinking of Rose, so he bunked with the devils. Tick locked her in to keep her safe. He wasn't exaggerating when he said Rose would kill him if he lost her.

They closed in on the ship, grappling hooks flying through the air, gaining purchase on the railing of the unprepared fisherman's boat. It was a quarter of the size of Nemain's Revenge, sheltering very few men aboard.

Earhart and Black situated a plank between the two ships and Phantom was the first to step upon it, swaggering to the other side.

The fishermen were unarmed, at least outwardly, but Phantom understood deceptive appearances better than anyone.

Serena jumped off his shoulders, screeching at the men as they ducked away from her, then landing on the highest point of the mast.

Phantom pulled out his sword, scraping against the railing of the small ship. It filled the silence in the air, causing the Draiocht men to step back in unison. Had they no pirates in these waters? Were they so unprepared for an attack?

No, considering the state of the world, they could not be so innocent.

Phantom tossed his head at Earhart, who immediately reacted to his captain, ordering Hyne and Tick to follow him but keeping Black and Clare at Phantom's side. The captain's hand went out, stopping his first mate before he stepped aboard the ship.

"Keep a weather eye out."

Earhart nodded, a grave solemness hardening his features. The look had been there since Phantom lost—

He couldn't think about her right now. He had to keep his head on straight. These men's help depended on their survival. He doubted leaving their carcasses spread out on Draiocht's wall would grant him passage.

Although, it remained an idea he enthusiastically wanted to test.

"Well, don't you all look like a school of sardines surrounded by sharks?"

There was something in their wide eyes Phantom couldn't quite determine. He'd brush it off as a mistranslation considering these men likely didn't know Brettanian, but something was wrong. He sensed it.

"Where is your captain? I'd very much like to speak to him."

"Who wants to know?"

From behind the helm cabin, a woman emerged, skin as dark as a Draiocht goddess, curly hair cascading down her shoulders, but she wasn't in sailor's clothing the way Phantom expected from a female captain. She donned an ivory, gauzy material befitting a princess.

Phantom eyebrows rose high.

"Sita, never thought I'd see you again in this lifetime." He crossed his arms, staring down the Draiocht princess with a stoic expression. A small man Phantom failed to notice babbling in Draion, but upon seeing Phantom's disregard, he changed to Brettanian.

"You will address Her Highness as Amariah Sitamun from the House of Rán, rightful heir to the throne of Draiocht, chosen by Sobek himself to watch over the realms of men."

Phantom's eyes drilled into Sita as her chin lifted. "Sweet Nemain, that is quite the mouthful. Apologies Princess, but I think I shall keep calling you Sita. Saves time."

Her eyes narrowed. "And where was your concision when you were persuading me to join your crew?" Phantom was aware of the curious eyes of his devils. He had not told them of his failure or the brawl he started in defense of the Princess's honor. Of course, that night he still took a devil home. It just wasn't the one he expected.

A sharp pang zapped his heart at the thought of Jon, followed by piercing anger at the devil's betrayal. Phantom didn't let any of this show on his face, a smirk etching his mouth where a frown should be. He spread his arms out wide.

"I've grown busier since we last spoke. Time is of extreme importance now."

"I couldn't agree more." He recognized that look. Even one conversation with the Princess two years ago and he understood that if she showed any emotion on her face, it meant so much more than it seemed. And her eyebrows had risen.

She wanted something.

"Join me in the cabin, Captain. We have much to discuss." She turned, not waiting for his response, but expecting his obedience. He didn't enjoy being ordered about, but as Princess, she couldn't help it. It was the possibility of entrance into the city that had him nodding to Black behind him and following Sita.

Black understood the order, sheathing her weapon, but remaining close by. The fishermen before them offered little danger, but a vigilant eye was always necessary.

He entered the cabin to be greeted by Earhart, Hyne, and Tick on their knees, gagged and restrained with two Jon-sized Draion men towering over them.

Palace Guards.

He recognized the uniform after running from them, but he didn't consider their size.

"I don't take well to snooping aboard my ship, Captain. They'll be released to you when you leave."

"How kind," Phantom drawled, but it was apparent his devils were unharmed, so he continued to the desk at the back of the dimly lit cabin. Everything in the cabin still screamed fisherman, like the excess rope and wire lying about in piles or the pungent smell. The desk was simple, nothing more than a few planks of wood with a candle and papers neatly stacked in the middle, but there were rings and marks on the wood that suggested other objects used to inhabit it.

"Modest accommodations for a princess, don't you think?"

She lowered herself to the old wooden chair behind the desk, waving her hand to suggest he sit in the opposing seat. He refused, opting to stand before her.

She sighed heavily. "Most of my people are dead, Captain."

He turned his head. "I warned you." He knew the signs, just like he knew in Koi No Yokan. Just like he knew on Samsara. Draiocht's fate had been sealed. "I have to admit, I didn't think you'd save any of them."

"That's precisely the problem. I am in debt to the saviors of my people. They had this citadel made before anyone knew Nephthys was coming. I blame myself for not heeding your words." A darkness fell over the Princess's face, a guilt he recognized flooding her. "But now, the royal family is dead, save for me."

Phantom's brows rose high on his forehead. "Then why aren't you in your palace, Princess?"

"Because the scarab of Rán is missing. It has been for years now. We cannot instate a new monarch without the gods' approval."

Phantom had heard of the scarab; he'd coveted it at one point. A blue and violet stone that was said to turn to solid gold when possessed by the rightful heir of Draiocht. People believed Rán's blood ran through the royal lineage, making their dominion a sacred birthright. A tradition the people took very seriously.

"So, you came out to sea on a fishing boat because—"

"I have reason to believe our new saviors have the scarab as a way to block my rule."

"Who are these saviors?"

She stood, apparently disliking Phantom's advantage over her. "How did you know the necromites would come?" Phantom narrowed his gaze, recognizing her ire. "You knew, and they knew. Something that even the priests could not see. How. Did. You. Know?"

He raised an eyebrow, aware of the guards at his back. "Are you suggesting I possess such a treasure? I assure you, if I had the scarab, I wouldn't be standing before you. I'd be in your city, hopefully leaving with what I came for."

"And how badly do you want what you came for?"

He held her eyes. "Desperately."

She lifted her chin, the battle of wills becoming tiring. They clearly needed each other, even if his reasons weren't yet stated.

"Listen, Princess," Phantom drawled, not missing the way her body tensed at the title. "I am a simple man. I want simple things. Like to get into your city. With accommodation, of course. I realize you set a trap for me, so you need something from me as well. Just tell me what it is, and I'll decide if I would be so inclined to grant your request."

She scoffed. "Sounds like you already named your price. I wager there is very little I might ask that you would deny me."

He snapped forward, placing his arms on the desk and leaning down until they were at eye level. Her guards flinched forward, pulling on their swords, but not completely advancing since he didn't touch her. They were fools not to recognize his threat to her. If they had, they'd restrain him as well. Or they would try.

"Careful, Sita. I like you, but not that much, and I care very little for the fate of Draiocht. If you cross me, I won't hesitate to lay your cold body at the gates and force my way in with fire and destruction. The necromites will be the least of your worries."

She eyed him for a long moment, letting the threat hang in the air before she relaxed, a soft smile on her lips.

"That's exactly what I needed to hear, Captain." She gestured for him to sit again, but the tension stiffened his body, putting him on edge. He wanted a fight. For her guards to lunge, so he had someone to blame when he painted the deck in blood. But the stoic, regal look on her face returned, unwavering, until he forced himself to sit down.

He adopted a relaxed composure, propping his elbow on the arm of the chair so he could run it over his scruffy beard.

She reached the table behind her, and he noticed that she'd failed to sit with him. She came back with a bottle of rum, filling two glasses and handing one to him. He accepted, but swirled the liquid in the glass rather than tasting it.

"I need that scarab, Captain. I propose an alliance. One where I get you into the city, and you get me that scarab."

His gaze travelled to the guards at his back. They truly stood tall, unnaturally so. They had to hunch just to fit into the cabin. "Your giants can't get it for you?"

Sita's face flickered with surprise before leveling out. "My giants have their own troubles in the citadel."

Phantom leaned back in his seat, crossing his arms. "Well, leave nothing out."

Sita's face twisted in discomfort. "I only have a few at my disposal. Most have chosen current ascendancy as their sovereign."

An eyebrow rose on his face.

"Now, do we have an accord?" Sita bit out the words, losing patience with him, no doubt.

Phantom put a finger to his lips, an idle habit. The deal was uneven. She would get her country back and he got into the citadel. He needed that regardless, but she had no choice but to accept his terms. Not without an army or the loyalty of her people.

"Should I be inclined to accept, I would expect that our alliance would continue to benefit us both until my departure? I expect shelter for me and my devils, along with food or other supplies, as I see fit."

Sita offered a gentle shrug. "There are barracks reserved for my guard that I can spare temporarily. Food will be rationed and delivered there." She lifted a hand. "I will provide you with what you need, Captain. If you're half as good of a thief as your reputation proclaims, I'm sure you'll have the scarab in my possession soon." An underlying threat infused her tone; failure on his part would lead to complications.

Even as a pirate, he wasn't about to go back on his word. There was a code among thieves, and he didn't want to lose his credibility.

Phantom stood, extending a hand. "I do believe we have a deal."

She reached for his hand, but he drew it away. "Just to be clear, if this deal should endanger any of mine," he paused, letting the meaning of the word settle with her, "our business is finished."

Her face gave away nothing. "Agreed."

He took her hand in a firm shake. The next second, Sita nodded, releasing the devils.

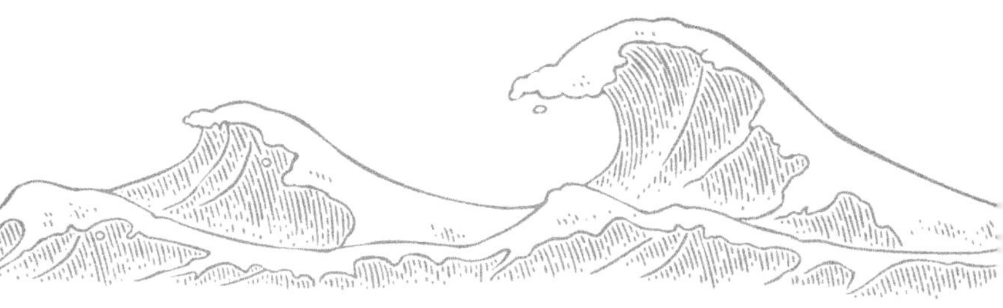

CHAPTER 3

CONSEQUENCE

SEBASTIAN

Sebastian found it hard to look at Ravana's door without an overwhelming sense of dread pooling in his stomach. Tonight, it choked him with its intensity, threatening to spill out of his mouth to the polished black marble of the Temple floor.

She had called on him again. Though she had yet to take him to her bed since poisoning him with her vile potions, it still caused him a tidal wave of anxiety when she called on him, particularly to her chambers.

Another part of him wished she would invite him, let down her guard now that he was immune to her or anyone else's magic. He'd seize the opportunity, slicing her throat open and letting her bleed out in the Temple she regularly desecrated. But alas, she had not let herself be vulnerable enough yet, and he wasn't willing to take a risk that would see himself dead.

Should he sacrifice himself, he would take her down with him. He wouldn't allow it otherwise.

A loud caw drew his attention to a high temple window. A crow perched on the ledge of the window, tapping the glass.

Before he paid the bird too much attention, a group of acolyte priestesses came around the corner, covered in their lilac robes, huddling close and smiling to each other.

One looked over to him, but he turned away before she could inspect him further.

Sebastian trained his face into the passive neutrality he had seen from her other spelled guards. The ones with no self-preservation or any sense of self-awareness. It was alarmingly easier to exist as nothing. To let the world spin around oneself while having no reaction to it. He wondered how long he felt numb to it.

Maybe it happened the day he killed the Draion boy in the courtyard of the Fortress. He was only a boy then, the last moments that he was Bash, a slaver's orphaned child with no place in the world. Not until James showed him a better way. A way he betrayed that day by killing a harmless boy. One his parents would have exploited.

Yet, he would not have made a different decision.

The Minister whispered to him while James was screaming at him not to do it.

"Kill the boy, or I'll make an example of your friend."

Sebastian didn't believe what he was hearing, staring at the man who clothed and fed him, gave him the education Mama Owen couldn't. He liked James, Bash saw the favoritism the Minister bestowed upon him, yet the insult of an ignored command couldn't be forgiven. Bash's obedience alone kept James from death.

So, Bash chose James over the nameless boy. Even as their paths deviated from there, he couldn't find it in himself to regret that action, even if he was ashamed of it.

Sebastian stood at the side of the door at parade rest with his arms behind his back and his dead eyes focused on the wall before him. He knew clearly enough that Ravana did not like to be disturbed, only waited on, so wait he did.

It didn't take long for the blasphemous Priestess to appear in silver robes, her hair like a waterfall of blood falling down her back and her eyes as cold as stone.

"Come, Commodore, we have work to do." Her eyes flashed, a maniacal undertone to her words. He followed loyally, his dread only expanding at her disinterest in taking him to bed. He was counting on it, and it had yet to happen. Though his hands flexed at his side, eager to pull the sword from its sheath and end her now. He'd thought about it hundreds of times. He just needed the opportune moment.

"I have a task for you, Commodore."

Technically, the title no longer belonged to him. But since Lockness had taken over the palace, the existence of the Navy at all was questionable. With half of them still under Rose's spell, and the other half disappearing into the crevasses of Samsara's underbelly, the state of the officers was turbulent. Lockness didn't even need them with his army of criminals keeping the people from taking the Fortress for themselves.

Ravana breezed out the door to the cliff beyond, bypassing the forest to their right where a pair of crows were perched on a bare branch. The cliff dropped to the sea just beyond the Temple, close enough for an unruly pirate to jump off. But the descent was lengthy. It was a miracle he survived. Most wouldn't.

At the edge stood two Temple guards with a disheveled man between them, one with a torn officer's uniform. A torn uniform held significance. A dishonorable discharge or a blatant rebellion, but a simple recognition told Sebastian what category this man belonged in. Mr. Jones. One of the men who'd been freed from Rose's enchantment.

Rebellion it is.

He spat at Sebastian's feet. "You bloody son of a bitch! You knew what was happening to us. Yet you did nothing."

Sebastian refused to let the insult, or the accusation cause a physical reaction. He was nothing and no one now. So long as Ravana's snake eyes focused on him, he could only be empty.

Mr. Jones pulled at his restraints and the men at his sides, jerking them forward and away from the ledge. "I trusted you, Commodore." He spat the title out like it poisoned him. "And you would rather stand by and say nothing than stand up for your men. You are the vilest of men, more than the villain beside you."

Ravana laughed at the attention. Sebastian wanted to scream. Every moment his men had been subject to Rose's song, either during mass or when they were dragged one by one to the bowels of the Fortress to receive their 'treatment', he wanted to stop it. He wanted to fight, and he tried. Time and time again, he had tried to draw his sword, intent on rebellion, and his muscles had not obeyed. They wouldn't move with any command from his mind that had opposed the Minister.

The men had lost their minds, but he was trapped in his, watching his men be destroyed. But now? He was able to act but chose not to. All for the chance to destroy the monster beside him.

Ravana's hand slid up his arm causing unpleasant gooseflesh to crawl up his arm. "Consider this a test, Commodore. If you are truly mine, then I want your boot on his chest." She circled around him, pressing her body to his. "I want you to kick him off the side of the cliff. Davina can decide his fate."

Sebastian's mind flashed with many thoughts at once. First, the man had a family, one he'd met. Two sons and a gentle wife. Second, the restraints would ensure his demise, erasing any hope of survival, no matter Davina's involvement. Third, refusing would not save the man, only taking the guilt of having to kill Jones himself. Fourth, refusing would reveal himself to Ravana, possibly causing his own death before he could cause hers. Fifth, she doubted him. Perhaps, it was the reason she had not called him to her bed. Sixth, earning her trust could give him the perfect opportunity to end her.

In the next breath, his boot landed on the man's chest, a look of betrayal flashing across Jones' dark eyes before he was falling backwards. It took longer than he expected before the audible splash could be heard. But Jones never screamed, taking his dignity with him to his watery grave.

Sebastian resisted the urge to close his eyes in respect for the man. He was a good man, but the fate of Samsara mattered more than his life. If he knew why, he would have agreed.

He'd work on being able to live with himself once Ravana's grave was cold.

Her hands clapped in the air before landing on his face, searching for his humanity. He buried it deep within himself, letting the exterior become absent to anything even as the true man beneath screamed at him to reach for her. To run his sword through her belly, or to snap her neck.

"I didn't think you were much fun when you were still you. Now, I miss your stoic glares," she mused, as if speaking to herself, before sucking in a breath. "This is exactly why I keep you around, Commodore. You have a small army of defected officers hiding somewhere on the island. Traitors, the lot of them." She tossed her hair over her shoulder, turning back to the Temple. "Your task is to hunt them down. Bring them to me and kill anyone who resists." He didn't have to ask what her treatment of the officers would be. A glance at the unmoving guards still at the cliff side made him shiver. In their bodies, only raw obedience remained. They'd stay on that cliff day and night until someone told them otherwise.

That marked the end for his soldiers, if Ravana had her way.

He wouldn't allow that. He wondered how he could get his hands on the potion he first took, the one that blocked the poison's influence. Were he to supply it to his officers, they'd be granted the same immunity.

Ravana's hand flicked to the side, her draping sleeve following the movement. A clear dismissal.

He veered from the path to the Temple, opting to walk around it when her hollow voice called to him.

"And Commodore." He halted, not turning to her. "If I don't have at least one officer by week's end, the consequence will be — unpleasant."

He swallowed. Threats weren't needed for a man lacking his free will. She still suspected him. He turned to face her, cursing himself for not doing so sooner.

"Yes, my lady." He dipped slightly, a respect she had not earned yet expected of all her guards, so he adopted it.

She nodded, satisfied for now.

He left, eager to escape the unsettling feeling of being near her, like a spider he saw but was unable to kill. But he will kill this spider, no matter the cost.

***

Sebastian made it back to his chambers at the Fortress.

Even though it had been seized by Lockness, the old officers were still allowed to live in it, as per the alliance between Lockness and Ravana. He'd had little trouble with the resident criminals since they treated him no differently from an object and most of them occupied the east wing of the Fortress. It was filled with lavish guest chambers, drawing rooms, and other finery the criminals insisted on seizing.

They might possess the island's riches, just not its people.

He had to relocate twenty displaced youths who were housed in the same bunks he was familiar with. It was odd, seeing the Minister's orphans. He usually hid them away so well. Ravana's priestesses were their caretakers, but with Fortress' new tenants and the Temple unavailable for "unruly miscreants", Sebastian had been left with one option.

Though, instead of displeasure marring Mama Owen's features, she had lit up from the excitement. The neglected house seemed warmer just with the return of the children.

Just another cog in the wheel he was operating, but as long as he kept it moving, maybe he could save everyone.

Not Jones.

He beat back the reminder of his failure and the officer's sacrifice. He had to prevent that from happening again.

He entered his simple room to discover an officer seated upon his bed, perusing the book on his nightstand, despite its weeks of neglect.

"What does a man with no will of his own require of light reading?" Felix flipped through the pages as if looking for some clue tucked into its pages.

"Should I be asked, my mind shall be sharp enough to provide insight," he said with as little emotion as possible. The book on battle strategies, especially having to do with sea fearing, would have been a more helpful tool if he had an armada at his disposal. Had Ravana not dug her claws into his mind, he would have started a project to build ships. As it was, he'd rather not willingly present her with more power.

Felix hummed, suspicion radiating from his tone as he snapped the book shut and stood.

"My role as Commodore was short-lived," he mused, walking

up to Sebastian and pressing the small tome into his chest. Sebastian's hands came up to take it, outwardly ignoring the bitterness and warning dripping from Felix, but mentally making a note of it. "It seems Ravana is more interested in your — infallible obedience for leadership."

Felix stared, looking for an emotional reaction in his features alone. As if that would be enough evidence to take to Ravana. But Sebastian was aware of his methods, having survived the bully at the orphanage then again in the Fortress as they grew up together.

He stared back in that unblinking way the other enchanted guards had done, willing his muscles to relax until he was unnaturally still.

"If you are unsatisfied with your role, I'd suggest you take it up with the Priestess."

He watched Felix swallow, fear shining in his eyes. He wasn't a fool. Ravana would tear him apart for questioning her judgment, and his failed promotion would be the least of his worries.

"No need. I'll simply show her how capable I am. Where you fail her, I will not," he bit out, a smile following his words. "She's already given me this."

Sebastian looked down to see him pull a sexton from his satchel. He'd recognize the golden shine of magic anywhere. It was entrusted to Lockness to find the witch sons. What was Felix doing with it?

"Apparently, she still wishes to round up the little wretches and I will find them all for her." Pride beamed from his smile. "And once I figure out how to expose you for the imposter you are, she will have no choice but to acknowledge me."

Sebastian worked to keep his face straight. It only meant death for him if he was discovered, and he'd have no chance at saving the island. Was it not clear to the scoundrel that this benefited him?

After studying him, Felix knocked his shoulder against him as he left the room. Following his departure, Sebastian exhaled.

Felix would be a problem. One he needed to find a way to deal with.

But for now, he was exhausted.

Sebastian stripped from his uniform, letting the air kiss his bare chest when he felt eyes on him. On the ledge of his open window stood a crow eyeing him curiously.

"Can I help you?"

He really was going mad, talking to birds.

The creature cawed at him, spreading its wings before flying into his room. He moved to shoo the bird away, but before he prevented it, it snagged his discarded shirt, the fold of the sleeve tucked away in its beak.

Sebastian lunged, and the crow jumped away then flapped its wings, struggling with its new cargo and soaring out the window.

"Bloody bird," Sebastian swore, leaning against the window to watch the bird land on a half-dead tree at the edge of a forest. A figure stood beside the tree taking his shirt from the crow's beak. A full black hooded cloak adorned the figure; however, only one Samsara resident controlled crows.

Indigo.

"Witch."

"Commodore."

"Was that really necessary?" He reached for his shirt in her grasp, but she pulled it away.

"You didn't answer my call," she mused, as if it was self-evident.

"And who are you to call on me?" He crossed his arms before himself, uncomfortable outside his room, his chest bared to the bitter air. He hadn't thought the crows were of any consequence, let alone a summons.

He reached again, and the shirt disappeared from her grasp. He groaned, blaming himself for believing a simple retrieval of his shirt was possible, then considered how much he needed it.

"I rather like you this way, Commodore." Her gaze shifted down his chest and arms before returning to his eyes. "Leaves you rather, vulnerable."

"What do you want, witch?"

She flinched back, mocking offense. "Keep calling me that,

makes me all tingly." She smiled at his exasperation. "You once told me that you serve Samsara's people, not its leadership. Is this still true?"

"On my life."

She reached a hand to the crow on the branch beside her, stroking a finger over its feathers. "Then what did my darlings witness on the cliff side?"

He straightened. Was she able to see through the eyes of those creatures? He'd have to keep that in mind.

"A test of loyalty. Ravana believes me to be under her complete control. If she were to believe otherwise, my life would be forfeit and my position at her side lost. I cannot help Samsara from the grave."

She picked up a crumb from the satchel at her side, feeding it to the crow. "Neither can Mr. Jones. Who's to say your life is worth any more than his?"

His irritation grew along with his guilt. He knew he did what was necessary, even if he didn't like it.

"I am the only one close enough to her to land the blow. Trusted enough."

"She cannot be killed. What is your reason now?"

He swallowed, reluctant to reveal what he knew, but the gleam in her eye told him there was some vital information he was missing. This was another test of loyalty. Not to her, but to the people.

"She was once willing to take me to bed. I'm waiting for her to call on me, then I will end her life."

"And if she never does? If she's grown tired of you?"

He lifted his chin. "Then I will find another moment. Even if it takes my own life, I shall drop her soul in Hell before my own parting."

She scoffed, followed by a laugh. "Oh dear, you are a self-right-eous one, aren't you?" He frowned at the comment but lacked a reply. "Very well, Commodore. Come with me."

Before he could take a step to follow her, his shirt materialized on his chest, the fabric rougher than he remembered. A look down confirmed that it wasn't his shirt but instead, one of lower quality, nothing noteworthy. Something that James would put him in as a disguise.

"Where are we going?"

"To see the reason Mr. Jones came to the Temple in the first place."

<hr>

Indigo led Sebastian through alleyways and shadows in Samsara with a crow perched on her shoulder. The night remained eerily quiet, as if the people were holding their breath waiting for a monster to jump out of the shadows.

Sebastian sensed the restlessness stirring even in the quiet.

Indigo opened a back door, presumably to an establishment or home, but it was on the outskirts of low town, near the sea. A precarious spot for storms, but the building seemed intact.

The crow flapped away from her shoulder with a great caw, refusing to enter the home of its own volition. Sebastian concluded that it didn't bode well.

They crept into the thick darkness shrouding the inside before he heard a whisper.

"*Illuminos*." A flame burst to life in a nearby lantern, urged by Indigo's magic.

Sebastian grunted. "You needn't use magic around me, witch."

"Apologies." She feigned regret, placing a hand to her exposed collarbone. "Next time, I shall let you wander about in the dark to spare your gentlemanly sensitivities."

He groaned, taking in the surroundings, shapes coming into view with the minimal light. "I do hope we don't make this a habit."

She failed to respond, taking in the room. It was a simple home. A few chairs to relax, a cabinet for storage, and bags of sand to prevent flooding during storms. This was a home. It was clear enough that a couple resided here with their children.

The Jones'.

He had never been to their home, but conflicted feelings rose up inside him at the sight of all his former officer had. Shame for having to kill the man, though regret remained absent, and duty. He owed the family an explanation. The children needed to comprehend that their father perished protecting them and the rest of the islanders, even if they didn't realize his involvement.

"Where is the family?"

Indigo didn't answer, but her mouth pinched together. A simple nod, and he followed her down the hallway to a door from which soft moans emanated. Not any imaginable for enjoyment, but the type born of suffering.

Was that Mrs. Jones? One of her sons?

Indigo halted him before he opened the door. "I must prepare you for what you will witness. Mr. Jones came to the Temple to plead with Davina to spare his family. There is a plight controlling them that no potion can erase."

Sebastian raised an eyebrow, a habit he picked up from James, but it worked. "What is behind this door?" His hand drifted to his sword.

Something flashed in her eyes. "Death."

She opened the door, and the screeching began, pulling a gasp from him as he witnessed Mrs. Jones lunge for him. He lifted his sword, but she didn't pay any attention to it, impaling herself on the blade, reaching for him. No blood seeped from the wound, as if she had already been drained of it. Her skin showed a deathly pallor, and her eyes were clouded.

"What in Davina's name in this?"

"Mr. Jones came to me for help, seeking a cure for them. But their souls no longer exist in their bodies."

Sebastian struggled to maintain his hold on the writhing creature before him. She inched closer, seemingly desperate to sink her nails into his skin. And the sounds — wails as if from a nightmare.

"How can a living body contain no soul?"

"Because they are not living. I examined each of them. Their hearts do not beat."

"This happened to the boys as well?"

She nodded grimly. "There is only one thing like it."

Sebastian placed a boot on the creature's navel, pushing her off his sword and slamming the door before she could attack. She slammed into the door with more force than her small body should be capable of, screeching at the door.

He looked at his sword, holding it in the lantern's light. Thick black blood coated half the blade. There was only one thing that bled black.

"Nemain's plight has finally caught up to us," Indigo whispered.

"Necromites."

CHAPTER 4
WELCOME PARTY
BLACK

Davina's silver moon filled the sky as they drew close to the wall built into the sea around Draiocht's shores. Black clutched at the pommel of her sword, nerves building at their approach.

Captain's old friend turned out to be a Princess, one with a slipping grasp on her people. She was desperate enough to seek help from a band of pirates. Black shook her head at the idea, but it would get them into the citadel, so she cared little as to why.

The devils dressed as sailors, though the disguises were hardly helpful seeing as none of them looked remotely like a dark-skinned Draion. Even in the dark of the night.

But the Princess insisted it was necessary.

"I don't like this," Sophia whispered from her side, staring up at the moon as if taking her complaints to the Goddess of Fate herself. Her face was bathed in the moonlight, highlighting her high cheekbones and full lips. Lips that Black had yet to taste but imagined quite frequently.

"Which part? The useless disguises or the fact that we're entering a country with unstable politics?"

Sophia's eyebrows scrunched together. "Neither."

Before Black asked her what she meant, a guard from the wall called to them.

"*Min hunak? La 'ahad yestatie aldukhul.*"

A giant of a man, one of the Princess's guards shouted back. "*Maftuh lil'amirmah Sitamun.*" A figure stood behind him, hiding beneath a heavy cloak.

Skepticism wrinkled the guard's face; the conversation was not going so well, it would seem.

The figure beside her let her hood drop, revealing dark curly hair. "Let us in, Asim." Her tone was light and graceful, emanating royal decorum. The man paled at seeing his Princess, or perhaps it was that she knew his name.

"Apologies, your Highness, I was only following orders."

She sighed. "Who's orders exactly?"

Asim swallowed thickly before shouting orders to the others to raise the portcullis. The gate shifted upwards, revealing a water-logged tunnel they were to sail through. It was a clever way to control the ships coming in. Only small ones were able to make it through. *Nemain's Revenge* wouldn't.

The Princess offered a couple guards to hold their vessel until they returned. By the threat in the captain's eyes, they'd better be willing to release it when the time came.

The captain had meant to leave Lara aboard his ship, but she insisted on joining them, huddled in her cloak beside Tick and Hyne, who'd hardly left her side since she boarded the vessel. It was almost cute seeing how protective they both had become.

The ship sailed through the gate with little resistance, the guards eyeing them suspiciously. Black wondered if the 'saviors' of the city held the loyalty of the guards on the wall. It was highly likely. As strategies go, that would be the first thing to take care of.

A few minutes later they were docked in the city of Amal, the captain was the first off the ship. He wore a cloak much like the Princess, hiding his face because recognition might cause unwanted trouble.

He sauntered down the dock, his devils keeping tightly behind him. A creeping sensation on Black's spine made her restless, like eyes trailing their every move.

Upon entering the city, life filled the streets, Draion singers with long notes and drumbeats filled the streets alongside the chatter of a crowd. Carts filled the sides of the street, an array of colorful goods on display. Rugs and tapestries were hung against walls or dangled from lines. Pills of spices decorated tables in cone shapes. Clothing and scarves covered poles and hooks. It was a market for ethnic goods. Even animals scattered about, filling the street and hoping for a scrap of food. Monkeys snatched fruits, sneaking away. Dogs begged or barked at attendants who ignored them. Colorful birds perched on tents and windowsills, more exotic than Black had ever seen.

A wafting of earthy spices or floral perfumes covered the growing stench of sweaty bodies and animal waste also littering the street.

The people filled the sandstone road and buildings, leaving very little room for the devils to brush past them. Vendors and merchants held out their goods, speaking rapidly in their native tongue.

The music shifted, becoming louder, and people doused their lanterns and candles, casting the busy road into darkness. It was unsettling to adjust to the darkness in the middle of a crowd.

The strings of a bandolim mixed along with the other instruments, drums and flutes. It became apparent something would happen as the natives gazed skyward. She followed their gazes but saw nothing.

The music built, edging towards a crescendo and the voices of the crowd dropped to a whisper.

Black tugged on Wilson's robes. "What are they waiting for?"

Wilson's features twisted as if he scented something foul. "Something is coming."

The music crescendoed, and the crowd cheered. Flares erupted in a cacophony of colors, filling the street with blues, reds, oranges, greens, yellows, and everything in between. The light flashed across the devils' faces, fading in and out as they took in the ritual around them.

Wilson's hard glare was intensified by the flashing lights.

Hyne smiled at the wonder of it.

Earhart blinked slowly, adjusting his sight to the assault.

But Phantom? He looked ahead as if none of it mattered. A

short whistle had the devils following closely behind as he waded through the thick crowd of merry people, some beginning to dance. A row of women in colorful robes blocking the path before them.

The citadel's overpopulation became obvious. Too many people had been stuffed into a small space. Phantom veered away from the main street, opting for the darkness of a nearby alleyway.

Once all the devils made it there, he glared back at the crowd, searching the bustling street.

Earhart put a steadying hand on the captain's shoulder. "We'll find her, but this is no place to start." Phantom glared at him as if he wanted to bite the hand that touched him.

Muffled whispers drew Black's attention further down the alleyway to the shadowy corners where movement rustled. Inching further, she narrowed her eyes. She had to confirm the danger before taking the devil's attention away from the street.

"*Shhhh.*"

Black caught the breathy warning, her eyes finally adjusting to see — children. Two girls were huddled against the dirty sandstone wall, clinging to each other in the desert night chill. They wore rags; worn potato sacks by the looks of them. Their faces were dirty, and hair matted, but their eyes...

The music in the street halted, then changed to something more powerful. Drums beat heavily in a style purely attuned to Draiocht. In fact, it sounded like a royal march.

Something was wrong.

After one last glance at the girls, Black peeked back into the crowd to watch two giant guards leading the procession as Sitamun followed with a veil covering the lower half of her face. Her back was flanked by two more outrageously large guards. Black eyed the procession carefully or, more accurately, the surrounding people.

Tension choked the air, and the world fell still as the music abruptly stopped.

Her gaze traveled back to Sophia behind her, only to find unfamiliar panic in those dark eyes.

"Ey ey ey!"

Calls broke out all around them filling the air with war cries. Men appeared on the ledges of buildings, masks resembling wild animals hiding their faces. Though the animals were closer to nightmares than any creature she envisioned. They climbed down ropes into the fray of screaming citizens.

Phantom drew his cutlass. "Kill all but one."

Blue flashed across Black's vision as if one of those firelights got too close. Resolve settled in her stomach. *Kill all but one.* The command was clear, the captain had meant the masked assailants. The ones currently fighting their way to the Princess.

The guards huddled around her, fending off the attacks but they were quickly becoming outnumbered as the assailants surrounded them.

The devils poured in, pushing the masked men back as civilians screamed and ran into nearby buildings.

The assailants hissed through the hole in their masks. Black squinted. Were they otherworldly or only pretending to be so? The intimidation would not work though, not with the new determination in her gut.

Black raised her sword, deflecting the blade of another and soon there were two more blades crossing with hers. They were stronger than they should have been, pushing her back harder than any man who had crossed her blade before. Still, she was not afraid.

Twisting her blade to the side, she caught hold of theirs and disarmed them before pushing them into the nearest tent. A plume of colorful powder exploded around them.

Before she had a chance to breathe, another assailant jumped from a nearby window and she deflected the blow, rolling the metal in her hand until the masked man lost his blade, tossing it to the middle of the street, far from his reach. She managed to catch the second blade just before it was buried in her gut, drawing the pistol at her side before he was aware of it.

She shot him down before he reached for a third.

Gunfire, firelight explosions, and metal crashing filled the street along with screams and war cries. It was an all-out battle with little strategy.

Phantom buried his cutlass into the belly of one such beast, pulling out a black-coated blade. He stared down at the blade for a couple seconds before his panicked eyes found Black's. They *were* otherworldly. The masked assailants were not human.

"Behind you!" Phantom yelled at her.

She turned to find the two she had gunned down were rising. Panic surged in her chest. What were they? They moved too fluidly to be necromites, yet her weapons had no effect. Even the Captain's opponent was rising to rejoin the fray.

Black lifted her blade just before metal met her skull.

"What are they?" Phantom ran to her, helping with the weight of their blade by slicing his cutlass across the chest of one.

"I don't know. They bleed like necromites." Phantom stuck his blade into the second one before it could react. She expected it to try to run, but she supposed a creature who thought itself invincible wouldn't need to.

"But they aren't walking corpses. What exactly are we dealing with, Captain?"

Phantom whistled. A long note summoning a particular devil.

A loud screech sounded over the people, freezing everyone and turning their eyes to the sky. Serena dipped low, her white scales rippling in the moonlight. She opened her maw, burning the head of one masked demon before taking to the skies again.

A hand wrapped around Black's arm. "Back them all up against that building." Black followed her captain's gaze. The street ended abruptly at a building, curving inward with no assumed means of escape. "Get them there. I'll handle the rest but remember to keep one."

He left before she got a chance to question him. Ideally, Serena would burn them all, but would that work? For a dragon, her size was quite small.

Her resolve beat her logic to the punch as her limbs moved of their own accord. She whispered in the ear of every devil she could find, encouraging them to spread the word while fending off the creatures and forcing them down the street.

The devils moved efficiently, bending to the new orders and forcing the masked assailants to the wall.

It was clear that even though the ambush and their immunity to weapons was meant to give them the advantage, they lacked the actual skill necessary to win a long-winded fight.

Wilson disarmed five in under a minute, the other devils fairing similarly.

Once every assailant was shoved against the wall, weaponless and hissing, Black searched the masks for the one to spare. At least, until the captain was done with the wretched soul. But it had to be more than a lackey. Someone significant enough to be privy to specifics. In the crowd of faces, not a single one was remarkable.

Not until she noticed one was not hissing at them. The bare-chested man stood predatorily still, with a mask that looked more like a jackal than the other misshaped animal faces. He turned his head, as if he were a newborn puppy, assessing his new surroundings. The move was so intentional, so inhuman, it made Black's skin crawl.

Black stepped out, wrapping her hand around his arm and pulling him into the fray of devils. Still, he did not hiss, accepting his role to be taken as if he expected it.

Wilson and Hyne tied his hands together, seizing an arm each.

Sophia stood at Black's side along with Earhart, waiting for the captain to show. He was absent, along with Serena.

Finally, Black took note of three barrels lined up at the rooftop of the building behind the assailants. They tipped over, one by one, gallons of fine colored powder pouring from the barrels to the men below. Soon, they became coated in blue, red, and yellow powder.

Phantom appeared kicking the middle powder barrel off the roof and staring down at the masked assailants below him. They hissed upwards, seeming to understand who the real threat was.

"Are you familiar with this powder?" He called below him, all voices going silent to hear what he had to say, to see what he would do. "The Draion villagers use it for their firelights. Now, in other countries, colored powder and gunpowder are used separately. But here, the color protects the powder from catching fire in the heat of the sun."

He whistled then. The long whistle that summoned the only dragon left to exist in the world.

Sweet Davina.

"Tell me friends, who do you work for? Perhaps I'll be merciful."

Serena screeched, the sound echoing across the high walls of the buildings as she flew in from the opposite end of the street. The assailants below broke into chaos, attempting to escape, but a line of devils stood in their way.

"Tell. Me. Who." Phantom yelled down; desperation unfamiliar to Black crawled up her spine. She itched for a fight yet needed answers more. "Or burn."

Serena closed in, circling the air above them. They hissed, not even one of them willing to betray their master.

"Very well." Phantom stood straighter, looking down to Serena who hovered in the air above the powder covered men.

"*Que ardan.*"

Serena's blue fire erupted from her before the complete command was spoken.

Many had theories of what the blue flame of white dragons was like. Some considered it cool like ice, hitting its target like a thousand knives. Others claimed it resembled a ghostly fire, burning one from the inside out.

They were both wrong.

Serena's blue fire was so hot that it burned Black's eyes to look at it for too long, coming down on the assailants like a blast of cannon fire. She incinerated the men before her, their shrieks of pain harsh and unnatural. Every powder coated figure beside them engulfed in flames, blue turning white, then yellow and orange as they burned alive, screaming until their voices failed.

The smell was horrific. Burning flesh assaulted her nose, so Black used her sleeve to block it out.

Once Serena was satisfied with her work, she flew up to Phantom, landing on his shoulders and creating a picture of power with two moons at his back. In the next breath he was gone, and the devils waited until he appeared again from the darkness of the alleyway beside the burning remnants of his enemies.

"Bring the survivor forward."

Wilson and Hyne pulled violently at the final masked man,

throwing him to his knees before his still burning and ashen comrades.

"Remove his mask."

Earhart stepped forward, pulling the jackal mask from his face by the nose. Black expected what would be underneath to be infinitely more grotesque than the mask.

However, it remained a typical human face with bronze skin and brown hair. He had a square jaw with a dusting of hair across it. His face appeared youthful, no older than twenty-five judging by his looks. He glared at Phantom with cool detachment.

"Are you human?" Phantom asked.

"No," the man answered immediately.

"We have that in common then."

Movement grew Black's attention to the street beyond, one that had been cleared of all civilians. Yet, one man walked towards them, covered in white robes with a flaming torch in his hand.

"Her Highness, Amariah Sitamun, has prepared arrangements for you. Follow me."

CHAPTER 5

RUN, LITTLE MOUSE

ROSE

Scratching. The grating noise roused Rose from her place on the prison cell pallet. Opening her eyes, she found the same sandy cell she kept hoping was some drawn out nightmare. No such luck, apparently.

To the left the scratching continued. A little desert mouse hopped along the sand, stopping every few inches to scratch at the sandstone wall. It must have fallen through the hole at the top of her cell.

Eat it.

Rose wretched at the thought. *Isabeya.* She certainly didn't come up with that idea.

"Are you crazy?"

You are being starved. Never mind that your power depends on you being well-fed.

"The little creature wouldn't provide me with more than a bite. Besides, I can't exactly eat the poor thing raw."

That's what Scarlett is for.

Yellow flared in her vision. *I want no part of this decision.*

"Using Scarlett's fire would use up more power than I would gain from this poor creature."

The mouse sat up, staring at Rose as if assessing her as a threat.

If the creature understood her, it would be furiously trying to escape.

You need only to let her start the fire. It would not take long to cook.

Rose's stomach rolled with the idea, both from a moral standpoint and a physical one. She couldn't possibly eat something so cute and — hairy. She didn't even have anything to cut the rodent up.

The mouse's nose twitched a bit, inching dangerously close to her.

Unbidden, her hand came out slowly as if to snatch the creature. She pulled it back before her fingertips skimmed fur. Green climbed into her vision like a rush of fast-growing ivy as Isabeya fought for control of her body.

She squeezed her eyes tight, clenching her fists to keep them still. No, she was not doing this. She wasn't nearly starving enough for it. There was no need to traumatize herself further than necessary.

But Isabeya had different ideas.

Her body jerked forward, her foot heel slamming down on the creature's tail. It squeaked in protest, drawing lines in the sand in its attempt to get away. Rose grunted, trying to regain control of her foot to let the mouse go, but Isabeya held firm, reaching for more of her body.

She usually wasn't so forceful, but when she decided it was her turn to take control, she was relentless.

Give up, flower. *This is for your own good.*

She wrestled against Isabeya's hold. "*No me jodas.*"

Sweat beaded her brow as she kept all her muscles locked and tense against her frame. All, but the leg Isabeya currently had control of.

"Let me go!"

The door flew open, startling her enough to lose focus. Isabeya took advantage, swooping forward to grasp the creature in a fist, then hiding it behind her back. It screeched but was quickly silenced when she squeezed her fist tighter.

In walked a man dressed in complete black, but nothing like the leathers and assorted fabrics James liked to wear. This man draped himself in an obsidian black robe, a cape flowing behind him. His hair had a short, neat style, but Rose didn't miss the black irises staring back at her. The matching set to Colt's dark eyes.

Colt embodied energy, constantly moving around the room like a butterfly, unlike this very still man. He seemed to float into the room instead of walking, his face devoid of emotion.

It distracted her from the squirming mouse in her fist until the blasted thing started scratching at her.

"Ow," Rose snapped before releasing the fist, the little creature running through the now open door.

Congratulations, there goes our bloody dinner.

It scampered by another pair of boots, these dirty, the wearer much less graceful as he followed the first visitor in.

Her eyes scanned over his body, seeing a uniform like ones worn by naval officers, but the pattern and colors were all wrong. It was his face that both relieved and unnerved her. His eyes, dark brown, not black and otherworldly, bored into her as if she were a lamb for slaughter, and he the god to whom she would be sacrificed.

"Miss Davenport. I apologize for not visiting sooner. You see, I had to be certain your power had waned enough to make you vulnerable." Although the man didn't laugh, his subordinate let out a breathy chuckle. "My name is Dante. What I will attempt to do is experimental. I have no doubt that my efforts with you will fail, but I hope that this experience will provide the necessary information to succeed the next time we meet."

Rose scrunched her brows together. Dante's words were said peacefully, as if he did not mean to cause her to panic, but the content of those words made her heartbeat rapidly.

"What exactly do you plan to do to me?"

He took two measured steps towards her. "I will enter your mind. I will draw each of your past lives to the surface, force them to integrate one by one until you are a whole entity once again."

Confusion riddled her mind. Integrate?

Kill you, he's going to kill you after you kill us. Kill the parts until they become the whole. Was he going to kill them from the inside?

Coldness bled through her veins as red nearly blinded her

sight. Skye panicked. Rose panicked. He was going to reach into her mind and pull out each of them like a goddess-damned candy jar?

"I'd rather not," was the only response she came up with.

"I assumed as much, which is why Cain is here."

Cain stepped forward, picking his teeth with a fingernail as he smirked down at her. Every inch of her skin crawled at his stare. "During our sessions, he will ensure cooperation." The man was an oaf, six feet of hard muscle and leering looks. "Should we need it."

It didn't matter if he was a proper giant, they all fell to her song. James alone was able to resist.

"His hearing has been temporarily impaired during our sessions."

Rose didn't let the fear take her as it threatened to, instead she leaned on anger, letting Scarlett surface in a flare of yellow to share in the fury.

"*You can still burn.*" Rose and Scarlett said at once, small sparks spitting off her skin. The oaf paled upon reading her lips and it was her turn to smirk.

Before she turned back to Dante, power like a drowning wave crashed into her, knocking her back until she laid on her pallet. Dante's hand was out, the surge of energy coming from his fingertips. Even unseen, she sensed it.

Cain laughed behind him, but she ignored him, focusing instead on keeping Dante out.

The more she resisted, the more painful it became, like a headache that grew gradually worse with every second. She screamed against the pain, letting some of the tension leave her body that way, but it only worsened.

A small crack in her defenses proved enough.

Dante's presence came rushing into her head, relieving some of the pain, but not all of it. Her memories flashed before her in a blur. Meeting James as Captain Phantom. Lara mutilation when those guards pinned her down and destroyed her hearing. Losing her virginity to an officer. Watching the light leave Sebastian's eyes as she sang to him.

All of them flipped through her head, the next one being worse than the last.

What are you truly afraid of, child?

His voice was in her head, louder than her other selves had ever been capable of. She felt them fighting his hold on her memories, trying to push him out. Rose screamed, though her body was too far away for her to hear it.

What about this?

Rose entered a memory from five years prior.

"Why must you always resist, Rose?" It was her father's voice; in a tone she came to loathe. He spoke to her like a petulant child when she resisted singing for him. In fact, when she was a child, she didn't resist. She let him burn out her power on making him pretty things and wealth that he'd never use in his lifetime. She sacrificed her childhood for his greed.

Only when he wanted her to take away someone's free will did she resist.

"You are as useless as your mother said. Even as a babe, she said you would grow to become a princess all but in name. She was right. I give you everything. Whatever you desire is yours. Yet, when I ask you for a favor that costs you nothing, you stomp your golden shoes and tell me no. I shouldn't have spoiled you so much."

The memory was so real. He gripped her wrist, pulling her down the steps of the hidden library. He cared little for the books there; what he wanted was a place to conduct his less savory deeds. She wouldn't consider his grip painful, neither did she find it comfortable. He always toed the line of abuse, then made Ravana carry out the acts, calling himself a saint for never hurting her himself.

"One little song, Rose. Then I'll send you to bed without another word. He's a bad man. Only you can make him a good one. You won't just be saving the people around him, but the man himself."

The Minister rounded a corner into a stone walled room where a man sat gagged and tied to a chair. His muffled cries filled the room, yet the wall he faced made her stop. Chains were imbedded in the stone with four cuffs as if a person might be strapped to the wall to resemble a star.

Fear rose in her belly. By then, Ravana had taken a knife to her, but only on her arms. This would allow her a lot more skin.

Still, she did not ask about the chains.

"*What has this man done?*" The younger version of her sounded so innocent and naïve, still blind enough to listen to her father. It made her cringe.

"*He has committed crimes against us. Threatened me. Threatened you.*" The man shook his head vehemently, tears watering his eyes and trailing down his cheeks. His eyes pleaded with her, begging her to reconsider.

"*Are you certain, father? I do not wish this on an innocent man.*"

The Minister stood before her, blocking her view of the man. "*He is far from innocent. He* preys *on the innocent. If he had you alone, my child, he would do much worse things to you than kill you.*" A shiver ran down her spine, even if she now understood the words were lies.

That naïve version of Rose nodded in agreement. The Minister moved out of her way as she stepped up to the man, but he remained unaware of her suspicion. The night before she had snuck into the Temple and stole the Stone. She had learned a new song that night. A song to reveal the truth.

She had started humming before her fingers drew down the man's gag.

SPEAK NOT OF POISON AND DECEIT
NO MAN CAN LISTEN

The man's eyes trained on her, captured in the inescapable pull of the song, powerless to do anything but listen.

BREATHE NOT THE FALSEHOOD OF THE ERA
FOR THERE IS NO AIR

SPEAK WHAT THE HEART CANNOT SAY
TO LIVE ANOTHER DAY

The song ended, and the Minister spoke first once the trace ended. *"That is not the song, Rose. What have you done?"*

That naïve, yet clever version of her ignored her father for the first time in her life and looked to the man below her. *"Do you deserve this?"*

"No!" He was quick to respond, looking to her then the Minister. *"I only asked what happened to my bunkmate."*

For a moment, she wanted to take it back. To live in the world where she believed her father was flawed, but not wholly irredeemable. But it was too late. How many had she condemned in her ignorance?

"Rose, let me explain, I did not know you could do that." The Minister blinked away the effects of her song. *"No, wait, I meant, I didn't think you clever enough to figure it out. No, that's not what I wanted to say."*

Tears trickled down her cheeks, the truth hurting far worse than she imagined it would.

Frustrated, the Minister lunged, pinning her arms at her sides to shake her. *"You put me under your spell, you witch. Take it back."*

Rose sniffled. *"It will fade soon."* But the memory would not. Since that day, the Minister was careful with his ability to hear, always bringing plugs with him. And Rose never trusted a single thing her father said again.

Ravana also made more frequent visits. Her torture eventually made a daily appearance.

Rose was snapped out of the memory like a bucket of cold water dumped over her head, the flashes returning, but Dante's presence withdrawing.

There is both fear and lies in this memory, yet the subject does not appear. Skye doesn't live in this memory with you.

Dante ripped away from her mind then, leaving her exhausted and breathless. Her head stung and her stomach soured like she contracted some kind of illness from the violation, yet he stood above her without even a bead of sweat on his brow.

"This session failed. We will try again tomorrow."

CHAPTER 6

HELL IS EMPTY

PHANTOM

The first thing Phantom noticed was the distinct smell of smoke in the air, like a forest was burning to cinders nearby. The next was the jagged rocks beneath him. His final memory prior to sleep involved a cot, which he no longer occupied. The third was the sound of dripping water.

Darkness greeted him when he opened his eyes, but his surroundings came into focus after his eyes adjusted. He was in a cave with two faint sources of light. The one to his left burned brighter than any simple torch, yet it did little to lessen the darkness. The light on his right felt as chilly as a sea breeze; however, it shone with a bloody red hue.

Nemain's moon.

His head stayed blessedly quiet, not a trace of his normal counterparts.

"Sam? Are you there?"

Only silence and his own thoughts filled his head, but he hadn't drunk the poison Ravana had created for him, so how was this possible?

By instinct, he followed the moon, where the sound of dripping water came from. Soon it turned into a familiar lap of waves and the mist of the sea. His body instantly relaxed when he spotted the opening to the ocean, though it differed from his familiar sea.

The water was dark, almost black where Nemain's crimson light did not reach it. Beside the cave opening, a shipwreck had crashed into the rock wall, looking torn and shredded to pieces.

With narrowed eyes, Phantom recognized the ship. A ship with deep purple sails, but before the disrepair and the grime, they had once been lilac. The tentacles on his neck seemed to pulse in response.

Macha's Demise.

Wariness had him turning his head around the area, searching for the crew that went down with it. The crew he had personally ensured would end up in Hell.

"Maahes..."

A voice like wind drifted in the breeze, carrying the stench of death in its wake. He turned his head, looking for the source of the voice.

"Who's there?"

"Your master." This time the voice was clear and coming from directly behind him.

He pivoted, coming face to face with a dangerously beautiful woman. Her skin matched her dark hair and eyes. White seashells wove together to create a dress to cover her slight curves. Some of those shells had been braided into her hair too.

What caught his attention, however, was the burn marks across her brow.

Recognition and a memory came to him. A candle that had burned in that witch's hovel.

Phantom held up a finger, pointing in her direction while taking a step back.

"I remember you. You gave me those vague words in the witch house. You said I wasn't ready."

The corner of her mouth twitched in a shadow of a smile before she schooled her features again. "You are late."

His brow quirked upwards. "I do apologize. I've been a bit busy, you see." She brushed past him, walking into the water, her dress floating on the surface behind her. This had to be one hell of a dream.

He followed until water lapped at his knees. She pointed to the sky. Besides Nemain's crimson moon, a star existed as the only other celestial body. One lonesome star, but he recognized it.

The Star of Nemain.

"I even showed you the way."

The pieces finally clicked together as he stared at the being before him. He hadn't looked hard enough before. If he had, he would have seen the glimmer of red under toning her skin like waves of shimmering blood.

"Nemain?"

She didn't confirm or deny his claim, instead she turned to the sea.

Her accent rang as she spoke. "Some call it *La Mer Rouge*. Where I keep my pets. You met Hafgufa. He dragged this ship here. All because of you."

The tattoo around his neck flickered with movement, reminding him that it was not placed there by human means. "You owe a debt. You will come to pay."

"That's not what I'm coming for. A priestesses has violated Your power. She's cheated You and become immortal."

Phantom didn't miss the flicker of rage in Her eyes.

"Come to me. We will discuss this once you have walked the gates yourself." She turned away from him, walking towards the shipwreck instead. "I have brought you here for another purpose."

Phantom hesitated to wade further into the waters, but he doubted whatever monsters inhabited the sea would attack while he remained with Her. She all but confirmed Her divinity.

The water never grew deeper. They waded through thigh high water until reaching the ship where She crawled through a gaping hole in the side. Water dripped around them as they reached a door, the smell of rotting kelp putrefying the air.

"Your purpose lays inside. Do not waste My gift." Her eyes locked onto him, looking like the entire ocean dwelled inside them. "And return to Me." He inspected the half-soaked wood door infested with barnacles and algae. "And Phantom?" He turned back, Her gaze chilling his bones. "Return soon, or I will send for you."

He turned to ask Her meaning, but only darkness remained where She had been.

"It's just a dream," Phantom reminded himself, turning the doorknob to where something awaited him. Even if only a dream, he wished to observe its conclusion.

Through the door was a room he assumed had been the captain's quarters, but it had been transformed into a torture room. Weapons and devices of all kinds lined the walls. Contraptions from ages past and some that had yet to be invented, but all with a singular purpose in mind.

Torture. Raw, unrestricted torture.

"I hear this had been your personal collection."

In the room's far corner existed a dog-sized cage containing a person in tattered garments, bent low. Though, by the sallow look to his face, the cramped space was the least of his worries.

If the man had once been recognizable, he wasn't now.

"Who told you that?"

The man laughed, but it turned into a vile cough. "She did."

He didn't have to elaborate. The Goddess of Death.

For a goddess, She didn't have much to say. Honestly, he pictured something more elaborate.

"I told Her you weren't a resident of Hell. You were born and raised on Samsara before you took to pillaging. I never did quite believe the outlandish tales Ravana would spin about you."

Phantom examined the man closer, seeing him clearly now.

"Minister?"

He coughed heavily, blood splattering on his hand. "Not anymore."

He wasn't the same man at all. Reduced to skin and bone on a once round frame. Especially without his adornments and fancy robes, or even the space to raise his posture. No, he wasn't that man at all.

And yet—

Phantom stilled. Anger that had been fueling his every action pulled stronger. This time, no colors obstructed his vision.

Then, he understood. Nemain didn't need to verbalize Her

meaning; She was able to demonstrate it to him. The Minister *was* the gift, but the ship — this particular ship — was a threat.

"Lost, my boy?"

Phantom hadn't heard the endearment in many years. As if he were that boy again wanting the Minister's approval more than anything. The idea that he ever wanted his man's approval made him sick.

"I'm not surprised where I ended up, Lieutenant."

"Why?" Phantom snapped. "Can you list your sins, or should I carve them upon your flesh?"

He'd been dreaming of doing that very thing ever since he found out what the Minister had allowed to happen to his daughter. Maybe he had not struck her with the knife himself, but he ordered it. He controlled it. It was within his power to stop it.

"I understand you have reason to hate—"

"I don't think you understand, Minister." Phantom stalked the cage, knowing instinctively that a key would be in his pocket. He reached for it without ever letting his eyes wander from the Minister's sallow beady ones. "You are a lamb, trapped in the lion's den. And I'm ravenous."

That faint dripping noise continued as Phantom unlocked the Minister's cage, letting the man crawl out himself before dragging his bound hands to a metal hook. He lifted the chain until the Minister's uncanny frail body hung from the ceiling, his toes an inch from the floor.

The fire fueling his rage simmered, happily burning in his core as satisfaction dripped over him.

He turned, pulling a dagger from the wall, one dull enough to draw out the pain. All while the Minister prattled on. "I did what I had to do. You, of all people, should understand. You do what you must for your people."

Phantom shushed him, putting the knife to his cheek, just hard enough that it didn't break skin — yet.

"You see, that's where you are wrong." He watched with sick satisfaction as fear flooded the Minister's eyes. "I would have let them all die, if it meant saving *her*."

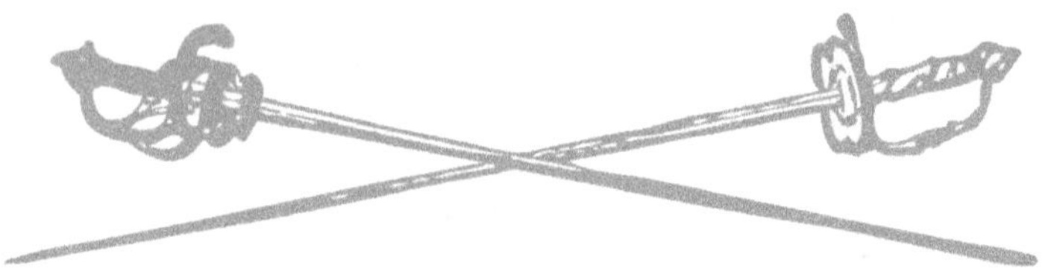

CHAPTER 7

ALL THE DEVILS ARE HERE

BLACK

Maybe it was the unsettling presence of their captive, or the girls Black had seen in the alley earlier, but somehow, she had ended up with her hood over her head, creeping across rooftops in the middle of Amal.

She hadn't even tried to sleep. Instinct pricked at her gut, insisting she seek out the girls she saw earlier. She'd *seen* that look in their eyes before, on the faces of children she'd rescued in Samsara. They didn't always ask for help, but their eyes always gave their fear away.

Those girls needed her help, of that, she was certain.

It had been some years since she'd been the Black Shadow. She wouldn't say she missed working alone, but in some cases, it was more efficient. Like now, with the streets quiet, it paid to be soft footed.

But even for the witching hour, the streets were eerily quiet, as if everyone was shut away from the monster spotted roaming the streets. She imagined it had to do with the assailants earlier and their strange animal masks. Their eyes held an otherworldly quality—Black dismissed the thought, concentrating on locating their earlier hiding place. The girls had likely moved on, but it provided a good place to start. There was a lack of good drainpipes to climb down like she was used to in Samsara, but the roofs were much flatter. Both simplifying the journey and increasing her vulnerability.

Finding the alleyway, she gently lowered herself by windowsills and protruding rocks to get down into the unforgiving darkness. Luckily, she blended right in.

Searching, she found a discarded red blanket that she recognized as the rag they had been sharing for warmth. Black didn't think they would willingly leave the scrap behind. She twisted it in her belt, fully intending on giving it back.

Movement drew her eye deeper into the alleyway where a man shuffled inside a nearby building, having pulled a tapestry away to enter.

Curious, Black waited a few minutes before following.

Under the worn tapestry, a stairwell descended into darkness. She hadn't considered that there would be an underground to the city, especially being so close to the sea and sands. It made her wary to venture further, but this was the best lead she had for those girls.

With a deep breath, she continued, taking the steps slowly with a hand on the hilt of her sword.

The stairs led to an even darker tunnel. Running her hand along the wall, she located a torch and a flint next to it. She lit it up, holding the torch out to see the tunnel only offered more darkness.

It's going to be a long night, she thought while traversing through the darkened tunnels.

After nearly an hour in the dark, Black had passed by twenty more staircases, all leading upwards and four forks. She had taken a left each time just as an easy way to remember her way back. Or had she? Did she do it every time?

"*Maldita idiota,*" Black cursed herself. "This is the way you die. The devils don't even know these tunnels exist, and you get lost in them. Brilliant bloody idea."

Black sank her head against her hand, mentally berating herself for going out at all. Until she heard a distant sniffling, as if someone cried. When she got to a chamber, she slipped inside searching for the source.

In the corner of the room, the two girls huddled together. A closer inspection confirmed that it was the same two girls from earlier that night, except their eyes were filled with fear, flinching away from her.

"No no," Black started, lowering her hood and sheathing her sword to put both hands out. "It's okay. I'm here to help. I can get you home." She didn't exactly speak Draion, but she hoped her hands conveyed the universal gesture for peace.

It didn't appear to work, the girls shivered and clung to one another harder.

She should have brought Earhart. Or Robin. Hell, Wilson would be better at this than she was.

"I promise, it's okay. Any chance either of you girls know how to get out of here?"

"*Khalfuk!*" The older girl screamed, pointing at Black as if she was a horrifying monster. This really was a terrible idea.

"I swear I won't hurt you."

"I can't say the same to you." Black turned just before a nasty brute bludgeoned her over the head with the hilt of his sword. She ducked before he could touch her. "Spry little girl, aren't ya? Maybe I'll put you in the fighting pits instead of the fields. The lifespan isn't much shorter."

Black put a few steps of distance between them, drawing him away from the girls. He was at least a foot taller than her with massive shoulders and arms as thick as tree trunks. He wasn't Draion. That was clear by his pale skin and blue eyes. Brettanian, likely. Slavers?

"Did you get him, Captain?" The ruddy fellow she followed into the tunnel poked his head out. "He followed me a long while, I reckon."

"You bleeding idiot, this is clearly a woman." He pointed to where her short hair curled around her nape and swept across her brow. Or perhaps it was the kohl lining her eyes. He was unable to see her form under her cloak.

The ruddy man squinted, taking a few steps closer. "Is he now? Couldn't rightly tell with that hood on now, could I?"

The brute pushed him aside. "What are you playing at, princess?" His eyes flicked to where Black's hand rested on her sword. She hadn't drawn yet, trying to take her own advice for once and ask questions before cutting them down.

Ask questions first, kill later.

"Wanted to play tough like the men?" He taunted, clearly wanting a reaction. She steeled her features, even if she wanted to kick his fat nose in.

"What do you want with them?"

The brute chewed on his cheek as his gaze moved to the girls then back to her. "Why, I'm saving them. Orphans don't live long in a place like this. Soon they'll be necromite food. I'm just taking them someplace better."

"Right," Black said, shrugging. "Like fighting pits or a field." Her tone was laced with disbelief, but apparently the ruddy man didn't catch on.

"See, she understands. We'll be on our way then." The next second, his face flew forward as the brute clapped him on the back of the head.

"Idiot! She was mocking us, weren't you, girl?"

Black was made for action, so this 'asking questions' bit was further out of her skill set than she cared to admit. Sophia proved more adept at this kind of thing.

"I'll ask again." She pulled on her sword, slowly unsheathing it while she secured her torch in a metal hold on the wall. "What do you want with them?"

"Oh, kitty has teeth." The brute lifted his own sword. "Let's see them pearly whites then."

Still like the sea before a storm, Black waited for her opponent to make the first move. It wouldn't be long by the way his breathing grew rapid, working himself up before he had even struck. Amateur mistake.

He moved, aiming for her head, Black ducked, rolling away. Grunting loudly, he lunged for her again, but this time she blocked, only shaking a little before getting hold of her opponent's strength.

"Come on, girl, show me what you've got," he egged on, ready for more.

Black leaned over the clashed sword. "Just remember you asked for it."

Her foot came down on his boot — hard. He reared back, giving her enough leverage to shove him away. Then she moved to him, letting him get a few more good swings in before she relieved him of his sword.

It skittered across the stone floor, away from the girls and the idiot manning the only entrance.

"How d'ya do that?"

Black offered another shrug. "You fight like you rely on your strength alone to win you the match. Your footwork was disgusting and the angle you held your sword left nothing to be desired. I could go on, if you'd like."

His face paled, finally registering the threat before him. "Who are ya?"

Black almost responded that she was a devil of Nemain's Revenge, and it would have the desired effect, but something else possessed her to say instead: "The Black Shadow. I'm fresh from the docks, just getting settled, so don't be spreading my name just yet."

She intended for quite the opposite, hoping these men would spread their rumors to spite her. By next week, *she'd* be the rumor that made men wary of hurting children like these girls.

Black lowered her blade, deciding she didn't know enough about these men to kill them. They might be just spiteful bastards.

"You're letting me live?" The brute said, shuffling to his feet before scrambling to the other man's side.

"The girls go with me. If you have a problem with that, I'll reconsider."

For a moment, they looked like they wanted to argue, so Black raised her sword again, taking a stance between them and the girls. This was where they decided the worth of their lives.

"No problem, Miss Shadow, sir," the ruddy man responded, letting his tone drop in a way that made her skin crawl. "We best be on our way." He elbowed his companion until he finally took his eyes off her.

A glance passed between them before he refocused on Black. "Yes, take the girls, we'll be off," he forced out. They both gave curt nods before scurrying away.

She had no doubt in her mind that they'd be back, which meant solo missions would no longer be an option. Her mates gave her the advantage.

If they attacked again, she wouldn't allow them to live a second time.

Turning to the girls, one attacked her leg, or so she thought, until she realized the older girl held her calf captive in a firm embrace. The younger followed suit, hugging her other leg.

"Alright, ladies, you're going to need to help me out of here," Black said, patting them on their heads like they were hounds back from a hunt.

Their eyes turned up to her, bright as moons, but none of her words registered. Black put her hands on her hips. "This is going to be a long night, isn't it?" She asked, not expecting an answer.

When she didn't get one, she sheathed her sword, reaching for the torch on the wall.

"Well, we'd better get started."

The older one pointed to herself. "Aya."

"Aya," Black repeated, earning an excited nod from the girl. Then she pointed at the other little girl. Her sister, possibly?

"Dalilah."

"Dalilah," Black repeated, assuming those were their names. "Alright, Aya. Dalilah." She leaned over to pick up the small girl, easily holding her to the side while Dalilah wrapped her arms around her neck.

Aya tugged at her pants, urging her to the door and pointing more.

"Do you know where to go?"

Aya pointed at the entrance again, so Black took that as a 'yes'.

Another hour of wandering the tunnel under Amal and Black's feet were aching, her stomach growling. She'd tried to ask Aya how much longer they would be down there, in fact, she asked if Aya even had any idea of where she was going. Both responses were a blank stare tossed over her little shoulder.

Bloody brilliant.

Luckily, the girl moved with such confidence that Black believed she understood the path. Dalilah clung to her like a baby monkey, one that she had to switch from hip to hip whenever her arm got tired. She began to believe that she wasn't cut out for motherhood, not that she'd ever desired any children of her own.

"*Nahn huna!*" Aya exclaimed, jumping up and down in excitement.

So far, all Black saw was brick and stone, some sand maybe. Nothing to get excited about. No signs of parents.

Metal sang just before the tip of a blade stopped her from taking another step. A Draion man stepped out from an alcove, his eyes steel cold as he inspected her and the girls.

Black let Dalilah slide down her body and run to her sister. The man was okay with that, but advanced further when she put a hand on the hilt of her blade. He moved close enough to nick the skin of her throat.

"*La tufakir fi dahlia hataa.*"

Black didn't have to be familiar with Draion to understand the meaning. She raised her hands, keeping well away from her weapons. Aya led them here, which meant this might be their father. Unlikely, going by the scared look in their eyes.

"I didn't hurt th—"

"*La tatakalam,*" he spat, clearly not interested in hearing words beyond his comprehension. Before he decided what to do with her, Aya tugged on his tunic.

"*Laqad 'anqadhatna,*" Aya said, earning her an incredulous look. Her brows crashed together. "*Laqad 'anqadhatna,*" she stressed, saying it louder.

He hummed before taking his blade away from her throat but not sheathing it. His brows scrunched in displeasure, but whatever Aya said seemed to have done the trick.

"Do you know who these two belong to?" Black attempted, hoping he understood a little trade language to understand. His glare was answer enough. "Right, thank you for not killing me."

Aya tugged on her cloak again, followed by Dalilah. She must have understood their location, because she was being towed through the alcove and upstairs until she entered a new building.

A large room, more like a common area, held numerous burning candles and torches. On the far side, two women were engrossed in conversation, one looking utterly distraught, until Aya shouted at her.

"*Almu!*" Aya ran to the woman, followed by Dalilah, their little hands pawing at her. The woman wailed, falling to her knees, she embraced the girls with open arms.

"Thank you," a soft voice purred. Black turned to find the other woman standing next to her, a white hood concealing her features, yet her voice sounded familiar. Sitamun? The Princess? "They got lost during the display tonight. I didn't think they would be found."

Unease prickled her spine at the thought. "Do children often go missing here?" The mother kissed her girls repeatedly as they embraced.

"Children. Women. Grown men. Most won't go looking for them anymore. One less mouth to feed means the rest live longer."

"You can't believe that."

The stranger lowered her hood, confirming Black's suspicion. Sita's amber eyes locked on hers. "I don't, but I understand why they do. Which is why I must save them." A distant look swept over her eyes before she refocused on Black. "Where did you find them?"

Black pointed behind her. "The tunnels, about an hour away from here. There were two men with them who said something about fields and fighting pits."

Sita closed her eyes slowly. "It's a miracle you found them then. We'd have lost them to slavers after that." Her brew grew pensive as she lifted a finger to her chin.

"With all due respect," Black started, earning Sita's curious dark gaze. "What are slavers doing in the city? It was hard enough to get in and we had your help."

"Yes, how did they get in?" Sita twirled a chain around her neck. "It's as if someone let them in." Silence rang around them as

Black took in that answer. Why would anyone let slavers who steal children into the city? On a regular basis too.

"But you're not asking the right questions." Sita faced her then, blocking her view of the girls' reunion. Black narrowed her eyes at the Princess, uneasy. Sita's eyes flicked to the tunnel at Black's back. "What you should be asking is where that leads."

"And where is that?" Black kept her tone neutral, uninterested, even if she was intrigued.

"Everywhere."

CHAPTER 8

BROKEN WINGS

ROSE

Rose carved into the rock beside her with one of the chain links of her manacles, counting how many times the sun rose. The number had become more daunting with each passing day.

By her count, she had been there for three weeks and two days. The only company she had was the voices in her head and the men who came to visit her.

Dante entered her mind nightly now, peeling back every wall she'd ever built and pulling her deepest, darkest memories from where they should have rotted away. She tried to remove the sense of violation. Especially since, by the disappointed curve of his mouth the last time he visited her, he hadn't located his target.

Dread pooled in her stomach right before his visits. It was worse than facing Colt. At least then, she didn't relive her greatest fears.

Rose received meager meals once a day, some dried meat and bread with a single glass of water.

Colt had explained they didn't want her to grow powerful enough to presume she might challenge them. After all, they didn't want to "damage" her by putting her down.

Whenever Dante dug around in her head, he sought Skye. As if the right memory, even if it belonged to Rose, had the potential to bring her out of hiding.

Colt would crouch before her and attempt to persuade Skye to come forward. She never did. If Colt got annoying enough, Isabeya or even Scarlett would surface, fending him off.

But their attacks were fruitless.

The old hinges of the door complained as it opened, revealing a stone-cold face and black robes. Dante must have been old, so old in fact, that he no longer understood what it was like to be human.

He spread his arms, the robes dangling from his limbs.

"Shall we begin?"

Rose didn't bother nodding. He didn't require permission. Her denials were ignored so often that she no longer bothered to say them.

His eyes narrowed before his power pushed into her mind.

It was like a bee flying directly into her eye, then through it to her mind, buzzing all the while. It could not be ignored, nor avoided, as he buzzed around in her mind.

She wanted to fight against his hold, but she had no idea how. Could she sing him away? With the right song, maybe?

"*Relax, firebird, you need not sing to me.*" His unwanted voice rattled in her head.

While in her mind, he heard her thoughts, plucking them out of her head like feathers on a dove.

Dante flipped through memory after memory skimming over the ones he'd already subjected her to live through and giving her a pounding headache.

He searched longer than before, taking his time rifling through her more horrendous moments, until he finally stopped.

Rose looked out across the open horizon where the water slapped against the cliff side. Her heart ached for that horizon, for the possibility that someday she would get on a ship and never look back. An odd moment for Dante to choose. Rose was no older than fourteen and faced no danger. Then, her father was kind and although she missed her mother, the world had been far simpler.

Until she looked down—

The cliff side drop reached a hundred feet, at least. If she slipped, she would die upon the rough waves and jagged rocks. Survival was impossible. Rose was not close enough for fear to seize her, yet she trembled from head to toe.

No, move back.

It was the first moment Skye spoke to her. She took control of Rose's body, flinging her away from the ledge and landing her in the mud.

I can't.

"There she is."

The memory dissolved and Dante withdrew his hold, but it wasn't only Rose looking through her eyes anymore. Red eclipsed her vision.

They fell forward, scrambling away from the wall to make room for the newly sprouted wings as pain pierced her back, burning like heated blades.

Dante moved forward, causing Skye to flinch away from him, but it was the key in his hand that kept her still. He unlocked the shackles on her wrists and ankles. Rose watched carefully as he slipped the key back into his robes.

He raised a hand to the hole in the ceiling, the tempting notion of freedom so close.

"Fly. Show me the bird can fly. I won't stop you."

Skye heaved, a dry sob spilling from her mouth as her hands shook violently.

Rose pushed at her, urging her to use her wings. They once did it together, flying above Samsara and freeing the officers she had imprisoned with her voice. Since then, Skye refused, not even wanting to think about the skies and their endlessness. Maybe it was being back there. After centuries trapped in strange lands, she was back in Draiocht, the place where she died.

"No," Skye breathed, her throat scratchy from screaming. Had she been screaming?

"No?" Dante's disappointment was evident, yet no anger arose. "Do you not want to be free? To be amongst the clouds and the stars? It's right there, waiting for you."

"No." Skye spat, falling back inside Rose again, clamoring into a ball and hiding herself in the darkest parts of Rose's mind.

Rose sucked down air to calm her sporadic breaths, the change taking too much power, too much energy. She wasn't getting nearly enough food for this kind of exchange. A look back confirmed that the wings had vanished as well. So much for taking advantage of them.

Dante crouched, like how Colt always did, the movement throwing her off. He refastened the manacles to her wrists. Then he stared at her, resting his elbows on his knees.

Rose saw, given his dark hair and handsome features, how Dante likely got what he wanted from humans. There was so much calculation working in his mind, so much malevolence, that Rose shrunk under his stare.

"The work has only just begun."

Before she backed away, his hand landed on her head, his magic diving into her skull like cracking open a watermelon. Waves and waves of pain crashed into her to a point that was so overwhelming she no longer remembered where it came from.

Falling. She was falling, with her hair whipping around her face in a flurry as she plummeted to the ground. The scream tore from her throat, but it did no good, getting lost in the suffocating air. She was falling so fast, she saw the ground rising to meet her and yet, too distant. She was stuck in this perpetual state of falling and could do nothing to escape.

Her wing was broken, tossing uselessly in the wind, red streaking behind her as it bled and bled.

A mental door slammed, locking Skye behind that endless falling prison as Rose was dragged back to her physical body.

Dante released her mind as she twitched in an attempt to stop the fall. With both hands on the ground for stability, she breathed rapidly. Then heaviness overpowered the adrenaline. She tried to keep her eyes open, too afraid to let Dante out of her sight, but she had no strength to hold.

Skye's screams echoed from the back of her head. That was *Skye's* memory. Not hers. She shouldn't be able to see it and yet, she did. She looked up at her captor. He blurred the lines between them.

Dante examined her. "We'll increase your food intake now that I can access Skye. You'll need it. I can't have you passing out just as I am making progress. Once *she* has had enough, we will continue, but sleep for now, firebird. I'll see you again tomorrow."

CHAPTER 9
TWO SPIRITS
PHANTOM

Phantom woke with a start, flinging forward in his bed. Serena's scaly body was curled up at his feet, a light snoring came from her nose. She didn't stir with his outburst.

His hands still felt wet with the Minister's blood, but when he raised his hands, they were dryer than the desert surrounding them. He had carved sins of every kind in the Minister's flesh. There were a lot of crimes he had to answer for. His screams had filled the ship, retribution tasting sweet.

The fire built in his belly again.

He wasn't nearly done with the Minister. He'd only listed his darkest deeds, but he still had to pay for them.

Where did you go? Green flecked the edges of his vision as Sam rolled into his conscience. He had almost grown used to their absence.

Phantom reached for his canteen. "I haven't gone anywhere." His voice came out graveled. Partly due to the burning rage in his gut that wasn't nearly sated.

You normally dream. I can at least sense your emotions in those dreams, but tonight, there was nothing like you weren't in your body at all.

Phantom's brows crashed down on his face. Not a dream then.

The Minister's cries still echoed in his head, but he pushed those thoughts away before Sam grasped them.

And just now, you woke up angry. That usually doesn't happen until you remember where Rose is.

Anger split through his spine. He hadn't forgotten his purpose or why sand was in every crevice of his clothing.

"Thank you for reminding me." Phantom stood, pacing as much as the small space would allow him. His restless energy only grew worse with every passing moment he didn't have Rose returned to him.

I'm only saying—

"Maybe our connection is weakening." When there was no response, he continued. "Maybe I'm learning to shut you out."

Orange and yellow flared in his vision, a rebellion for his words, but neither Draven nor Kayden had anything to say. If they could be separated from him, they would be.

That will only happen when—

"When I've merged with each of you; until we are one, yes I know."

Blissfully, Sam quieted.

His patience grew thin. He'd spent all this time traveling and now he was finally here. That incessant pull from Davina urged him to save Her daughter.

But where?

The bloody princess had disappeared. At least she got them into the citadel and provided them with the barracks for shelter.

Serena snored herself awake, finally noticing Phantom's absence from the bed. She stretched by putting her front taloned feet in front of herself and letting her haunches rise behind her. Phantom would have found it cute, but he had little time for such sentiments.

"*Muevete,*" he commanded, and Serena jerked, jumping to land on his shoulders. She had taken to always staying at his side. He wasn't sure if it had to do with normal dragon imprinting, or if she sensed his turmoil, but he wouldn't complain about the flying weapon that wouldn't leave him alone.

He pulled back the curtain in his room to find the newborn

sun warming the sky. Soon it would hit the streets and bake the people here, although most of them didn't seem to mind considering the alternative was to brave the necromites outside the walls.

Around him was a training yard with small closet sized rooms made for the militia. Now, they housed pirates.

He whistled sharply.

The surrounding rooms rustled with his devils waking. Some had already awakened, including Wilson, who stood leaning against a wall with his staff in his hand. Phantom's next lesson awaited.

"Get up, you bilge rats!"

Hyne rolled out of his room, pushing back the curtain and rubbing his eyes. "What's going on, Captain?"

Phantom finally noticed the meal Wilson had prepared for them, laid out on a table with bowls of rice on a sandstone slab. At least one of his bloody crew understood the rush they were in.

"Eat. I better see each of you ready to leave in no more than ten minutes."

Russet looked like death, with the addition of sunburns across his forehead. "Where are we going?"

"We are going to meet the fine leaders of this city and see if they are aware of where our new friend came from."

They had him tied and gagged in an extra room with shifts for guarding him.

"Captain?" Black asked, darkness bracketing her eyes. She looked tired.

"Didn't sleep well?"

She stiffened before licking her lips. "I found tunnels beneath the city."

Phantom's brows rose up his face. "Did ya, now?"

"I rescued two girls from some slavers smuggling them in the tunnels."

"And where do these tunnels lead?"

"All over the city."

A ghost of a smile tipped his lips. Something like that would be useful, but not until they knew where to use it.

"Good work," Phantom praised before turning his attention to their makeshift brig and the prisoner they had stashed there.

Serena jumped off his shoulders before he reached the room. "I'll join you soon. For now, scout the area and find out how we gain an audience with these mysterious leaders. Any sign of Jon, inform me immediately."

"Aye aye, Captain!"

He itched to go with them, wanting to be out there searching with his crew. If Rose turned up in any form, he wanted to be the first one to see her. But he wouldn't find her with hope alone.

He first had to discover why the Princess had been attacked.

The prisoner was awake, staring through the curtain, as if he knew Phantom was about to walk through it. He sat on an empty cot, his hands tied behind his back and his ankles bound.

Phantom kissed his teeth, dissatisfied with the blank look on the man's features, before leaning against the adjacent wall.

"Do you know who I am?"

The man's head turned, more animal than man. "It depends. What name do they call you in this life?"

Phantom let a humorless chuckle leave him. "Captain Phantom is the only name you need." He shifted off the wall, inching closer. "Is there a name I can call you, or shall I just call you the jackal? Has a ring to it, wouldn't you say?"

No reaction. Only stone-cold eyes, as if no soul existed behind them. "West."

Phantom smirked. "West? That's a direction on a compass, not a name."

He inspected Phantom but didn't answer.

"How did you sleep?" The question made his smile fall. West was aware of more than he revealed. "I imagine well." Phantom didn't want to give away what he was truly doing while he slept, especially since he wasn't yet ready for Sam to know about it. "Did his screams satisfy you?"

James, what is he talking about?

Phantom kept his rage in check, drawing his sword to hold at West's neck. "What do you know of it?"

West blew and flecks of embers flew from his mouth, landing

on the sword and heating up the air. A blast of hot air slammed in his face. Colors blasted behind his eyelids before fizzling out. Phantom's counterparts vanished before he opened his eyes.

"Now we are alone."

Phantom pressed his blade harder to the man's throat, letting a trickle of blood drip down his chest. "What are you?"

West turned his head in that unnatural predatory way. "What lies in the West, Captain?" Many things existed in the west. Samsara. Kalon. Atlas. The native tribes beyond. "The true west."

The Star of Nemain.

The Gates of Hell.

Some sailors use Nemain's Star more than the Northern Star, tracking their location at night, yet avoiding it.

"Nemain grows impatient with you."

"Yes, well, I'm quite occupied at the moment. Perhaps some assistance from Her could speed up the process."

"Do not test Her. The years carry on and you've yet to return to Her. Now, She has gifted you a reminder of your former self, and you still remain here."

Phantom huffed out a sigh. "You see, someone I care about has been taken from me and I have no idea what they want her for or what they are doing to her right now." He'd already imagined the worst. Those ideas haunted him, focusing his mind.

He pressed the sword deeper, a pool of blood collecting at the base of his throat.

"So, tell me, where is she?"

West smiled, his eyes bitter cold. "You're a fraction of your potential. What can you do to me?"

He couldn't hurt West, but there was someone who could.

A wall inside his mind kept out his three voices. His own essence crashed like waves against it. But the wall was not solid. With a slow intake of breath, he mentally reached through the wall, pulling at the warmth of a sunset.

Orange drifted into his vision.

"Tell me what you know of him," he commanded. West's brows furrowed, but Phantom ignored him.

He is not himself. Two spirits lay beneath the flesh. One is in posses-sion of a soul. The other is a soldier of Hell. A demon.

Phantom lowered his sword, too aware of the innocent soul hidden beneath the flesh. Guilt clawed at him. How many of the men he burned were innocent? Possessed suits for these creatures to wear.

They lacked innocence, but no, not all of them chose to be there.

Phantom's guilt stirred further, pushing his feet to move. He started pacing before the demon.

"Can I kill it?"

West's eyes shot at him, his head tilting in confusion.

You cannot kill what is already dead. However, we can banish him back to Hell. It will take him some time to crawl back out.

"Tell me about your master."

West smiled then, sharp and inhuman. "My master is death. She is the sea and the storm."

The sentiment sounded awfully familiar.

A demon's information is worthless. He will only tell you what he wants you to know.

"Then I no longer need him. Teach me."

Draven pushed into their consciousness, sharing space inside Phantom's head. He dropped the sword, but Phantom couldn't determine by whose order the sword now lay at their feet.

West finally looked uneasy.

Relax.

Phantom let his shoulders drop as the room grew darker. The corners enveloped light, moving closer. *Shadows are skittish things. They will retreat if they sense emotional instability.*

"What good will they do me here?" He kept his voice low, calm, like the soothing cadence of Draven's tone.

West's eyes widened. "Which do you speak to?" Phantom noted the panicked edge to his voice.

As the shadows close around the body, they can force out the demon and spare the human. Feel for them.

"What do they feel like?"

Like the coolness of death.

Phantom did as instructed with Draven's help, but the

shadows were reluctant to obey, like a dog with a new master. He pulled on them with his mind, willing them to focus on the demon and leave the human alone. He winced at the icy touch they left on his skin, leaving gooseflesh on his arms.

"What do I do with them?"

West tugged on the irons they had secured to his wrists.

Once he is separated from the body, let them consume him. They will drag him to Hell. There, he will be punished for his failure or until we decide to take pity on him.

Ah, that was why the demon trembled.

Phantom smiled as the shadows grew darker, snuffing out the light seeping through the curtains.

"No," West breathed, recognizing the shadows.

"All those souls I burned; the demons are released into the world again."

West pulled at the restraints, whimpering as the shadows took hold of his essence.

"But this is worse, is it not? Being forced to return to Hell for punishment."

West screamed. It was shrill, shaking the surrounding sandstone until bits of it crumbled.

The two spirits separated, followed by a sickly satisfying sensation. One he could get used to. The man's body fell to the ground, but the demon's true form lingered before him, trapped by shadows. A rotten smell permeated the air in its true presence.

Now, use the shadows to swallow him.

Phantom focused on the demon, the shadows latching around it like a cage until it darkened so deeply that no light escaped.

Good, now let go.

His focus shattered, the shadows dissipating. The demon was gone. Light crept back into the room as the shadows slithered back to their appropriate places. Phantom may never see shadows the same again.

"What are they?"

Shadows are Nemain's reapers. I've heard you say Nemain's Carriage. Think of them as that. They are shapeless entities that transfer souls to Her realm.

Phantom's brows rose. That, he had not expected. He wanted to ask Draven more questions, but the man before him moaned in pain. Right, this one was human.

"Smith," Phantom shouted.

Smith hobbled in, favoring his good leg. "Sir?"

"Where am I?" The man behind him asked. As Phantom suspected, the innocent man likely had no idea what had happened to him.

He put a hand on the doctor's shoulder. "See to it our guest is taken care of. Once he is ready, he is free to go."

Doubt etched Smith's face, making his white whiskers flinch. "Captain? Is he not our prisoner?"

"Not anymore."

Phantom walked past him before the doctor asked more questions. There would be time for all of that when he had Rose back. Until then, he needed to do something. For now, searching the streets of Amal would do.

CHAPTER 10
IT WAS WRITTEN
SEBASTIAN

Sebastian hauled another decapitated body to the alleyway. His pile was four strong now. Four more than there should have been. Onyx blood seeped around the corpses, all decaying in some manner. The stench assaulted his senses. He poured rum over the bodies before lighting them on fire. That's how he could ensure the outbreak's containment until he determined its origin.

This week alone, he had burned eleven walking corpses.

The stories his mother used to tell him ran through his mind. If the legends were true, one had to be bitten to be infected. It was the venom in their fangs that spread the disease.

If that's the case, who was the first victim? Did someone bring a necromite from the mainland?

He watched as the bodies burned and sparked in the pyre. Something about necromites, perhaps their darkened blood or venom, fueled the fire, making it burn hotter. Thankfully, Samsara's ever-present rainfall prevented the fires from spreading.

"I was told I would find you here."

Sebastian had his sword drawn before he turned, facing—

Lord Casimir.

"Oh dear, what did I do?" The lord may have been the kindest man Sebastian had ever known, in addition to being incredibly brave. Their relationship involved the transportation of slaves off the island. Lord Casimir remained a discreet smuggler, though with new developments to their situations, they didn't need each other.

The slave trade stopped when Lockness or the Minister no longer funded it.

Sebastian calmed his racing heart, lowering his sword. "Apologies, William. I wasn't expecting to see you. Or anyone."

"Anyone you wouldn't greet with the tip of a blade, that is?"

"Something like that," Sebastian breathed before replacing his sword and resting his hand on the hilt.

William hummed before coming to stand beside Sebastian. "That's quite the mess." The last vestiges of clothing and flesh burned away, but the smell was unmistakable. He waited for his friend to ask about the pyre, but instead his brows furrowed with a different kind of concern.

"Excuse an old man's theories, but I've been watching the signs, Commodore. Nemain's moon appeared out of sequence. The few plants we have here, rotting away. People are getting sick. Tell me truthfully, has Nemain finally sought to punish us?"

"Yes." William reeled back as if he'd been struck, even though he suspected the truth. "Necromite breakouts are happening all over low town. Thus far, I've been able to contain them."

His eyes widened in horror, accentuated by the firelight reflecting off his face. "You've done this all on your own? My boy, why did you not come to me?"

Sebastian placed two fingers against the bridge of his nose, exhaustion weighing him down. "Ravana needs to be dealt with, but I'm on precariously dangerous terms. If she finds out you or anyone else has helped me outside her knowledge, she will take you down with me."

"You are still the Commodore, order your men to help."

"I'm not. Not truly. Even if my title remains intact, I cannot give any command outside what the Priestess demands. Not without giving myself away." Sebastian's mouth thinned. "I suspect Ravana to be the cause of all this. It coincides with her ascension to immortality. Nemain doesn't like being cheated, and we are paying the price."

William nodded, as if his ramblings made perfect sense.

"So, you think she's aware and does nothing?"

Sebastian rubbed his chin. "I think Ravana has no love for the people. In fact, I'm unsure what she wants. She's likely waiting until someone asks for help so they can be indebted to her."

William cringed, then placed a hand on Sebastian's shoulder. "Well then, it's about time Samsara protected itself." Sebastian focused on the Lord, finally noticing that he lacked his normal clothing. Lords dressed to impress, even on days they didn't leave their estates. But William dressed like a low town fisherman.

"William, who told you to find me here?"

There was only one with his location, as much as the partnership made gooseflesh pebble his skin, he needed her help.

"Interesting story. I was investigating some disappearances with my fishing boats. Many of the men had been ill in the last week. I went to their homes and found their families hadn't heard from them. Then this woman, a frightening one dressed in black and purple, appeared and told me to find you here. She said you would know what happened to them." He looked down at the smoldering pile of ashes. "I suppose I have my answer."

Sebastian's lips twisted. When he had cut down these necromites, he noted that they were all male with sailor's uniforms.

He blinked up at Sebastian. "In what state did you find them, Commodore?"

"A grave one, I'm afraid."

Fear and horror-struck his face. The older man collapsed to the ground, holding a hand to his heart.

"Are you certain the families are unaffected? This disease spreads fast."

He held a hand up. "I'm certain." Sebastian closed his eyes for a moment. At least, there was some good news. Though the families would still be hit hard by the loss. With resources dwindling, they'd find living on Samsara a dreadful experience. "It's real. Nemain's siege. The necromites. It's all real, and it's here."

Sebastian had witnessed so much; seen atrocities some men wouldn't survive. It occurred to him that Lord Casimir might not be ready to accept the truth, even if he had suspected it.

William's silver lined eyes stared up at him. "Samsara is not prepared."

Sebastian held out his hand for the man, pulling him to his feet. "They will have to be. Death is already here."

William blinked away his tears, standing straight once more, even if he couldn't look at the pile of ash anymore. "Before I lose myself entirely, that woman had a message for you."

Sebastian had to resist the urge to check his surroundings for a spying crow. He found them lurking around him often. Perhaps he only noticed them more now. Either case, he was certain Indigo had been watching him. He didn't like it even if their arrangement remained intact. For now.

He took a breath. "What did she have to say?"

"She insisted that you find her."

His jaw clenched. "How am I supposed to know where she is?"

"She seemed to believe you would know." William's confusion echoed in Sebastian's expression.

Until a crow landed beside them, cawing.

"Of course. I have to follow the bloody bird."

Lord Casimir followed Sebastian as they trailed the squawking crow down the center street of low town where the buildings of the witch district darkened their path. Though there weren't many people out during this time of the night, the bird's incessant chatter drew curious eyes.

"Are we not meant to be inconspicuous?" William asked in a whispered tone, sticking close to Sebastian's side as if one of the citizens of low town would reach out and grab him.

"I would have preferred it. I'm not a welcomed face here."

Sure enough, people poked out of their homes to glare at him. From toddlers to men two steps from boarding Nemain's carriage. "William, keep your head down." If there were to be some uprising due to his presence, then it would be best if Lord Casimir avoided it.

Finally, the bird landed on the windowsill of a palm reader's shop.

The crow peaked at the window incessantly until the door finally opened. Sebastian rushed inside with Lord Casimir a breath behind him.

He shut the door, peeking through the window to have his concerns confirmed. The people had grown in numbers, all looking his way.

"Well, that isn't good." William gulped beside him, inspecting the tide of a mob forming outside. None had grown restless yet though. As if they were waiting for a reason to approach.

"Indigo better have a damn good reason to call me here."

"I do."

Both men turned to find Indigo sitting at a table. Candles surrounded her; a layer of sand covered the wood before her, upon which lay various bones and shells. When she looked up at them, her eyes had darkened, paint dripping down her cheeks.

"Something is changing tonight." Her eyes flicked to the masses forming outside her window. "They can sense it. They know it happens here."

William shuddered beside him, clearly regretting his decision to come with Sebastian. "What, per se, is happening?" William's voice trembled as he inspected the witch's home.

This was Indigo's home, the lavender and lilac colors surrounded by dark umber and blackened wood gave it away. Or the array of dried sea stars and shells. It even smelled like her, incense and salty air.

Indigo blinked a few times before she refocused on the men before her. "Our coven sage is in her chamber, asking Davina for guidance." She looked down at the bones before her. "My own divination claims that she will be successful, but it will come at a cost."

Sebastian tensed. This was exactly why he didn't want anything to do with a witch's magic. There was always a high price involved. "I didn't come here to act as a bodyguard if the civilians come looking for blood." He pointed a finger at her. "I want no part of your nonsense."

Indigo stood slowly. "It's clear that you are important when it comes to the success of this. If you do not hear the words yourself, then they will do nothing." She looked back down at the bones and shells, a tear mixing with the paint on her face as it rolled down her chin. "Believe me, you are the last person I want here."

Sebastian watched that tear like it personally offended him. He closed his fist to keep himself from reaching out to her. Until the second one fell, and his hand involuntarily brushed it away. Her lips parted in shock at the contact of his skin on hers.

A rattled crash drew their attention to the far door.

"Mother," Indigo said as she whipped to the door, swinging it open just as an old crone stepped through the threshold. She stood a foot shorter than Indigo, partly due to her stooped posture, attired in what Sebastian presumed to be ritual robes. It was dark fabric, threaded with silver so light it reflected the candlelight surrounding them.

The woman huffed with shortened breaths, buzzing around the small apartment like a bee searching for flowers. Indigo followed her, cooing at the woman to sit.

"Please, mother, talk to me. Did you reach Davina?"

The old crone must have had Indigo late in life to have such an age difference. It was unheard of to see someone as old as her still breathing.

"Yes, yes, yes, yes, yes," the woman chanted, stirring up the kitchen by banging on pots and pans.

"Well, what did She tell you?"

"Yes, yes, yes, yes, yes," she continued to chant, ignoring her daughter altogether. Finally, it occurred to Sebastian that the woman was looking for something. He approached, getting right in her path.

Sebastian stopped her by gently seizing her shoulders. "Hello, what is your name?"

"Celeste," Indigo answered, concern twisting her features.

"Celeste, what are you looking for?" The woman kept chanting, but she didn't try to pull away from him. "What do you need?" He leaned in closer, bending to reach her height.

Celeste's eyes landed on him, unnatural violet eyes that were clouded over with age. Her brows furrowed as she took in his features, then she reached out, cupping a palm to his cheek. "That day, you showed such courage. Your mother was so proud."

Sebastian pulled back, dropping the old witch like she was diseased. "How do you know my mother?"

Celeste blinked a few times. "I don't, but I get a sense of her last thoughts of you. They surround your aura. Your father's too—"

"Do not speak of my father," Sebastian snapped. The reminder of his parents was the last thing he needed if he remained around witches.

Luckily, her attention turned from him to her daughter. Indigo shuddered. "Your father loved you, even in death he loves you. I did not understand why Davina never allowed us to have a child until late in life. Now, I understand your destinies are entwined." She reached out a hand to Indigo, the two clasping hands as she led her daughter to where Sebastian stood rigid.

The crone reached for his hand next. For some reason, he let her take it, drawing it closer to where she held her daughter's hand.

"I understand," she whispered as she laid Indigo's hand atop his, holding them both in her hands. Fire crawled up Sebastian's arm from where he touched her. Indigo's tear-filled eyes chilled his blood as she looked back at him. He wanted to pull her in and wrap his arms around her until she stopped crying. He wanted to destroy whatever caused her despair.

"I don't understand, for the record," William chimed in, breaking whatever spell the witch cast on him. He jolted away, taking his hand back. It was a spell that made him think all that. He didn't care for the witch. It was another manipulation.

He would have said so, when the crone fell to her knees, her eyes rolling back.

"Mother!"

Sebastian noticed something on the crone's neck as her heavy head landed on her daughter's shoulder. He pulled back the robe to find a spiderweb of black veins traveling up her neck.

He'd seen them before. He recalled nothing as vividly as the black veins consuming his mother's body before her death.

"What? What is it?"

Sweat poured down the woman's face as the fever began to take hold.

William leaned over Sebatian's shoulder. "Sweet Davina," he whispered before he retched, holding his stomach as he walked to the other side of the room.

Indigo's hand reached for Sebastian's, gaining his attention. "Tell me what is happening to my mother." Her eyes were so desperate, so pleading that he didn't want to be the one to tell her.

"I'm dying, pet," Celeste provided. "I've had enough time. A witch cannot gain such knowledge without sacrifice." She pulled up her sleeve, revealing a bite mark across her forearm. Indigo sucked in a breath at the sight of the indented fangs, teeth, and the blackened skin surrounding it.

William looked over again, only to retch. "I'm going to be sick."

Sebastian ignored him, focusing on Celeste.

"Now, I'm like my sisters during the war. They gave their lives to find this place." She looked up at her daughter. "I give mine so you can keep it."

Full-bodied tears streamed from her face. "Don't talk like that, mother. We can fix this. There is still time."

Indigo's devastated eyes turned to Sebastian's, begging him to fix this. He wished he could.

Celeste reached a hand to her daughter's face. "You know as well as I, the prophecy will only reveal itself at my last moments. If there was anything to be done, I would not let you do it."

"*Mama*," Indigo said, sobbing into her mother's shoulder.

Sebastian wanted to scream that it wasn't worth her life. Even if she only had a handful of years, she could live them, but he knew better than most that her fate was sealed when she let a necromite bite her. And if it had already spread to her neck, she had moments left.

"It's alright child. Promise, you will listen."

"I-I will." Indigo held her mother close for another few minutes before those violet eyes glowed. Celeste sat up; weakness forgotten. A jewel matching her eyes sliced through the skin of her forehead, glistening in the candlelight. Blood dripped down her face from the hole that allowed it through, the sight grotesque but he was unable to look away.

"*Listen,*" she commanded, her voice otherworldly, before her head tipped back.

"*The sea is a grave. All the dead have come out to play. Red as blood. Orange as the fading light of day. Yellow as fire. Green as the warning of the ray. Blue as sea. Violet as the coloring of decay.*"

The surrounding air began to thrum with energy as she spoke. The flames of the candles bent, leaning to the side as if following a breeze that swirled around them.

"*Santa doncella, madre, y anciana,*" William swore, causing Sebastian to take in his surroundings. The flames had formed a complete circle around the three of them.

"*Once friend, now foe,*" Celeste continued to speak upwards, her hands out on either side of her. "*The final reckoning will begin at the flash of green at sunset and Death's war begins. Only the heart of the truest witch can save what could be lost. Only lovers can destroy love's equal.*"

The candles all blew out at once.

Her back bowed, snapping backwards like she was split in half. Indigo reached for her, but Sebastian grabbed her hand before she could get too close.

"*Mama!* No! Get off me!" Indigo kicked and screamed while Celeste's body writhed on the floor, followed by an unmistakable moaning sound. Indigo stopped her attempt to escape to watch her mother roll onto all fours before rising to her feet. The violet of her eyes had vanished, replaced by cloudy white. Her skin had a sickly yellow and pale tone, and her mouth drooped, saliva leaking from the corners.

William had gone still where he had flattened himself against the wall. "Sweet merciful Davina," he swore again, echoing everyone's thoughts.

"We have to get out of here." Sebastian pulled at Indigo, trying to get her to move.

"I can't leave her. She's my mother," Indigo cried, turning to face him. Within her silver lined eyes, her irises glowed violet, like her mother's once had. That didn't seem like a coincidence.

"She's gone. There's nothing left of your mother." He put a hand on her cheek, wiping away a tear. "Let me give her a proper death." More tears sprang from her eyes, but she stopped fighting him. Choosing instead to lay her head on his shoulder and sob. He held her close, keeping an eye on the necromite in the room still struggling to find its footing, but its eyes were locked on them.

"William," Sebastian started. Lord Casimir jumped to his side as close as humanly possible. "Take Indigo outside. She doesn't need to see this."

"No," Indigo objected. "I can be strong for her." She swiped at her tears, smearing the black kohl all over her face. "I—I can do it." She pulled a knife from the waistband of her shirt.

Sebastian placed a hand over hers. "You can, but you don't have to. Let me do this." The necromite moved now, one slow step at a time. He pried the knife from her hand, and she relented. "Go with William. I'll be out soon."

She nodded once more before shuffling beside Lord Casimir who offered her kind eyes and a sympathetic smile. Once they had left, Sebastian focused on the necromite before him. The one he had just spoken with as a human.

"May your journey be swift, Celeste," he whispered before plunging Indigo's dagger through her mother's forehead, right where the jewel had left a gaping hole.

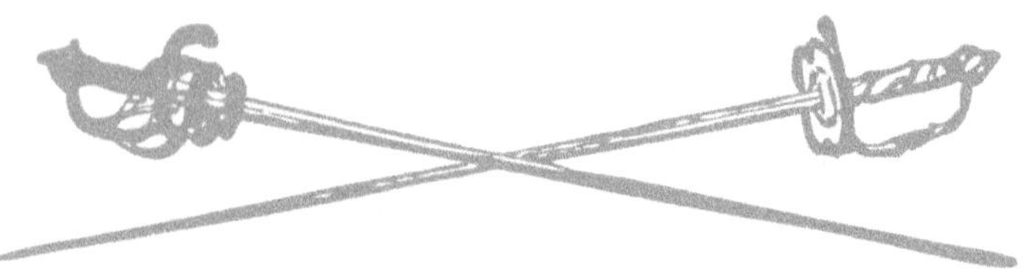

CHAPTER II
THE STREETS OF AMAL
BLACK

Black's mind kept retracing her steps in the tunnels, wondering if she could guess where each offshoot connected to the surface as the devils prowled the streets of Amal.

The sun beat down on them, the desert heat making her skin itch with dryness. The devils had split into groups so as not to draw attention.

Black traveled with Earhart, Ramirez, and Sophia. The huntress has insisted on taking the high ground, hoping the flat, closely placed rooftops.

Thin white drapes shrouded each of them, shielding them from the sun and sand while also concealing their identities. If Amal remained unaware of its infiltration by the Eleven Devils, it would be best to keep that knowledge safe.

Ten Devils.

Black scolded herself for the slip up. She'd never dreamt that a devil would betray them. It didn't just involve the captain. Every single one of them watched as Jon destroyed their trust. What must have been so important to throw everything away? Or had he been playing them from the very beginning?

Black shook the idea from her head, focusing on the task at hand. They scouted the citadel, searching for clues. Might the slavers she found last night have Rose? That seemed unlikely. Jon wouldn't make enemies like Captain Phantom for a bit of coin.

Black watched the Draions on the street. Numerous individuals were homeless, some clad only in rags. Even some with distended bellies, the kind that happened when a body was starving. All these people had been shoved together in a citadel unsuitable for so many.

Before her, Earhart halted, bending to a small child who had curled into a ball. His dark skin contrasted against the light sandstone walls, his brown eyes blinking at them through thick lashes.

The first mate pulled out a ripe red apple from his vest, holding it out for the boy. The devils didn't have much themselves, surviving on half rations ever since they hit a storm on the way there. To forgo an apple in a city gripped by severe poverty wasn't ideal, but Earhart's generous nature couldn't be helped.

The boy smiled at Earhart who returned it. "Hey, do you know Brettanian?" The boy's smile faded, then a string of words fell from his lips that made no kind of sense, but they didn't seem pleasant. Earhart put his hands up in mock surrender. "I'm not looking for trouble." But the boy didn't stop, his words turning to curses before he spit in Earhart's face, tossing the apple into the street.

Finally, Earhart took the hint, backing up.

"That didn't exactly go well," Black drawled as he hurried away from the cursing boy.

"I don't think they like outsiders."

"It's the language that offends them," Ramirez said, rounding the corner to join their quickened pace. "I suggest we keep communication to a minimum." The old man looked almost native with the way he tied his shawl to his head.

"How can you tell?" Earhart whispered.

"I picked up a little Draion on our last visit," Ramirez said, swiveling his head as he took in the glaring faces around them. "Then, they weren't so intolerant of Brettanians."

Earhart squinted against the sun as he looked around at the glowering faces around them. "Yeah, I recall them being more friendly."

Ramirez took on a thoughtful expression before he leaned

down to the boy. "*Pehea to korero... rangatira. E mohio ana koe?*" He cringed at the words as they fell haphazardly, but the boy's eyes brightened with understanding.

"*Imari,*" the boy hissed before running away, disappearing into the crowd before them.

Ramirez scratched his beard, as if he might divine some answers from it.

"Well, what did he say?"

"*Imari.*"

The devils turned their heads to the new voice. The captain had appeared, lack of sleep darkening his eyes in a way that made him look haunted.

"It's the Draion word for treasurer." His jaw clenched. "Apparently, the country is being run by the old royal treasurers rather than actual royalty."

"Ones who speak Brettanian," Ramirez added, as he eyed the captain. "Do you think Brettania has the means to conquer?"

"No," Phantom answered, nodding his head to the giant guards passing them by. Once they passed on, he continued. "If Brettania were here, their soldiers would have taken up residency. No, these treasurers have an agenda all their own and are not to be underestimated." He pulled out a weather worn map of the city. "I'll speak with our ally, find out what she knows of them. Before that, I'd like to get a good look at this palace. Last time, I had been too occupied fleeing guards to visit."

He turned to walk down the street, directed by the map in his hand, the devils following close behind.

Treasurers.

Black didn't miss the irony. If they were the masters Jon had returned to, then they would be in possession of Phantom's *tresora.*

The tradition was widely practiced in Samsara. If one claimed an individual as their *tresora,* it meant more than a lover or consort. It would be to declare one's soulmate. Once claimed, the relationship rarely failed.

A sweetly tuned whistle brought their gazes upwards. Sophia's signal.

She stood on the rooftop, looking down on them. Her bow lay strapped to her back as she pointed at the door they stood beside.

Ramirez pushed open the door, and it led them to a staircase ascending into the building. There was no better way to describe the inhabitants than refugees. People from all over the country had come to the last remaining city in hopes they would survive. Every room was packed with people, most with very little to their names.

Black wanted to ask about them, but she had little to offer. She remembered the tunnels and wondered if they chose to remain in groups for protection.

They reached the rooftop, and Black didn't shift her face before Sophia spotted the sorrow there. Was Samsara much different? Or would this be what became of it?

Somehow Sophia managed a reassuring sad smile. She nodded and Black understood. Just maybe, they could help these people.

Her dark eyes turned to the captain. "We can see the palace from here. I scouted its perimeter."

"Did you see a way inside?"

"Unfortunately, the palace is fully reinforced. By the looks of it, there is no way in. Even the servants are well searched before entry." Sophia pointed down, past the building next to them. Phantom retrieved a scope from his pocket to inspect the building. "There is a front entrance, but by the sand building along the bottom, I'd say those doors haven't opened in years."

Phantom passed the scope to Black, who squinted to block out the blinding sun to see stone doors, thick by the looks of it and more ancient than anything she'd tried to break into.

"Any chance your tunnels can lead us inside?"

Black found the captain's sharp gaze on her, but Sophia's, just beyond him, morphed into confusion.

"Tunnels?"

Black ignored her. "It's hard to say for certain, but I could find out."

"Inform me the moment you do."

She nodded, aware of Sophia's stare on her face as she refocused on the palace through the scope.

Inscriptions were carved into the walls on either side of it, but it was too far to make out, even if she could read Draion. There were a few symbols of note, but most of them consisted of birds or plant life she'd yet to see. Though they must exist somewhere in Draiocht for them to—

A tall, broad figure stood at the edge of the entrance, reading over the carvings as if he wasn't a native who passed by them daily. It might have been minor as far as suspicious activity went, but instinct pulled on her gut, begging her to pay attention.

There was something about his arm and the red scarf wrapped around his bicep—

"Bloody bastard," Black said, pocketing the scope before rushing back to the rooftop entrance.

"Black, where are you going?" Earhart called out to her, but she didn't want to get their hopes up if she was wrong. It was a long shot.

Still, she heard them chase after her, but she didn't slow her steps. If she was right, there was no time.

"Move," she yelled, not caring about their offense, as long as they moved. But she found it more efficient when she drew her sword, none of them wanting to get in her way.

Finally, she made it out of the building to find the street more packed than it once was. The gathering crowds formed a kind of parade, bright colors flashed across her vision as women danced in the street. Handmade puppet creatures, including a dragon resembling Serena, danced along with the entertainers.

Black nearly pushed half of them down in her rush, but it caused a commotion when people started screaming at her. Guards dressed in matching white robes came to block her path. With their drawn curved swords and matching red ribbons on their pommels, it was clear they had no intention of letting her pass.

She halted when they filled the street to stop her. The surrounding people shrunk away from the guards, shrieking at their foreboding appearance.

"Ah, so you're the infamous palace guards?" She smiled brightly at them. "You're shorter than the legends say."

They advanced, perfectly in step with one another and all stood over a foot above her.

Black retreated a step, trying to work out her odds of four against one. It wasn't looking good considering this was the bloody royal guard.

An arrow bolt rammed into the shoulder of one giant, taking him to his knees. Ramirez, Earhart, and Phantom stepped up to her sides, ready to fight.

"We can handle them," Earhart got out before taking the brunt of a sword. The guard towered over him, but it wasn't wise to underestimate the first mate.

But it was the captain who commanded her, his eyes flashing a brighter shade of blue. "Go."

Black took the chance, swiping her blade to block another guard and slide out from under his arm. She got past him, looking back to see the devils descend on them. It wouldn't take them long to take the guards down and keep them from chasing after her.

Normally, Black would be in the thick of the fight, but she had one goal in mind. The devils could handle themselves.

She finally spied the figure again, running and pushing people down to get away from her. That confirmed her suspicion, adding energy to her veins. A power she didn't truly understand propelling her forward.

No, she was too focused. Instincts screaming at her to *run*.

She jumped over fallen baskets, sliding under toppled pillars, taking every shortcut imaginable to catch up.

Soon he was just before her, and she grabbed a fistful of his wrapped turban and pulled. She didn't get a hold of him before he jumped, landing in a flowing canal in the center of the city. She stopped, knowing she would lose him in the waves if she did not see him come up.

After a few agonizingly long minutes, she spotted him across the river. His wrap fell into the water behind him. She pulled her scope out, focusing on his face.

Breath left her lungs as she watched Jon run into the shadows.

CHAPTER 12
TEMPLE POOLS
PHANTOM

"**M**y palace is taken by *Imari*, how predictable."

Phantom had found Sitamun lounging in an underground hot spring. After being shown to the barracks by a priest, he'd understood where Sita was staying.

The priests of the temple were loyalists to the royal bloodline. After all, they believed the bloodline was directly descended from their gods. Rán specifically. If the bloodline truly ended, the priesthood would have to call for a new order.

Since Sitamun still lived and currently waded in a sacred pool, the priests who shifted around the edges of the pool needed only the scarab to sanctify her reign.

"You would have me believe that you weren't aware of them?"

"I've had my suspicions, but I've been in hiding since Draiocht fell and Amal became the last city standing." Her eyes narrowed on him. "My people have needed my help outside the city as well. Until I have obtained the scarab and can prove my birthright, there is little I can do for them."

The princess floated among lotus flowers, stalks of papyrus reeds, and bones, larger than he'd seen before. It was the bones of giants, mostly their skulls, as large as a boulder, taking up most of the space in the pool. Swirls of yellow and green floated among the ripples.

Phantom knew the spot was highly sacred to them. In fact, swimming in its waters was one of the crimes he'd committed during his last visit. Yet, he never did find out why.

Sitamun was fully clothed in thin layers of white that did little in the way of coverage. Once, he had been interested in the princess and her beauty, but that was before he found his songbird. His *tresora*.

He was uncertain whether it was pure coincidence or Davina's influence, yet he couldn't shake the sense that these treasurers held what he valued most.

"What are those lights in the pool?"

Sita turned, the white cloth floating around her. She had yet to dip completely, walking around the shallow pool in lazy circles. A glass of wine was poised in one hand while the other drew swirls in the colors surrounding her.

"Some say they are spirits of the old giants. But I believe it is their *heka*, the magic of the gods that is left behind. Giants with powerful enough blood. The diluted version of giants we have today would not produce the same effect. These *lights*, as you so disrespectfully put it, can judge a soul and punish one if need be." She turned about the water. "As a child of Rán, I am immune, but a normal human soul would easily perish at the slightest touch."

Phantom raised a brow. "Wouldn't that be enough to prove your legitimacy?"

She scrutinized him, her gaze running over him. "I'm afraid not. An ordinary human soul might survive if the *heka* deemed the soul worthy. Though it is rare, it is not impossible."

A thought occurred to him. "You once dared me to enter the waters. Tempted me quite a bit, if I recall correctly." The night would have been much more fun if guards hadn't interrupted them, but he never forgot how they burst into flames upon touching the waters. "You didn't expect me to survive, did you?"

"My, do you have a delayed perception. Yes, Captain, I tested you." Anger rose at the idea, though dangerous pride followed at the idea that he passed the test. Whatever 'being worthy' meant. "Though I hadn't tested your *worth*." At Phantom's frown, she continued. "I had suspected that you weren't entirely human."

Phantom froze. She'd heard the rumors, but this incident had happened before those whispers circulated the city. "Maahes is a legendary demon, after all."

Phantom smirked. "You knew."

"Of course. Just like I knew you would delight in an opportunity to rob royalty."

The conversation began to bore him. He was about to face the *Imari*, and he needed information.

"Enough reminiscing, Princess. What can you tell me of the *Imari*?"

She took another sip of her wine. "The *Imari* was a vindictive bunch to begin with. They were our tax collectors. They controlled where money flowed throughout the country. For eons, the order served the royal bloodline. They must have seized control while I was bringing my people here."

She leaned against a giant skull, unbothered by the death surrounding her.

"Now, they rule with an iron fist, controlling the food supply as if there isn't enough." She breathed a calming breath as Phantom's thoughts wandered. He had seen the hunger on the streets. Their response to Brettanian. It was the language of trade, so it would make sense that a treasurer would be familiar with it. But to deny their citizens food?

"How do you know there's enough food? I've seen the people on the streets."

"As have I," she bit back, anger flashing in her gaze, the yellow lights around her flickering in a way that reminded Phantom of Kayden. "But I also know the city's resources aren't depleted. They are controlled. With the necromites numbers beyond the wall, it gives the people little choice."

"Do you believe they have your scarab?"

Her features turned venomous, as if she could cut down her enemies by only willing it hard enough. "They were entrusted with it."

Phantom leaned back, a new scent wafting to him. Vengeance went beyond anger. That kind of emotion was rancid enough to smell like burning flesh. They had something in common.

Someone they trusted had betrayed them, but he wasn't going to let his story end as hers had.

"What else should I know of them?" His veins burned as anticipation mounted. He had to face his enemy and find out where they kept Rose, but something about this wasn't adding up with this story. Why would a group of treasurers want a woman who lived in an entirely different country?

Sitamun kept that glass of wine near her lips, clearly deciding whether she should tell him something or not.

Yellow flared his vision as white-hot anger pierced him. She would dare keep something important from him. He should force the answer from her; see how the *heka* would react if he drowned the precious princess in its sacred water.

No one would stop you. Kayden encouraged his dark thoughts. *Hold her under until she's willing to talk.* The water just beyond his boots flared with him, yellow swirling more fervently.

"Calm yourself, Captain. I'm a willing ally, but I'm not yours to command."

Sunset orange crept into the corners of his mind like creeping shadows. A pinch of guilt made it past the walls he'd built around his heart. He could be cruel, but that kind of behavior would not earn him allies.

Green joined the colors in this vision. *I fear what you will become.*

Phantom willed his voices to retreat, forcing his familiar smile back into place, even if it was becoming harder to maintain. When his vision cleared, he saw the swirls before himself, orange and green had joined in with the yellow.

Sitamun examined the colors closely. "Quite a mess you have in there."

Phantom then noted the colors surrounding her. Yellow and green. Although Sita had no counterparts to speak of, the concept was still applicable. In this case, the colors referred to her heart and her sternum, where the energy for love and anger were stored. Love for her people. Anger for her situation and betrayal. It seemed she had some aligning to do herself.

"Just tell me what I need to know."

Sitamun lowered her glass, letting the contents spill out into the pool, where they steamed in reaction. Apparently, libations were unworthy. "The *Imari* would survive the pool's waters, but not because they are worthy."

Phantom heard the words she didn't say, Sam finishing them in his head.

They are not human.

CHAPTER 13

TEACH ME, DEAR CREATURE

SEBASTIAN

Sebastian had come to learn the name of the crow who would wait outside his window. Its name was Begonia, and like the oddly perky name wasn't confusing enough, the bloody bird answered to it.

"Begonia!" She turned her beady eyes on him expectantly, answering with a caw of her own. He often wondered if Indigo saw through those eyes but thought it was best if he didn't know the answer.

He'd already learned too much about witches; the scene with Celeste haunting his nightmares regularly, especially the despair in Indigo's eyes when he first arrived. She *knew* that her mother was about to die, yet she did nothing to stop it.

Witches are all the same.

William had vowed to keep quiet regarding what he had seen, promising to help in any way he could. There hadn't been any more necromite sightings since, but he doubted the worst was over.

Begonia took flight, cawing into the night sky as she flew towards the shore. He almost took after his friend and shot the beast down. Would Indigo truly mourn the loss?

In truth, the last thing he needed to deal with was an angry witch, so he followed and hoped the creature didn't draw too much attention.

The bird flew past high town and onto the rocky steppes that led to the cliffs. The barren area held little life, and what grass and trees it possessed died slowly. Before him a woman stood at the edge of the cliffs, a bitter wind whipping her hair and clothes into a frenzy. More alarmingly, a murder of crows flew around her head, raucously.

The bird he had been following joined them. He was no witch, but he took it as an omen.

He climbed the rocks and dead grass until he stood beside Indigo. Grey morning light washed over her face, shadowing her deep freckles and a frown. He followed her fixed gaze to the water below where the sea lapped against an alcove in the cliffs. There, a large body rested across the sand. A whale the size of five buildings had washed ashore, its remains so decayed rib bones protruded from the blubber.

Finally, the stench hit his nose, like the rotten flesh of necromites.

"That creature was no mere whale." Sebastian's eyes returned to the witch. She spoke with such sadness in her tone.

"He was a witch's son." A tear fell down her cheek. "We've been doing this for so long, convincing ourselves that they were better off as animals. We should've known."

"Known what?"

The whale jerked then, black blood flowing out of its open flesh. No creature living would survive that level of decay, which meant—

"Animals cannot be turned. Only a vessel which contains a soul."

"Which means all those creatures out there, children—"

"Will fall to Nemain, same as us, and we sent them into this world with no protection. They cannot access their magic in this form." A sodden breath left her. "We have damned them, and they will serve to end us in return."

Sebastian let his gaze travel over the witch's features. She really was beautiful, but there was a deep sadness on her face. Something more than sympathy for a nameless boy.

"Who was he?"

More tears slipped from her face, and he had an urge to wipe them from her cheek. He found he didn't like her sadness. It differed from when Celeste died. Then, he didn't think about the comfort he offered her. Her wound was too open, too raw. This time, her sadness permeated in the air like the death of potential.

"My brother. My mother changed him when I was very young. He had been an infant. I hoped one day I would find him, and I might change him back."

"Is that him?"

"No, thank Davina. But I may already be too late." She sniffed, wiping away her tears. "I always thought they were the lucky ones. Safe in Kheli or the sea. I was wrong, so very wrong."

A few more moments passed where neither of them said anything. Only the sounds of the wind, waves, and cries of the dying whale disturbed the silence.

"Why do you hate me so much?"

The question blindsided him, making him unsteady. She kept her eyes on the sea, tears still streaking down her face. Of course, he hated witches, but at this moment, he didn't feel much like he hated Indigo.

She'd allowed him into her home at her most vulnerable, he owed her at least the truth.

"When I was young, about seven or so, I lived in high town among the wealthy. My father had been a well-known slave trader, even if he never wanted to be. He told me that he had to do this so I would never have to." His throat tightened. "My mother was kind, often trying to convince my father to abandon the trade. One of my father's men came back from Kalon ill. It was too late when we found out he had been bitten."

Sebastian closed his eyes at the memory, the screaming from all over the manor as the outbreak spread. "Any infected were killed, except my mother. My father used every resource and expense to cure her, but any attempts failed. Desperate to save her, he called a witch, offering her everything, all the money he possessed, even a cut of future endeavors. She accepted."

Indigo's eyes finally turned to him, the unnatural violet glow of them reminding him of her true nature.

His throat closed, making the next words harder to say. "After she arrived at the house, she gave my mother some potion we thought would cure her. While we awaited the news, she attacked my father, ripping the heart from his chest and cursing him for the work he did as a slaver. I watched him die before running back to my mother. The witch found me and told me the potion eased her passing. There was no cure. When the looters and rioters came, I ran. They burned the manor down with my parent's bodies still inside."

He refused to look at her. To see the magic brewing in her eyes. "I don't hate you, but I hate what you are. Not just witches, but magic has only ever bred evil." Memories of his time with Ravana, of the malevolence against Rose to use her magic. Though he didn't blame Rose for what her magic did, he wished she possessed none.

"Ravana," Indigo whispered. He found her vibrant eyes sympathetic. "What did she do to you?"

His body shivered with the memories of the vile things he was forced to do under Rose's spell. He had not been with anyone else intimately, and he didn't intend to. Ravana had broken that desire in him.

"She broke me," he answered, letting the answer lay heavy with questions he hoped to never answer. Indigo remained silent.

The sun shined down on them, the morning fog parting to reveal a clear sky. Indigo wiped her tears, straightening herself before facing him. Were those tears left over from her own troubles, or were they for him?

"This is not why I called on you." She sniffed away the last of her sorrow. "You are in need of a sacrifice."

Sebastian stiffened. "I have no need for sacrifices," he bit out. The mere suggestion had his insides rolling, an anger so bitter it made him sick.

"Correct me, Commodore, but Ravana requires a defected

officer by today. If you return empty-handed, she will suspect your ruse." He'd been avoiding that very idea all week. Those men, his men, already had their lives taken from them. He remembered what it was like to be trapped in one's own body. He never wished to inflict that pain on anyone, especially the men he'd failed once already.

Assuming Ravana wouldn't just kill them.

"I will handle Ravana."

There was no mocking tone, only sadness as Indigo stared at him. "At best, she would kill you. At worst, she'll use you as a weapon against us. I'm very sorry, but you are too important for this war against the dead."

Her eyes left him, focusing on something over his shoulder. He tracked her eyes to find a man walking along the steppes, one he recognized immediately. An orphaned boy who lived with Sebastian back when he was Bash. A boy he had grown up with, Thomas.

"No."

"Sebastian—"

He advanced on her, and she didn't even flinch. "You cannot force me. I didn't earn my free will to do this." Sickness threatened to overcome his stomach. To kill a comrade who'd already been caught was one thing, but this man had a chance of survival. "The officers are included among the people I am to protect."

"War requires sacrifice, Commodore." This time, she advanced on him, and he took a step back. "We've been at war since before you were born." Her eyes traveled back to the whale and the sad moans leaving the creature. "We are overdue our reckoning. Now, it's time to act."

Thomas was only a few more paces from earshot.

"He understands what he must do," she whispered as if the notion helped. "I wish there was another way."

Thomas arrived, placing a hand on Sebastian's shoulder. "Hello, Bash. If you don't mind me saying, I want to thank you for helping us."

"I didn't—"

"I know. But you also never gave up on us and if it wasn't for you, we'd still be trapped under the spell." Sebastian wasn't certain that was true. "The way I see it, if I have a say in how I die, I want it to mean something. If this will serve to help you, it'd be an honor."

A tear gather at the corner of Sebastian's eye and he let it fall, the man before him deserved it.

"Do you understand that death is only one outcome to the many things Ravana could do to you?"

Thomas swallowed and dread pooled in Sebastian's gut. Death was the preferred option among Ravana's many sins. Thomas feared her like all the other boys of the Fortress did.

"I am prepared, Commodore. But I ask that if you can, you kill me."

Sebastian nodded, hating every moment, every second of this. When he imagined being the Commodore as a boy, he never imagined it like this.

When he turned to Indigo, she vanished. Not even a crow left behind.

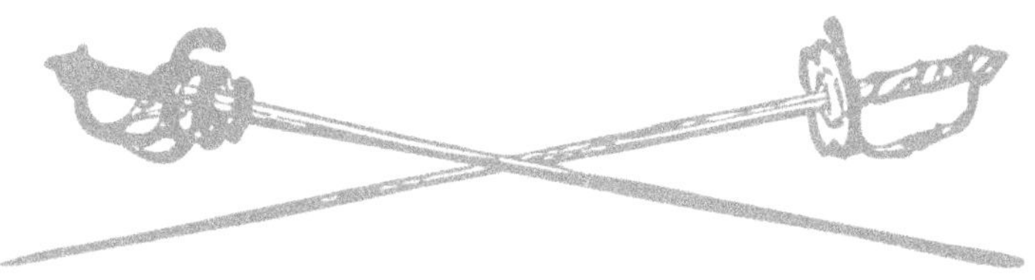

CHAPTER 14
THE MISSING DEVIL
BLACK

Amal was a maze of corridors, buildings and packed streets. Black berated herself for not noticing her surroundings enough to determine her position, especially since asking for directions was unthinkable. The last thing she needed was to start a riot. All that considered, she didn't regret it. Her hunch had been right, and she had barely confirmed it.

It not only confirmed that Rose was nearby, but if they managed to capture Jon, perhaps this trip wouldn't be too lengthy. That would require the devils to find him again, but if anyone would, it was the captain.

The sun had disappeared, two moons rising to create a blanket of silver and lilac across the sand and stone, by the time she found the training yard of the barracks.

Black caught the tail end of Sophia's description of the palace. Ramirez was off to the side, smoking a pipe.

"There are symbols along the gate, ones I couldn't read, but with the wide berth locals gave this area, I wouldn't be surprised if there was some religious connotation." Black stopped before stepping out of the shadows, the news she had would distract them from the conversation. She could wait a moment.

"Ramirez," Phantom asked. "What did you make of them?"

The old man let smoke trail out of his mouth, Robin coughing beside him. "I took a look, but the hieroglyphics are old, ancient even. Only a few of them are still used today. I noticed the symbol for death repeated numerous times."

A skull on a spike. Black had seen the unsettling symbol.

"But there was a curious one. It sat at the very top of the entrance as if it represented the gate altogether. A snake in a circle, eating its own tail, but in the middle of the enclosed snake body there was the head of a lion with a crown atop its brow, more detailed than normal hieroglyphs. I would call it a coat of arms."

The captain's brow furrowed.

"I might have seen someone who can explain," Black drawled, inching out of the shadows.

Sophia's head whipped around. If Black wasn't mistaken, her shoulders dropped in relief even if her face didn't let on.

"Where did you run off to?" Earhart inquired, relief relaxing the lines around his eyes. Though Black half expected to get scolded.

When she locked eyes with the captain's, the dark ocean of his eyes churned with intensity. He already knew what she was about to say.

"Where is he?"

———

The debrief with the captain left Black uneasy. She wasn't sure why. Maybe it was the fact that she didn't catch Jon like she tried to. Maybe it was the hungry look in his eyes and how they brightened slightly. She remembered what it looked like when the captain was scheming. He would catch Jon eventually and when the time came, she hoped Jon survived, despite his betrayal.

The moment Phantom retired to his room, and the crew scattered. A hand on Black's forearm pulled her into a room. The curtain was drawn over the entrance, blocking out the moonlight so Black wouldn't see anything. The flick of a match and lightened candle was enough to show Sophia's pinched brow.

She threw a fist into Black's arm — hard.

"What in the hell were you thinking?"

The corner of her mouth twitched upwards. "I missed you too."

Sophia's full lips pursed, irritation drawing a growl from deep in her throat. Black much preferred her this way. It was much better than the stone-faced woman from earlier. Even though she wasn't keen on the hitting.

Black nursed her arm. Sophia hit hard.

"It has been hours since you took off without a word. I didn't know where you went or how to help you. No one could follow you. You could have been hurt." Sophia's hands landed on her hips, drawing attention to the beautiful turquoise fabric she recently acquired. It exposed her midriff and frankly, looked stunning on her.

"You look beautiful today."

Sophia's jaw dropped, a slight red tint coloring her cheeks. "Are you even listening to me?"

Black refrained from smiling at the small victory, knowing Sophia was worried about her and it threw her off enough to be affected by a little flirtation. A rare win.

"Yes. I apologize. I did not intend to make you worry. It took time to retrace my steps, I ran all the way to the canal."

Sophia blinked, finally relaxing enough to come to her scenes. "I wasn't worried." She crossed her arms, building that wall back up again. "I was rightly concerned, but I would have been for any of the devils."

"Right..."

Black didn't believe that for a second. Her singular goal around Sophia had been to break her icy shell. Black liked being the reason she got riled.

"Are you hurt?" She said the word so curtly, but the fact that she said them at all reassured Black that her walls weren't back in place yet.

Black stretched her arms out either way. "You can check me over if you'd like." Sophia's glare made her lips curl up in amusement. "No, I'm in excellent condition, actually." That part she said with a healthy dose of surprise.

She wasn't certain how she built the stamina to pull off the sprint she did. Perhaps it wasn't as impressive as she believed.

Either way, she should be more tired. As it was, she could run under the moonlight.

Black expected her to deflate with relief, but instead she chewed on her lip.

"What else is it?"

"Tunnels? When did you find out about tunnels?"

Black blinked at all the questions. "I found them last night, there were these—"

"Last night? You went off on your own?"

She breathed in a suffering sigh. "Yes, these girls needed my help. I saved them from some slave traders."

Sophia pulled at her hair. "Take me with you next time." Her dark eyes glimmered in the candlelight. "Promise me, Gwen. Let me have your back."

Black's heart squeezed at seeing Sophia so concerned. She didn't think the huntress wanted to come with her on missions like this. "I will, I promise."

Sophia breathed out slowly, her tense body finally relaxing. With her back straightening and her eyes cooling, Black watched her walls snap back into place. She moved to the curtain.

Black's hand snapped out before she thought it through, wrapping around Sophia's arm and pulling her until they were face to face again. This had been the first time Black had her alone in weeks, she wasn't about to let her go so easily. Black took a step into her and their eyes locked, the huntress captured in her gaze.

Sophia retreated, backing up until her back hit the sandstone wall. The room had only been big enough for a small bed and table.

Black's arm came up on the wall, blocking Sophia's escape route. They no longer touched, but Black surrounded her, only a breath's length away.

"You told me to come find you," Black whispered, her tone sultry. Sophia sucked in the smallest amount of air at the sound of it. If she hadn't been paying attention, she would have missed it.

"And find me you did." Sophia said flatly.

Truly, she never thought Sophia would agree to be hers. There were many reasons, but they all boiled down to the idea that she would never be good enough. Not that Sophia asked for anything more than to be respected.

"When are you going to acknowledge this thing between us?"

Sophia's eyes floated to the ground. "I have no idea what you're talking about."

Black reached for Sophia's chin, pulling it up until they locked their eyes. "*Los cojones.*" *Bullshit.*

Sophia jerked back from the vulgar phrase, but there was no better way to call out her lies. As Black expected, those walls of hers reinforced themselves as the ice returned to her gaze.

She raised a finger, halting the spitting words, no doubt about to roll out of Sophia's mouth. "There is a connection between us." She leaned in, whispering into her ear. "You're in my *soul*, Sophia Clare." A shiver raked her body. "How about this time, you can come find me?" Black leaned away, a smirk on her lips.

It would be entertaining to watch Sophia come to her, but she refused to believe in miracles, especially with the fight still simmering in her gaze. Though now it looked more like surrender tempted her.

Black backed away from her, giving her space to walk out.

Sophia's brow rose. "You will be waiting a long time, *Black.*"

She inwardly cringed as Sophia used her moniker.

Black resisted reaching for her. "I'm willing to wait centuries for you, Sophia." No flirting tone, no jest entered her words. Her heart throbbed against her chest with the confession. If it took that long, so be it. She had never met anyone like Sophia, someone so self-assured, yet in that silent way, she cared for many people at once. Black even recognized the wisdom in her young eyes, so beyond her years. She was fearless, talented, magnetic even.

They made a good team, too. One day she'd get Sophia to admit to that, but it wouldn't be tonight.

Sophia blinked slowly, her mask cracking before it slid back into place. She didn't say anything further as she brushed past Black, exiting into the training yard.

Black stared at an empty room that seemed much bigger without her huntress in it.

CHAPTER 15

BY ANY OTHER NAME

ROSE

A piercing scream woke Rose in the middle of the night.

Rose searched the chamber, but it was just as empty as before. No mice in the corners, not even a breeze. Silver light poured into the cavern, as if searching for her. A strange thought to have, but the light seemed... alive, somehow.

The scream echoed again, making Rose flinch, but she remembered where it came from. Skye had been trapped in some kind of mental barrier in her head. Sleep deprivation settled in on the third night of restlessness. Sometimes, she would jolt awake after a sense of falling.

Dante hadn't been back, leaving her in endless torture.

Green consumed her limited vision. *When he returns, she will give in.*

Rose's stomach clenched. What was the point of all this? What did they want?

They want to kill us.

Rose grunted. "You keep saying that. Why? Who am I to them?"

Silence answered like it always did. Interrogating her past selves seemed to be the only solution. If only they weren't so stingy with the details.

Rose tossed her empty water cup across the chamber before

burying her face in her hands, frustration bubbling inside her. The manacles shifted down her arms, she realized how small her wrists had become, the bones protruding on the sides.

Lifting one manacle, she inspected the iron ring that had caused her skin to bleed and redden. It was loose; loose enough to—

Rose slipped her hand from the manacle, the metal rubbing against her skin. She stared at her wrist, relishing the range of motion she had been missing for weeks. She pulled her second wrist out before trying to work on her ankles.

Those took a bit more work, the metal scratching her heel as she pulled on them, but eventually, they gave too.

Both her ankles and wrists were raw from the irons, blood oozing out of the. scratches she made. She tried not to think about how thin her wrists had become in the last few weeks. Her body was strange and feeble as she stood.

Stars twinkled beyond the hole in her cell, the moonlight fading as it drifted away. Since it was the middle of the night, this just might work.

Rose padded to the door. She tried to turn the nob, hoping against the odds that they underestimated her enough to leave it open.

She only jerked against the lock.

Green seeped into her vision like vines crawling up a stone wall.

Right, because they would leave your cell door unlocked.

"It was worth a try."

She practically heard Isabeya scoff. Then footsteps behind her made her more certain.

"You need to find two small metal rods. Is there anything around here we can use?" Isabeya's tone was lighter than usual, hope brightening both their spirits. When Rose turned, her counterpart's projection glared at her. Rose came to believe that was simply her natural state.

She scanned the room, but she'd been staring at these walls for weeks, there was nothing but sand and stone.

"There's nothing here. Do you really think they would put an object like that in my reach? They know *you're* in my head."

Isabeya's mouth twitched, but the smile didn't reach her eyes. "Those two have failed as many times as we have lived. Look harder."

Rose searched again, eyes trailing over nothing but sand.

"Find anything?"

Rose's nose scrunched, irritation bubbling. "I'm finding your voice outside my head to be more annoying than it was inside."

Isabeya's glower was dramatic enough to give Rose a spark of amusement. "Shall I leave you to it then? You are familiar with lock picking, naturally."

Rose blinked and Isabeya was gone, but her presence remained close. The hints of green in Rose's vision gave her away. Still, she needed Isabeya. When *they* returned to see she had escaped her irons, she wouldn't be able to slip away a second time.

"Fine, help me, *please*. What am I missing?"

Isabeya's voice was slow to return, but no matter their differences, they all wanted to be free of this place and the inevitable end that would come with the success of the treatments.

"Look closer at the door." Rose whipped her head to the door, and the only wood in her cell. Several planks of wood to be exact. The door itself was barred with metal, so the likelihood of getting the planks to separate was unlikely. "I bet there are loose nails in there."

Rose's hands glided along the wood, picking at nail heads with little success. Her fingernails were brittle, cracking under the slightest pressure. Another symptom of her body's rapid starvation. She growled, landing on her knees before the door.

It would be so much easier if she just sang. She knew the song to unlock a door, but the well of power inside her was dangerously dry. She wanted to dig deeper as Dante and Colt forced her to do every time they visited, but doing so would bring her closer to death. It was best to save her magic as a last resort.

"Why can't Scarlett just light it on fire?"

Yellow sparked across her vision at the mention of her name.

Happy to.

Isabeya tsked. *That would use more power than an opening song.* Rose growled again, frustration building. *You don't even know if it would work. It may only be a waste of precious energy.*

"But I can't stay here."

Then pick the lock.

Rose stared at the door again, looking for a nail she would focus on. A weak point. The door was solid, not a line out of place, but not the door frame. Rose touched it, letting her hand drift over the rough ridges and splits. The wood on the frame was old and frayed. The door itself had likely been installed recently. Right before her arrival, she imagined.

But the frame had been there for years.

A small nail poked out from the side of the frame, protruding from the wood, only marginally. She got her nails beneath the head, lifting it.

The tips of her fingers dripped with blood, but she ignored it because the nail moved. It rose from its hole before finally releasing into the open air. Rose pressed down on her nail beds, willing them to recover even if the movement smeared blood over her clothing.

Let me see it.

Rose opened her palm and studied the nail, not for her own examination, but for Isabeya's. Blood streaked across her skin, partially covering the nail.

This will do. Now, listen to me very carefully. This is a very old style of lock.

Rose knelt before the door, looking over the door handle and lock.

Push it in slowly, lifting once you reach the back wall. You must lift each tumbler in succession. If you miss one, you will have to start over.

"Why are you letting me do it if you can just take over?"

Isabeya paused for a moment, but Rose had been living with the woman in her head all her life, that pause was nothing more than her gathering patience. *Because it uses too much energy for us to switch. Even a small amount might make your body lose consciousness at this point. We can't risk it.*

Rose breathed in heavily. She had grown too accustomed to

being able to use her power. Spoiled by it, her father would say. No, she didn't want to think of her father and his turbulent love.

Just focus. You can do this.

She pulled in a breath of air, praying that the air in her lungs would fuel her power in some small way. Then she followed Isabeya's instructions, pushing the nail in. It barely reached the back, moving it up and down proved to be a challenge.

Keep your ear close to the lock to listen for the tumblers clicking into place.

Rose leaned close, hearing the faint scratches and metal sliding. Finally, the first one set, a satisfying click signaling her success. She went on the next one and the next.

Footsteps interrupted her work, coming from the other side of the door.

Stop. Rose froze, her heart beating wildly in her chest. *Don't make a sound.*

The footsteps grew louder before they moved on, fading. Whoever it was, passed them by without even slowing.

Rose went back to work, only one tumbler left. It clicked into place. She turned the knob, and the door swung open. If she wasn't so focused on escaping, she would have celebrated but still needed to find a way out.

The hallway outside her door possessed no more adornment than the cell. The hall was small, only wide enough to fit three people walking side by side. There were only two ways she could go and no direction to indicate which way was the smarter choice.

"Any ideas from the counsel?"

She sensed more than saw Isabeya's flare of annoyance. *Just pick one. Being wrong is better than standing here.*

"Debatable."

She turned left, the deciding factor having to do with not wanting to run into whoever walked past her cell before.

Sharp pebbles pricked her bare feet as she walked, her body moving slower than she remembered. A cold breeze blew into the hallway, making her shiver and wrap her arms around herself.

Light appeared, lilac moonlight spilling into the hallway as it opened to a large room. The moonlight came from a high window, with again, no way to reach it. She took a short breath, glaring at the window.

Her gaze fell to see a door, more like a double-sided gate made entirely of metal, below the window. Rose smiled.

Yellow flames licked at her vision. *That looks an awful lot like a way out.*

Rose scanned the area, unnerved by the lack of guards. If this was the entrance, shouldn't there be someone standing guard?

"Where is everyone?"

She inched closer to the door, giving it a tug, but unsurprisingly, it was locked. A hole through the metal allowed her to see outside. She closed one eye, looking through the hole.

A half rotting head started back at her.

She jolted, taking several steps back.

Yellow assaulted her vision, responding to her sudden fear. *What the hell was that?*

Isabeya answered. *That is what we've been fighting.*

After her heartbeat slowed, Rose looked through the hole again. The decaying body wrapped in swaths of fabric moved to reveal a sight that drew the breath from her lungs.

Hundreds of bodies hobbled around in the sand, most in a grotesque state of decay; others didn't even resemble humans anymore. They weaved around one another, completely aimless. She heard them now, low moans like those of a dying man.

If she escaped through this door, she wouldn't get past them. Rose had been trapped in that cell, but seeing how impossible escape truly was made the air leave her lungs. She fell to her knees at the door, sucking in as much air as she could, her breath too shallow.

Shhh. It's okay.

Rose no longer paid attention to who was speaking in her mind. It didn't matter, because she would never escape.

Don't give up yet. There are other places to search.

She held up her hands, their trembling growing stronger, more demanding. Useless power thrummed in her veins. Everything she had ever endured only led her here, where they would pick apart her mind until there was nothing left.

You will not die here. I won't allow it.

A multitude of colors blocked out her vision as if every past version of herself came to console her. But what did they know? Each one of them had died, young even. She needed to live. She'd figure everything else out later, but if she died here, none of it mattered.

Skye screamed in the back of her mind, fueling the panic on her own.

Calm down. Everything will be alright.

The sobs started, pulling from her body like a hand constricting her lungs, further stanching her ability to breathe.

Red fully washed her vision so violently that she wondered if she was bleeding from her head. It made no sense why she would be, but her racing heart told her it wasn't impossible. She was dying anyway.

Let it happen.

"What? Let myself die?"

No. Your body is reacting to your own panic. Focus on your breathing. Picture it like a wave, washing over you, but you're no longer drowning, you're floating.

Rose tried taking longer breaths to push against the pressure in her lungs.

That's it. You're floating on the waves, letting the current take you.

Rose imagined herself in the water, waves lapping at her skin, but the water wasn't cool or warm, it only rose and fell, she with it.

Breathe in.

A hand grabbed hers as she floated, but she didn't have to look to know who floated with her. She let her fingers tangle with his, the warmth of his palm shutting everything else out.

Breathe out.

He wasn't there, but the thought of James calmed her more than the ocean did.

Survival was second nature to her pirate. He'd done it despite the odds and kept his crew surviving with him. That included her. Hope crept in. He would come for her. He would do it for any one of his crew. A crew she was now a part of.

He would come.

She exhaled, and everything seemed manageable again.

A slow clap had her eyes snapping open.

Colt leaned against the wall before her, covered in shadow. His bellowing laugh echoed around him as he stepped into the moonlight, lilac light spilling over his inky hair.

Rose was too numb to panic again, but his presence frightened Skye, who had escaped Dante's mental prison. *How did that happen?*

"I see you've discovered your little... dilemma." Colt crossed his arm, but there was a painted smile on his face. Though she had no doubt that this entertained him. "See, we've underestimated you time and time again."

"We've used many strategies against you." Dante appeared from the hallway to the left, darkness clinging to his edges like it didn't want to let him go. But unlike Colt, Dante didn't smile. "This time we have constructed the perfect prison from which you cannot escape."

"Well," Colt said, tilting his head and gaining Rose's attention again. "You can actually escape." His brows rose, as his eyes lifted to the open window above her head. Too far to climb to but even if she did, she'd have a host of necromites to get past. "All you have to do is get that skittish little girl inside you to fly."

Rose shook her head. Maybe in different circumstances, one where Skye might breathe without fearing everything around her, but here? No chance.

"Why does it matter? What do you two get out of this?"

They looked at one another before Dante knelt, getting on Rose's level. She flinched away.

"You see, little bird, we're trapped here, in the mortal realm."

"Because of a curse, your *Mother* inflicted on us," Colt interrupted, his smile finally dropping.

"My mother?" Her mother was the kindest soul she'd ever met and in possession of no such power.

"She cursed us right along with you as punishment for our crimes against you over a millennium ago."

Rose blinked, at a complete loss. "What?"

Dante tilted his head at her like a curious dog. "They haven't told you? At the very least, Isabeya should have, but they all know the truth."

Silence echoed around her lonesome thoughts as her counterparts kept their mouths shut.

"What is the truth then?"

Colt chuckled, raising his palm to the sky. Rose looked up to see his hand gesturing to the silver moon waxing just out of sight. "I present to you the Mother of All, the Queen of Gods, Keeper of Fate, and the most annoying pain in my ever-loving ass, Davina."

Rose stared at the moonlight, beaming just above her head, but not touching her. Davina was her heavenly mother in a religious sense. All of creation belonged to Her aside from Nemain and Her domain. Somehow, Rose understood that wasn't the context they referred to.

"My mother is the Goddess Davina?"

"Bingo!" Colt yelled out, the sound echoing down the hall. Rose didn't understand what the word meant.

"What he means to say," Dante started, an apologetic look crossing his features, "is that you are correct. Davina created everything else, but you, She physically birthed you into the world. Well, the *whole* version of you."

Rose tried to wrap her head around the ridiculous notion. She wasn't some forsaken goddess. Laughter bubbled up her throat, but the men ignored it.

"Not to be rude, but you are only part of what Angel was. She was as fearsome as a goddess herself."

Angel. The name sounded so right. The original life?

"She had the divine right to it, too."

"Once you've ascended completely, you'll regain your original memories and every life you ever lived, making you whole once again."

That word again. *Whole.* Like she wasn't a complete person now.

"We don't make the rules, birdy."

Was she glaring? Probably.

Dante pushed off his knees, standing again. "That's where we come in."

"Davina tethered our power to your ascension. It's poetic really. We conspired to kill you centuries ago, and now we have to watch you die over and over again until you finally conquer that little head of yours." An edge sharpened Colt's words, less buttered than before.

"Do not mistake your luck. We are patient above all else. If you prove to be incapable, we will kill you to speed up the next cycle."

Rose's gaze snapped to Colt, hoping to find something else on his face. Unfortunately, he smiled again. "And around and around we go."

Anxiety split through Rose's chest, that familiar panic wanting to resurface. Even if it meant she would return in another form, dying meant losing everything and everyone she gained in this life.

Except one, Isabeya reminded her. *He'll find us again. Like always.*

"Was — James cursed, too?"

Both of their faces scrunched up in confusion. "James?" Colt asked, looking at Dante.

"I believe that is the name he goes by now. Our Sam."

The corner of Colt's mouth bent upwards. "Oh yes, he was cursed worst of all." This time it was Colt who approached her, crouching down to her level. Those inhuman black eyes were so unnerving. "He was cursed to fall in love with the same woman over and over again." Rose swallowed, not liking the implication. "Don't you wonder?" Colt bit his lips, that familiar cruelty spilling from his gaze. It caused a pit to form in her stomach. "How is it possible for him to fall in love with you time and time again?" He leaned in whispering. "I'll tell you a secret."

Rose doubted that it was much of a secret if he told her.

"It's not real love. It's only Davina's hand. She cursed him to serve as your bodyguard throughout lifetimes. Making him fall in love with you was the surefire way to gain his loyalty. If he loves you, he'll protect you at all costs."

Rose's heart sank.

"So, you see, birdy." Colt drawled, rising to his feet again. "Once we finish with you, all of us are free, including him. And that love he *thinks* he feels for you—" he snapped before her face, making her flinch "—it will be gone. All you'll be is an unpleasant memory."

Fear penetrated her heart, flowing all the way to her toes and threatening to spill over again.

A tear slid down her face. Colt leaned down to catch the tear on his knuckle. "Don't worry." His knuckle traveled to her chin, lifting it to capture her gaze. "If you ask really nicely, I'll kill you before he can get the chance to."

Dante drilled into her head before she responded.

CHAPTER 16

GIANT'S BONES

PHANTOM

The streets of Amal darkened, the tall buildings preventing moonlight from penetrating its depths. Lanterns lit the inky corners, but it wasn't enough.

The surrounding shadows whispered in the cool night air as they answered the call of their master. Draven was close, tinting the edges of his vision in shades of orange, matching the firelight around them. The shadows answered him alone, Phantom had not yet earned their loyalty.

But with Draven currently at his disposal, it didn't matter.

Make them listen to you.

Phantom scoffed, earning the concerned glances of his devils beside him. Black walked on his left, Earhart on his right, their twisted brows mirroring each other as they entered the tavern. Perhaps they hadn't grown accustomed to his *situation* yet.

The shadows spoke, whispering the location of his devils. The sound of their hushed tones traveled like breath over his ear instead of in his head.

Russet sat at the bar, halfway through a pint, Hyne joining in his laughter. Tick resided near the door, cloaked in darkness, but watching warily.

Wilson stood outside with Sophia, the two keeping watch.

Phantom had followed Davina's call like a string tugging at his gut to a tavern with the face of a golden cat on its swinging sign. He had to admit, the controlling Goddess did have Her advantages as an ally.

The tavern buzzed with the thrum of excited patrons. Though Jon was not small in stature, he hid well amongst the crowd.

"Hey! Everyone this time!" Russet yelled from the bar, his beer sloshing in his glass. Although, one would not recognize the burly red bearded fellow. Russet had put considerable energy into changing his appearance, using kohl to deepen the lines around his eyes and spreading it across his beard to hide his signature ginger color. A hat, more like a Brettanian sailor than a pirate, sat upon his head, flopping with his jerking movements.

From the looks of things, Russet had managed to charm the nearby sailors by teaching them a song. He taught them the chorus, pounding his fist on the table. They echoed it.

Phantom shifted through the revelers and drunkards to the far end of the bar, away from Russet and Hyne's antics on the other end.

The sailors took on the beat, comfortable with it now as Hyne took the first verse.

HOIST YOUR SAILS AND READY YOUR SPEARS
TONIGHT, WE EARN THE SHARE OF OUR YEARS

The sailors sang in a low cadence.

FOE HO
THE BLOOD OF THE OLD GODS IS HERE
BUT WE'LL SHOW THEM WHO'S REALLY TO FEAR
FOE FUM
WHAT WILL MAKE US RICH AS KINGS?

The sailors and Russet joined with Hyne.

THE BONES.
AND THE CREW OF THE GIANT'S BANE.

The air grew thicker, people hoisted their hoods over their heads or shimmied out of the tavern as discreetly as possible. Wilson and Sophia stayed there to check their faces as they left, instructed to signal at the first sight of Jon. Since they stood as sentries at the tavern entrance, they weren't difficult to notice. Jon would try to find another way out.

By now, Tick would have secured every other door, using a lock pick to secure any open doors. Jon wouldn't leave without a scene.

Russet took the reins of the song, starting the second verse.

**THE CAPTAIN CRIES ALL HANDS
ALL HANDS!**

The sailors echoed. Earhart and Black took their cue, cutting off from Phantom to find their respective posts.

**WE MAY LOSE NO MAN TO THE BEASTS OF THE SANDS
FOE HO**

"Can I get you something?" The glittering eyes of the barmaid caught Phantom's.

"I'll have what they're having," he drawled, pointing to Russet and Hyne as they continued to sing their hearts out. She gave him a quick nod, not lingering.

Phantom scanned the surrounding faces, hoping to pick Jon out of the crowd, but with so many covering their faces, it was a gamble.

"Here you are," the barmaid slid a stein across the counter into his awaiting palm. He tossed her a coin worth fifty times what the beer cost. Chugging the contents of the beer halfway, he found her blinking at him in shocked wonder.

He flashed her with a winning smile. "For the damages."

The barmaid's eyes widened as Phantom faced Russet, giving him a subtle nod.

Russet reacted immediately, slamming his stein on the counter with a single low tone resonating from his throat. It halted the sailors, the rhythm they expected suddenly changed.

On the second beat, Hyne joined in, slamming his own stein and adding harmony to Russet's song.

On the third beat, the rest of the crew joined, stomping their feet or smashing their drinks against the wood tables.

The tavern quieted, malice drifting in the air around them as fear took hold of the patrons. Many of them knew descendants of giants or were part of that diluted gene pool themselves. There wasn't a more offensive and horrifying song to hear than the one their murders used to sing whilst killing them.

Russet took the lowest note; a depth that impressed Phantom.

FOE FUM

The song took on a slower quality as the devils continued to keep up the beat of the song like a collective heartbeat. Earhart sang,

DON'T HESITATE.
DEAD MEN EARN NO COIN.

The devils answered,

FOE HO

Black stepped out of the shadows, taking on the tones of a tenor to contrast the rerouting notes of the basses.

STRIKE THE HEART AND BRING THEM DOWN.

Phantom took a pull from his stein before abandoning it in favor of his sword. The sound of unsheathing echoed as the other devils joined. Color drained from the patron's faces. A few put hands on their own hilts, ready for the fight. But Phantom's fight was not with them. He sang his own lines,

WE SEEK A BEAST AS TALL AS THE PINES
HE'LL MEET HIS END AT THE TIP OF MY BLADE

MARK ME WORDS, THIS CREW OF MINE
BRING ME HIS HEAD, OR IT IS THE DEVIL TO PAY

The devils joined in.

FOE FUM

The crowd shifted, heading for the door, most standing to leave when they witnessed others escaping. Wilson and Sophia still inspected faces, but they spared most from the upcoming melee. The devils still chanted the song like it was an execution march. Phantom stepped around the fleeing patrons, his knuckles white on his hilt. He sensed a battle brewing, the tension rising in the air.

The barmaid from earlier stepped into his path, blocking his view. Her eyes glistened with terror, her placating hands up to halt him. "Please. We want no trouble. Take your business elsewhere."

He realized his eyes must have been glowing orange, because she stared at them in awe. Just behind her, at a nearby table, a man with a white cloth covering his head and face looked over, interested in the exchange. The small mistake earned a look at the man's eyes.

The eyes of the *cerbalus*.

"Gladly," Phantom growled before brushing past her to pull the cloth from Jon's head. Jon didn't react fast enough before Phantom used his strength to pull Jon from his seat by his shirt and slam him against the tavern's dirty floor. His head knocked against the ground hard enough to disorient him.

The remaining patrons screamed, barreling out the unguarded door as Wilson and Earhart took up each side of Phantom, disarming Jon as he lay there.

They pulled him up to his feet, the other devils closing in to block him in case he broke their hold.

"Bring him outside, the lady insists." They obeyed and blue splashed against his vision with the orange. He turned back to the dumbstruck barmaid, her customers fleeing rapidly. "When they ask you what happened here today, tell them Maahes has returned."

Her eyes snapped to him, witnessing the mix of colors in them.

Before she regained enough of her wit to ask questions, he turned to his devils as they pulled Jon through the door.

Silver moonlight hit the side of Phantom's face. Jon struggled against the devils as Black approached with a poisoned tipped arrow. Before she managed to drug the giant, Jon slipped out of Earhart's grasp, elbowing Wilson in the ribs hard enough for him to loosen his grip. Within seconds, he broke through the crowd, running down the alleyway.

"After him!" Phantom shouted.

The devils sprinted before the words fully fell from his mouth. He whistled and Serena descended from the top of the nearest building, screeching at the surrounding crowd. They scattered as she hovered over Phantom. He planted his boots in the sand before she landed on his shoulder, a stream of blue fire billowing before them.

"Find him," he whispered to the beastie. Perhaps it was the moonlight or the shadows around him, but he might have sworn blue glistened in the little dragon's gaze. She launched from his shoulder and into the night sky.

Phantom followed where the shadows whispered for him to go.

The orange light flickered with Draven's waning presence.

"No, not now," Phantom hissed.

Make them listen. The shadows are yours now.

Draven drew away from his consciousness, the shadows retreating without his familiar presence.

Phantom stopped abruptly, focusing on the dark masses around him. Although they shrunk away from him, they only retreated to their normal occupied spaces, the darkness of corners, or unlit alleyways and walls. They laid in wait for death to call on them. They had no shape, yet they traveled. They had no voices, yet they spoke. They had no souls, yet they showed loyalty.

Loyalty to whom? Draven?

His mind quieted, the other voices in his head silenced to allow him to focus.

Phantom fell to his knees in the darkened alleyway, letting himself focus only on their presence around him. He needed them. Jon was out there, possibly getting away while he rotted in this alleyway. And Rose...

Guilt hit him like a knife to the gut. His insides spoiled as he thought of what might have happened to her. He hadn't let himself think of the possibilities. Was she being tortured? Torn apart bit by bit? Had someone taken advantage of her vulnerable position for their own pleasure? Or maybe she was already dead.

It was his fault.

He hadn't stopped long enough to accept the idea, but now, he let his mind drift. He had brought her onto the ship with Jon; made her vulnerable to him.

That little box in his head opened, spilling over and drowning him. He tried to fight the onslaught of emotions. He needed to focus on the shadows. Make them listen to him, but now that the box was open, it wouldn't close.

The shadows drew closer to him, lacing around his fingers like wisps of smoke. They approached like a soft caress, as if they cared and understood the weight he carried.

Phantom rose to his feet, the shadows still wrapping around him as if getting acquainted with him, not Draven's presence, but his. There was still much to understand about the shadows and the man who first wielded them.

"Tell me," he pleaded with the vessels of death. "Where is Jon?"

CHAPTER 17

YOU ARE WHAT YOU DID

PHANTOM

The shadows found Jon instantly. Once the connection between them had forged, the whispers came easier, as if they were less reluctant with the information now.

Jon hid amongst a seller's stock of tapestries, rugs, and fabrics. He thought himself hidden in the deep corners between goods, but that made him all the easier to find. Phantom smelled the tangy scent of fear that he always found strange on a *cerbalus*. Now he understood why.

"Was everything a lie?"

Jon's gaze snapped to the direction of Phantom's voice, but it wasn't until he let the shadows recede that Jon gazed upon the man he betrayed. A fire lit in his chest, burning brightly. Kayden's yellow flames flickered.

Kill him. Traitors deserve only death.

Phantom ignored him, wanting more from Jon than his death would provide.

"From the moment I invited you to join my ship, my crew, did you *know* you would one day take from me as you did?" Phantom inched closer until he stood a foot away from the giant of a man. "Did you *know* when she first stepped foot on my ship what you would do with her?"

Rage rose the hairs on his arms, stronger than ever before. His fingers twitched next to the hilt of his sword, longing to plunge it into the man who took Rose from him.

Jon rose to his full height, moonlight beaming across his face. Although his features were stony, his scent reeked with how potent his fear had become.

"I knew." Two words and they hit like knives to Phantom's chest. "I didn't know it was her until I witnessed it myself with her nightmare. Rose—"

"Do not speak her name!" Phantom's patience grew taunt. Alone, he might convince himself that Jon had been bewitched. That his actions were not his own, but hearing that it had been the plan from the beginning—

"I did what I had to."

"Had to?" For a fraction of a second, Phantom witnessed a sliver of regret pass his features only to disappear again. Then, the eyes of his devils tingled the skin of his neck. They had found him. "How much exactly is Rose's life worth?"

He didn't answer.

Kill the traitor.

Though only Kayden spoke, the other two echoed their agreement. All of them would have killed Jon if he had done the same to their version of Rose.

Only Phantom hesitated. Perhaps that made him weak. The thought bristled against his mind, corrosive and rotten.

Phantom pulled his blade, the metal reflecting moonbeams.

"Where is she?"

Jon said nothing, not offering the one thing that might have convinced his former captain to show mercy. "You were supposed to be loyal to *me*! Where. Is. She?"

Jon flinched at the shout, but the words pulled from his throat. "I don't know." Phantom narrowed his eyes, unconvinced by a man who had only been a liar to him. "I took her to the palace, but I haven't seen her in weeks. I don't even know if she's here."

Phantom took one step towards his *cerbalus*. The giant sprinted away, finding the only opening a devil did not cover.

"Stop!" Blue crashed over his vision like a cresting wave.

Jon halted in his tracks immediately, not turning to face his punishment, but not running either. The devils lunged towards him, but they halted with the raise of Phantom's fist.

Why did he stop? He had no reason to obey. A stirring sensation filled his stomach, Davina had turned to watch. Fate unfolded before them.

He inched towards the giant of a man, turning around him, but Jon didn't move a muscle. His breath heaved in his chest as the fear took him completely, his scent rancid.

Instinct tugged at Phantom's chest, something primal that wanted to show dominance.

"Kneel," he seethed, more blue filling his vision until the world looked like a fourth moon had entered the sky, brighter than the sun.

Jon fell to his knees in the sand, his eyes never leaving Phantom's. Instead of fear, there was submission in his gaze, his head falling to his chest, but not before Phantom noticed, the blue in his own irises.

Well, that's new.

Power stronger than he'd ever received from his counterparts thrummed through his veins. It wasn't distant magic he only reached through their connections. This sparked from him, flowing from his throat.

"Captain?" Earhart stood next to him, looking like he'd never seen his best friend before. He didn't like it.

Phantom brushed past the former devil, not looking at his crew as he sauntered away. "Make him hurt but keep him alive. Then drag him to the palace."

The shadows still whispered in Phantom's head as he marched through the streets of Amal. Sunrise was not far off, the walls already littered with tents for the next market day as people set up their shops.

we ssssee you

Draions shifted out of his way, seeing him on the war path to nowhere. The shadows flew around him like insects buzzing around his head.

the sssssword of death

Colors bloomed in his vision, an array of orange, yellow, and green. They all spoke at once in his head.

What's going on, James? Did you just command him against his will?

This power has been inside us all along?

Maybe we'd been cursed for a good reason.

They all spoke at once and over each other, but their questions and theories faded as the shadows captured his attention.

come, let usssss help

Phantom veered from the street into a darkened corner. The shadows swelled around him, like a trained dog returning to its owner. He leaned against a wall, putting his head in his hands and breathing out. Slowly his heart rate calmed, but his mind didn't keep up.

His command was undeniable. Jon was unable to disobey a direct order.

And he left his crew there to pummel the traitorous bastard.

You should have done worse. He deserves to be in his grave.

"It's not his fate I was careless with." He didn't look at any of them as he walked away. His devils. They regarded Jon as a brother. They should have had some choice about the violence they inflicted on him. "They trusted me. Look how I've rewarded them."

Kayden's flames returned. *With this power, you have no need for trust.*

Phantom rammed his hands into his eyes, banishing the hateful bastard from his mind. Kayden tempted his fury like no man could. One of these days, he might even listen.

He needed Rose back. She would calm his fury, just by seeing her alive and well.

An idea drew his head back up, looking at the heavy darkness around him. "Can the shadows find Rose for me?" They pulsed around him as he remembered how quickly they located Jon.

ssssshadowsssss cannot sssssseee her

"What? Why not?" Where might she be beyond the reach of shadows? When no buzzing answered his questions, he looked inward. "Draven. Tell me what's going on."

Orange filled his gaze, cool like the setting of the sun. Instead of speaking in his head, Draven pulsed behind his eyes until Phantom allowed access to his body.

After a couple heartbeats, Draven looked through deep blue eyes, staring at the darkness surrounding them, thick enough to block out the rising sun. "This is not what I intended."

Phantom pushed back on his body, trying to regain control, but Draven held firmly to consciousness. Only then did Phantom realize that he had not meant the possession of the body. *What did you not intend?*

"The shadows have taken to you quickly."

That's what you trained me to do! Phantom lowered his voice, choosing to ignore Draven's concern for a more pressing question. *Why can't they find her? Can I make them?*

His command worked on the devils, perhaps it worked on reapers as well.

"If they say they can't, they can't."

Phantom tried to raise his arms with no success. *A lot of help you are.*

"You do not understand. Everything touches darkness. Light sources create shadow. They only way to not have one is to be surrounded by the dark, in which they thrive."

What exactly are you trying to say?

Draven put his hand out, the shadows instantly curled around him, as if they had missed his touch.

"The enemy knows our strengths. They understand who we are and are powerful enough to shield her location from us."

Phantom snapped back to his body, shaking out his limbs from the intrusion. He had to get to the palace. What better place to be for an entity that powerful?

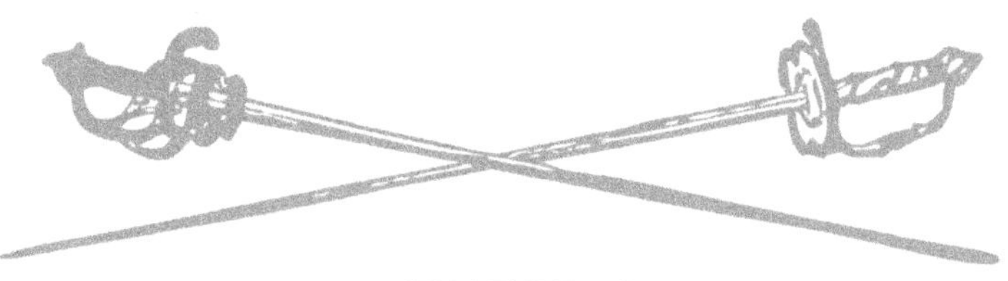

CHAPTER 18

AWAITED ENTRANCE

BLACK

The captain stood at the unused palace doors with a hand on the pommel of his sword, early morning light washing over his stoic features.

Black and Wilson had personally seen to Jon's ties and gag. Wilson had a special knot he swore no man would break. The traitor in question had been beaten within an inch of his life, left eye already swollen, body covered in scratches and bruises. His arm was even dislocated, limply hanging from its socket.

She had never experienced rage so visceral. It came on swiftly, choking any other emotion until all she could see was Jon. He committed the most horrendous act imaginable for a devil. They found each other when others wouldn't accept them. A family, trusting one another above anyone else.

That is what Jon betrayed.

They dropped him at the entrance, and he slumped against the stone, unable to hold himself up.

"Fix his arm," Captain ordered.

Smith jerked his limp arm back into place without so much as a warning. Black had never seen the doctor act so brutally with anyone, his face twisted in wrath.

Jon sucked in a sharp breath, his gag too tight for much else.

"I want to make something perfectly clear." Phantom leaned

131

down to Jon, giving him little space to breathe. "I welcomed you aboard my ship. I didn't have to, but I saw something in you. A lost soul, a devil, same as the rest of us. A lost soul ready to find your true place among us. Yet, you betrayed us." He seethed, his anger palpable. Black thought he might take a swing himself, but he kept his distance.

Jon coughed into the rag tied around his mouth, blood seeping around it.

Phantom gaze lifted to Hyne, who understood immediately, pulling Jon up by the back of his shirt until he haphazardly stood, facing the markings. He pulled the traitor's gag down until it hung around his neck. "How do I get in?"

Jon inspected the door, his eyes catching on to the symbol at the top, the one Ramirez had said was like a coat of arms. "I don't know."

"Now, that's not true." Phantom's patronizing tone didn't bode well for Jon. "This is the language of your people Jon." His hand drifted over the symbols, squinting at them.

"You recognize some of them, don't you?" Jon asked, boldly. A muscle in Phantom's jaw ticked, his patience waning. "They may be older than even you, Maahes. But you sense it. Like it belongs to you. Don't listen to it."

"And why should I not?" A hint of a smile tugged at the captain's lips, but his eyes remained cold.

Jon's eyes refocused on the door before him. "These doors haven't opened in centuries, perhaps a millennium. But it isn't the symbols you should concern yourself with. It's the legend surrounding them."

"And what legend be that?"

Black's gaze roamed over the crowd. They whispered between themselves, pointing to the symbols on the door then at the captain.

"This door is a symbol for chaos among the people."

Catching a few gazes, unease crawled into Black's gut.

"The legend says that only one can open the doors. A man with many names. Many have tried and failed, seeking the favor of the gods and the people, but none prevailed."

Phantom looked at the crowd around them, noticing the audience.

"Maahes is a symbol of justice for the people." Jon leaned closer so the crowd would not hear. "If you open that door, they will think you have returned to them." The surrounding crowd kept growing, everyone staring at him. "These people are angry. They are on a slippery slope, waiting for the right nudge. Knowing Maahes is among them — many will die."

Phantom's eyes narrowed at Jon's, ignoring the crowd completely. Then a dangerous smirk lifted his features even if it didn't reach his eyes. "Maybe that's precisely what they need."

The captain turned from the traitor, standing before the entrance. "Devils, with me."

Each devil stood at attention, standing behind their captain, with Hyne holding Jon's shirt to direct him.

Phantom leaned forward, pressing a palm to each door as he pressed into them. A chill cooled the surrounding air, warning them to stay away. The captain shouted in agony as pain disoriented his features, but he wouldn't let it go, pushing the doors inward.

The rocks shook around them, pebbles springing free and sand slipping to the ground. Wind swept around them as if the elements were trying to prevent this from happening.

Phantom roared, sounding more animal than human as it echoed along the sandstone walls. Finally, the two sides budged, swinging open with the sound of grinding rock.

His arms dropped as he stepped through the opened doors, the devils fanning out behind him.

Silence surrounded them before a large cheer rose up behind them. Some with shouts of rage, some of joy. They would no longer go unnoticed in the city.

Walking through the doors was like stepping into an entirely different world. The floor below them shined with fresh polish. The columns beside them glistened with white alabaster stone. A dome above them let in sunlight that reflected fragments of gold and precious jewels carved into the floors and walls. Statues lined the walls, paying homage to the ancient gods, the ones Black gambled with in Kazeboon.

It surpassed all the wealth Samsara possessed.

Black looked back to be certain it wasn't an illusion. Servants pushed closed the doors the captain had opened, a crowd of people trying to push their way through. A row of guards appeared, beating them back until the entrance closed once more.

Dread pooled in her stomach. This may have been a trap. Her eyes found Sophia, but the huntress's eyes were focused forward.

Black followed her gaze to the two thrones at the end of the expansive room. Windows allowed sunlight to flood the floor from behind the thrones, making it hard to tell if anyone was seated upon them.

Music drifted to them, a sensual beat of tambourines, drums, and a flute. At least five half-naked women danced to it, entertaining the others in the room. Men and women lined the sides, all dressed in black robes with gold embellishments like bangles, tassels, or other accessories. They stopped their conversations, halting the next sip of their wine to take in the strangers who made an entrance that wouldn't soon be forgotten.

None said a word, and the guards didn't attempt to stop them, even with their show of weaponry.

Black kept her sword close and her eyes sharp.

A clap reverberated through the room, echoing off the walls as the music halted.

A man stood from the left throne, silhouetted by sunlight until he stepped off the dais.

"I cannot believe my eyes." The man spoke abruptly and with a strange cadence that reeked of arrogance. "Maahes, is that you?" Whispers echoed in the room.

He reached the same height as the captain, dark brown hair dusting his head and sharp jaw. His thin frame stood at an angle rather than keeping his feet planted. But most of all, Black noticed the things that didn't make sense. His skin was much lighter than that of a local. Lighter than even most of the devils. And his accent—

He was clearly foreign, but Black was unable to place his

accent. His tone was too rough to be Brettanian even though he spoke the language. Atlas perhaps, but she couldn't place the district he belonged to.

Still, it was odd for an Atlatic to be this far east.

The captain stood resolute, sizing up his new enemy, or maybe something else kept him frozen.

The man laughed. "I do believe it is. Damn, after all these years, too." He turned behind him as the sun rose behind the thrones, allowing a visual of another man on the right throne. "Dante, look who it is."

The second stranger sat on the throne like he was born to it, his black robe sat on his shoulders like a cape, his face impassive. Dante's accent was decidedly Brettanian. His clean-shaven, fair-skinned face contrasted with his well-maintained long hair.

"Yes," Dante drawled, no excitement to his tone. "I watched him walk in."

The first man tossed a hand behind himself. "Ignore him. He's excited to see you too. He just doesn't know how to show it." He turned his back to Phantom, spreading his arms out. "Bring it in. Don't leave your old man hanging."

The words he said were all Brettanian in nature, but he arranged them in a way that made little sense. He didn't want the captain to hug him — did he?

Black's eyes focused on Phantom, finally seeing the closed fists at his side.

"Captain?" Black asked, close enough to his side that she contemplated placing a hand on his shoulder. He turned abruptly, locking eyes with her, green blossomed in his irises. They didn't even dilate like she'd seen before. No, green swirled around the blue, blocking out the whites of his eyes.

Sam gazed at her along with the captain. She'd spoken to him a handful of times on their voyage here, but never had he looked at her as he did now. Undisguised fear. But when he turned his gaze to the *Imari*, his features turned stoney, his eyes blue once more.

"Who are you?" Phantom's voice came out in a growl, barely audible.

The man put a hand to his chest, whispering his words so the courtiers wouldn't hear. "I apologize. Sammy knows me, but we haven't met yet." His other hand came around, offering it to Phantom. "The name's Colt."

Phantom glared at his outstretched hand like it personally offended him. "Release her, and we'll be on our way." A threatening edge sharpened his tone, one that Black wouldn't refuse.

Colt smirked. "That's my Sammy. Straight to the point. Don't worry, your little birdy is safe. As long as she does what she's told, she'll be fine."

The captain moved faster than Black blinked, his sword drawn and at the man's throat. The devils followed suit, drawing weapons, but facing the guards who advanced on them.

"Stop," Colt ordered, and the guardsman halted, forming a semi-circle around the devils. The devils held back too, waiting for the order, but if the captain lunged, so too would they.

"Come now," the impassive one, Dante, said as he rose from his throne. "There's no need for that." He flicked his wrist and Black's sword flew from her hand, along with the pistol at her side. They slid across the floor along with the other devils' weapons, including the sword that had been pressed to Colt's neck.

The clanking continued for long enough that it drew attention to Hyne.

Weapons still fell from his belt and pockets. Knives. Pistols. An axe. A grappling hook. A cannon ball? A sheepish smile appeared on his face. Wilson shook his head beside the devil.

"You said you would let her go." Jon's voice echoed in the throne room. His bindings had fallen, likely thanks to Dante's witchcraft. The giant hobbled his way to the dais, facing both men. "That was our agreement. The siren in exchange for my sister."

"Actually, we said we wouldn't kill her. Do you really think he would release leverage?" Colt chimed in, a bit of humor to his tone. "You have your coin, *cerbalus*, you'll get nothing more from us."

Jon straightened weakly, looking down his nose at Colt. "Have you no honor?"

Colt squinted, unfazed by the threat. "Debatable."

"It matters not." Dante refocused the attention on himself. "The terms of our agreement dictate that her first life be restored before the return of your kin. *That* was our arrangement. Thus far your *siren* has been... uncooperative."

Phantom growled low in his throat, moving towards them, but he wasn't fast enough before two guards seized his arms, keeping him in place. Other guards moved to isolate the devils from him even as they fought to be at his side, Jon included. The captain struggled against their holds, the guards strong enough to restrain him. "Let her go, now."

Power echoed in the command, electrifying the air.

"There he is!" Colt laughed, the sound echoing in the silence. "We've been missing you, buddy. The real you. Things just aren't as interesting around here without you." Colt put a hand to his chest, as if calming the laughter, then it faded with whatever he saw on Phantom's face. "What? Did you think that would work on us?"

Dante's decidedly monotone voice carried the thought. "He is unaware of how to use his abilities. They likely only just manifested."

"I'll say. He thinks he can command us."

"Leave us," Dante snapped, and the audience filed from the room, shuffling into hallways. Black had nearly forgotten about them. "Guards included."

The guards filtered from the room as well, dropping the captain's arms and returning their swords to their hips. They took the devils discarded weapons. Soon, only the devils and the two men remained.

They were outnumbered, even if the devils no longer had their weapons.

Yet, Phantom didn't give the order.

"You can't beat us," Colt said, inching closer. "*Sammy* must be telling you all about it right now."

"Don't sacrifice what little crew you have for a foolish errant," Dante continued for him as if they were of one mind. Now that they stood next to each other, there was a certain symmetry to them.

"Shall we tell him?" Colt asked Dante, who nodded his head. Colt clasped his hands, rubbing them together like a fly would.

"Just like old times."

Dante waved a hand, and the room darkened, the windows around them blocking out the light they once let through. Then he stepped up to Phantom. A flick of his wrist had the captain's shirt and vest popping open, revealing a toned and hairy chest.

Phantom raised an eyebrow. "Not exactly what I expected."

Dante gestured from his navel to head. Lights followed his movements, one by one colors illuminated from under his skin, the bottom one just barely visible above the belt line of his pants. That one glowed red, more brightly than the others. Orange radiated at his gut, yellow at his core, green in the center of his chest, and blue at his throat. Faint lights flickered between his eyes and at the top of his head, too muted to make out.

"Your power of persuasion is limited and connected to your essence." Dante pointed to the blue light at his throat. "Once you merged with Maahes, you began the process of integration, allowing you access to your newest magic."

"That you, um..." Colt leaned over to Dante, whispering, "what was his name again?"

"His name is Captain Phantom," Black said, a pang of offense punching her gut. They should know the man who will kill them. "Leader of the Eleven Devils and Captain to Nemain's Revenge."

The man in question remained silent, allowing Black to speak for him.

"Right, quite a reputation you've built. But that's not the point." Colt circled Phantom, who tracked his movements carefully. "The point is the persuasion part of your abilities, it's a power earned, not given. Essentially, once a man," he pointed to the devils behind him, "decides to follow you with his entire heart and soul, he belongs to you. As in, they will do whatever you command of them. Hell, they'd kill their own families if you wished for it."

Black sucked in a breath, looking at her captain, who refused to meet her eyes. Is that what happened earlier? She recalled fury more intense than ever before, but she attributed it to seeing Jon in person.

"Then why can they still betray me?" Phantom glared in Jon's direction, who shook where he stood, barely holding himself up. He seemed so much smaller this way.

Colt stood before the captain, stealing his glare away from the traitor. "You have to speak it for it to be true. If you had told our dear Jon not to betray you, he physically would be incapable of it. Since you never spoke the words, he still could. Although some of your emotions, if strong enough, will transfer too. He likely felt your betrayal like he stabbed his own heart."

"Good," Phantom said, not a hint of remorse showing.

Colt chuckled. "This guy." He pointed to Phantom as he looked back at Dante, who didn't return his amusement.

Dante let out an exasperated breath, like a disappointed mother. "I warned him not to get attached. He did not listen." Jon's eyes narrowed on Dante. "Though in truth, Maahes would not have trusted him if he had managed to keep his distance."

Colt spread his arms out. "Sam didn't have that nifty little ability. It would have made his task much easier. Although Sammy always did work better on his own. Our little assassin."

"But since he betrayed me, doesn't his loyalty end?" This time, Phantom refused to look at Jon, allowing him the dishonor of talking about him even though he stood in the same room.

"No," Dante answered. "The bond is irrevocable."

Jon sat on the bottom step, nearly falling as he did. Black locked eyes with him, but she only saw sadness there.

"Is there anything else I should know?" Phantom changed the subject.

"There is much you do not understand," Dante said, but Colt picked up the pieces of that pointless answer.

"For starters, this bond between you and your crew, it's more than blind obedience." Colt approached him again. "That power within yourself."

Dante lowered his hand, and the illusion faded, the room brightening with the sun again.

"My *heka*?"

"Ah, so you do know something, good. Yes, your *heka* is filled when you take a life. Not a difficult conclusion, you answer to Nemain no matter what face you're sporting or who cursed you.

But..." Colt inched closer, lowering his voice, as if he hid his words from the very Goddess he spoke of. "This bond allows you to benefit from the kills they make as well. It's like shares of treasure. You split the kills you make fifty-fifty with the Goddess of Death Herself, lending to Her godliness and yours. All these people you gain the loyalty of, when they make a kill, you get some of that power as well."

Black listened, thinking back on her lessons in accounting from her father. There was always a bit of wealth shared with the footmen as well. She looked at her own hand, wondering if there was something else to this bond.

"It's a genius system Nemain created in you. The more you use your devils, the more powerful you become." Black sensed Sophia's stare before turning to her. She looked at her hands too. "I dare say, the little birdy would've benefitted from it."

Instantly, the room grew darker.

"I will get her back." Phantom growled. "No matter what obstacle I must face. No matter what atrocities I must commit. I will have her back and if I find she is not as she existed when taken from me, I will bring you both down to answer to Nemain Herself."

Dante's eyes narrowed, as if searching for something in his words.

"And what will you do if we kill her?"

Darkness spread from the corners of the room, filling the once glittering floors with shadows. Black looked up to find it wasn't Dante's shaded windows. This darkness consumed the surrounding light, rising from the corners of the room like smoke.

This time when the captain spoke, it was like the night Rose had returned to Samsara. His voice contained many at once.

"We will bring this entire city down until there is nothing left but ashes."

Colt hollered and Dante... smiled?

"There he is! That's the man we've been waiting for!" Colt was as giddy as a child, the oddest reaction she had seen to a threat. "I knew he'd come around, eventually."

"Yes, it would appear so."

The darkness only grew further, inching to snuff out the

remaining light in the hall. Colt stepped up to the darkness, reaching a hand into its depths and pulling it back. The shadows moved like smoke through his fingers. They moved upon him until consuming his form completely.

Black reached a hand behind her, taking Sophia's. She'd never feared the captain before, but perhaps she should. Sophia's hand trembled.

A moment later, Colt stepped out of the smoke, his gait stronger than before. His black eyes resembled two pools of endless ink. A stream of shadow left his mouth as he blew it out like a smoked pipe.

He nodded to Phantom. "Not the result you hoped for?"

The captain's breathing grew ragged as he stared at Colt.

"Call off your dogs, Captain. We won't kill her," Dante amended.

Phantom's jaw worked.

"She's, unfortunately, valuable to us."

"And your little pets won't work on us. We have no souls for them to extract."

Phantom's brows rose.

Reluctantly, the shadows crept back to where they came from. Black had to blink several times to be certain she saw them move. By the confused looks on the rest of the devils, it wasn't only her.

"*Enu hyeo tashin*," Wilson spat.

"How is she valuable to you?"

"That information is private," Colt remarked, his early humorous tone gone.

Phantom growled, a bit of his beast showing. "There is nothing about her that can be kept from me."

Dante and Colt's faces turned sad. "Davina did a real number on you, but don't worry—"

"We intend to break Her hold on you." Dante finished his sentence.

Phantom stepped back from them. "Even if you do, it changes nothing."

Dante let out another breath, as if reserving patience. "You say that because you have no choice."

"We'll free you, Sammy." He winked before they both lifted their hands, sand from the crevasses of the stone lifting and swirling around the devils. "I promise you that."

The sand multiplied, until a small sandstorm encased them, Phantom included. It swirled around them until the thrones, the walls, the columns, everything disappeared. Even the ground beneath them liquified, turning to sand itself.

Sophia latched on to Black's arm, as if letting go would separate them. She glimpsed Sophia's scared face right before the ground opened beneath them, swallowing them whole.

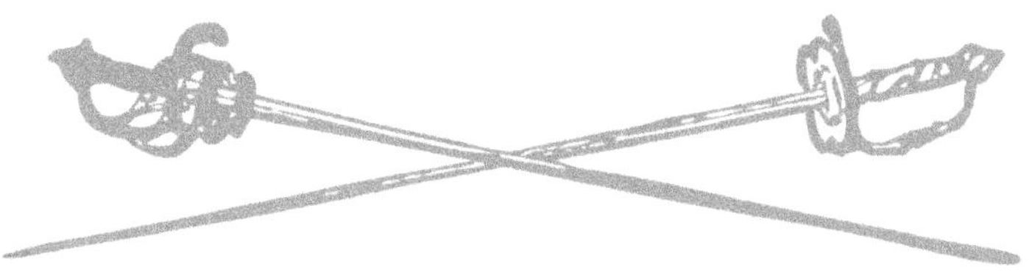

CHAPTER 19

ROTTING SANDS

BLACK

They fell through the floor, sand everywhere.

Black closed her eyes to keep the particles out, but her hand stayed clasped in Sophia's, the huntress's grip holding her just as tightly.

Finally, they fell in a bed of sand, both soft and scratchy. Black found that she didn't like Draiocht much at all. Sophia panted heavily but seemed otherwise unharmed. It was odd seeing her without her weapons.

They appeared in the middle of rolling dunes a mile outside the walls of the city.

"I'm wasted on these bloody sands." Russet brushed granules from his beard, crimson already blooming across his nose and brow. "I'm built for fjords and snowstorms."

Earhart squinted at the blinding sun, lifting a hand to shade his eyes and see his mate better. "You steal my blankets at night."

Russet's brow crinkled. "What's your point?"

The rest of the devils recovered from the drop in various degrees, Hyne coughing up all the sand he inhaled while Wilson was already standing, staring off into the distance behind her. Black followed his fixed stare.

At first, there was nothing but endless dunes. It amazed her that an entire country had been built on this wasteland.

Then she saw it, little dots of movement, heading their way and multiplying.

Necromites.

"Captain!" Earhart shouted, everyone noticing at once. "Orders?"

Phantom's gaze shifted all around them, taking in the dunes and the sandstone buildings between them. They must have been abandoned from how little life existed out there.

Black took stock of what they had, but that would add up to nothing. All their weapons were seized by the *Imari*. Even Jon had disappeared before they were somehow dumped outside the city. This witchcraft went far beyond anything she'd witnessed before.

"Bastards wanted to kill us after all," Russet spat, cursing profusely.

Phantom finally spoke. "We aren't dying here mates." But even he didn't look certain. He held his head, pulling at the hair at his temples. "What do you mean the shadows don't work on them? Your power is as useless as you are." Phantom stared at the ground as he shouted, drawing more attention to them.

Black would have thought him insane, had she not known he was consulting one of the voices in his head.

He beat his head once more, the necromites drawing closer.

"Run," he growled. The crew blinked at him as if they had never heard the word before. "Run!" This time her vision tinted blue as he said the word and the urge to run solidified in her heart. Her feet moved before her mind had made the decision, every devil running with her, all of them heading for the city wall.

A look around told her this was only a desperate idea. Smith lagged, his wooden leg not meant for running. He tripped on a steep dune, rolling down it. Black wanted to turn back, to help him up, but the compulsion in her veins didn't allow for deviation.

Phantom's face morphed into determination, turning back to retrieve his lost devil. "Black, with me!"

Black turned, running after the captain.

Phantom pulled a knife from his boot, throwing it into the closest necromite's forehead. It stopped the creature before it took a bite of Smith's intact leg. Apparently, the *Imari* had missed a blade. The necromite fell like a tree struck by lightning, rolling the rest of the way down the dune. Black and Phantom stopped on either side of Smith, hoisting him up.

"Thank you, Captain," he rasped. "I wouldn't want to lose the other leg."

Phantom managed a smile. "Don't want to go down in history as No Legs Smith?"

Black's lips twitched up, even as she supported half the doctor's weight. "I would prefer to avoid such titles, yes."

The necromites hobbled only a few paces behind them, and gaining, closing the gap of space.

"Captain?" Smith asked, half out of breath trying to help them to be faster. "I do believe if you whistle, Serena can find us."

"From way out here?" Black asked, knowing Phantom couldn't possibly whistle that loudly.

"You'd be surprised at the instincts of a dragon."

Black looked behind them. A few necromites drew close, too abundant to be opposed by a single knife. Black would fight with her bare hands, but she'd never had to fight even one off before.

Phantom caught her gaze. "Go ahead. Get them to safety."

"Cap—"

"I'll survive," he said, dropping Smith's arm. "Now go!" Again, blue assaulted her vision, unmistakable against the sand surrounding her. Her feet moved a little slower with the added weight, but Smith's breathing grew more ragged, trying to help as much as possible.

Phantom whistled, long and loud, calling Serena to his side, but they were still so far from the city. Silence answered, nothing to indicate she'd heard his call.

Black's hope diminished just as she saw Sophia running in the wrong direction. She sprinted towards them.

"What are you doing? Get everyone across." Sophia had Smith's other arm before the words slipped from Black's mouth.

"Not without you, now run!" Sophia instigated a different urgency than Phantom's words did, forcing Black to keep hope until the very end.

Phantom whistled again and Black wanted to look back, to see how many necromites he'd killed so far.

Silence answered again.

"Damned beastie!" Phantom shouted before whistling even louder.

A roar rattled the city, echoing along the sand dunes. Blue flames sprouted from near the wall, showing them exactly where she was.

Hyne hooted his excitement at her arrival.

Finally, she sailed over the city wall, her wings spreading further than Black remembered. Another roar signaled that she spotted Phantom, rushing to his rescue.

They reached the wall just as Serena reached Phantom. He ran in their direction with more necromites on his heels, but he ran fast.

"Damned rich bastards took my grappling hook!" Hyne cursed at the smooth sandstone wall, not an inch jagged enough to climb.

"*Mierda!*" Black screamed, slamming her palm against the rough stone.

The hordes of necromites advanced slowly, but they were too numerous, even as Serena blasted them with fire. The creatures possessed no fear, reaching towards Phantom even as their limbs burned off. They took too long to fall. Serena screeched at them in frustration.

The devils searched the wall, looking for an opening or a gate of some kind to allow them access. They found nothing. They'd have to run down the length of the wall, but which way?

A hand reached out from the wall, grasping Tick's wrist. A shriek echoed, but it wasn't from Tick. Hyne had been sympathetic enough to scream for him.

A part of the wall opened, revealing a woman, heavily dressed in local drapes, her face only barely visible through the hood. She waved, motioning for them to follow.

Tick clasped her hand as if he didn't want to let go. Her hood fell when the devils didn't follow, revealing Samsaran tan skin and brown hair.

Lara.

"Hurry, time is of the essence." Just behind Lara, another woman peaked her irritated eyes out. Sitamun stood there too, shouting at them to move their asses.

A glance inside showed a set of stairs heading downward, a part of the city's tunnel system.

Lara motioned frantically and the devils finally followed, filing into the dark tunnel beneath the wall. Black gesture to the opening, insisting Sophia go first. She needed to be certain Phantom made it through. He sprinted towards them, his coat billowing out behind him. Serena delayed the dead long enough for him to get ahead.

Phantom veered into the tunnel, whistling to call Serena off. She immediately moved, flapping her membranous wings until they carried her into the air. It was enough for Phantom, allowing the door to close.

A swift click told Black that Sitamun had locked the passageway, the door thick enough to keep them out. Still, they heard the eerie moans and cries of defeat from the creatures.

CHAPTER 20

TWENTY-FIVE

SEBASTIAN

The sunset displayed an array of purples and oranges. Davina's moon, a mere sliver, offered colorless light to dilute the display.

Sebastian preferred these sunsets. Had he someone to be romantic with, he would plan a picnic for them to enjoy. Sadly, such a fate was never meant for him. Rose would have been the closest, but it had been clear to him that she did not want his affection. Once they had been at least friendly with one another. That is until she captured his free will with that enchanting voice of hers.

He shivered at the thought of those dark nights.

It made sense to him that she should be with James. They both had an adventurous spirit, one that craved the sea and experiencing new things.

Sebastian didn't have the luxury to consider such things. Not when Samsara always needed him. Although, this time was different. When James had left, he had asked for Sebastian to come with him. Though his heart wanted nothing more than to say yes, someone had to protect the island. Now, more than ever.

He rounded to the docks which were suspiciously quiet. Sunset wasn't a particularly active hour for fishermen, but the docks usually remained busy for most hours of the day. But now? Deafening silence. Only the sway of abandoned fishing boats against rocking waves showed any life at all.

Sebastian's eyes narrowed on the boats, searching for any signs of the fisherman who occupied them.

"Hey ho!"

William Casimir called from the shore, but Sebastian cringed. His instincts told him to remain quiet.

"My apologies, Commodore. I received a surprise guest at dinner tonight."

Sebastian raised a brow. "In all our years working together, never once have you been late. Who might be so important?

"I'll have you know—" William raised a finger, intent on scolding Sebastian when he saw the slight smirk on his face. "Oh, you were joking." His answering smile made their situation a little easier. Maybe there was something to not taking things too seriously. That, or James had left an impression on him. "You can't do that to an old man, my boy. My distracted mind can't begin to keep up."

Sebastian let out a small chuckle. "My apologies. Who joined you for dinner?"

"The strangest character. Mr. Castellanos himself." Sebastian's smile faded. "And not the imposter the Minister discovered." Sebastian didn't bother correcting him. The Minister's sins were too numerous to count accurately. The lord didn't need to know the Minister had tasked James with impersonating Lord Castellanos.

"He claims that the Minister paid him off to drop the impersonation charges and to remain out of sight in his home. He went so far as to say the Minister threatened his life if he set foot in the city."

Perhaps he did need to know.

"I, of course, told him such a thing was impossible. Although I do not agree with the late Minister's actions during his reign, I assured him that the Minister would not allow such dishonor on his house."

Sebastian wasn't certain his wince remained inward. The man's death left the island's leadership in a state of utter disarray.

There seemed little reason to dwell on those decisions, but Castellanos was practically a stranger to Samsara.

"What brought him to town then?"

The two walked to the dock as William elaborated on his story. "Aside from the threat to his life being gone, his cattle are dying." Sebastian wasn't entirely surprised by the development. Everything else on the island was dying, it would affect the rich as well. "He claims that, unbidden, they just started falling over, the meat rotting before he could make use of it."

Had he not had bigger problems, Sebastian would have visited the farm to make sure Castellanos wasn't trying to sell the meat of his dying cattle. Any number of diseases could accumulate from such carelessness.

Issues like that reminded him of what being the Commodore once had been.

Sebastian investigated the vessels beside him, noticing the neglect. Abandonment understated the state of them. A rancid scent wafted to him on the sea breeze, death. Dead fish littered the deck of the boat, all rotting in various degrees. Seagulls flapped around them as they picked at what edible parts remained.

"What happened here?"

William held a handkerchief to his nose to block out the smell. "I believe we found the source of the outbreak, Commodore."

Sebastian roamed his gaze over the ships, searching for bodies. "Look for survivors."

Fishing traps and nets laid around the deck among the rotten fish with little care.

On the far end of the deck, the net — moved. A low groan came from the pile as a man rose from the splitting knots of the net.

"One is still alive," William muttered through the cloth, placing a boot on the boat's railing to board, before Sebastian stopped him with a gloved hand.

"I'm afraid not."

The man rose, his head snapping at them, and William jerked back. The man's jaw loosened from one side of his face, hanging on by the remaining skin and tendons of his right cheek.

Nausea churned Sebastian's stomach, but he kept his dinner

down. He noticed the other signs now. The ashen skin and clouded white eyes. The other wounds ripping his flesh apart, particularly where the creature was entrapped in the netting. It moaned at them, the sound turning gurgled with the lack of facial muscles the creature possessed.

William gagged beside him but remarkably kept his stomach contents where they belonged. "Is there a cure?"

"Tell me something, William. If your body had decayed that much, would you want to return to it?"

William coughed, still struggling with the nausea. "I suppose not. But I'd let the man decide for himself."

Sebastian stepped aboard the boat confident the creature wouldn't escape its self-imposed trap. He released the sword on his hip, the metal singing into the silent hours of twilight. The necromite groaned at him, reaching to bite him with half a jaw.

"No, there is no cure, other than death." His sword cut into the man's head, severing the hold the disease had on the fisherman's decaying mind. He'd fought enough of them to understand how they worked. Even a severed head would continue to reanimate, but a damaged mind would end it all.

The necromite lost its strength, falling into a heap on the deck.

Sebastian sighed. These executions grew too numerous.

"Commodore," William called, but the man had moved on, peeking inside the next fishing boat. "The rest are empty."

Sebastian wiped the black blood off his sword, following the man. "I would hope so. I don't want to keep putting them down."

William's frantic eyes locked on to Sebastian's, finally reading the panic in them. "You killed four of them yesterday."

"Yes," Sebastian said.

William's arms rose, gesturing to the six ships at the harbor. "I have thirty fishermen who employ these ships."

The math made Sebastian's heart sink. "Which means—"

"There are still twenty-five of them on the island."

Sebastian's arms burned, pain lacing them as he swung again, cutting the head off one of the former fishermen. The head rolled, jaw still moving to latch onto anything. He put a single boot on the head, ramming his sword into its brain before it managed to do any damage.

"Twenty-five," he breathed, collapsing to the ground just as the sun greeted the sky.

He'd spent all night tracking every one of those necromites down. With some kind of Davina-born luck, they hadn't breached the city, only an outcropping of trees a mile away. They stuck together like a herd. As if they understood their chances of success heightened in a group.

Sebastian spent hours picking them off from the sides until he killed them all. It required quick reflexes and a sharp sword. He'd even shot a few of them down, but his sword seemed to work more efficiently.

"Come on now," William said, pulling him up. "You cannot join the dead yet." The old man had more strength than Sebastian gave him credit, lifting a man who well surpassed him in weight and height. William had spent the night a few paces from the Commodore.

He claimed it was to help if the need ever arose, but Sebastian refused his help. He wasn't sure why he let the old man keep him company during the task, but he appreciated it all the same.

Sebastian's energy waned, but he forced enough strength into himself to straighten, refusing to fall asleep covered in black blood.

"How do you suppose this spreads?" William's question brought him out of his own mind.

"What?"

"Forgive me for mentioning, Commodore, but you've been wounded." William pointed to several cuts laid out on his arms and face. Nothing serious had occurred, thank Davina. "And you are covered in a black substance I can only assume is their blood. Can the infection spread to you?"

It occurred to Sebastian how alarmingly ill-prepared they were for this inevitable situation. The necromites had been a reality for most of their lives. Yet, the island had treated the threat like it would never happen.

Another one of the Minister's sins.

"No," he said, wiping some of the blood from his face with the back of his hand. "My mother used to tell me stories of the necromites." He used his sword to lift the lip of the nearest body, revealing a set of elongated canines. "That is how the disease is spread. They must sink their teeth into you, but short of severing a limb, there is nothing that can be done after that."

William's brows narrowed.

"What is it?" Sebastian leaned against the nearest tree, keeping his breathing as steady as possible.

"You recall those slaves you liberated that I, in turn, smuggled off the island."

"That was only weeks ago. Yes, I remember."

"Well, what escaped your memory involved the slaves themselves." The old man stared at the bodies surrounding them. "I've spoken with many of them. They like to talk if you sit with them long enough."

Or pester them long enough, which was likely William's tactic, but Sebastian refrained from interrupting.

"But I asked them, 'why would you want to return to the mainland?' After all, being a slave on a safe island must be preferable to fighting for one's life against these creatures. But their answers remained the same. They claimed that the Goddess Macha protects them against the dead. They even showed me the marks on their bodies, some with teeth marks such as those."

Sebastian didn't dare to believe a cure existed. And what did that mean for the two dozen fishermen he'd just slaughtered?

He sheathed his sword, blood and all, since there was no hope of cleaning it anytime soon.

"You believe that some of them have been bitten and survived."

William shrugged. "It makes you wonder why they were so valuable."

One person besides the deceased Minister clearly understood their worth.

Lockness.

"I think it's time to pay homage to our new leader, don't you think so?"

William clammed up. "But... He's just a criminal."

"A criminal lord who just became the richest man in Samsara." Sebastian gained enough strength to walk, a fire in his stomach giving him the energy he lacked before.

"You... you can't just waltz into the Fortress covered in... in that!"

Sebastian was beyond caring. If he visited a bathhouse right now, he would succumb to his exhaustion. And he needed to talk to Lockness before that could happen. He was certain this outbreak wasn't the only one. Protecting the island came before anything, most of all his appearance.

"I'm going, William. Are you coming or not?"

Even from the gate, Sebastian smelled the contraband and heard the revelries of the looting criminals of Lockness' butcher houses. Drunken laughter and merriment blasted from the entrance.

Of course, no one minded the gate. And why would they? The gate existed to keep them out and now they occupied it.

Sebastian grunted as he strode through the entrance hall, determination drumming through his veins. Turning off from the throne room, he chose to enter through the servant's entrance. He needed to reveal himself to Lockness, but the rest of his criminal enterprise need not know he wasn't Ravana's loyal lapdog anymore.

Opening the door, he slipped through, keeping to the shadows as he inspected the throne room. Several tables and chairs were set out as if poised for a ball, but plates, cups, and clothing items were scattered around without a care.

The criminals, drunk off their asses, had women dripping off them. Likely some whores they brought from low town. Very few women participated in Lockness' dealings, but he wouldn't put it past them either.

Across the throne room, Lockness slouched into the Minister's throne, though he already had it remade into something more befitting the lord of crime. Shaped from a slab of jagged rock, jewels and layers of gold encrusted the edges. It made Lockness appear to be sitting on a pile of wealth. Luxury and a statement.

He'd earned every cent of it off the backs of the less fortunate.

Anger, hot and commanding, boiled his stomach, adding to his depleted energy reserves, but he was still too damn tired to fix any of it. His face. His stance.

Lockness turned to Sebastian's darkened corner, taking in the black blood covering him.

He showed no surprise on his face as he stood, walking down the dais and murmuring some excuse to his men before heading to a nearby door. He took a final glance at Sebastian before entering the doorway. The signal was clear enough. Sebastian crept along the edges of the room, following the crime lord.

Lockness led him away from the main throne room into an adjoining chamber. A room once used for meetings or other stately matters. Now, it suffered from disarray by its new residents.

Lockness poured two drinks from the decanter on the table, handing one to Sebastian. He shook his head, refusing the libations. The last thing he wanted to do right now started with dulling his senses and ended with remaining cordial with a criminal.

Lockness sipped his own drink, placing the second on the table, within Sebastian's reach. "You've had a busy night, I see."

Sebastian pulled his blood-soaked blade from its sheath, adding it to the mess of a table beside them. "Do you know what that is?"

Lockness raised an eyebrow, then made a show of scrutinizing the blade. "A sword?"

Sebastian narrowed his eyes. "The blood on that blade belongs to a crew of fishermen. But they were no longer *men* when I cut them down."

Lockness blinked, lowering his drink. "Are the other docks the same?"

"I have resources that say the others are still functioning. But I'll take those men out of danger as soon as I can."

"No," Lockness blurted, then took a long sip of his drink. "You think like an officer, Commodore. But I need you to think like a Minister."

"Isn't that your job now?" Sebastian growled, some of his rage returning.

"I've yet to be voted in, but if there are no more people to govern, I'm afraid it will all be for nought." At Sebastian's furrowed brow, Lockness continued. "We are running drastically short on resources. I'm sure you've heard of Castellanos' true debut. He barged in here, claiming that his cattle are dying." Lockness finished his drink, setting it aside. "Not only is that bad for business, but with the lack of food coming from Kheli, and this recent fisherman—" his eye tracked Sebastian's appearance — "incident, we are quickly losing resources. Those remaining docks may be the only thing keeping this island alive."

Sebastian let a breath roll out of his lungs. Lockness' assessment was accurate, however his methodology—

"Are you willing to risk the remaining fisherman we have for that?"

"We will all die if they don't." Lockness lit his pipe, letting the smoke linger around them. The Minister likely rolled his grave. "In fact, we'll use those abandoned fishing boats to make a trip to Kheli. If the fish in this area prove to be troublesome, perhaps some vegetation will be necessary." Sebastian was about to argue further. "Also, I've contacted my sources in Brettania. They will bring us a shipment themselves."

Sebastian circled the criminal lord. A trade deal with Brettania? The Minister never managed to accomplish an agreement.

"How did you manage that?"

"Why do you think I collected Kalonite slaves?" Lockness took another hit of his pipe. "For such a time as this."

"Why exactly are Kalonites so valuable that Brettania wants them?"

Lockness' eyes turned heavy. "Turns out Macha *does* protect them. Kalonites are immune to the bite of necromites." The air left Sebastian's lungs. "Brettanians use them for breeding, protecting generations to come. A plan I had for our fair little island as well, if not for a pesky rat thinking he was some kind of hero for saving them."

"People are not for your *breeding*." Sebastian bit out, his throat suddenly dry. He'd saved them. It was the right thing to do, no matter the cost. Lockness' understanding dark eyes told him the criminal lord was aware of the rat's identity.

But he didn't mention it.

"Now that my men are fed and happy, I have work to do."

CHAPTER 21

ELECTRIC TOUCH

ROSE

Rose screamed as power laced her veins, shooting through her body like spider-webbed lightning. It was worse than anything Ravana had done to her. Colt stood over her, the one she had associated with pain. She preferred this one though. The other demon only brought her insanity.

"Wow, you are really holding on today. I'm impressed, I dare say."

The pain came directly from his fingers as he dragged it across the bare skin of her arms. It appeared as a tender touch, yet her blood boiled.

She breathed through her teeth, screaming when he reached the sensitive skin of her underarm. He had every inch of her on display with her arms and legs spread apart and pinned against the wall.

He raised her ratted shirt, exposing the scars she always sought to hide. She flinched when his fingertips traced the scars, but no pain followed.

"Someone's already carved you up, huh?" Sparks of pain warned her of what was to come. "I wonder where he has touched you. Where he has kissed you." Colt leaned forward and her breath grew frantic. Fear gripped her as his mouth connected with the large scar that ran down her middle. Though no damage was visible, the white-hot agony reopened her skin as the original injury had.

Yellow swarmed her vision. *Let me out! I'll burn him to a crisp!*

Rose focused on the voices, letting them ground her and take her away from the pain and intimacy Colt fused together.

Green splashed with yellow. *No, you will only hurt her further. Let me go, I can get him off you.*

Both of them pushed against her mind, begging to be set loose on the foul man. Rose held them back. Colt's goal was to bring out the other women inside her, one in particular avoiding his every attempt.

Scarlett slipped most of all, using her fire to drown him in flames. Fire that he deflected time and again. Isabeya tried as well, catching him off guard a few times, but she had no weapon. With their hands bound, her skill did very little.

Colt pulled back with a satisfied smile; the pain reduced to only sparks as his hand held her thinning waist. She focused on a blemish on the wall to distract herself from the need to retch.

He inspected her flat belly. "You're looking a little hungry, birdy. Are you not willing to even beg for another meal today?"

What she'd eaten didn't qualify as a meal, stale bread and a couple crumbles of cheese. They hadn't even given her enough protein for any of it to sustain her. Yet her magic still pulsed, right on the surface, waiting for her to use it. She wouldn't risk it though. Nothing stopped him from inflicting pain, and she needed that magic to get out of this damned prison cell.

She glared, raising her chin and looking down on him. "I will not."

Colt cooed. "Tough, are you? Let me guess, you know pain? You've convinced yourself you can handle it." He ran a finger along her mess of scars, sending light shocks through her skin as he did. "Clearly, you've endured quite a bit. But these will seem like kitten scratches when I'm through with you."

She *could* handle it. The pain was worse than Ravana's blade, but more hope stayed with her in this dry cell. She used to scream as her father watched, knowing he would do nothing to stop it. But now? A pirate out there dared to track her down. No matter what they did to her, he would find her, and he would put back together whatever pieces of her remained.

Her head lifted, glaring daggers at him. "You can't kill me, and he'll come for me. When he does, you better pray to whatever goddess you serve that She will be merciful, because he won't be."

A darkness stirred in James that she understood like a reflection of her own. She may not have known what he was capable of, but she knew what atrocities she would commit if he'd been the victim of their cruelty.

Colt's head tilted. "You really believe he'll come for you, don't you?"

Rose masked her features, refusing to let his words diminish her hope. It was the one thing giving her enough strength to keep waking up.

Sand shifted under Colt's boots as he released her and crossed his arms. "The wandering pirate. The notorious lady killer and raider. That's the man you've put your hope into?" Rose's jaw tightened, but she didn't need to confirm it. "I hear he's got a dying island to worry about. If he's not the pirate I've heard so much about, if he's truly a good man, he'd be working to save the entire island, not some girl he met a couple months ago."

Rose's heart seized in her chest. "Dying?" He might be lying to her, but something about the way he said it made her believe otherwise. Colt's mouth curved, finding his opening. "You didn't know?" He scoffed. "You mean to tell me your precious pirate didn't tell you?"

She refused to allow such pettiness to take her hope away, even so, she listened.

"Samsara is dying, Kheli right along with it. Someone broke the deal, and now the island will fall just like the rest of the world." Rose blinked a few times, her eyes watering, her mouth too cottony. "That's why you were all heading to mother dearest. Sorry, following Nemain's Star. She is waiting patiently for him, but you, my dear, are in the opposite direction. He couldn't possibly save you and the islands. Which do you suppose he loves more? *You*?" He laughed as if the idea was too foolish to consider.

"How do you know all this?"

Colt smiled, reaching out to trace her collarbone. She flinched, but no pain followed. It would soon enough. "Nemain, you see, is our master."

Rose's brows scrunched. "What does Nemain want with me?"

"Your head, I would assume. And the assurance that you would never reincarnate, but I suppose that's where we come in. If I can get you to break the cycle and kill you before your pirate can save the world and get over here, he'll lose you for good." A tear fell down Rose's face, slipping past unbidden. Colt reached for the tear. "Assuming he cared for you enough to come for you at all."

"He cares for me. You must be unfamiliar with the sensation if you believe he would leave me here. He loves me," she hissed out, pulling her face away from his touch.

She closed her eyes as his thumb returned to her cheek sending chills down her spine.

"*Do I?*" The familiar cadence warmed her aching heart as she snapped her eyes open. It was Phantom before her. Her pirate standing in the sand with a thumb on her cheek, wiping away her tears. Unfiltered joy shot through her as she looked upon the face she had dreamed of each night. The one she always hoped to see when she woke. His thumb shifted until he cradled her chin in his grasp.

"I've had time to think, love." Finally, she noticed the glint of anger in his eyes. They no longer turned red, but the look was unmistakable, though he'd never directed it at her before. Except once, when she'd attempted to bend his mind to her will. "Your absence has made it easier for me to see. Your influence, the curse Davina inflicted upon me, that's the true source of my affection for you."

"What?" Rose let the question drift out before her. This was a trick. It had to be.

"I don't love you, Rose. I never have. Davina forced my heart, nothing more." It was one of Colt's lies. She understood that, but it didn't stop her heart from breaking. This fear she kept close to her heart. If his love for her had never been real, what was the point?

Rose shook her head, averting her eyes from his piercing gaze. "No. You're not really here. You don't mean that."

James seized her chin, making her look at him, at the eyes that were too familiar and the anger that was not. "I do. Don't worry, love. I'm not indifferent to you. I hate you." His palm was around her throat then, but what had once been a tender touch became unbearable. He pushed her back into the sandstone wall behind her. He squeezed her windpipe, trying to snuff the life from her. "Time and again you take everything from me. My inflicted 'love', as you call it, draws me to make decisions I wouldn't otherwise."

Rose gasped for breath, but none came through her constricted airways, but it didn't hurt nearly as much as the pain inside her.

"You never loved me," he said, bitterness dripping from every word. "She cursed you along with me. You feel no more for me than I do for you."

He allowed her enough breath to speak. She gulped down a lungful before protesting, "That's not true! I've loved you in every lifetime." But she couldn't deny his other claim. She had worried about it herself.

"Liar!" He growled as his palm constricted again, cutting off her air. Then he dropped his hand, stepping away from her. "You're pathetic." She slumped in her chains, gasping for breath. Aching bruises were already forming on her neck. "I could never truly fall for you."

He stood as she choked on her sobs, the tears flowing freely now. She hated them. The tears. Whenever they came out around Ravana, they felt like a failure. Even now, she was giving in to hopelessness. This was a trick.

He said nothing further as he pulled a lever that loosened her chains and deposited her body on the ground.

She watched as his boots stepped through mounds of sand, his black coat shifting behind him. She knew it was Colt, but he still looked like James as he left her there, sobbing into the dry air.

Rose reached her bound hands for the locket around her neck, the rose engraving a familiar texture beneath her fingertips. Her mother's voice, a memory, surfaced.

My dear, whenever you are scared or hopeless, open this locket and sing with it. It will ease your heart and frighten away all those fears that plague you. Keep it with you always, and I will be with you.

As a child, her mother would sing it to her every night, or whenever something bad happened. She let the notes carry her heart, making it lighter as she sang through the tears.

RAINDROPS FALL ON YOUR CHEEKS
THE SEASONS CHANGE IN THESE WEEKS
BUT NOTHING WILL KEEP YOU FROM ME
MY DARLING DEAR

No blue clouded her vision. No ribbons or tentacles sprang from or around her. Her voice was too muffled by her sobbing to be effective, but she didn't care. This song wasn't for the world around her. It was for her alone.

THE SEAS MAY RAGE, MY LOVE
THE STARS MAY FALL FROM ABOVE
STILL, NOTHING WILL KEEP YOU FROM ME
MY DARLING DEAR

Time passed and her sobs eventually stopped until she no longer felt so empty.

She shifted until her back hit the stone behind her. The voices tried to speak, but she drowned them all out. They would not help her today. With her tears spent, there was nothing left for her to feel.

CHAPTER 22

DEAL IN DEATH

PHANTOM

The Minister's screams were music to Phantom's ears, filling the hole in his heart that she had left.

He couldn't say her name, not even in his mind. Not since he found out she was with *them*. Phantom growled as he sliced another notch into his victim, letting all that pain fuel the vengeance in his veins.

The *Imari*. The self-proclaimed treasurers were from Nemain's court in Hell, her personal lap dogs. Phantom remembered them from the stories Sam told of his life. They had stolen him as a child and raised him to become the ultimate soldier. The hope was to prevent his connection with Isabeya, but Phantom knew all too well the strength of their bond. It was the truest thing he had in common with his counterparts.

They had one purpose in taking Rose. Break the bloody curse. He hated to think of what methods they would use to achieve that goal.

Phantom shouted his frustration, stabbing the Minister in his thigh. The answering whimper of pain only slightly relieved the tension in his head.

Sam had seen the *Imari* and given him one warning: *Do not engage. They will kill you and every devil here.*

It was enough to still Phantom's hand, even though the shadows spilled into that throne room, a tempting offer he almost took. But he knew he wasn't strong enough. Not nearly.

He would do what he did best, be a pirate.

A plan started brewing in his mind. Especially after seeing the tunnels for himself when they escaped the necromites. First, they needed a way into the palace. That was the most likely place they would keep her. She was too precious to keep out of their sights for long.

It wasn't until the Minister fell silent that he realized how distracted he had grown.

He pulled the hook from the man's shoulder. "Apologies," Phantom drawled. "I had forgotten about you."

The Minister whimpered, clearly running low on energy. "You don't think I know your scheming face by now, Hawkins? You're fixing a plan. I can see it."

"Maybe I'm just coming up with a new way to spill your insides on the floor."

The Minister coughed, blood splattering over his lips. "I have no doubt, but whatever truly has your mind has nothing to do with me. It's Ro—"

Phantom's free hand wrapped around the Minister's neck before he spoke further. A coughing sound confirmed that his grip was too tight. "Do not speak her name. Not if you wish to keep your tongue."

When the Minister's face turned as pale as Davina's moon, he let the bastard breathe. For now.

He coughed up chunks of blood, sucking in heaps of air between them.

Then that sickeningly wet laugh.

"You must like pain, Minister."

The Minister's laughter continued. "You have no idea how freeing it is that you are my only concern, Hawkins." Blood flowed over his chin, dripping down his neck. Phantom relished in the sight. "What more can you do to me? Managing that damn island was much harder, as I am sure you are aware."

Phantom returned to his tools, placing the bloodied hook on the table. He needed something that put enough fear into the Minister that he missed the island, but something about the words distracted him.

"I'm not actually."

"Not what?"

"Aware. I left the island almost as soon as you died. I believe Lockness has taken your place. But not I."

The Minister scoffed; the act powerful enough to rattle his chains. "That charlatan wouldn't know how to run a country if it played into his hands. He's too busy making sure his criminals are fat and happy. But that's still not what I'm referring to."

Phantom pulled a hot poker from the fireplace next to him. If Kayden's powers had been accessible in this Davina-forsaken place, he would have set the room on fire, torturing the Minister while he burned. But alas, the heat scorched his skin. It would have to do.

"And what, might I ask, are you referring to?" Phantom shoved the hot poker through the Minister's thigh, letting the heat cauterize the hole he made before pulling it back out. Only a bit of blood leaked out from the wound as it sizzled and crackled. The Minister screamed again.

On an agonized whimper, he responded, "I know what my death means for the island."

"No more games. Speak plainly." He shoved the poker in the Minister's other thigh, always being sure to keep his work even. It made it more satisfying. This time when he pulled it out, the hole bled more, the poker less hot than the first time. He frowned at the unevenness.

"I—" the Minster started before clearing his throat. "We have no walls like Atlas. We couldn't seal our borders like Brettania. I pleaded for our lives. I made a deal with Nemain for protection. In exchange for wards against those nasty creatures for Samsara and Kheli."

His eyebrows rose incredulously. "What exactly did you offer the Goddess of Death in exchange for thousands of lives?"

"One soul." The Minister swallowed. "I gave Her Rose's mother."

Phantom stood back, amusement leaving him. "You're the reason she died?"

The Minister breathed heavily. "You misunderstand. When you bargain with the Goddess of Death, it's not without loss of life. She could have taken my wife whenever She wanted." Phantom blinked, hoping this was a dream, and he wasn't hearing it. That he would have to tell — *Rose*. "I traded her soul. Then Nemain took her life." His eyes found Phantom's then, witnessing the horror there. "Yes, the most undeserving woman was thrust into Hell."

Phantom shook his head, dropping the poker. "Why? What is so important about one woman's soul?"

"My wife, Josephine Hart was Princess of Brettania and younger sister of the late Queen and traitor, Isabeya Hart."

Silence stretched on. Sam might not have been in his head then, but he'd heard the story plenty enough times. Isabeya ordered Brettania to be locked down but refused to be on the safe side. Instead, she sailed away, intent on retrieving her sister in Samsara.

"Before the war, Josephine's marriage to me was to be in good faith and encourage Samsara to be a trade port." The Minister coughed again. "She was meant to organize the trade routes. She was much better at that sort of thing than I ever dreamed to be. But when the time came to choose between the survival of my people and my wife, I chose them. I've yet to regret my choice."

Phantom narrowed his eyes, appalled at his callousness.

"But it matters not. The wards are gone. The deal was attached to my life. Now that I am dead—"

"The protection is lifted," Phantom finished for him, pressing his eyes shut. He hadn't even read Sebastian's last letters. Was he dealing with the implications of that?

His mind wandered back to Rose's mother. Was she nearby? He doubted his connection to Hell would grant him access to her.

If Isabeya had given up her country for her sister, who knows what she would do to get Josephine out of Hell. And Rose — that was her mother. A woman she'd cherished dearly. He knew once he told his songbird, she'd march straight into Hell to get the condemned woman back.

"She'd do it." The Minister disrupted his thoughts, staring down from his chains. "I know what you're thinking. I've thought about it, too. If anyone can get my Josephine out of there, it's Rose. What do you think I have been preparing her for?"

Phantom's anger flared. "Preparing her? You tormented her while you used her to control your own people."

A tear slid down the Minister's cheek. "I had to. If anyone left the islands, they would die. If anyone dethroned me, the deal would be done, and they would die. If anyone killed me, they would die." The tears ran furiously down his cheeks. "She looks just like Josephine. So beautiful. Kindhearted like her, too. Unwilling to take a person's free will, unless persuaded. I couldn't watch when Ravana—"

Phantom seized his face, pulling him forward roughly. "You let that witch into your home. What was done to Rose was *your* doing." He threw the man's head back, a crack sounding. But it didn't shut him up.

"I never denied her anything. Jewels. Clothes. I knew food would keep her strong, so I fed her at every opportunity." Phantom remembered watching the Minister participate in gluttony, piles of food being stacked everywhere, but he never suspected it was for her.

Now that he thought about it, she must have been eating quite a bit to keep the officers enchanted for so long.

"You think that makes you a good father? She was enduring torture *you* ordered."

The Minister blinked slowly. "If I had any choice—"

"You had every choice!" Phantom screamed at him, and the walls crumbled around them. He stared at the once formidable man that now hung from the ceiling like a sad excuse of life.

More puzzle pieces fit together, adding to his already unending list of reasons to hate the man before him.

"The men you ordered off Kheli, you never needed them, did you?"

His wrinkled features twisted, finally showing some fire. "I was saving them."

"By taking their lives away from themselves, from their families?"

"I had every intention of returning them to their island as decorated officers who had the skill set to properly defend the island." Phantom scoffed, remembering the apathetic former Commodore who risked the lives of everyone on Kheli to bring those men in. "That is until you defected."

Phantom laughed, his chest tightening. "Don't put the blame on me."

"Rose's enchantment would have faded without regular doses. And with your regular visits, you wouldn't have allowed that to continue on Kheli. Eventually, you would have recruited all of Kheli to rally against me. But as a pirate who scared the people away from trying to leave? That was useful. Especially when you insisted on protecting Kheli too."

The puzzle pieces fit together. "So, you started taking too much from Kheli, so I would raid it back?" He whistled. "Didn't think you were much of a gambler, Minister."

"It wasn't a gamble. You always fancied yourself the hero, even when you called yourself a criminal. *Captain Phantom,*" the Minister scoffed, like the moniker he'd built a reputation around was nothing more than a child's nickname.

"But now you're dead, the island is no longer yours to protect."

The Minister breathed out fiercely. "May Davina have mercy on their souls."

There was one part of the puzzle piece that didn't quite make sense. "Why did Ravana kill you? I've read the immortality spell myself. It requires a sacrifice, but that could have been anyone. And if she knew about the deal you made with Nemain, why would she risk it?"

The Minister's eyes were growing hazy, blinking as though he was about to pass out, likely from the blood loss. Or the position. "Clearly, you did not translate the text correctly. The word is *yajna-niyati* which translates to 'sacrifice of fate'." At the skeptical look forming creases around Phantom's eyes, the Minister responded.

"Yes, I studied the book myself. I've memorized it, even if I didn't perform the rituals. No mere human would do. Your own life or that of my daughter wouldn't have sufficed either. You both were born to die. One must intervene fate with a death powerful enough to fuel the spell."

Phantom crossed his arms, not liking his implication. "Your deal with Nemain, how long was it meant to last?"

"I bargained for sixty years. I thought it would be enough time to build a Navy large enough to protect the island."

"Ravana intervened."

The Minister nodded, barely holding his head up. "I was cheated halfway through my bargain, but my last thirty years were absorbed by Ravana, fueled by her magic enough to extend it with every life on that island."

Phantom's head began to hurt, finding this interaction with the Minister more tiresome than ever. He recalled seeing her fight Serena until the beastie blasted her knife with blue flames. Ravana had then turned on the Minister, slicing his throat open in front of his subjects. It had made no sense at the time other than the completion of the immorality spell that she'd been determined to complete.

Now her choice of sacrifice made sense.

"Her immortality is simply the years she took from the people of Samsara who will now die thirty years too soon?"

He nodded. "Yes, and the ones who haven't been born yet."

That weight on his chest grew, threatening to let in the guilt he'd been shoving away for months. "I can go to Nemain and demand she reinstate the deal you made."

The Minister half opened his eyes. "Not if you bring my Rose. She won't allow her mother to stay there." The man's eyes closed completely, the strength leaving him, but he left Phantom with one last parting phrase. "And you don't have what it takes to make a sacrifice like that."

The Minister's eyes closed, but Phantom stared at him, thoughts whirling through his head. There might not be a home to return to. Samsara might have Sebastian, but Kheli? They had the angels, but not their fearless leader. Sophia was with the devils.

Angelica led them in the meantime, but they would need help, eventually.

So would Samsara.

Phantom closed his eyes, knowing he needed to find a way to reinstate the bargain, but he wouldn't sacrifice the same thing. He would never allow it.

There had to be another way to save the islands.

Then there was the problem of Josephine Davenport. She was being held against her fate in Hell. Rose would come for her. Nemain didn't even need the bargain to get her hands on his songbird.

No—

After he got her back, he wouldn't lose her again.

Watching the Minister's broken and bloody form take its last breath, he stepped away from the mangled spirit. This was the last time he'd let the Minister consume another thought of his. It was useless revisiting the past like this. Hell was free to take what was left of him.

He needed to find Rose.

First step, get into the palace.

⁂

Phantom awoke with relief and a pooling sense of dread. He'd never see the Minister again, but the bastard had left quite a mess. Josephine Davenport would have to wait. In the meantime, he had secrets to keep.

Green assaulted his vision. *What's wrong? Why are you thinking of Josephine?*

Phantom ignored his counterpart, opting to put his plan in motion instead.

He moved the curtain of his room aside, revealing the morning sun and a collection of devils in the sandy yard around the barracks. He scanned the faces but couldn't find his swordsman. Wilson was cooking up something that spiced the air around them, his stomach growling in response.

I know you can hear me. Ignoring me won't shut me up.

He strolled beside Wilson's makeshift stove, taking a bowl of steaming stew. The cook eyed him wearily. Phantom took a bite of delicious lentil soup with a raised eyebrow, challenging Wilson to speak his mind.

But the cook shook his head saying, *"Eh ya."* Like it wasn't worth the effort. Phantom wasn't sure if he was relieved or offended.

"Captain." Earhart was before him, his barrel arms folded before himself. Yes, there were things he hadn't told the devils yet. It wasn't that he was avoiding the conversation, but he'd hardly been able to grasp the idea himself. Commanding Jon to his knees without his will getting in the way was most convenient, even if the *Imari* had decided to keep the traitorous bastard.

You're hiding something from us.

The first mate's brow twisted in concern at whatever he witnessed. "Is everything alright?"

"Yes." Phantom answered a bit too harshly, taking another spoonful. "I just have a ringing in my ears."

Earhart shifted on his feet. "Something the doctor can help with?"

Phantom let out a breathy laugh. "I'm afraid not." He straightened, facing his first mate with renewed energy. They needed him at his strongest capacity. *She* needed it. "I need Black. Where is she?"

Earhart nodded. "I'll find her, Captain." He wandered off towards her room.

Inspecting the devils again, Phantom found them clustered around the communal table eating from their bowls. Russet swatted at flies the size of his thumb between bites.

"Away you foul beasts! The blood shall remain inside my body!"

The insects were interested in his meal, but none of the devils bothered to correct him.

Hyne and Tick were closed in around Rose's handmaiden, Lara. Phantom was still against the idea of her being present. Rose would have his head if anything happened to her, but she did prove to be useful. She had sought Sita out, who then used the tunnels to get them back inside the citadel.

Lara stood beside the two devils, moving her hands as if she were—

She was teaching them how to use their hands to speak. It never even occurred to him that they would want to. It would be a useful tool to be able to communicate that way with them. Perhaps she would teach the entire crew.

"Hi," Robin jumped in front of him, appearing out of nowhere. "Are you Draven right now? I wanted to talk to him..." Phantom looked around the barracks. They weren't close to a building. How did he drop from the sky? "... but then I thought. No, he doesn't want to talk to me, but it was amazing. The shadows in the palace. Even if it didn't work, I mean, he made the lights dimmer."

Orange burst into his vision. *The shadows aren't some light show.* Draven pressed against his consciousness, wanting to correct the boy.

"Wait, how do you know it was Draven?"

Robin blinked rapidly. "Oh, ah, your eyes. They turn orange for Draven." He stood up straighter, counting on his fingers. "Green is for Sam. I see that one the most. Yellow is for Kayden, but he's the angry one, so I don't talk to him."

On cue, yellow flames danced across his eyes. *I am* not *the angry one.*

"Oh, there he is now." Robin took a step back, wary of Phantom's weakest counterpart.

Weakest? Let me out once in a while and I'll show you—

Orange interrupted his tirade. *As entertaining as that would be, I believe he was asking about me.*

Phantom took another bite, looking over Robin's shoulder for Black again. Earhart had yet to return.

"Anyway," Robin continued. "What are the shadows? I mean, they can't just be the lack of light if they can move like that."

Phantom inspected the powder monkey.

Clever, isn't he?

Indeed, he was. "Death," Phantom answered. "Shadows are the reapers that take your soul to the next life." It was then that

Phantom noticed the silence around the yard. The other devils were listening.

"*Chido*," Robin breathed, awestruck in the way only a teenage boy would be. It wasn't exactly the word he would use to describe the shadows.

Earhart finally appeared with Black in tow.

She nodded at him. "What do you need?"

He smiled, ready for action. "How certain are you that the tunnels can get us into the palace?"

CHAPTER 23

TRINKET

ake up, girl.

Rose blinked rapidly, taking time to clear her head and the green swarming her vision with Isabeya's incessant yelling. Was someone touching her?

Finally, her vision cleared in time to watch a hand pass before her eyes, a slightly hairy hand with protruding veins, but it was the dangling chain that made her jolt, reaching for the pendant.

Colt pulled it away before she could. "Ah ah ah," he drawled. "What is this?"

"Just a trinket. It's not worth much." Before she lunged for it again, he stepped out of her reach.

He smiled, a glint entering his eyes. "But it's not worthless to you." Whatever was on her face was confirmation enough because he turned his attention to the rose engraving. "It is beautiful craftsmanship, but that's not it. What could possibly—" He clicked open the latch, the tones of the music box flooding out. "Ah, there it is."

The music made her mother's image return to her. It was a faint copy of what the Stone did, but it was comforting all the same.

"Music is a magic of its own, wouldn't you say?"

"Give it back," she bit out, but her demands fell on deaf ears.

"You wear this every day, yes?" He turned the necklace over to the backside where the metal had deteriorated, turning the color of brass. The edges of the rose petals were the same color. "I'd say you never part from it until today."

"It will do nothing for you. If you take it, I swear to Davina, I will end you."

Colt stepped back, a palm to his chest in false surprise. "So, the birdy finally shows her talons, and over a necklace? Well, it seems I struck a nerve."

He snapped the locket shut, cutting off the music mid-verse, then slid it into his pocket. "What will you do with it?"

"Well, I believe it will make a wonderful gift for a friend."

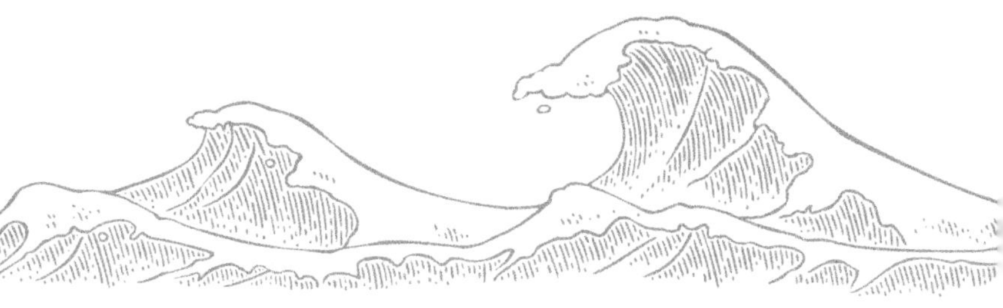

CHAPTER 24

RAVANA'S LAPDOG

SEBASTIAN

Working with Lockness was the last thing Sebastian expected to do. Though, truth be told, everything had gone wrong. He couldn't quite place when events turned for the worse, but Lockness was thinking rationally, even if Sebastian didn't agree with his methods. Survival was important, but if he tried to save everyone, they would all die.

It didn't mean he had to abandon his morals, though.

He learned that lesson when watched Thomas die by firing squad, one he had no choice but to command. Memories of them as boys in the orphanage flashed in his head as he watched the life leave him.

Never again. He couldn't do it again.

Sebastian rubbed his freshly washed face, letting water trickle down his bare chest. The cool water helped awaken his senses. He dreaded seeing Ravana again.

She summoned him this morning. Although he hoped for an opportunity, it was becoming clear that she no longer desired him in her bed. Maybe she knew all along and waited to see how long he'd keep up the ruse. How many men he would sacrifice for it.

Frustrated, he slapped the bowl, knocking it to the ground.

He had to think of another way to get Ravana's guard down,

and quickly. He needed those men she was hunting. They were the only ones with the motivation to protect the island.

Sebastian pulled himself together, looking into the foggy mirror to steady himself. Until he saw someone behind him. A violet-eyed witch who was currently ogling his bare chest.

"I wouldn't complain if you decided to make this the new uniform."

Since it was Indigo, he didn't bother to turn, continuing his routine like she wasn't there. "What do you want, *witch*?"

She breathed out, annoyed that he didn't bother to react to her flirting. Truly, he didn't know why she bothered, but he suspected it was to make him uncomfortable. Surprisingly, he found comfort in the airiness her flirting brought to a room, even though he'd hardly admit that to her.

"We're allies. Remember that, Commodore. Especially when you decide to bed with the criminal lord of Samsara." She didn't bother moving from her spot at his door. He would have cared that someone would see her, but with the Fortress packed with criminals, they would hardly question her presence.

He turned, throwing a towel down on the table. "I'm not bedding anyone." It was such a crude term used mostly for political arrangements, but the sparkle in her eyes told him her amusement on the subject.

"Clearly. When was the last time you lay with a woman?"

He growled, picking up his shirt from the bedpost and throwing it over his head. When he glared at her, she smiled with that hint of mischief in her eyes, her teeth biting her bottom lip as her eyes trailed his chest before he covered it.

"It's a real shame."

He wasn't sure if he should be flattered or disgusted. To his horror, he was neither. Instead, the room felt a little warmer.

"I have a meeting with Ravana. She will grow suspicious if I am late."

The humor drained from Indigo's face, yet her tone remained feather light. "Oh, are you about to end your celibacy, Commodore? And with a priestess no less."

Sebastian held her stare, daring her to say it again. "I hope that's her intention, so I can slit her throat open."

A small smile ticked the edges of Indigo's mouth. "I'm not here to talk about your nonexistent evening activities." She approached, moving like a cat, graceful but predatory. Her face collapsed, solemnity taking over. "I found another one."

"No," Sebastian snapped. "I cannot do that again."

She pressed her lips together. "He is a willing sacrifice. This one is from Kheli. His only kin is a sister he has no way to return to. He wants to do this for her."

Sebastian pressed his eyelids shut. *A Khelitian.* He had worked hard to protect Kheli at one time, feeling sympathy for families that no longer had their husbands, fathers, brothers, nephews and uncles in their lives because the Minister commanded it.

Now some of them were finally free, and they would line up for slaughter. Not to mention it was a useless sacrifice. He needed them in the field, protecting citizens as they were meant to.

"Did you convince him of that? That his death would mean something?"

"Sebast—"

"Don't. I'll let Ravana have me but let me protect *someone*." He pressed his fingers into his hair, letting wet strands fall forward. "Lockness is sending a party to Kheli. I'll get him on the boats heading there. Then he can be with his sister again instead of dying for *my* cause."

Indigo took two more steps, placing herself before him. She was so much smaller than him. Her hand landed on his forearm, the small contact making him suddenly feel unbearably human.

"We'll send him to Kheli. But I will find another." He blinked at her, not understanding why she was really doing this. "Mark my words, I will sacrifice hundreds for you."

He glared at her. "Why?"

Her hand moved to his cheek, the contact strangely comforting. "Because we need you. Samsara *needs* you." Her mouth opened to say more but it closed again. "You cannot die on me, Ashby."

He nodded, removing her hand from his cheek though he was reluctant to drop it. "I will still get him on a boat to Kheli."

Indigo's face twisted, a small frown bringing down her features. "You're too noble for your own good." Then she turned, walking into the hallway like she belonged.

He found the room to be much colder without her presence.

Sebastian entered the temple, having adopted his mask of nothing by the time it was within sight.

Ravana sat on a settee as blood red as her hair, but she was not wearing what she normally did. Instead of a color that honored one of the goddesses she desecrated, she wore black silk that clung to her body like a second skin, plunging low enough on her chest to see her sternum beneath her breasts.

Sebastian fantasized about plunging his sword into that vulnerable spot, but he didn't let the idea show on his face. He was nothing, after all. He felt nothing, including that burning anger that saw fit to end her life.

It took a moment for him to recognize the look of disdain on her face.

"You're late."

He bowed uniformly. "Apologies, my lady." He left it at that. Excuses were for someone who had something to fear. He felt nothing.

"You lack performance with your mind at limited capacity," she said through clenched teeth.

He said nothing. The only response he had was another apology, but the sentiments did not need repetition.

"It's come to my attention that my army of mindless slaves may be unsuitable. Your officers will slowly begin to regain themselves soon, so it seems I am left with insufficient men." She stood gracefully, like how Indigo moved, but where Indigo's fluidity resembled a bird in flight, Ravana's was like a snake. One that would strike at any moment. "I must do things the old-fashioned way." She threw a cloak around her shoulders before walking past Sebastian. "Come, you will help."

Sebastian followed closely as she exited the temple, heading straight for the Fortress.

CHAPTER 25
DEATH OR ME?
SEBASTIAN

Ravana's magic poured violently from her, spreading open the doors of the Fortress like a gust of wind.

The midday sun revealed a group of miscreants in various degrees of undress. Some were asleep, others were still swaying on their feet.

"Miserable souls," she spat before clapping her hands together, the attention of the room fixating on her and subsequently the Commodore behind her. Some of them had enough sense left to straighten and search for their weapons.

"Ladies," she commanded, clapping slowly. "Good work, you've left them pliable."

The women of the night, as naked as the day they were born, stood, not bothering to cover themselves. Sebastian kept his eyes forward, looking at anything but the bodies drawing closer to him. He nearly winced when he felt their hands on him.

"Such a brave Commodore," one cooed, but he refused to acknowledge her.

A hand trailed along his arm, curling to reach his chest. "You're so fit."

A sickness started overtaking his senses. These women either had no idea the amount of control Ravana had over them or they were willingly brazen.

"We can treat you tonight."

Davina, spare him.

"Don't waste your breath, ladies. He's unresponsive." She spat, snapping her fingers. The girls were suddenly dressed in robes of blood red. They were priestesses, every one of them. He recognized their faces, but it was difficult to pay attention to the complexities of their facial features when he was averting his eyes. Now that they were covered, it was clear.

One continued to caress his chest, looking like she would enjoy drawing a response from him. It made him shrink away from her. Ravana snapped, and the girls left, gossiping and laughing as they left their mistress with the wolves.

"They were priestesses?" One man with a crooked jaw and a hairy chest came around a table. He had managed to right his pants, but his shirt was still missing.

"Did you enjoy them?" Ravana questioned before walking further into the throne room. It occurred to Sebastian that Lockness was nowhere to be seen. "In case you believe any of your secrets are intact, don't. My girls specialize in getting information."

The criminals paled.

"Also, to keep you all in here until I arrived." She picked up the nearest bottle, holding it upside down, not even a drop fell from it. "By the looks of it, I needn't have bothered."

Some men had assembled themselves enough to stop Ravana's perusal. "You got some nerve coming in here. You started this whole mess, didn't you?"

Her lips twisted. "What you call a mess I call organized chaos. Though I do find myself in need of something new." Ravana's hand came down on the man's long stubble, her nails biting into his skin. "Something only the underbelly of Samsara can provide." She poked his round belly to make her point.

"You conniving bitch—" The man reared back before his fist flew towards her face. But when it reached her face, it flew straight through her, red mist dispersing where she once was.

"Now now, boys, no need to use names." She appeared on the throne Lockness had made for himself. "We're friends here." They took a collective step back, a few of them running to the nearest exit. "Ashby, dear."

He withdrew his sword, blocking the exit as the other doors slammed shut, noticeable clicks echoing in the silent room. The men stopped in their tracks, unwilling to cross blades with the Commodore.

Ravana inspected the throne. "Lockness has no taste." With a wave of her hand, it changed, transforming until black rock jutted out behind her, red tipping the ends. The entire throne looked like it was carved out of black crystal, red decorating the surfaces.

Robert Westerwood marched out to face her himself. As Lockness' second in command, he retained the most respect amongst these thugs. He stepped up to the dais.

"Don't get comfortable, witch. That's not where you belong."

Ravana's mouth curved into a smirk that shot ice down Sebastian's spine. He knew the look and what it meant. Red mist gathered around her like a magical blanket, causing the moon pendant on her throat to glisten.

"It would be wise to hold your judgment until you hear what I have to say."

Robert's arms crossed over his chest. "What would tempt us enough to support your ass on that throne?"

"Let me explain this in a way that even your thick skulls can understand." Anger rose in the room with the mounting tension. "When our former leader died, he took something very important with him, Nemain's blind eye." She shifted in her mist, appearing behind Westerwood. "Now, She sees us, and She wants us all dead. Her infection has already taken root. Unless you rats haven't bothered to pay attention to the island you live on." She twisted around, the mist following in her wake.

"A disease you brought to our shore. Is that what you're admitting?" Robert pulled a sword from his hip. "Why don't we sacrifice *you* as penance?" The savages hooted at the idea of spilling her blood. Sebastian wouldn't stop them if they tried.

The sword in Robert's hand turned into red mist, leaving him with only a handle.

"Aside from the fact that you can't, you'll lose something far more precious than your meaningless lives." She faded into the mist again, reappearing next to one of the thugs. "A chance at eternity."

Robert laughed, the sound echoing in his men. "You must think us thick if you believe we would fall for such outlandish promises."

"I believe I was clear in my opinion of your mental capacity. But that isn't my point." She circled the men, her feet not quite touching the floor as she slithered across the room, red mist smoothing out her edges. "What I did was only the start. Without a true patron, my immortality will always have an expiration." More chills ran up Sebastian's spine as the air grew colder. "No, I'm thinking *bigger* than that."

She made her way back to Robert, where skepticism was written over the lines of his face.

"The Moon Goddesses have been ruling too long. It's time for the next cycle of gods to arise." Ravana returned to the throne, moving to it like a cloud. "Once the deed is done, you will be rewarded for your loyalty. You'll each be granted immortality, beginning a new race of superior beings. You'll have gold," she paused, flitting her hand over her head as gold coins dropped from the ceiling, the men reaching for them. "You'll have all the flesh you desire." The women from before manifested like apparitions around them, naked but not fully corporeal. They smiled and laughed as they floated around the men. "You'll each have your own country to govern, as big as your worth is. All of this will be provided by your godly patron."

One fair-haired man spoke from his spot on a far table. "And who would that be?"

Ravana's form grew until she filled out the wall behind her, as tall as a dozen men. "Me, of course."

It was a terrifying thought to consider. A world dictated by a blasphemous, pedophilic lunatic. He had little faith that she could achieve such dramatics. Ravana was still human, even with her impressive tricks. The Goddesses would punish her for her ambitions soon enough.

The criminals laughed, mocking statements rattling around the room, reflecting his own thoughts.

"Idiots!"

The air was swiftly taken from the room, sucked out like it never existed. Sebastian breathed in, but nothing filled his lungs, the sensation uncanny as panic flooded his veins. The surrounding men did the same, clutching at their throats and falling to the floor.

"Nemain is coming for you. I offer you a chance at everything you ever wanted. You would choose death over greed? Over lust? Over power?" Her voice boomed through the airless room. "Do you require proof? Here is your proof!"

The air rushed to Sebastian's lungs as he gulped greedily, the men around him doing the same as red mist surrounded them completely, swirling like a storm.

Shapes appeared in the red mist around them. Images of a red sky, Nemain's full moon shining like a beacon above their heads.

Ravana's voice floated over them. "This is what is to come."

Sebastian refocused on the surrounding walls to find them gone completely. The walls had crumbled around them, scattered in the dead grass surrounding them. Necromites filled the available space, moaning and reaching for someone to infect. Red outlined their forms, but Sebastian couldn't tell if it was from the moon or Ravana's dark magic.

One such beast walked straight through him. He recognized the necromite as Lord Desmond, the same white hair but nothing of his boisterous smiles. Only clouded eyes and the remnants of high fashion falling from his thinner limbs.

Was that what happened when they became a necromite or was he starving by the time death came for him?

Sebastian looked on, focusing on where high town was visible. It was burning, half the buildings had already crumbled to the ground, the other half blazing. Low town was too distant to see, but he imagined it was much the same.

Some of the very criminals around them saw themselves in the form of monsters, breathing heavily and reaching for any still beating heart. He'd never thought he'd see the day when criminals fell to their knees with prayers on their lips.

Sebastian looked around for his own body, praying to Davina, he wouldn't find it.

The clashing of swords drew his eyes to the right, where the temple stood in the distance. Metal clashed from afar. Two figures, neither of them a necromite, faced each other in battle, the moon itself highlighting their duel.

The figures were too small to make out their identities.

Red swarmed the vision, returning to its swirling nature. "This is what awaits you, unless you follow me. I will see that you not only survive but thrive for centuries to come." The red died out, leaving behind the Fortress walls and the sun where it shined through the windows.

Sebastian blinked to readjust to the light.

Ravana sat on her throne, looking bored with her hand holding up her head and her legs crossed, red mist swirling at the edges of her robe.

"I will only offer this once. Who will follow me? Will you choose death or me?"

Silence greeted her for a moment, no one willing to give in. But by her argument, did they have a choice? What could Lockness offer against eternity? And even if she was lying about that, if she was their best chance at survival, what did it matter?

Robert stepped up to her. His expression didn't change from the quizzical brow, yet he nodded his head. "Aye, Mistress. I will follow you."

Another piped in, walking to stand behind Robert. "Aye. I will serve, Mistress."

More lined up, one by one pledging their allegiance, until their voices took up the entirety of the room. As they swore fealty to her, magic electrifying the air like static from a storm.

Ravana's smirk grew, filling her face as they stood before her.

Once the last one swore, she rose from her throne. "Oh, and one last thing. Let's keep this development between us. Follow Lockness' orders like good little thugs for now. I'll let you know when the time is right." Her mist circled her as if she was about to blink out of existence. Sebastian wondered if it was too much to hope that she would get lost in that red mist of hers. "And before you go running to your lord with this information, do know, the punishment for betrayal will be — severe." She giggled to herself as if she hoped one of them would try. "Come pet," she cooed.

Sebastian marched to her side, hating the idea of being transported by her mist. Alas, he had no choice but to obey.

They were swept away, but before red consumed him, he witnessed the throne flicker back to its original state. The way Lockness wanted it. Even Robert's blade had returned to its hilt, as if Ravana had never been there.

He attempted to keep the despair from his face as the evidence disappeared. Lockness was the most powerful man on Samsara, and she had managed to take that power from him in one move.

Sebastian knew he had to be the one to tell Lockness, but he wouldn't remain on the island after he did.

CHAPTER 26

CHALLENGED

PHANTOM

The air crackled with anticipation as Phantom sauntered to the palace, the grandeur of the building pressing down on him with an unseen weight. The mask slipped on, his painted smile mocking the lack of emotion behind it, a chilling contrast to his confident gait.

The unused door he used last was a direct route to the throne room, but stirring the locals to attack was not on his agenda. He was still scheming on how to use it to his advantage but not today. This time he decided to use the main entrance.

He stared at the building, its many windows like dark eyes staring back, wishing he sensed Rose within those walls.

Green assaulted his vision. *This is a bad idea.*

There was a guard at the gate, eyeing him with scrutiny. He was a large fellow with a shaved head and tattoos covering his head in a pattern of runes and boxy designs.

"What business have you?"

Phantom rose his brows. "Brettanian? What gave me away?"

The guard grunted, looking him up and down. "You have look, like drowned rat in desert." He spit on the ground at Phantom's feet. "You not survive long here."

Phantom twisted his features in disgust. Spit was a high form of insult in the desert. He resisted the urge to fix his hair after the 'drowned rat' comment. "Well, I have a challenge for one of your dear treasurers. I'm sure one of them can spare a moment?"

The guard's brutish features twisted into a smile before he broke into laughter. "For you? I take you to dungeon. See who accept challenge there." He continued to laugh, the sound rolling off his tongue.

Phantom ground his teeth together. He didn't want to have to use his old name, but at desperate times — "And for Maahes?"

The guard laughed *harder*.

"*Mus zibbi*," he cursed between breaths. Though clearly intended as an insult, the words washed over Phantom, unfamiliar and meaningless.

He was about to resort to his third plan, when a silhouette came out from the gates.

"Watch your language, Rahl. There might be children present." Colt slipped out beside him, striding for Phantom. He contrasted against the sandstone in fine crimson silks, a red stain against the city. Whispers echoed around them as the people began to take notice. Colt shrugged dramatically with hands in his pockets. "I never could resist a challenge."

Colt strode through the sand like he was in no hurry at all. How did he not notice the animosity of his people? They glared at him, their hatred near palpable.

"You must be brave, to face a people that hate you so viscerally. That or idiotic."

More slid into the street, keeping to the buildings with watchful gazes.

"You've forgotten who I am if you believe I have anything to fear from them."

Phantom kept an eye on the demon before him, but his attention kept wandering to the people gathering. They'd already doubled in size. "I don't know about that. Numbers should not be taken lightly, especially when you've left them with little to lose."

Colt's smile didn't fade as he assessed the crowd, turning his eyes to witness the scene they created. He circled Phantom, the rhythmic thud of his boots a counterpoint to their anxious whispers.

"You mentioned a challenge. What exactly did you have in mind?"

"A game of Kazeboon."

Colt kissed his teeth. "The stakes?"

"If I win, you give Rose to me."

Colt's brows rose. "I'll expect something of equal value."

"What do you want?"

"Tell you what," he started, spreading his arms out. "I'm a generous demon. All I ask is one night of complete obedience."

Phantom bristled, every instinct in him screaming for him to refuse. "And what would you make me do?"

Colt laughed like they were old friends sharing a joke. "I'm not going to tell you. It'll be my little surprise. It's only fair considering what I might lose."

Phantom didn't like it at all, but he needed this game to take place. But compliance might cost him dearly.

"Come on," Colt taunted. "Where is all that swagger and arrogance now?" He chuckled, bringing his thumb to chin. "Ya know, when you took out the big bad pirate captain, I thought to myself, *wow, we have got ourselves a badass*. Now that we're face to face, I don't see it." He scowled, a visible expression of his displeasure, but Phantom remained unmoved, ignoring the provocation.

"How do you know what I've done?"

"You mean how you summoned a creature from Hell to take down good ole Captain Pike?" A shiver played across the skin of his neck where the tentacles seemed to flinch. "I wrote the damn book, boy."

Phantom fought to keep his face impassive, not giving away his shock. His silence must have been evident since Colt's mouth split into a toothy grin. He continued circling, the crowd around them growing thick in numbers.

"Dante and I wrote down all the spells we learned on this *god-forsaken* rock, except it comes with a catch." He pointed a finger at Phantom. "But you already know what that is."

Green vines obscured his vision. *Fealty to Nemain, marking the castor for damnation.*

A pregnant pause followed; the silence thick enough to taste.

"The grimoire's one spell to delay the human inevitability of death and the following torment that awaits them in Hell requires *your* blood. It was an eventuality that the book would one day find you."

Phantom shuddered, a cold dread gripping his heart.

Colt spread his arms out wide. "We sensed the moment you gave yourself to Nemain. We'd been waiting for it. It was only a matter of time until you found your little birdy. We just had to get a sleeper agent onto your ship."

Jon.

It was a set up. The entire bloody thing. From the moment he had cast the spell Rose's fate had been sealed—

She was always meant to end up here. It was well and truly all his fault.

And he needed to get her out of this mess.

"Now you have the chance to dismantle our entire plan with one game, and you hesitate. For one little game. One wager. One possible night of obedience. Is she worth so little to you?"

His eyes flashed yellow. "She's worth more to me than your vile mind can comprehend."

"Well then." Colt's eyes, gleaming with barely leashed anticipation, seemed to burn with a hot, restless energy. "Do we have an accord?"

He held his hand out to Colt. "Agreed."

Colt smiled widely before accepting his hand. That knowing glint of mischief in his eyes... it was the same look he'd used on his enemies before.

"Rahl, be a gentleman, and get the door for us."

Rahl nodded before stepping to the side and lifting the portcullis. As they entered, Phantom heard the whispers. He tried to block them out, but it was hard to ignore the restless energy in the city. A wave of people surged behind them, their collective murmur rising to a roar before the heavy portcullis slammed shut, a metallic shriek cutting through the air.

He had to get Rose out before a rebellious riot tore the citadel apart.

Colt led him through halls of white stone lined with the modern version of the symbols Phantom had come to associate with the Draion language. If he were here under different circumstances, he would have loved to learn what each meant. Alas, he had a mission to achieve.

We'll free you. The words rang in Phantom's head ever since he heard them in the throne room of the palace. Strange words coming from men who obviously wanted to see him submit.

"What did you mean, when you promised me freedom?"

Colt grinned as he opened a door, welcoming him into what looked like a parlor. Embroidered cushion seats sat before a balcony that faced a courtyard. The palace had its own oasis, complete with a swimming hole with more greenery than the rest of the city combined.

Right before the balcony, two chairs sat adjacent to one another. A table sat between them, but it was the pile of runes that drew his attention.

"I knew you were the man to talk to. Your other versions have been less inclined to believe it, but you strike me as different." Colt leaned on a nearby table, choosing from a selection of expensive cigars before lighting one.

"Different how?"

Colt offered him a cigar, but Phantom shook his head. "*Freedom is worth its weight in gold.* Isn't that what you told our *cerbalus*? You are cursed to follow the whims of a goddess you do not belong to. It is understandable you would value freedom so much." Colt spoke around the roll in his mouth, smoke wafting around him.

"You feel it, don't you? Davina pushing you. Right now She's urging you to hunt down the little birdy."

For once, he and Davina were on the same page. It's Her interference he didn't like, but he caught the meaning in Colt's words.

"You believe I'm not here of my own volition?"

"Let's just say, I don't believe you are controlling your own emotions." It was absurd. He sensed Davina whenever he made a move for or against Her wishes. If She controlled him to such an extent, things would not be the same. Instead of voicing that, Phantom chose to play along, allowing his opponent to let down his guard.

With a flourish, Colt gestured towards the table laden with

Kazeboon runes, their ancient script etched into smooth stones. He picked up a tile that wasn't part of Phantom's set. With a sickening realization, he saw the rune mirrored the symbol, crudely embossed on the rusted manacles Lockness had used to imprison him. The angled square made his skin crawl with memories. It reminded him of the failure that had nearly ended Rose's life.

"I don't remember that symbol being in the game."

Colt examined it. "An alteration, popular since the fall. The Maahes tile was added as a wild card, so to speak. It can become any of the three factions, so long as it doesn't match the opposing tile. Though, it matches the tile in strength. Trickster god, after all."

Phantom scoffed. It made the chances in a game harder to interpret. He shouldn't risk so much. Colt was entirely too confident.

"What? Don't tell me the mighty Captain Phantom is going to walk away from his own challenge?" The game had begun long before they'd entered this room, he wasn't about to show his cards this soon. Instead, he mirrored Colt's smile with his own. That familiar mask slipped right into place.

"Why risk it? You clearly need her."

Colt raised his hands in mock surrender. "As much as Dante would kill me for it, I'm a gambling man. I'm willing to risk a little to get what I want. Are you? What's one night on a leash compared to her life?"

It was as good of an answer as he was going to get. Phantom let in a long, steadying breath before settling down into his own seat.

"Excellent! One last thing before we begin."

Colt tipped his head and agony ripped into Phantom's palm, searing his skin. He held in a scream at the boiling pain, refusing to let Colt see him flinch. When he lifted his hand, blood dripped from his hand to the table between them before it sizzled away.

"Consider this a contract between the two of us. If you win, it will disappear."

On his palm, where he expected to find the skin seared and melted, he found black ink in the shape of a circle, a rose depicted at its center. He'd seen its likeness but couldn't pinpoint where exactly.

"And if I lose?"

"This will keep you to your word, of course."

The tattoo around his neck itched as if recognizing the presence of a new deal.

"And if I should not keep to my end?"

It's a question he'd had for years, though he was never brave enough to defy Nemain, especially when there seemed to always be more lives for him to take. As if She supplied him with them.

"Well," Colt started. "I tethered birdy's life to it. So, if you aren't a man of your word, it'll cost her this life." It was an echo of words he once said to her.

I am a man of my word. Are you a woman of yours?

"You're bluffing. You need her."

Colt smiled, like a cat toying with its prey. "Am I? I live forever and she will be born again shortly. As will you. Then we can start this process all over again. I'd prefer to have a speedier time frame, but as I said, I'm a gambling man."

At that point, she wouldn't be Rose, and he wouldn't be James. They'd be reduced to another voice in the next poor soul's head.

"What's keeping you to your word?"

Colt put a hand on his chin, rubbing the stubble there. "Every gambler worth his salt knows that in order to keep playing the game, one must treat their word as law."

Phantom narrowed his eyes. "No tricks?"

Colt's mouth twitched, but he ignored the question.

"Shall we begin?"

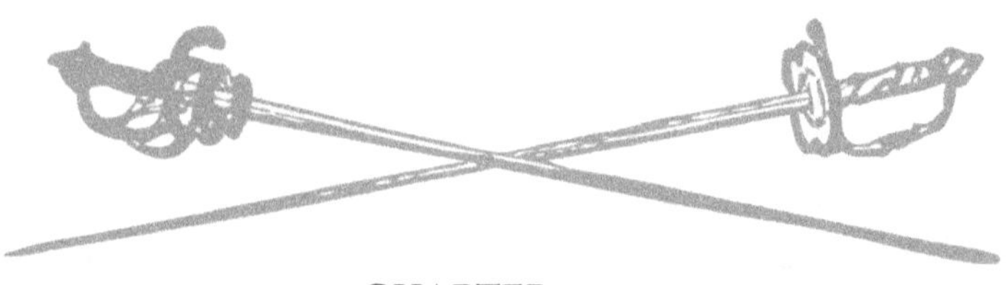

CHAPTER 27

TUNNELS

BLACK

"Once you get inside, do not get caught." Sitamun adjusted the black scarf around Black's head and face. It helped her blend into the shadows while also marking her as a common thief rather than a pirate. If seen, she likely wouldn't be traced back to the devils. "I cannot allow the *Imari* to know of the tunnels. It's a miracle they don't yet."

Sophia and Lara were dressed in servant's dresses, intending to blend in with the palace staff. Samsarans were common enough among the servants to not draw suspicion.

The garments barely covered them in a thin sheet of gold with a white sash around the waist. Both women filled out the dresses well. It was a look Black appreciated seeing on the huntress.

By the hungry looks from two of the devils, Lara's appearance was also noticed.

Black intended on staying a step behind to make certain they weren't disturbed as they searched the higher levels.

Hyne, Tick, and Earhart were to search the dungeons and lower levels.

They had two things on the agenda. Rose was the priority, a fact the captain had drilled into them, and the scarab.

"Remember, it will look like a large blue beetle."

Black nodded, admiring the soft lines of the princess' face. She really was a beautiful woman. Sita smiled softly at her, and it made Sophia stiffen beside her. It was almost imperceptible, but Black had spent enough time studying her to understand her tells.

The huntress is jealous.

The thought made her smirk, a reaction mistranslated by the princess before her.

"Good luck to you all." She stepped away but didn't take her eyes off Black. *"Al bakot lille, al baca Lila."*

Dalilah peeked her head out from behind Sitamun's robes, those round cheeks spoke of the joy and health she regained after returning home. Her dark hair was braided away from her face, and she chewed on her nails as she smiled up at Black.

Unable to help herself, Black offered a small wave. She had missed the two girls she'd rescued from the tunnels. A jolt of pressure on her calf brought her attention to the other girl, Aya clutching at her pant leg, the older girl smiling up at her.

Black reached down to pat her head. "I missed you too," she whispered, knowing they would not understand, but wanting to say it.

Their mother shooed them away, and they laughed as they ran off to another room.

"This is your guide, Almu. She will take you there and back. Bring her back in one piece for me." Sita locked eyes with Black in solidarity, who nodded back. She would bring her and everyone else back in one piece.

Almu gestured to the tunnels behind her before leading the way.

CHAPTER 28

THE TRICKSTER GOD

PHANTOM

Phantom had lost two turns already. Colt had lost one.

He was a difficult man to read. He'd bounce his leg beneath the table one round with a low-ranking Geb. Then he would do it again with a high-ranking Duat. He was doing it on purpose to throw Phantom off. The entire point of the game was to read one's opponent, and he was failing, but the game had barely begun.

There was still time to sort him out.

"Are you familiar with the Draion gods outside this little game?" Colt asked, pondering the tile before him.

Phantom did little to hide his irritation as he sat back in his chair.

"I'm afraid not. I know a little of Maahes' history here. I remember his life, but the locals seem to have fantastical ideals."

Colt chuckled, the sound ending in a soft growl. "I suppose they do. They still think their gods are alive. They make sacrifices and honor them, when in fact, the reign of Rán ended some time ago."

Phantom bit his cheek, tipping his head back. "Is that so?"

Colt placed a high-ranking Aaru tile down, effectively destroying Phantom's Geb. Luckily, he anticipated that move, but he still let a glimmer of disappointment show in his half-frown.

Two could play this game.

"It's the natural way of things in this realm. Gods rule until someone more powerful knocks them down and takes their place. Time runs out."

He placed a new tile down and Phantom countered it with his own. The Duat tile crushed the low-ranking Aaru easily. He let a small smile bolster his victory.

"You mean to say this has happened before?"

"Many times," Colt scoffed. "Before the Draiocht kingdom even crawled across the sands, the Yokan gods ruled. Two, I believe, but I forget their names. It's hard enough to keep the recent ones straight as it is."

Phantom won the next round as well.

"How exactly did the gods of this land fall?"

Davinian priests didn't teach anything pertaining to other gods, let alone a cycle, but Maahes was aware of their existence, even if he lived outside their rule.

"The very Goddess who cursed *you*, destroyed them," he began, sipping on a glass of bourbon. "With the help of Nemain, that is," he amended. "Nemain, of course, was known as Nephthys. And Davina, she was Rán's beloved wife before She condemned the whole lot to Hell with Nemain."

Green flared in his vision. *They're in Hell?*

Colt noticed the color in Phantom's eyes, smirking to himself before picking up a used Duat tile. Delmec, the God of the Gate. "A special kind of Hell. I've seen it myself. They rot there, once gods, now no more than the sand beneath our feet."

Colt won the next turn.

Phantom inspected his tiles again, recalling that he had the Maahes tile. He wasn't sure when to use it or what good it would do. If he were playing the game against one of his devils, this would have been his last tile, a gamble to see what happened. With Rose's life on the line, he wouldn't take such risks.

Regardless, it had to be played. The game wasn't over until all tiles were in play.

"If Davina and Nemain are Draion Goddesses, then where did Macha come from?"

"Now, you're asking the right questions." Colt threw back the rest of his bourbon. "You see, Davina was the original Goddess of Life and Fate, but She wanted Her own child. Not a created copy as Nemain liked to do. Davina wanted a flesh-and-blood child She could raise like the humans do."

Phantom lifted his brows. "And Rán didn't help her with that?"

Colt snickered. "He would have been eager, but Davina found a fault in Herself. She created life with Her power, but She failed to do so with Her body. It seemed that was the consequence of the power of life."

Colt won the next turn as well.

Mierda. He couldn't tell if it was him or one of his counterparts who swore, but the sentiments were mutual.

Colt continued with his story. "So, She selected a human she favored, bestowing Her power of life to the creature we know as Macha today."

The rest of the puzzle pieces arranged themselves. "That left Davina with—"

"A functional womb, yes. Apparently, She was with child for decades before She finally popped out your little birdy." He shrugged. "Her original form that is."

Phantom blinked, the darkness behind his eyes burning with the memory of the vision he was gifted. The one provided by the Davina pendant. His *original* life.

He eyed the man, then looked at his hands. Shadows deepened around his palm, ready to respond to him. If Rose was the child of Davina, what was he?

"You know me," he said, voicing his thoughts rather than asking.

Colt laughed, spitting some of his bourbon out in the process. "You could say that."

"Who was I in my original life? I know Maahes wasn't the first."

Colt pondered his tiles. "In a way he was, but yes, I remember you when you were a vessel of strategy, cunning, and of war. You spread chaos in your wake at the very mention of your name." He set the tiles down for a moment, relishing the story rather than the game. "It was that order Nemain gave you that sealed your fate."

"What order?"

Colt finally put down a tile. Nephthys. Easy win, at least in most cases. "To kill Davina's child. Not an easy task considering she was immortal. You first had to convince her to give up her immortality, but you've always been a charming son of a bitch. I'd like to think you picked it up from me." He leaned back in his seat, content that he had won the round even if Phantom had yet to reveal his tile. "So, you pretended to be a human, and she sacrificed her immortality to be with you. All according to plan until the final blow came, and you wouldn't do it." Colt hissed out the last words, still angry with a centuries-old grudge. "You fell for your own con! Your hesitation cost us everything. Davina found us and cursed us."

"*Us?* You were created by Nemain?"

Demons. Kayden's yellow flames consumed his vision.

Colt spit out his next laugh, reeking of bitterness. "You think you were the only one She blamed for the separation from Her daughter? Oh no. You were cursed to be reborn with Her daughter and we were cursed to watch. Cut off from our Nemain-given powers, forced to learn earthly magics until we can restore the *daughter* to her rightful form."

Colt leaned over, turning Phantom's tile and exposing the symbol he detested.

"Ah," Colt cooed, a grin decorating his face. "You have learned something." The Maahes tile matched Nephthys in strength, but with the power of Aaru backing it, it defeated the Goddess of Death. "Perhaps, we can all be more powerful than we appear."

Phantom moved the tiles into his own pile. "What exactly do you mean by that?"

"You've aligned with Maahes. You're on your own journey of enlightenment. Once complete, you'll be strong again." A serpentine smile flicked over his features. "We can start the next cycle. Destroy the goddesses who control us and take our place as conquering Gods." He played his last tile. It was the last turn, and they were tied. "Once the daughter has been aligned, we will be restored and more powerful than ever. The winds are changing, *Captain*. It is time to change course."

"Your plan is to dethrone the goddesses and replace them?"

Phantom played his last tile, but it didn't matter. The King of Gods had yet to make an appearance. He closed his eyes, cursing himself for not seeing it sooner.

"It is, but I will need you to do it with us." Colt took the liberty of flipping over each tile.

"Why?" If he was offering godhood, there couldn't be a good reason for it.

"Dante and I are beholden to our patroness, but you—" He smiled widely, as if this was the moment he'd been waiting for. "You can defy Nemain."

He flipped over the tile of Rán, and Phantom's heart sunk in his chest. Colt, the demon, smiled wider than ever, the sentiment genuine behind it.

He'd failed.

If Phantom thought She would listen, he'd pray that Davina would give his devils better luck.

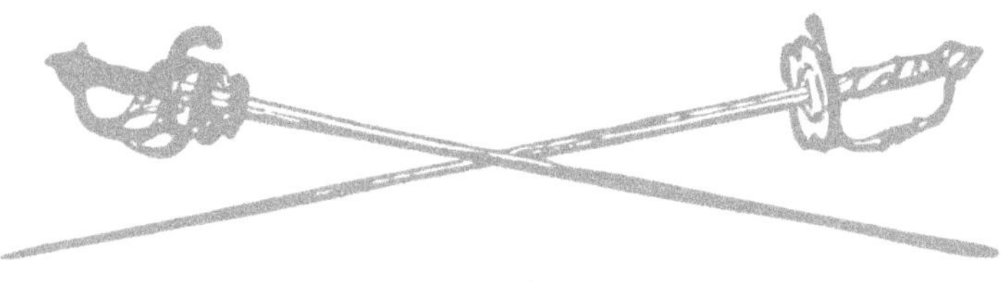

CHAPTER 29

SHUYET

BLACK

The boys separated from the group once Almu parted a tapestry in the main hall of the palace. The alabaster stone was painted with liquid gold that sparkled.

Lara and Sophia had an empty basket each that was covered in cloth. Black followed several steps behind them, moving along shadows and behind furniture, one hand on her sword, ready to defend if anything went awry.

The guard who had towered over the girls marched down the hall in the opposite direction. Black tucked herself behind a table and a large plant. Her time as the Black Shadow made her acutely aware of her surroundings and the lighting. The growing darkness was enough to deceive the guard's peripherals, but anyone standing close enough would see her.

The giant passed by her with no trouble, not paying attention to anything but the path ahead. Black let out a soft breath before looking for the girls. They had disappeared around the corner, their shuffling feet too distant.

Mierda.

Checking for anyone else roaming the halls, Black slunk back into the hall, increasing her pace to catch up with the girls. They wouldn't have gone far. Sophia would have slowed their pace.

Sure enough, past the bend, Black spotted Sophia and Lara walking down the hall.

"Oh yes, he might have killed us, but we got away." A familiar mousy voice drew Black's attention to a door that was cracked open to reveal the two men she met in the tunnels. They sat before a table, both radiating nervous energy as they looked up to someone.

"And the people believe this man to be the *Shuyet*?"

The speaker's face was obscured by the chair he sat upon, but the voice was unmistakably the quieter *Imari*. Dante.

A fourth voice joined the mix. "They keep saying he is an omen." This man had a noticeable lilt like that of a Samsaran sailor. "Some servant of Nephthys to help clear the path of Maahes." His pronunciations of the Draion god names were butchered, but her understanding of the accent helped her catch his meaning. His voice was familiar too, but perhaps that was the accent. "We have a character like this where I come from..."

Black checked on the girls who were almost out of sight.

As if some sixth sense alerted her, Sophia turned, noticing that Black had stopped at the door. The opportunity to listen was too great to pass up, but she'd be damned if she let the girls be caught alongside her.

She signaled that they should hide nearby. At the command, Sophia and Lara quickly ran into the nearest vacant room.

The fourth man still spoke, but Black didn't catch some of it. "Tell me, Dante, do we have anything to fear from this *Shuyet*?"

"The *Shuyet* is a spirit, not a man. The people will soon realize this and brand him as an imposter."

The fourth man whistled. "I would not underestimate your people. They reach in the dark for something to believe in. It is bad enough with these rumors of a god among us. I would not let this one spread."

"Very well," Dante said with a heavy sigh. "See that it is done."

The two slavers practically bounced in their seats from excitement. "I will catch him, mister, sir."

Dante raised a hand to stop them. "We don't make martyrs,

gentlemen. We make examples. Keep that in mind as you hunt the Black Shadow."

Black's heart pounded in her chest, her palms growing sweaty. They were looking for her. The slavers had lied about her gender, likely too embarrassed that they lost to a woman, but they clearly noticed.

Why were they calling her the *Shuyet*? More bloody questions to ask Sitamun upon their next meeting. It seemed to be related to the ordeal at the palace gates when they dragged Jon in.

"We will take care of your little problem, but I must warn, we will depart from here soon. Business is calling me home."

Wood creaked with the telltale sound of men getting up from their seats. Black rushed away from the door, finding an alcove to hide in.

"Understood," Dante drawled. At the door, he shook the men's hands, sending them off. "I'll want a full report before you leave." From this angle, Black couldn't make out who the fourth man was. She leaned out as far as she dared, only to see a nondescript back.

"You will."

The slavers walked down the hallway in a direction that made it difficult to watch them, but Dante remained. There was a furrow between his brows as he looked up and down the hall.

"You can come out now. No need to waste time."

Mierda. Mierda. Mierda.

Her heart beat out of rhythm as she tried to conjure an escape plan. He knew she was here. Turns out, he wouldn't need the slavers to get the job done. The *Shuyet* would fall right into his lap. Mentally slapping herself, she hardly noticed when a door clicked open.

"Apologies, sire." Sophia stood in the hallway; eyes downcast as she curtsied before the approaching *Imari*.

Black had a hand on her sword, ready to intervene. Her blood boiled when she caught the way his finger tilted Sophia's chin up.

"Have we met?"

Sophia took on the role of a submissive servant easily, avoiding his gaze as he inspected her face. "Not formally, sire. You must have seen me around the palace."

He stood unnaturally still for a moment, making the air tense with caution. "It's more than that. I would recognize a face as beautiful as yours."

Black's skin itched to intervene. She needed to get Sophia and Lara out of here before he put it together.

Sophia said nothing, letting him evaluate her. Footsteps drew their attention to the next bend, where two forms emerged. The other *Imari* and the captain, who paused upon seeing Sophia face to face with Dante. They were out of time already.

"One of yours, Captain?"

Phantom opened his mouth, but before he denied it, Dante's hand shot up. "Do not deny it. I saw her amongst your crew."

Damn it, Sophia.

The captain came up beside her with a hand to her back to lead her away. "We'll take our leave then."

As the two scurried away, the *Imari* had some silent conversation, nodding to each other at their agreement.

"Captain, come to our party tomorrow." There was an edge to Colt's tone, as if he was giving a threat instead of an invitation.

"And bring her with you," Dante added, turning his eyes to Sophia's again.

Over my dead body.

The captain offered a mock salute before rushing Sophia away.

Black's heart finally calmed at seeing Sophia disappear towards the exit. Once the *Imari* retreated, she found Lara and got her back to the tapestry.

Almu waited for them with a worried expression. The boys hadn't made it back yet. Hopefully, they had more success.

Anger and dread warred in her stomach as Almu led them through the tunnels, and Black marched back to the barracks with Lara in tow.

Sophia should not have come out to the hall. What was she thinking? Black had a lecture ready to pour from her mouth the moment she got Sophia alone. Why would she risk herself?

Lara grunted, pulling her hand from Black's in the middle of the street. The handmaiden massaged her wrist. A pang of guilt struck Black in the gut. She hadn't realized she was holding on so tightly.

Lara abandoned her wrist in favor of moving her hands around wildly. She was clearly saying something, but Black had only learned some basic words and she wasn't able to process the motions as fast as Lara used them.

"Hold on," Black interrupted, holding up her own hands in a global gesture of surrender. "What's going on?" Hoping to aid Lara's lip-reading, she pronounced each word carefully. Instead, she received an indigent frown.

Black took in the busy street they were on. There was nothing special, no vendors or beggars, just a street people passed through. Even so, they had drawn more than one pair of eyes.

Lara grabbed her wrist and moved them into a dark alleyway before her hands moved again, but she spoke too. Her words blended together, and her voice was scratchy from disuse, but Black understood her. "First, slow down. You look suspicious. Second, why are you so mad?"

A scoff ripped from her throat before she realized that Lara couldn't hear it. *Damn*, she was bad at this.

Her jaw tensed. "Sophia. She shouldn't have gone out into the hall. Why didn't you stop her?"

Lara's mouth dropped open. "Don't blame me. I tried to stop her."

Black's nerves frayed further. This conversation wasn't helping. "What was she thinking?"

Lara's brows rose, and it occurred to Black that she used her facial expressions just as much as her hands. "She was trying to save you, you idiot." She reared back as if the little handmaiden had struck her. "If you were found, you might have died. Sophia had the best chance of surviving."

Black spread her arms out. "We don't know if she will. Dante has his eyes on her now. All because she was trying to protect me." Lara's eyes glazed a bit, putting together Black's words.

Then her eyes softened. "Would you not have done the same?"

Tears pricked at Black's eyes, but she didn't let them fall. If she said anymore, she wouldn't be able to hold them back, so instead she reached out her hand. "I'm sorry for dragging you before, but let's get back before they start to worry." This time, she was thankful Lara couldn't hear how her voice trembled, even if the handmaiden tossed her a knowing look.

Lara took her hand and Black adopted an unhurried pace as she attempted to blend them in with the crowd.

Only a few minutes later, they arrived. Phantom and Sophia stood at the communal table with sour expressions.

He sat facing the entrance with his elbows on his knees and palms facing skyward. He stared at his hands as if they held some answer for him. Serena nestled her head against his arm, but he didn't reciprocate her affection.

Ramirez came from Black's left, concern drawing his brows together. "What happened?"

Black threaded her fingers through Sophia's, giving her a firm squeeze. Her huntress was trembling. She had been so angry; she didn't stop to think about how scared Sophia might be.

"We didn't make it far before running into Dante. Hopefully Earhart's team has better success." It was the abridged version, but it encompassed the important parts of what she knew. Except — "Oh, and the captain promised the *Imari* he'd take Sophia to a party tomorrow night." Anger flared again. She needed to figure out a way to get Sophia out of this mess.

Finally, Phantom looked up, meeting Sophia's eyes and his jaw tightened.

Ramirez turned. "Captain?"

Hurried footsteps and heaving breath tore their attention away, landing on the first mate clamoring into the yard, Tick and Hyne in tow. Something eased in Black's chest at seeing them make it out alive.

Tick ran straight to where Lara stood beside Black, his hands moving. The language seemed to be easy to pick up for him, but since he didn't verbally speak, it was probably a relief to know how to use his hands. But as they moved, Black noticed the slight tremble to them. Hyne followed him, concern etched into his features too, but he was less fluent in the language.

Lara grabbed Tick's hands, stopping whatever he was saying. He looked down at his hands, freezing in place. She didn't say anything to him, instead she smoothed her hands over his arms and kept eye contact with him.

His shoulders dropped marginally before he nodded.

She reached for Hyne's hand, giving him the same expression. It seemed to be her way of telling him she was fine.

Black let them have their moment, focusing instead on the first mate.

Earhart's dark eyes had that same haunted quality that Sophia and the captain had, only he didn't seem dumbstruck.

"It was a trap," he breathed out. "They knew we would try it." He pulled something from his pocket, a shining quality to it. A necklace. It was familiar in some way, and the tension in Earhart's brow said he knew exactly what it meant.

He maintained his grip on the chain, letting the pendant fall. It clicked open and notes of music poured out; a soft calming melody that reminded her of Samsara. The good parts of it, festivals in the spring, summer nights when it was delicately warm, the waves crashing against the cliff side and shores.

The dread lifted, easing her soul a bit as the music filled her.

She thought she heard the frustrated growl of the captain, but that wasn't right. Not when everything was okay. They could rest now.

The locket clicked closed, and the world came back into view. The sun was harsh and blinding and the air dry. Dread returned to her gut.

Phantom had moved before the still statue of the first mate, who blinked away his own reverie. The locket was clasped tightly in his hand. "I'd suggest that you refrain from opening this in the future."

Ramirez studied his captain. "What is it?"

"It's Rose's necklace. It's connected to her power. She's worn it around her neck every day I've known her." His whole body tensed with the unspoken words around them. "Until now." If that be the case, she'd never part from it willingly. Black didn't want to think about what that meant and how much of her they had to take to retrieve it.

Phantom heaved in a heavy breath as he clutched the necklace. Ramirez seized his arm. "What does it mean, Captain? What aren't you telling us?"

"I failed. I challenged a demon to get her back, but I lost. They expect me at the palace tomorrow. There, I will be beholden to their will for the night."

Ramirez shook his head. "Then don't go. You can't let them control you."

Phantom stared at the necklace in his palm. "He knew. The entire time, he knew."

Black leaned closer, looking at the pendant Phantom was transfixed on, but it wasn't just the pendant. There was a tattoo on his palm that matched the rose design on it. Almost as if the very design had been branded on him by the necklace.

"They played us for fools. Played *me* for a fool," Phantom growled, the devils straightening at his rising tone. "I will bring Hell upon them for this. They can watch the entire kingdom burn to the ground." He let his eyes travel to each of his devils. "They have toyed with the wrong crew."

"Aye!" Smith agreed, shaking his fist in the air, echoed by Russet.

"We will get Rose back and they will regret the day they made an enemy out of us!"

"Aye!" Hyne echoed, Tick nodding beside him.

Soon the devils chorused their agreement. Hope filled Black as he heard the sounds of her crew persevering. It made her feel like anything was possible.

Sophia's hand squeezed hers and she saw the light return to her eyes. Her brush with Dante had been enough to shake her, but not break her. Black lifted their joined hands to kiss her knuckles.

She leaned over to whispered in Sophia's ear. "Promise me that when this is over, we'll find a beach somewhere, just the two of us."

Sophia smiled softly before pulling her down to whisper back. "I promise."

CHAPTER 30

LOVE LETTERS

ROSE

They had been gone awhile. Longer than usual.

Yes, they had tightened the manacles on her wrists, but she held onto that nail she used to get through the door. Isabeya assured her that the same nail would work on the manacles. They hadn't thought to check her over when they returned her to the cell.

After what she had seen beyond the cell door, why would they? She was just as trapped in this cell as she was outside it.

Rose glared at the bit of dust floating down through a beam of sunlight onto the ground before her. It reminded her of her potential, those wings taking her into the sky above countless people. If she could only get Skye to come out, at least fully enough to spread her wings. But to get across a minefield of necromites, she would need more than a few seconds. Which was impossible considering the portions of food she was being given and the constant drains on her magic.

That's what she was focusing on, building her strength back.

The last time they drilled into her mind and forced her to use her powers, she had faked weakness, allowing them to believe she had reached her limit long before she did. She'd had more than enough practice clearing her mind so as not to give herself away, much to Isabeya's chagrin. It had paid off. They must have assumed she used her power during her escape attempt, draining herself. Now, she needed to hold onto whatever strength she had left to manage an escape.

I told you, Isabeya boasted.

James would be coming after her, but ultimately, she refused to do nothing.

The voices in her head refused to let her.

We need to find out how far away we are.

"From what exactly?"

Anything. Everything.

Rose inched forward to bathe her skin in sunlight. The nights had been so cold, her body wasn't used to the lack of fat or the bitterness of desert nights. She took warmth wherever she could get it even if the midday sun was harsh.

"If James isn't here yet, what does it matter? They will find me again and bring me back."

Then we must find out where he is.

Rose scoffed, leaning up on her elbows. "Right, because there are so many ways to gain information in this sand crypt."

Well, you won't find the answers in this cell.

She has a point. Scarlett chimed in, unhelpfully.

They are clearly distracted at the moment. Take the opportunity.

Rose grunted before rising. She dug out the nail from her bodice, the horrid underdress already too big for her, but the nail stayed in place.

Now that she was used to the movement, it didn't take long for her to unlock her manacles, then make quick work of the door. Before leaving entirely, green entered her vision again.

Bury the key in your cell. They will probably search you this time.

Rose turned back to the wall she had stared at for longer than she ever wanted to, finding a section of sand she could reach, even manacled. She buried it loosely, so it didn't look too disturbed.

Let's pray that will be enough.

Rose bit her lips before deciding it was good enough. Silently, she left the cell, turning to her right this time. There had to be something more to these halls than cells and a hopeless means of escape. After all, Colt and Dante had to go somewhere when they weren't tormenting her.

But specifically? A map would be helpful.

It occurred to her that there was supposed to be some sort of guard in these halls. Cain, the slimy one. She'd assumed he was the footsteps she heard during her last escape, but this time there wasn't a soul.

Maybe he was fired.

"Recent events have proved that my luck isn't that good."

Stay alert. He might still be here.

More cells lined the wall to her right, but each was empty, none possessing the sunlight hers did. She couldn't quite see through all the darkened shadows.

Sunset orange blossomed in her vision. *They're keeping you away from shadows as much as possible. That's why they left a hole in the roof.*

"Oh, so it wasn't just to torment me?" Rose whispered to her selves.

An added bonus, but if Draven has anything to do with it, his shadows will eventually find you.

Finally, a door appeared to the left, and she hoped it was not a cell like the others.

"Remind me to ask about these shadows later."

The door opened easily for her. Clearly, they weren't concerned she'd get into it. Once inside, she understood why. No one had used this room in years, maybe decades with the thick layer of dust coating everything. There was a small window letting in a fraction of light but ultimately left most things in darkness.

Yellow flames licked at her vision. *I can help.*

Rose cringed. "I don't think that's the wisest decision."

The last time Scarlett helped with a delicate matter, she had burned the entire book Rose had attempted to read. Since then, she tended to rely on her own powers, the blue siren magic, rather than Scarlett's fire.

A glance at her side told her there were matches on the end table. It seemed there was an entirely human way to solve the issue. She often forgot to look for those, but she needed to save her power for when it truly counted.

Fine, do it the primitive way.

"Gladly."

Rose lit a match before lighting the candle accompanying the matches. It was complete with a holder. It seemed the room wasn't entirely abandoned.

She went to the desk first, rifling through papers that were so old and exposed that the ink had faded from most of them. There had to be something useful though. She opened one of the drawers to find a leather-bound pad. Inside was a journal of sorts, but every page was addressed to an Amara and signed by Elijah.

It was clear they were love letters, many detailing intimate details of their meetings or of realizing that he was in love with her, but why were they bound this way instead of sent to his lover?

Until one entry made things clear.

My dear Amara,

You died two years ago, yet my soul is restless, mourning you even now. My country, Brettania, has abandoned me. I'm left in Draiocht alone, with nothing to my name but survival.

Though Draiocht stands, this region of land was condemned long ago, isolating the outbreaks of necromites. I do wonder what I have done that Nemain would seek to punish me so much that two countries should see fit to abandon me and yet, I still live. Perhaps if you were here, you could explain it to me.

The city of Amal is two miles to the west where the sea meets the sand. It is the only city that has survived the outbreaks on this side of the country. The others talk of heading that way. We will starve here soon if we don't, but the horde outside has only grown in number. It's like they know we're here. They will not make it far.

I've chosen to stay. What more could the world have for me without you in it?

I'll write these letters to you until I join you.

All my love,
Elijah

Rose wiped a tear from her cheek before she returned the journal to its resting place. She didn't want to know how much longer he wrote to her. What his final words were. Maybe he was finally with his Amara.

Two miles.

She sniffed, refocusing on the task at hand. She was two miles away from the nearest civilization. At least it was when this letter was written, but it was something to go off of. It was also to the west. If she recovered long enough to make the journey by air, she could fly to the city. But that would take fooling Colt and Dante. If they discovered she was holding back, they'd make certain to drain her.

Part of that included them not finding out about her getting out of the cell.

Rose quickly righted everything the way it was, blowing out the candle and placing it back on the end table.

Then she headed back to her cell. If she kept this up for a week, maybe it would be enough. Maybe James would be in the city by then too.

You can't fly out of here on maybes.

A cough pulled Rose from her thoughts. One of the cells was occupied. That was a new development. She hadn't seen or heard anyone in the cells before. She followed the sound, peeking through the small window on the door.

There was just enough light coming in through the window for her to make out a massive hunched over body, shirtless and in bad shape. Cuts and bruises marred his dark skin in so many spots she couldn't count them all. It was different from the torture she would have expected. This man had been beaten.

He coughed again, lifting his head.

Jon.

She gasped, flinching back and clasping a hand over her traitorous mouth, but it was too late. He heard her, and she was certain he had seen her.

"Rose?"

There was very little that happened between when she was taken from *Nemain's Revenge* to the feet of the two men who torment her now. It was as if she'd blinked, and everything had changed. It knocked the air from her lungs how fast she went from comfortable and safe, to betrayed and afraid.

All because of the man behind that door.

"Rose, I cannot begin to tell you how sorry I am." He coughed again, his voice raspy. She forced herself still, noticing the slight tremor in her hands. "If I had another choice—"

"Another choice?" She spoke before she intended to, but it was ridiculous. He'd had every choice, and he'd chosen to betray them. She looked through the window again, but seeing his face made it a lot harder to keep her shaking under control. "Do you know what they do to me?" She wished he could see the damage he'd caused. Anyone who looked at her body would see the immediate change. A change too unhealthy for anybody to endure.

Jon opened his mouth to speak, but panic gripped her, the air growing thin. Her hands shook violently. No, she couldn't do this. She was going to fall apart in this hallway.

She wrapped her hands around herself picturing the ocean like Skye told her.

"I know you won't forgive me. But you should know. The captain is here."

She blinked away threatening tears. "What?"

"The devils are in Amal, looking for you."

She sucked in air, hope flooding her heart.

"He's here?"

Jon met her stare, dark eyes filled with remorse. He nodded. "He'll stop at nothing to get to you."

Hope seized her chest, new tears falling at the relief. He was coming for her. It was one thing to know he wanted to, another to know he was close.

Two. Miles.

Jon's eyes widened. "Rose, run!"

Ropes drifted out of nowhere, snapping around Jon's mouth.

"That's quite enough of that." Dante came from the left, his hand outstretched, clearly controlling the ropes now binding Jon.

Panic surged in her chest at seeing Dante. Skye leapt to the back of her mind, encouraging the fear zapping through her veins.

She ran.

"That won't do."

Before she could get five feet away, ropes wrapped around her ankles, pulling her to the ground. She screamed, her chin hitting the hard stone floor. Pain shot through her jaw and teeth, blood spilling from where she bit her lip in the fall.

Boots stepped into her line of vision. She tracked the legs upwards until she saw Colt's half-smiling face. "Well, you clearly are doing better than we thought. If you can run, birdy, you can use your power. Let's see what you got in store for me today."

She was jerked backwards by her ankles, forcing her to drag across the sand and stone. It scraped at her skin, causing small scratches across her legs and arms.

She bit back a scream, not wanting them to have the satisfaction of knowing they hurt her. Soon, a familiar hole in the ceiling came into view. She was back in her goddess-damned cell. Rope bound around her wrists, slamming them together and lifting her to her feet, then further.

The ropes finally stopped when they landed on a hook, keeping her body above the ground. It was just off center from the sunlight pouring through the window.

Colt stepped up to her, seizing her chin. "Now look at what you did." His hands came back bloody as he wiped at the evidence of her treatment. "This won't do at all."

Rose's brows creased. They had never had a problem with her blood spilling before. What was different now?

"My apologies," Colt said, feigning embarrassment. "We had this big surprise for you."

Dante lifted his chin, not a hint of the same concern in his expression. "We're taking you to a party."

"What?" She let the word slip out unbidden, the pain in her arms already registering with the position.

Colt spread his arms out. "Surprise!" He laughed, seeming to amuse himself. "You're the main attraction!" His arms fell with his face. "But not like this. You have way too much energy. We need you nice and drained."

Dante began removing his gloves, dread pooling in her stomach.

But it was Colt, whose face suddenly morphed into the man she loved, that she flinched away from. "Stay awake, birdy. This is about to be a bumpy ride."

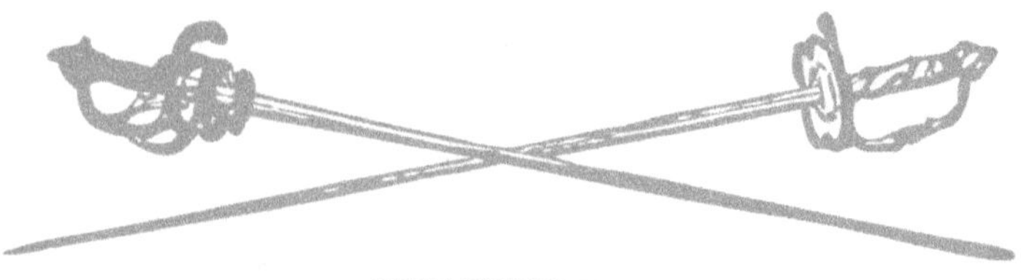

CHAPTER 31
MOONLIT LIAISON

BLACK

Sleep evaded Black.

She tossed on the small cot as if a new position would help her but it was no use. Sophia was now a target for the *Imari*, specifically an interest to Dante. The scene played out in her head on repeat, reminding her that she was useless when it mattered most.

The events distracted from her own target.

The *Shuyet*. Apparently, enough rumors spread around her appearance to warrant a kill order on her. It didn't concern her too greatly though. Other than the two idiot slavers, most believed she was a man or a spirit. She wasn't likely to be suspected.

With any luck, the rumor would die.

She did inform the captain that the *Imari* were working with slavers.

Footsteps drew her attention to the training yard, shrouded by the curtain pulled across her chamber entrance. She wasn't getting sleep anytime soon, so she let out a long breath before rising from her cot.

It took her a minute to adjust her boots before she peeked around the corner. The night was thick, darkness blanketing the surrounding buildings. One light came from across the moonlit sand. A single candle lit as Sophia, awake from her chambers, drifted to the exit.

Black fastened her sword to her hip before following. Ramirez stood on guard at the gate, taking long pulls from his pipe and staring at the stars. A simple nod allowed Sophia passage through. It nearly made Black angry. It wasn't safe for Sophia to be wandering the city alone. How many nights had Ramirez allowed her to pass?

She shook the thought from her head. Not only was Sophia not beholden to remain with the devils, but she was perfectly capable of handling herself. Though, he didn't miss Sophia's lack of a bow and quiver.

When Black stepped up to the entrance gate, Ramirez raised a single white eyebrow. Black pressed a single finger to her lips, requesting his silence, causing both his brows to wrinkle his forehead.

Ramirez kept his voice low. "Am I to believe you're following Miss Clare?"

Black ignored the question. "How often does she come out here?"

"Most nights it seems. Though always on my shift."

It was smart for one devil to know she was no longer there. Had she not returned, he would have informed the captain. But why wasn't *she* the devil Sophia chose?

Ramirez took another pull before nodding his head. "Go after her then."

Black flashed the old man a half smile before departing. She followed the single candlelight that shone in the distance and the silhouetted figure attached to it. There were sleeping homeless lining the streets, covering themselves in ragged blankets to stave off the bitter desert wind.

It was cruel how a land so heated in the sunlight would become so bitter in the moonlight.

Sophia traveled far, weaving through streets and alleyways, before turning into a building. Black kept her steps light, following the huntress with diligence, the flame guiding her until she reached a tower. The steps curled upwards before letting out at the top.

Black surprised herself with how well she handled the never-ending steps. Usually, it took more effort. Was her endurance not her own? When she reached the top step, she might have sworn it to be true. She hadn't even broken a sweat.

The top of the tower revealed a city asleep in one direction, and the world dying in the other.

Sand dunes stretched out as far as the eye could see, the mounds bathed in silver and lilac moonlight. Black had never considered how moonlight made sand look so beautiful, but the walking corpses upset the beauty of it.

Black hid behind the sun barrier that shaded half the platform. It seemed to be the spot where one would stand if they were standing watch. Mostly, Black was surprised this one was unoccupied.

Sophia sat at the very end of the platform, overlooking the sand dunes, facing a half-risen silver moon. She had laid her candle next to her, the flame doused. Her legs were crossed before her.

It was a similar pose Black had seen Wilson take, especially in those first months after his country fell. Sometimes he'd even chant, but he never told them what he was doing or why. Black stared at Sophia, her face so peaceful in this state. It was so rare to see her without the crinkles of concern or a displeased tilt to her mouth.

Black found her heart settling easier just watching her. She could have fallen asleep on that tower much easier than in the confined barracks chamber.

Her eyelids grew heavy when she heard Sophia's soft voice. "Gwenivere, I know you're there."

A jolt shocked Black awake. She didn't remember sitting at the base of the sun shader or leaning against it. Was that drool on her face?

Sophia was blessedly not looking at her, her eyes still closed. "If you must be here, come sit."

Black rose from her position, barely regaining her senses. She noticed Sophia was dressed in those white robes she had been in earlier. They contrasted with Black's dark attire.

She crossed her legs, mimicking what Sophia was doing. Even going so far as to close her eyes.

"What is it I'm meant to be doing?" She cracked an eye open to witness a small smile tip the edge of Sophia's lips.

"You're meant to be focusing. This is *kimiya* meditation."

"Oh." Black closed her eyes again. "What is the gimya?"

She expected Sophia to become frustrated, but instead an amused laugh left her. It was a soft laugh that only came from her when she was truly comfortable. Black had only been graced by it twice. Once, when they first met, and now.

"The *kimiya*. It's an energy that lives inside us. It governs how we feel, how we act, what we say." Finally, she opened her eyes, turning to focus on Black. A shock went up Black's spine at the attention. "There is a process for *kimiya* meditation. There are seven sources of it in your body." She leaned over, her hand hovering over Black's hair. "It ends here." Her hand trailed down Black's body, not making contact, but tracing her until her hand's descent ended between Black's crossed legs. "And it begins here."

Black flushed, heat rising to her cheeks. Sophia didn't fail to notice, smiling faintly, but Black was already mesmerized by her movements.

"Once you open each *kimiya*, you will gain full access to the energy in your body." Sophia leaned back, rested her hands in her lap. "Start with your root. What is it you fear?"

"That's an intimate question. Care to share dinner with me first?" The joke was meant to lighten the mood, but it only mildly annoyed Sophia.

"I'm serious, Gwen. Close your eyes and think of what you fear."

With one more look, she closed her eyes, focusing on fear. Simple things came to mind, like the necromites wandering the sand below them. Or what the *Imari* will do when the captain gets Rose back. Perhaps, there was a little fear for the Samsarans, and what the island was facing. There was plenty to fear when she thought of it. But none of it soured her stomach. None of it made her unstable.

She thought back to what kept her awake, of being out on the sand with no weapon and everyone she cared about surrounding her and in as much danger as she was. She knew fear then when she watched Dante approach Sophia.

Another fear lay dormant in her heart, but it was hard to put a word to it. Was it as simple as rejection? Abandonment? No, it was deeper than that. It was the same reason she decided she had to be the best when she picked up a sword for the first time.

"I fear I'll never be good enough." She kept her eyelids closed tight, afraid to see Sophia's reaction, or lack thereof.

"Good enough for what?" Sophia's voice was considerably softer.

Black let out a breathy laugh. "At first, I wasn't good enough for my father. That I would never be the lady he wanted me to be. When I found the devils — I wanted to be the best swordsman. I used to challenge Earhart and Jon, and even the captain to a duel just to be certain I was coming out on top."

"What did you find when you challenged them?"

Black thought back to those first days, when she would use a sponge to dust charcoal over her chin. When she used to bind her chest and hide her features beneath a feather hat. She opened her eyes, focusing on the sand below. "Earhart was swift and efficient. He'd used his height and strength to his advantage. Plus, he used to be a blacksmith, so he was aware of how different metals behaved. He was the most difficult to beat. Jon would last because of his height. I always had to find a way to gain an advantage over him. But the captain—"

Sophia's attention shifted to her, wind brushing her raven hair from her shoulder.

"I always thought he was letting me win. Like he wasn't trying hard enough. Or he didn't care to. Either way, my challenges to him always seemed—unfinished. I assumed it was because he was the only one who knew I was truly a woman. But I've seen him do the same, even with his enemies. Like he's always holding back."

Sophia let out a slow breath. "Unfortunately, I believe you're right. However, what you described is related to your shame. That is yellow, and it is here," she said before leaning over to touch the spot just below Black's chest. Her heart skipped a beat at the contact. Then her hand drifted away.

"What we are focusing on is your *fear*. The color of this *kimiya* is red, and it is influenced by Nemain's moon. Focus on that fear, go ahead, close your eyes again."

Black twisted her lips before obeying. It felt strange to do so when they were so exposed, but there was something peaceful about the tower she'd yet to find anywhere else in the city.

She looked inward until a pit of dread became visible. She focused on it, but she didn't recognize it. The unfamiliar monster inside her posed a threat she couldn't fight. Her breathing became rapid and her palms sweaty.

"What is it?" Sophia's voice was right beside her, calming her racing heart.

"I don't know. It's just there, like something will jump from the shadows at any moment and tear us apart."

Silence responded to her admission, before Sophia leaned in, wrapping her arms around Black's torso. "You fear an unknown threat. The possibility of an enemy you are unprepared for. It makes sense, but you can't let yourself dwell on uncertainties. Learn to accept that the unexpected can happen, but you are trained to adapt and you can handle it."

The faith she had in Black's skill was enough to calm her nerves and understand what Sophia was saying.

"Let go of this fear and ground yourself in the focus and skill you've trained yourself in."

Black's burden lifted marginally but she wasn't sure it had anything to do with meditation. Perhaps, it was Sophia's hands on her waist or the soft sound of her voice. Coolness replaced the warmth of her hands as she slipped away.

Black opened her eyes to see Sophia focused on her, a slight smile to her full lips.

"What *kimiya* are you working on?"

The smile faded. "One I may never master." Her eyes traveled to the waxing moon in the sky. "Even though I must if I am to be ready."

So many questions piled in her mind as Black stared at her. There was a burden weighing down her shoulders. One Black wanted nothing more than to take from her.

"Ready for what?"

A tear fell down Sophia's face, glistening in the moonlight. Black reached over, brushing it from her cheek.

For a moment, Black believed she would tell her, but she rose from her seat. "We'd better get back. We have a lot to do tomorrow."

She considered prying further, insisting to know every one of Sophia's secrets. Instead, she chose to change the subject, rising to her feet. "Don't go."

Sophia's face turned stricken. "It's not that easy."

"It is. Don't go. I'm going to be beside myself with worry. Watching you risk yourself for me was hard enough."

Sophia straightened. "That was my choice. It made the most sense. I wasn't about to lose you when there was something I could do."

Black chewed on her lip, wishing she hadn't overheard that stupid conversation about the *Shuyet*.

Sophia's eyes narrowed. "You never did tell me what you found that we had to stop for. I assume it had to do with Dante since you were so close to him."

Black bit the inside of her cheek. "He was talking with the slavers from the tunnels. Apparently, rumors of the Black Shadow have spread. They are calling me the *Shuyet*. But the slavers were too cowardly to admit I'm a woman, so most of them are looking for a man."

Sophia groaned. "They're hunting you?"

"Like they have a chance. If they figure it out, I'll take care of it."

She reached out to grasp Sophia's hand, lacing their fingers together like it was second nature. Black breathed heavily, steadying her nerves, although the warmth of Sophia's hand was doing more for that than the air.

"If something happens to you—"

"Nothing will happen to me." Sophia inched closer, her scent wafting over Black like a tropical breeze of coconuts and charcoal.

"You don't know that," Black insisted, pulling her closer.

Sophia's hand came around Black's face, urging it down to look at her. "I do. We will both make it out of here alive."

Black didn't bother to mention that Draiocht was the least of their problems. Samsara was bound to be a worse mess. Sophia's eyes were starkly intense, as if she knew without a hint of doubt that they would be alright.

They were so close that Black caught the very moment Sophia's gaze traveled down to her mouth, flicking back up again.

Drawn to her like a moth to flame, Black leaned into her, pushing her back into the wall. It was a shaded area where no moonlight reached.

"What are you doing?" Sophia asked but made no move to escape Black's arms.

"Releasing my fear," Black whispered before capturing the lips she had been dreaming about for months. Sophia flinched at the contact at first, the shock causing her to freeze, but she soon melted, softening in Black's arms as they came around her waist.

They sank into each other, savoring the moment like aged wine. Sophia's arms came around her neck, the contact sending shivers down her spine.

Black groaned, driving her hands into Sophia's thick ebony hair and pulling at the root, just a bit. Sophia's answering moan was enough to know she liked it.

Black had envisioned this moment with her, but nothing in her imagination matched the reality. The rest of the world melted away until it was only the two of them. Black's hands drifted down Sophia's waist to the flare of her hips, groaning at how perfect she felt.

A cool breeze drifted over her heated skin.

Sophia pulled back, eyes wide and lips swollen. She blinked once at Black before her gaze shifted outside where silver moonlight spilled at their feet. Then she jerked away, shimmying along the wall to escape down the stairwell.

Black ran right after her, but she moved swiftly. "What was that?" She didn't want to scream the question, but Sophia seemed intent on escaping her.

"A mistake." She called up before opening the bottom door and shooting out into the night.

By the time Black made it to the door, Sophia had disappeared completely. She wasn't in her chamber upon returning.

CHAPTER 32
RELUCTANT ALLIANCE
SEBASTIAN

Sebastian slept, even if only for three hours. It was a restless sleep at best.

The island was well and bloody screwed. He knew that now. The best chance he had was getting as many as he could to Kheli. It wasn't far enough to save them from Ravana's insanity, but it was a start.

Before he did that, Lockness had to be warned.

The sun was low in the sky when Sebastian made his way to the Lockness estate. He used a confusing route, shaking a tail that might have followed him. Rain clouds rolled in by the time he made it to the estate.

It didn't take Lockness' guard more than a moment to allow him entry. Apparently, the guard had been given orders to allow him access. Trepidation made him vigilant, though. Sebastian wasn't certain how many of Lockness' men had returned.

"Commodore," Lockness greeted the moment Sebastian entered, tracking rainwater onto the lavish carpeting. "I will pretend you didn't bring mud across my Yokan rug like a common street urchin."

Heat pricked his cheeks, but he mumbled an apology before Lockness led him into the estate.

"To what do I owe the pleasure?"

Sebastian wanted to unload the truth, but Lockness had quite a bit of staff present. Did Ravana offer them the same deal?

He gave the crime lord a slight shake of his head before taking on a casual tone. "I just came to check on you." Hardly a reason to stop by, but it was the only thing he could think of. The raised brow Lockness shot him said as much, but he played along.

"Good to know you care, Commodore." Lockness led him further in until they turned through his gallery. Priceless paintings and sculptures lined the walls. It was a collection of historical achievements. There were scenes of battling the dead, or of Macha creating life. Most were highly religious and spoke volumes of the time and place they came from.

Lockness shut the door to the gallery, locking them inside.

"We won't be heard or disturbed in here."

Sebastian took in the simple but expensive clothes he wore and his slicked back salt and pepper hair. He was made for this life, and yet he was about to lose it, including every priceless artifact in the room. "Aren't they beautiful? They are genuine pieces, unlike the Minister's collection." Sebastian didn't want to think about Rose and the countless riches she provided her father. There was always a sheen of falsehood to the creations.

"Do you have someplace safe to store all these?" He let his eyes drift over them. There wasn't truly enough time to take it all in.

Lockness smiled. "There is no safer place. I built this gallery for them."

That's what he was afraid of.

"But I doubt you came here to gawk."

Sebastian steadied himself, knowing everything was about to change. "You must run. Tell no one and leave. If you have no vessel, you can join me, but you must leave tonight."

Lockness' brow furrowed, mistrust lining his eyes. "And why is that?"

Sebastian hesitated, realizing how crazy it would all sound. "Your men are compromised. Maybe only some of them. Maybe all of them, but enough for me to know you won't live much longer. Ravana made them an offer they couldn't refuse."

"And what exactly did she offer to outbid decades worth of loyalty?" His brows rose. "I've been building this empire my entire life. You'll have to do better than that, Commodore."

Sebastian chastised himself for not thinking this through. Of course, Lockness wouldn't believe him. Giving him the warning was still the honorable thing to do.

"Immortality. She offered to let them live eternally," Sebastian spit out, losing all tact.

A moment of silence passed between them before Lockness burst into a fit of laughter. "Right, and I'm the King of Brettania. Do you honestly think I would believe that?"

Mierda. This wasn't working.

Sebastian rubbed the bridge of his nose. *Why does no one listen to me?*

"I came to warn you since your men were sworn to secrecy. It's your choice if you believe me, but if she finds out I told you, I'm a dead man. I'm getting the hell off this island and I'm taking as many as I can with me. If that's not you, so be it."

Lockness' laughter died as he inspected Sebastian.

He opened his mouth to respond, but before he did, the sound of breaking glass drew their attention. It came from beyond the door. Lockness put a finger to his lips to demand silence before shifting to a nearby window. It had a perfect view overlooking the main entrance where Robert Westerwood stood with thirty men, each holding a torch.

They were already flooding into the estate with ease, as if someone let them in.

Lockness blinked a few times before turning to Sebastian. "Immortality?"

It seemed this was what he needed to see to understand.

Sebastian nodded. "Perhaps, you shouldn't have made an enemy of her." Panic rose as he realized his warning came too late and now, he was about to be caught in the crosshairs.

They were supposed to report on Lockness' movements, not create a coup. Ravana would be furious. She should have recruited a better army than a band of criminals.

Lockness raked a hand through his manicured hair before

rushing over to his desk, gathering papers and books. "We don't have much time. But I am to believe that the Captain of *Nemain's Revenge* intends to set sail for the Gates of Hell?" Lockness raised his brows as the sounds of his mansion being torn apart reached them.

How did he — Not enough time to ask...

"Yes."

"Then he will need this." Lockness shoved a sheath often used for artwork in his hand along with a brown leather-bound book with worn edges. Stitched on the cover read: *Les Découvertes de la Pérouse.*

"Where did you get this?"

"Why do you think I took the Fortress? That library is beyond valuable. But for the sake of the island, I needed this, but it appears I am out of time." A rock hit the glass window on cue, shattering it. A flaming arrow followed, setting a priceless painting ablaze.

"Come," Lockness beckoned, leading him further into the gallery until they reached a door. Sebastian clutched the items close to his chest.

The crime lord wrenched the door open to reveal a set of stairs that led underground. He put a hand on Sebastian's shoulder before shoving him inside. "This will lead you outside. Don't let them see you."

Lockness began to close the door.

"Wait, you're not coming with me? I came out here to warn you."

"And it was much appreciated, however, they will not stop until I am found. It will make your job harder." His eyes flicked to the book. "And you need to get that to the captain." Windows crashed in towards the gallery entrance. Lockness reached for an ancient sword with a beautiful silver design. Apparently, he wasn't going down without a fight. "Get out as many as you can. Davina save us all."

The former crime lord slammed the door shut, and it wasn't long before Sebastian heard metal collide. He didn't stick around to hear how long Lockness lasted.

As he climbed down the steps, he slid the sheath and book into his coat pockets, trying to figure out how *the bloody hell* he was going to get them to James.

CHAPTER 33
A WITCH'S DOORSTEP

SEBASTIAN

Sebastian's fist pounded on the wooden door again.

"Indigo!" He shouted, impatient with spending the last ten minutes knocking. There was a candle in her window. Someone had to be home. "Come out, you bloody witch!"

"Oh dear." Her muffled voice came from just behind the door. "You are persistent." He contemplated the consequences of kicking it in, but the thought of hurting her in the process stopped him. Odd, but he had bigger problems to deal with.

"I need to speak with you. Urgently." He rubbed his eyes. After running from Lockness' estate in high town all the way to the witch quarter with very little sleep to speak of, his body was worn. Only the adrenaline of fear kept his feet moving. The longer he stood there waiting for her, the less likely that it would be true. "Please. It is of the utmost importance."

Silence followed his requests, and he began to consider other possibilities. Unfortunately, without her help, he wasn't certain he could organize an escape mission. He moved to walk away when she finally spoke.

"Say it again."

"What?" He wasn't sure which she wanted to hear again.

"I do enjoy you begging. It's convincing me to be more amiable." He ground his teeth together. He didn't exactly consider it begging, but he didn't correct her given the situation. "In fact, I might be most agreeable if I opened this door to find you on your knees."

Why was she speaking like a lady of high town? It was likely to mock him, but he found his dignity chipping away. There were lives he sought to save and if it cost him his pride, so be it.

"Please, Indigo. I need your help," he gritted out. Apparently, his pride went kicking and screaming.

She cleared her throat, but he could practically *see* her pointed look. Did she somehow see that he was not on his knees?

Goddess-damned woman.

He fell to his knees like he was on an executioner's block.

"Please."

Finally, she opened the door with a smug smile painting her features, but it died when she looked closer at him. Sebastian was confused though, because the image of her was blurry.

"Oh, darling, what happened?" She crouched down until she kneeled before him, hands on his face while she thoroughly inspected him. Her palms were warm on his face, but his eyelids grew heavy. Kneeling was a bad decision, or perhaps it was the incense in the air of the witch quarter. It wasn't that sense of safety that washed over him the moment she opened her door to him.

"You're an absolute mess. When was the last time you slept? Or ate?"

A day? Two? At the moment, I couldn't be certain.

Her brows furrowed, and he got the impression he said that aloud.

"Come along," she whispered, snaking an arm under him to hoist him up. "If you pass out in my entry, I won't be able to pull you elsewhere, you great oaf. Now, move those useless feet."

He did as instructed, agreeing that his dead weight would be no match for her.

As she sat him down on the brown settee before the fireplace, he attempted to blink away sleep. He had no time for it. Ravana would be expecting a new officer, and he needed to get them off the island before she went looking for him.

"None of your babbling. Drink this."

She handed him a bowl of... tea? Or was it soup? Whatever it was, it tasted delicious and made him forget what he was here to ask her. Something about the end of the world? No, that had already happened.

"My, I will have to see you sleep deprived more often. It is quite entertaining." He jerked away as something cold hit his forehead. Indigo had a rag pressed there, clearing away whatever blood or dirt he was covered in. He sipped at the tea again, not having the strength to do much more.

Once the tea-ish soup was gone, she took the bowl from him.

"Now, lay down. The world won't end tonight. You can tell me what you need to do in the morning."

Had he said it out loud again?

"Witch, you're reading my mind."

Indigo's smile was the last thing he saw before the world around him faded.

The hearty smell of bacon roused Sebastian from his slumber. Then the telltale sizzle and pop of the strips across the stove met his ears.

Blinking awake, he found Indigo leaning over a pan, cooking up what appeared to be meat and eggs.

"I apologize for the lack of bread, but high town is hoarding all the flour, and I don't intend to get arrested over your pathetic ass."

His head pounded, though he swore he hadn't taken any drink as of late, or in the last three years.

"What happened?"

Indigo's haunting gaze turned to him. "You showed up at my door appearing half-dead and ready to beg for my help." Ah, yes, he remembered that part.

She shoved a plate in his hand, bacon and eggs still hot, and a wooden spoon resting at the edge. "Eat. You're half-starved if I wagered a guess." Normally, he would argue with her, but this was one of the rare cases that she was right. He needed to be strong if he was going to pull this off.

Kneeling to sit at his feet, Indigo bunched her skirts to fall around her folded legs.

"What are you doing? There's plenty of room."

"I find myself more grounded this way."

Sebastian found it uncomfortable to witness what this angle did for his view. She had beautiful skin, just slightly tanned and her dress showed off her shoulders. He got the impression that this dress was more of an undergarment with how thin it was and how the sleeves hung low on her arms. It was beyond intimate just to witness her in it, especially when she had every opportunity to change.

He cleared his throat, choosing to focus on the fireplace behind her rather than the soft swells of her breasts over her neckline—

"I assume you access your magic from the earth. Does sitting on a settee really obstruct you so much?"

Her eyebrows rose, catching his strained tone. "Have you learned the ways of the magical arts since last I saw you, Commodore?" He didn't have to answer that, but she looked like she expected a response.

"No."

"Then don't *assume* you know why I do anything." She sat back on her heels, relaxing into the edge of the couch enough that her shoulder brushed his knee. He nearly groaned at the contact, even if the witch was doing it on purpose. He chewed on a piece of bacon, thankful for something to distract him.

"Now tell me, what brought you to my door in the middle of the night?"

Memories came back to him that he wanted to ignore like they were twisted dreams, but he knew it wasn't possible. He was the only one who could do something about it.

A spark of memory had him patting his jacket finding the weight of the book and sheath still there. A relieved breath left him, and Indigo raised a brow.

"Don't fret, Commodore. I did not steal from you."

"I did not mean—" he started, ready to explain his actions, but decided against it. The trust between them was shaky at best. He doubted her reaction would have been any different. "Ravana has taken control of the Fortress."

Indigo stopped breathing altogether.

"You're certain?"

"As certain as I am that the sun will rise again."

She flinched back. "Don't be so sure of the sun. He prefers to forsake this island." Before he could ask what her ramblings meant, she continued. "What happened to Lockness?"

He swallowed the lump in his throat.

"Dead, most likely. Ravana made his men promises they couldn't refuse."

Indigo stood, pacing before him, creating a draft that flickered the flames of the fireplace.

Before she spiraled, as he had, he offered his only solution. "I intend to rally all the Khelitian men and freed officers and take them to Kheli."

Her piercing violet gaze locked on him, at least she wasn't below him now. "How do you intend to do that? There are no ships in port."

Sebastian winced at the information he was about to share. "There are half a dozen fishing boats docked on the westside. Abandoned."

"And their owners?"

"Turned. Every last fisherman on the eastern docks. I killed them myself." That seemed like a lifetime ago. Was it only yesterday?

He watched her knees fall to the ground only inches from his legs, stricken horror crossing her features.

"How many?"

"Thirty. I'd say at least half of them had families." He swallowed at the next decision he had made before knocking on her door. "Once we assemble the untainted officers, if there are boats remaining, we must seek these families out and bring them too."

Her brows furrowed. "You chose the men over families?"

"Kheli is in, no doubt, a similar situation to ours, if not worse. They will need fighting men to hold the island. If Kheli falls, we all do." Sebastian hung his head, catching it in his hands. The decision was destroying him and everything he believed in. Those families were part of low town, an unprotected section of the city, one that couldn't even acquire flour. But displacement to Kheli would only hasten their deaths. Values seemed to pale in comparison to survival. Perhaps Lockness' ideals were contagious.

"And the orphanage?"

Another decision that plagued him too.

"I want to bring them too. If food is scarce, they will likely be the first to suffer." Them and the witches, but he didn't dare to bring them up. They had more defenses and resources than a house of orphans.

A warm hand drifted onto his knee. He lifted his head to find Indigo inches from him, her palm against his leg in a show of comfort.

Blast. She really was a beautiful woman.

"I will help you." Her thumb traced circles over his trousers, and he found it cleared his head. "How long do I have?"

"One day. I cannot stall longer than that."

She nodded. "Leave it to me."

CHAPTER 34

THE DEVIL THAT YOU KNOW

ROSE

Rose woke with a start, pulling oxygen into her lungs as if that would make her feel less weak.

She had no idea how much time passed, but by the numbness in her arms, it must have been hours. Blinking away black spots in her vision, the room finally came into view. She wasn't in the cell. Though there wasn't much indication of *where* she was.

Rope scratched at her wrists, reminding her what was holding her above the ground. They'd never used rope before. Fire could burn the ropes off and free her. They must have been confident in draining her magic to use rope.

"Scarlett," she said, wincing at the raspiness of her voice. "A little help."

Only silence greeted her.

She attempted to pull at the ropes, but her arms wouldn't obey.

"Scar," she called again. "I know we don't always get along, but I could use a little fire right now."

Nothing. Not even a flash of yellow.

It was too quiet in her head. Her magic was so depleted that even her voices could no longer speak to her.

Dante and Colt took everything from her in one night.

The worst part was that their methods were working. She could feel herself becoming Skye.

Fogginess lifted from her mind, reminding her of what her captors had said. A party? That must be why she was here. She doubted she was supposed to be a guest, but she feared what the alternative could be.

Rose tested her legs, curling one knee up, then the other, ignoring the burning in her shoulders with the movement. She was accustomed to outlasting pain. Cuts were not the only way Ravana had gifted her torture.

This opportunity was too good to pass up. Wherever she was, she doubted it was a prison surrounded by necromites. That alone would make her escape easier.

Her legs still moved, but the muscles in her abdomen were too weak to lift her.

"Scarlett, I don't know if you are awake in there, but if you can hear me, I need you to light the rope."

Fear and hesitance sprang up in her gut that she knew weren't hers. The one thing Scarlett lamented more than anything was the fact that she had dominion over fire but no protection from it. When she was alive, her skin had blistered and melted when it was too close to the flame. It was cruel, really. Even after two more lifetimes, no one had the ability to touch flames.

If Scarlet burned the rope even further up, it could burn her.

"I can take it. Just help me," Rose begged, willing feeling into her fingers so she could move them. There was just enough movement to get them to unfurl. Once she did, flame sputtered from them, the heat burning, but it was bearable enough as the rope holding her up caught the flame.

The dry air encouraged the flames, fire spreading along the rope, even around the parts that were wrapped around her wrists.

Rose winced as the fire grew hotter, burning the flesh of her hands and upper arms. She focused on her breathing to survive the pain. Flames curled around her fingertips, so she balled her hands into fists. The ropes loosened, jerking as part of them burned away.

She breathed in again.

The rope gave way completely, dropping her to the stone

ground. She held back a scream at the pain splitting through her arms and hands. A pail at the corner of the room provided enough water to douse the flames. The fire sizzled as she held her roped hands beneath the water. It soothed the fresh burns there.

"I don't know how you handled this all the time," Rose remarked to her fiery counterpart. With the fire finally out, her body tingled with the pain of hanging from the ropes for so long. She looked around the room for something to sever the last threads of rope to no avail.

She wasn't about to wait for her captives to find her like this. She used the only thing at her disposal, her teeth. She bit at the fraying fibers, spitting every so often to release them.

After a few minutes, the rope fell from her hands, freeing the scratched and blistering skin beneath.

Biting back tears she assessed the damage. Her fingers were blistered and red, her wrists were bleeding with fresh scratches, and pain shot down her arms and shoulders. But this was not the time to stop, and she couldn't afford to heal herself with a song. She was already tired from the small amount of magic required to burn the ropes.

What she needed was a decent meal to restore her reserves.

She shook her hands, convincing herself that she could ignore the pain if she focused on escaping.

Rose stared at the door, made of a thinner wood than that of the prison cell, biting her lip as she tried to turn the doorknob. It wouldn't budge, but new agony laced through her arm with the attempt to use the muscles of her hands.

She could open it so easily with a song.

Her heart squeezed in her chest. She could almost hear Isabeya chastising her for wanting the lazy way out.

"Fine, where do I get a pick this time?"

There were no visible nails in the door and no other places where nails would be. The room itself was mostly plain, with a small bed and a table with a chair. It wasn't like a prison cell at all. It was more like a servant's personal chambers. A window sat on the opposite end, but it was too high to reach and covered so no one could look in. It gave just enough light for Rose to know it was dusk. Good, the night would make it easier for her to go unnoticed.

"Come on, Rose, you're smarter than this."

Her gaze turned back to the door, inspecting it further. She placed an ear against the door, hoping to discover more about where she was that way. Distant music and chatter suggested there was a gathering. The party.

Nope, no way. She was not getting caught up in Colt's twisted games. Closer footsteps told her someone was nearby. Praying it wasn't Cain, she pounded a fist against the door, then hissed at the pain. "Hello? Can someone let me out?"

"Rose?"

Hope lit up her senses. She didn't recognize the voice, but it didn't sound like her tormentors. "Yes, I'm here!"

"Shhhh," the voice answered. "They'll hear you." He was right on the other side of the door. His voice sounded familiar enough that she knew he must have been a devil. "Back away from the door." She obeyed quickly, shuffling away from the door just in time for it to cave inwards.

Relief flooded her until she recognized his features.

Jon?

A half-bloodied brute stood before her with pleading yet determined eyes. Rose didn't believe what she was seeing until she noticed he held a hand out for her.

Anger bubbled up inside her. Not as potent as when Scarlett was close, but enough to have her glaring at him. He raised his hands in surrender.

"I know I'm not who you want to see right now, but I want to make this right."

She scoffed but found her knees growing weak. "Then you should never have brought me here."

"I had to, but I don't have time to explain. They will come for you soon. Let me get you back to the captain before that happens."

Rose couldn't see a reason for Jon to lie. He was breaking her out of her captivity after all, but every nerve ending in her body told her not to trust him. She could run past him through the open door, but she doubted she would make two steps before collapsing. Her body was too sluggish.

"I don't trust you."

His brows furrowed, but then he was becoming blurry. "I did it to save my sister."

Her vision turned hazy right before her knees gave out, but large arms were there to catch her before she hit the ground.

"Hold on, Rose, I'll get you out of here."

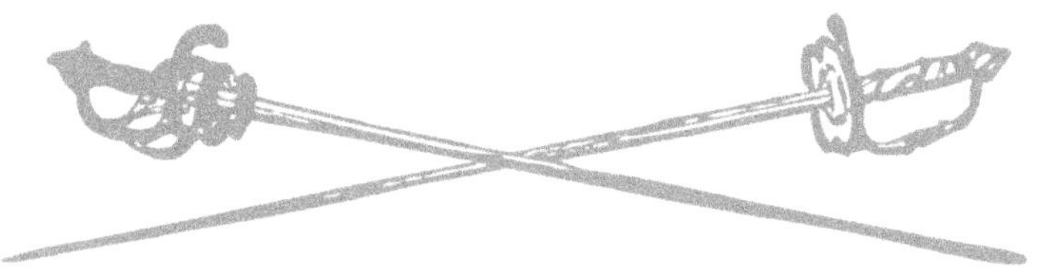

CHAPTER 35
MORE LIKE AN ANGEL
BLACK

Black hustled through the tunnels beneath the city, becoming more acquainted with how to move through them. She had memorized the path Almu had shown her, so there was little need to be shown again. Earhart, Hyne, and Tick came with her. The plan was like last time.

Find Rose.

Get out.

The captain would be forced to obey the *Imari* tonight, and he had to take Sophia with him. It still made her sick to her stomach. Every fiber of her being was telling her to find the stubborn huntress and drag her away from danger. It was only her duty to her crew that kept her on task.

"We didn't have a chance to check every door, but even so, Phantom is convinced she will be close by tonight. We must check everywhere and don't get caught."

They had dressed in some wealthy garments that would make them blend into the party, courtesy of the princess.

The big red door that marked the entrance to the palace came into view. Black pulled the door open, then peeked around the tapestry. Guests filled the halls in dramatically colored robes. Many of the men were completely shirtless with a sheen of oil across their chests and faces. The women wore even less with fabric barely covering their breasts and between their thighs. Black had attended many noble gatherings as an heiress, but they weren't this vibrant or revealing.

She closed the tapestry, pinning her gaze on Earhart who was wearing entirely too much to blend in. Then she looked down at herself.

"*Mierda!*" She swore. She opted for a man's robes, but they covered her nearly completely. She couldn't exactly go shirtless.

"What is it?" Earhart whispered before peeking behind the tapestry himself. He let out a heavy breath before pulling his robe off, leaving himself with only his pants and some chunky jewelry. The first mate was incredibly strong. It didn't surprise her that he was shaped like one of her father's statues.

"Come on, mates, shed your shirts. This is a different kind of party."

Hyne's face lit up, his excitement clear. "Yes! It's finally happened." He pointed a finger at Tick who glared at the devil. "You owe me twenty doubloons." Hyne pulled his shirt off, bouncing on his toes. He was also well-shaped man, and it didn't surprise Black when Tick revealed his own hard chest.

Black suddenly had the urge to vomit. She frowned at them.

"See something you like, Black?"

She *was* going to vomit.

"You're not exactly my fancy, mate. Save it for Lara." That shut him up as he shared a panicked glance with Tick. Choosing to extract herself from that mess, she refocused on the problem.

"You're going to stand out," Earhart stated with his enormous arms crossed before him.

"I'm not going in there dressed as a Carmean dancer either."

"That would be a sight," Hyne commented from behind her. It was all in good humor, but the thought made her skin crawl.

Earhart shrugged. "It wouldn't work. You walk like a soldier, not a noble lady."

Her brows shot up. "You do remember I *am* a noble lady? Kind of—" She wasn't about to argue the legitimacy of Lockness House, but she was still brought up as a noble. She just never wore that little clothing before.

"Listen, you should stay here."

"What?"

"You can't blend in and could give us away. Stay here and make sure our way out stays open."

Everything he said made sense, but *Goddess,* she didn't want to be left behind.

"But—"

Earhart lifted his hand. "That's an order."

The first mate didn't have the same power as the captain to make her obey, but he was still her superior. She nodded dutifully, then watched as the three men entered the lion's den.

CHAPTER 36

DOWN WITH THE SHIP

ROSE

ose's eyes fluttered in and out of consciousness. She wasn't sure which way Jon was turning. He could very well be taking her back to her captors. He did it the first time, after all. But with how utterly weak she felt, she had little choice in the matter.

"Hold on," Jon whispered to her. "I'm going to get you out, but you have to fight."

Rose's eyelids were so heavy. When was the last time she had eaten? Was it days?

She managed to open her eyes enough to see that they were in a different hallway, one with gold trim and fancy tiles. Was she in a palace? She laughed, so soft and breathy, she doubted Jon noticed. The fact that she went from a prison cell to a palace seemed like a metaphor of her life.

Footsteps pounded from the direction they were running towards. Jon looked around for a place to hide, but there was none. Only walls and it was too late to turn around.

Just as the guards came into view, he let her down. "I'll fight them off, but I need you to run. Find Phantom. Tell him I'm sorry." She wasn't sure she could do that. Her feet hit the tile, weaker than ever. She reached for the wall to steady herself while Jon faced the guards.

He had no weapon. No advantage. These men were close to his height and build, so his bare hands would only go so far against ten men. Or was it five? Her vision was doubling now.

"Run!" He screamed, and it instilled some kind of force within her because her feet moved back down the hallway. She still used the wall for support, but she was walking.

Jon screamed before the sound of pounding fists and drawing swords filled the hallway.

Rose kept moving, trying not to trip on the dress that was too big for her now. She took a different turn, hoping it would lead her to somewhere she could hide or find food.

Music floated to her, and her knees nearly caved in. The party they were talking about. It wouldn't do her any good to show up exactly where they wanted her to be.

She twisted door handles, her hand screaming in protest. Although the blood had finally returned to them, the burns still screamed with pain. Tears flowed down her face as she turned each door handle. All of them were locked.

Footsteps pounded. She could only assume the guards got past Jon and were now coming for her, but her feet wouldn't move any faster. She rounded a corner to find the entrance to the party.

Five hundred feet before her, guests spilled in and out, dressed in bright, wealthy, and revealing clothing. She'd stand out like a lighthouse in a storm if she tried to hide amongst them.

"Rose?" A voice turned her eyes to the right, down the hallway leading away from the party. A short man with burly arms stood with his mouth gaping open.

Earhart.

She nearly wept at his feet.

The first mate would do everything he could for her, and not because his captain would want it, but because she had once saved his wife. Relief hit her so hard she fell to her knees on the floor, a puddle of weakness and tears. She couldn't even make it the last few steps to get to her salvation.

He jolted, running towards her. Panic lit his eyes, but it wasn't until arms circled her waist that she understood why.

The guards. They were there, pulling her back, away from the party, away from the first mate.

The devil reached for her anyway, his fingers brushing with her outstretched hand before they forced her away. She tried to scream, but a hand closed over her mouth. Earhart's sword rang as he withdrew it, but even he couldn't fight off five men at once. Men who towered over him.

"Hold on, Rose," she heard him shout, his sword ringing as he fought them off just long enough to deliver his message. "Whatever you must do to survive, you do it! We're coming for you! You hear me, Rose? Don't give up!"

Her consciousness slipped in and out, blackness blurring her vision. Arms hugged her tightly, so much so, air couldn't enter her lungs. She had a vague awareness that she was fighting. Or it wasn't her—Isabeya was fighting with all her might, freedom too close to pass up. But even she couldn't fight off the weakness of their body.

Sorrow consumed her, even though she clung to Earhart's words. Yes, they knew she was there. James would do everything he could to get to her, but what if there was nothing left? She saw that look in Earhart's eyes. He didn't recognize her at first. She was afraid the next time she looked into a mirror. She wouldn't recognize herself.

Her limbs finally stopped moving as she gulped in air like she couldn't get enough. The guards dropped her, and she registered that it had only been a few minutes since they had recaptured her.

Footsteps drew her attention to two pairs of boots, one shiny and polished, the other old and unkempt, then she attempted to lift her head to see who they were attached to.

Colt and Dante.

More tears rolled down her eyes. She no longer cared to look strong. Maybe they had managed to break her.

"You just don't quit, do you?" Colt said with a smile, like it was a compliment. "You see, I admire that in a woman." He leaned down, crouching with his elbows on his knees, lifting her chin up with a single finger and letting the tears run down her cheeks. "We have plans for you tonight." More tears fell, knowing that the worst was about to come and right when freedom had been so close.

"Our guests are waiting for their — entertainment."

Colt shoved her face away like she was nothing. He stood, talking to the guards over her. "Send her to the maids to clean up. We left the dress out for her."

The two pairs of boots walked away, and arms came around her again. This time she was too weak to fight. They deposited her a few doors down, an army of women with solemn faces greeted her, shutting the door so the guards couldn't see. But Rose knew they stood right outside, in case Earhart reappeared.

The women didn't talk as they stripped off her clothing. Rose tried and failed to form sentences, but they all fell flat. As they threw cold water on her and scrubbed her skin from her toes to her hair, another woman offered her a bowl of soup.

Rose snatched it out of her hand before anyone could take it, her stomach aching. She drank the broth and the little bits of food inside. It didn't matter what was in it. She needed sustenance of some kind, filling her up. The food hit her stomach in an instant. More alarmingly, she felt her belly fill, like that little bowl of soup was all she could handle. Her strength would take longer to get back than it took them to take it from her.

She wanted to weep again, but something was coming. Something she had to be strong for. As Earhart had said, *anything to survive.*

She stared at the fresh burns on her hands. Years of muscle memory told her to sing, so she let out a *hum* that would heal her flesh. Her hands repaired themselves, the red receding enough to see smooth skin, but the magic stuttered out before the pain disappeared completely.

Damn. I thought you had more than that.

Rose let out a sigh of relief at Isabeya's annoyed tone. Even if her voices tormented her, they were a comfort she didn't know she was holding onto.

Once her hair was styled and her skin was covered in makeup, they brought out a dress. Though she would hardly call it that. It was a red cloth that strapped around her neck to cover her breasts, then hung between her legs. It left nothing to the imagination. This is what she was meant to wear before those guests?

It was nothing. Her breasts would fall out.

One look down confirmed that was no longer the case. In her nudity, she could see her chest was flat along with the rest of her, her skin clinging to her ribs instead. She was more worried the dress would fall off completely.

Once the atrocity was on her, she noted her back was completely bare, even her hair, which had fallen out in chucks as they'd brushed it, was styled into a pile of curls on the top of her head. It left her back exposed all the way to the curve of her ass.

Every one of her horrid scars was on display.

The women all lowered their heads, moving to the back wall of the bathing chambers, leaving Rose standing in the middle. At least she could stand on her own now, the food in her belly fueling her enough, but the weakness was still there. If she used one ounce of power, she would pass out completely.

The doors opened, and she turned around to watch a woman open the doors, allowing the guards in.

Her breath caught in her throat as a few of their gazes swept over her appreciatively. She glared at each one, imagining what a dagger in their chests would look like.

Her prison cell guard, Cain, approached her with chains rattling in his hands. Her wrists ached as she looked at the iron chains. Symbols took up the chains, decorating it in a way she didn't understand. Rope was out of the question now.

A collar attached to the manacles, all leading to the end of the chain. It was a *goddess-damned* leash.

She contemplated running. Even if the bloody dress fell off her as she ran, she would do it, but the guards took up the only exit like a blockade.

Cain offered a deranged smile as he snapped the collar around her neck, dropping the thick iron on her collarbone. She winced at the contact. Her wrists were next, sealing around her skin.

Skye surfaced, fear hitting her like a ton of bricks. It was too much. It was all too much. Rose focused her breathing as the shaking began.

"You're going to be okay," she whispered to her counterpart and, maybe, herself. "We're going to be okay."

Cain pulled on her leash, laughing. The dark chuckle was full of painful promise. "If you knew what the masters have planned for you, you wouldn't be saying that."

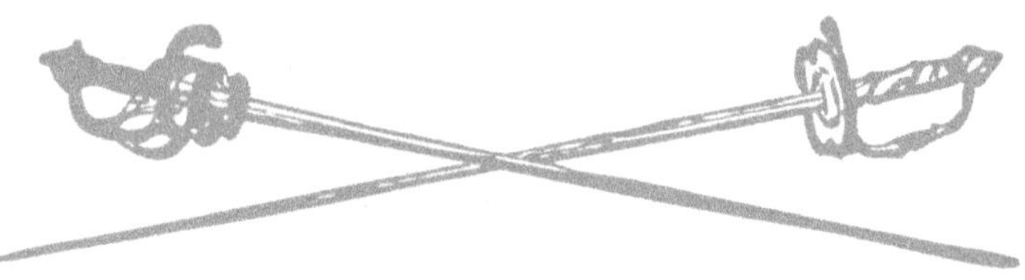

CHAPTER 37
KEEP YOUR POST
BLACK

Black paced in the tunnel with the door ajar, listening to sounds of guests talking and laughing amongst themselves. Worry plagued her thoughts. Logically, she knew it had only been half past an hour, but why hadn't she heard anything yet?

Sophia was in there as a guest herself. Black's skin crawled with the thought of people seeing her flesh on display. When they left the barracks, Sophia was dressed in a rich red dress that looked ravishing on her, but nothing close to what the women here wore. Would they make her change?

A guttural growl escaped Black's lips, the sound harsh and ragged, betraying her mounting frustration. Not knowing was worse because her mind kept coming up with terrible scenarios. What did Dante want with her?

An echo of music started, followed by the shuffling of feet. Soon, the murmur of voices faded. The guests were heading into the ballroom.

Black pulled back the edge of the tapestry to find an empty hallway. This was her chance to sneak in. She could get into the ballroom and check on Sophia. If everything was fine, she could just come back.

As quietly as possible, she slipped into the hallway, admiring the gold and white detailing. She walked like she belonged as she followed the tail end of the crowd into the ballroom.

Her jaw unhinged at the magnitude of the party. Colors of all kinds lined the walls in tapestries, drapes, and paint. The music was mesmerizing; a sensual undercurrent thrummed beneath the driving beat, a rhythm that urged feet to move.

Dancers filled the center of the ballroom, synchronized with their flawless movements. They had sheer and glittering shawls that dazzled in the candlelight.

Luckily, there were some who dressed modestly, helping her blend into the crowd.

It was nearly overwhelming and much better than anything Samsara could provide. Though Samsara did have its short-lived abundance, there was a second hand feeling to most of its style. As if none of the culture truly belonged there.

Here, it was like stepping into an entirely different world.

Black moved along the edges of the ballroom, searching for the huntress that was supposed to accompany the captain. A pang of jealousy came to her throat at the thought. If anyone was accompanying Sophia to an event, it should be her.

A door on the far side of the ballroom opened, revealing the newly arrived guest, including the captain with Sophia on his arm. He wore similar robes, except the accents on his were blue.

But Sophia—

She was dressed like Macha herself.

Lilac sheer fabric draped off her shoulders, a matching corset top revealing her cleavage and a skirt of equal magnitude floating around her legs, slits allowing her slender legs to walk through them. They had made her change.

Black bumped into another guest, losing her footing enough for the man to spill his drink. He briefly shouted at her to watch where she was going, but she ignored him, as did the other guests.

She searched for them, but they were lost in the thrum of bodies and colors.

Black shifted to a better viewpoint, finding a shrouded vantage point near where the wine was served.

She clapped with the others as the dancers finished their set.

They moved off the main floor, couples beginning to occupy it instead.

A tall, black-cloaked figure stood over Sophia, a hand out to her. Dante led her to the floor. Panic flared Black's senses as his hand came around her waist, pulling her flush to him.

Anger simmered as Black remembered what Sophia felt like pressed against her, how her lips had tasted. She didn't want anyone else to experience that.

"You feel it, don't you?" A voice pulled her from her stare.

Colt stood beside her, holding a glass of wine, but drinking in the sight of Sophia and Dante floating across the dance floor.

Did he recognize her as a devil? If so, why wasn't he calling for guards?

When Black failed to answer, Colt continued. "There's a worry in your heart. And I know, we're the bad guys. You would be wise to fear us both, but it's more than that." He drew closer, almost whispering in her ear. She had to ball her fists to keep from throwing them in his face. "That worry you feel, it's not entirely your own."

Black pried her eyes away from the dance floor, a crease forming between her brows.

Colt chuckled at the sight. "Oh yes, that connection you have with the good 'ole Captain, you can sense strong emotions from him. So strong, they drive his decisions. It's what makes him an effective leader." He lifted his glass. "Right now, he's worried about his dear love. He's frantic to get to her. He'll do anything to find her. Sound familiar?"

Her eyes snapped back to the dance floor, where Sophia and Dante moved like they were made for each other. Jealousy sprung on her again, but it was entirely her own.

"Oh, but the jealousy is all you." Colt laughed again, leaning against the counter. "You're here to check on her, the pull strong enough to make you follow her, but to see her here, dancing with a man. Now, don't mistake me, Dante is a fantastic dancer. But you hate watching someone else touching *your* girl."

Black had a hard time focusing on anything else as envy gripped her.

"Why don't you interrupt?"

Black spied a sly grin on the man's face, warning bells setting off in her head. A single look at Sophia drowned those thoughts. Dante's hand was spread over her lower back, nothing untoward, but the way he held her was too intimate, too familiar.

Colt chuckled. "Go get 'em, tiger."

Her feet were moving before she could think better of it, running off the raised platform onto the dance floor. She tapped on Dante's shoulder, who did nothing more to acknowledge her than a nod. He let Sophia go, bowing to both of them before returning to the dais.

Black faced her huntress, who glared back at her. Black assumed the position, putting an arm around her waist and pulling her close.

"What are you doing?" Sophia whispered into her ear.

"I had to see you." It was all Black could manage to admit.

"That's not a good enough reason. You need to be searching for Rose right now. The faster we get her, the faster we can leave this country." Black wanted to pay attention to what she was saying, but Sophia was clinging to her shoulder tightly, a slight tremor to her hands.

"What did he say to you?" There had to be something. The great Sophia Clare didn't cower to anyone.

"Nothing. I'm fine. You need to leave." Sophia avoided her gaze, choosing to stare at the floor instead.

"You're not fine. You don't think I can tell?" Fire burned her insides. Jealousy was a strong emotion, but the rage she felt because someone hurt Sophia—

That was irrepressible.

"Gwen, pleas—" Sophia pleaded, but it fell short, her eyelids growing heavy and her body going limp.

"I'll get you out of here," Black promised, taking her hand and leading her away. It showed how shaken Sophia was that she allowed it. They weaved through the laughter, the merriment, the shouting, and everything else until they were in the hallway.

One look at Sophia's face, now ashen and pale, sent a shudder through Black.

"What did he do to you?"

Sophia's knees gave out, falling face first toward the stone tile.

"Sophia!" Black cried, catching her before her head hit the hard floor. Soon, Sophia's eyes slipped shut. "No!" Black arranged her body to make her easier to carry, hoisting her up.

"Hold on," Black begged before she took off running.

CHAPTER 38

STOLEN VOICE

ROSE

Rose's throat burned as Cain brought her up several flights of stairs, stopping at a candlelit room with blood-red curtains blocking out one wall, but otherwise the only thing present was a hook at the center of the room.

A tear slipped past Rose's cheek, falling to the ground as Cain left, but not without leaving her with a parting phrase. "I doubt you'll be threatening anyone else." His laughter echoed in the halls.

Indeed, her throat was closing in on itself. There had been something in the soup. Panic seized her again, her breaths coming in rapidly, but none of them fulfilling.

"There, there, love. No need to worry." She knew that voice, but it was wrong. She knew by now not to hope for a miracle. It may have been James' voice, but it was not him.

Colt stepped into the candlelight, looking like the love of her life, but that hatred in his eyes told her it was not her Phantom. Not her James.

She opened her mouth to tell him not to call her 'love', since it was reserved for the real James, but the words wouldn't come forth. They caught in her throat, causing a knot to lodge there.

"The potion works quickly. I would be immune to your beguiling, but my guests sadly aren't." He put a hand to the dusting of stubble across his chin, but Colt got it wrong. It was too mani-cured, like when James was an officer, not the pirate she had come to love.

In fact, his entire outfit was wrong. He was still in his signature black tipped with blue accents, but it was a wrap style clothing that she had never seen before. It looked too clean and ceremonial for her pirate.

Instinct told her to demand he return to his true form, but she kept her lips sealed. It was only further humiliation to try, paired with the scraps of cloth they put her in.

Colt used a finger to lift her chin, caressing the metal on her throat as he dragged her to the center of the room. She was now familiar with the lift of her arms onto the hook and the ache in them when she was pulled from the ground. Colt didn't take his stolen eyes off her as Cain rotated the gears.

Rose looked to the ground, refusing to look into his eyes. She was beginning to see Colt in his 'Phantom' skin more often than his own.

His fingers wrapped around her chin, lifting it until their eyes met. She meant to snap her eyelids down, to dispel his effect. But she was drowning in the deep oceans of his eyes like she had so many times before.

"I want you to watch this unfold, love." His breath was hot against her lips as his finger traced down her neck to the iron collar encircling it. "Watch as I swear myself to your captors." His finger continued its descent, passing over the scar between her breasts. His touch was cold, eliciting nothing but revulsion and making her skin crawl. "And I want you to know, I'm doing this to be rid of you."

Tears pricked at the corners of her eyes.

It's not him. Green swirled in her vision. A reminder she was grateful for.

"When I make that oath, remember I'm doing it to break my own curse. Then," he paused, releasing her. Finally, she could breathe. "I will finally be free of you."

The air was thinner, not filling her lungs fast enough. Her panic brought a smile to her lover's face, all sharp edges and cruel intentions. He lifted his hand, and the curtains drew open, revealing a glass window that looked over the revelry. There were more colors than she could ever imagine. They blurred together with the tears in her eyes.

"Once he's seated, bring down his gift." She could vaguely understand Cain's agreement through the haze.

Before she could prepare herself, Colt's breath was drifting across her ear.

"See you on the dais, love."

Rose's mind whirled with the possibilities of what that could mean, but before she could lose herself to despair further, she cleared her eyes, blinking rapidly. It was humiliating enough to be strung to the ceiling, her arms burning from the abuse, her body limp in a dress that hardly covered her. But for Cain to witness her breaking along with everything else was enough to pull herself together.

As she suspected, Cain was smirking, clearly enjoying his view, apparent by the bulge in his trousers.

"I prefer you this way. Silent and crying. I'll ask the *Imari* to give you this potion before he lets me have you."

Rose schooled her features, not letting him see an inch of her fear. She wouldn't put it past her tormentors to go so far, but she didn't have a reason to fear it—until now.

"You see, he's already promised me my fun. I only have to wait until they say so." His eyes roved over her, heating in his lust.

Rose glared at him, and through the pain of her numb arms, she managed to raise a precise finger that told him what she thought of that. She ignored his goading laughter as if her protest was little to concern himself with. It wouldn't be enough with her voice locked away and her arms indisposed.

Then a familiar form caught her attention on the ballroom floor. The same black and blue outfit Colt was just in, but Colt was in his true form on the dais. He was wearing a white wrap like the black one she'd seen earlier. Which meant—

James.

Relief and dread mixed together until they were indistinguishable from one another. He's here. James was here.

CHAPTER 39
CAPTIVE THRONE
PHANTOM

If dread and guilt could swallow Phantom whole, they would do it here, at this richer-than-sin party in the middle of a starving city of desert folk. He still wasn't sure why he was here, but he knew Rose was close. He could feel her presence in the air, like a ghostly gaze across his skin. It made his skin prickle in anticipation.

If he saw her, he would steal her back, deal be damned.

The tattoo on his palm burned every time he even thought of defying it, but he couldn't risk her, no matter the consequences. He shook out his hand, hoping to ease the burn.

Rose's locket in his pocket burned in a different way, a sore reminder that she was suffering. He wasn't sure what the necklace meant to her, but it must have meant quite a bit if he'd never seen her without it. He'd cursed himself for not asking. They'd had so little time, just like the lives of their pasts.

"Ladies and gentlemen!" Colt's booming voice brought all eyes to the dais where Dante stood beside him. "Welcome to our humble abode. Tonight is not just about enjoying ourselves." They both were dressed in the traditional robes of royal white to remind their party goers of their status. As if anyone could forget the usurpers.

"We want to address a certain rumor that has been circulating amongst the population," Dante addressed, holding his hands out to the people. "Yes, Maahes has returned to our shores." Whispers erupted, circulating the rich and staff alike. As he listened, there was a slight panic to their tones.

"Maahes is not here to cast judgment. In fact, he's our honored guest, and I would be delighted to introduce you."

Kayden's yellow fire singed his peripherals. *That's your cue, pirate.*

Phantom walked forward, wishing he had a drink he trusted as the crowd shifted uneasily. They wanted a show? He'd give it to them.

Come to me, Phantom whispered to the shadowed corners of the room. They answered, filling the space and dimming the still-lit candelabras and chandeliers around them. They thickened around him like a cloak, making his appearance unmistakable.

Gasps and cries of panic rose up around him before silencing once again. No one wanted to draw his attention until he heard a sword unsheathe to his right.

"For Rán!" One noble screamed, a fit man with an old face. There was an eccentric fanaticism in his eyes that demanded justice. Or so he thought.

Kill him, Phantom commanded. Orange flared in his vision the same time a shadow took hold of the man. They latched onto his soul then ripped it from his body, leaving behind a fleshy corpse. He fell to the ground with a thud, the crowd lurching and screaming around him.

Phantom continued his ascent to the dais, the crowd parting for him easily. Green vines crawled at the edges of his vision.

Careful, Sam warned. *You're playing a dangerous game. One they are the masters of.*

Phantom ignored him. Sam could've told him about the bastards who raised him, but he chose to keep it to himself. Now, they were in this mess together.

"You've done enough," Phantom hissed, not caring if the guests heard him. He forced his own will in the form of a tidal wave in his mind, the current pulling them to the darker recesses of his mind. Now that he recognized his own power signature over his counterparts, he could use it in a way they couldn't counteract. He watched the flames and vines recede.

Phantom reached the dais with a clear head and determination.

Colt opened his arms to the crowd. "I present to you a god among men, Maahes, son of Nemain." The crowd cheered, a slow progression from their initial shock.

Phantom blinked at the term, inspecting the demons before him for the truth. Was this more lies to further their own narrative or was the truth potent enough for it? Colt's wink in his direction confirmed nothing.

Dante stepped forward, his voice more even, but no less assured. "Now, for the first time in a millennium, you shall hear from one of the gods."

The crowd quieted as the room charged with energy and all eyes pinned to him. He let his gaze drift over them, the rich cowards who sat in their towers and ignored the hungry around them. They didn't even have the stomach to stand against the *Imari*, for what?

A dying kingdom.

They were as desperate as the needy. He could smell it now, under all the flowers, incense, and expensive perfumes. The tangy scent of fear. It was an undercurrent to the entire event.

The last thing he wanted to do was assuage their fear and doubt.

But the tattoo burned on his palm until he was certain the skin would melt. Words poured from his mouth.

"You may think you know me." His feet began to move. "You may believe you know what I am here to do." Restless energy built under his skin but moving his feet along the dais helped. "You know nothing."

He hated them. He cared nothing for their fear and their limited existence.

"Give me a reason not to wipe your wretched souls from this plain. What good are you worth?" The tangy scent grew in its intensity. He sniffed, and the crowd gasped. Apparently, he behaved too animalistically for their liking. His claws itched to come out. He could show them just how beastly he could be.

"So much for the 'not here to cast judgment' part," Colt whispered from behind him.

Phantom ignored him, continuing to pace at the edge of the dais. Courtiers backed away from the platform as if they felt his lethal temper.

"I am here to right your wrongs." He turned to Colt and Dante and his words turned to ash on his tongue. The crowd held its breath, but he realized his words were not entirely his own. The burning on his palm confirmed as much. They were controlling his tongue, making him speak lies.

That was the deal. Obedience. Colt never mentioned how they would assure his compliance, but the foreign magic spreading out in electric waves from his new bargain tattoo was confirmation enough.

He curled his fist, using pressure to block out the pain.

"I pledge—" Colt's smile widened as he watched Phantom fight the words. He growled, the sound hitting the back of his throat as he lowered himself to his knees. "I pledge myself to the *Imari*." The words left his mouth growling.

He'd spoken so many lies in his life, and they had always been easy. Now, he lied like he was a stranger to it, because this was all wrong. None of these words were his.

"How do we know you are Maahes?" Phantom turned his head to the grating voice. It was the wrong time to test him. It agitated every counterpart taking up residence in his mind, the colors blending together.

"Do you require proof from us?" Our voices bled together, sounding like many. "We'll give you proof." We forced our body to shift, tearing through the little clothing we were given until giant ebony paws landed on the dais followed by a battle cry.

The crowd gasped and stepped back, cowering away from our clutches. The shadows responded, growing tighter around us like a blanket.

we sssssssee you

Phantom regained control of the beast, pushing the others to the back of his mind. This form was his now. He would no longer bend to it. Jumping off the dais and causing a cacophony of screams, he landed before the man who spoke. He was terrified now, staring into the ethereal red eyes of an unnaturally large lion. There was no mistaking who he was now.

He growled in the man's face. *Is this proof enough?*

The man fell to his knees in a show of submission. He lowered his head to the floor, his turban tumbling off. Phantom chuffed, deciding he did not need to eat the man, he turned.

The rest of the room followed suit, falling to their knees, some even crying out in reverence.

This was more than a show of power; these people believed him to be a god.

"Maahes," Colt called. "Come here."

Phantom growled at the blatant disrespect until the burning in his paw reminded him why he had to obey. *Rose's life. Not ours.*

Growling low, he whipped his tail as he climbed the dais again.

Colt and Dante raised their chins, smiles turning benevolent. He wanted to cut them off.

A trembling servant held out a robe to him and the shift happened before he could stop it. The damn tattoo was controlling more than just his words. Before anyone could look too long, Phantom wrapped a deep blue robe around himself.

Each word hit like a physical blow as he uttered the painful phrase, "Long may they reign."

The crowd shifted uncomfortably. Phantom turned, half-expecting the crowd to protest, but he should have known better. The lot of them echoed his sentiment.

"Long may they reign."

"Long may they reign."

It drifted through the dimly lit room, a chorus of cowards bowing to their captors. And he was one of them, the power of his deal keeping him on his knees.

"Rise," Dante declared, his arms lifting until they landed on Phantom's shoulders. He resisted the urge to rip the joints from their sockets. "You are one of us now."

Phantom barely registered the third throne being placed on the dais. Four servants struggled to carry the slab of rock before it thudded against the floor.

Colt's smile was too serpentine for Phantom to believe it was anything but a trap.

He reached out a hand, gesturing towards the new throne. "For you, son of Nemain."

Phantom's hesitance earned him a burning palm and a pulling sensation from his gut. He obeyed the silent command, walking past Colt to sit on the throne. As a small rebellion, he slumped into the seat, spreading his legs wide. Anything but the picture of propriety.

Dante leaned over him. "If you'd be so kind as to release the light."

It was a subtle enough command, and although it pained him to obey, he did so.

Recede, he ordered, and the shadows shrunk back into the darkened corners of the room they came from.

Colt blinked at the restored light before he addressed the crowd. "We have a gift, to show our appreciation and good faith for our new alliance." Phantom didn't like the way he spoke, like they were allies now. No deal could truly buy his loyalty. He would return to plotting their demise the moment he stepped out of the palace.

There wasn't a single 'gift' that could convince him otherwise—

Then the sun rose.

Rose stepped onto the dais. More accurately, she was dragged, led by a chain connected by the manacles on her wrists and collar. Her dress could barely be conceived as such, hanging on her frame like it might expose her with one wrong movement.

But it was her body—

Although there were no physical indications of abuse, her frame was so much thinner. She looked unlike the plump woman who had strut along his deck, challenging him at every turn. Her jaw, collarbone, and ribs were much more prominent against her skin, as if someone had sucked the life from her. Darkened circles shadowed her eyes through the makeup they painted her with.

Anger assaulted his senses so fervently it brought Kayden's flames to his vision. He wanted them dead. Colt. Dante. The entire bloody room. He'd slaughter them all.

He pushed from his seat, but before he could fully rise, a wince crossed her stricken features. The reddened outline of a rose appeared on her chest right where the necklace once sat. It was a reminder of what the burning of his palm truly meant. Her life.

For that, he couldn't risk anything.

Her mouth wasn't gagged or obstructed in any way. Why wasn't she singing?

He wanted to go to her, take the pain away, and reassure her that he would get her out. No matter what it cost him, he would get her out. He couldn't stand the look in her eyes, utter hopelessness.

Dante hovered over him. "You'd best remain in your seat, Maahes. We wouldn't want the innocent to be punished for your disobedience."

Phantom's fist curled on the arms of the throne, turning white with the pressure it took to keep himself planted.

"Not to worry, she's coming to you." Colt gestured with two fingers and the guard holding her chains approached, but Colt leaned into his ear. "This goes without saying, but if you attempt to take her, you or one of your loyal followers, her life is forfeit." Guilt licked up his spine until he had to banish the shadows that curled around him in comfort. She was in this mess because of him, and now, he couldn't save her. Not yet, at least.

Phantom marked the man carrying her chains, a large guard with the thrill of power on his face. He would die in agony. Holding her chains was enough to earn him a death sentence, but the sadistic gleam in his eye told Phantom that wasn't his only crime.

Rose's eyes widened as she took in the crowd and the scene. Fear. It was potent around her, more than he'd ever smelled on her. He hated it. It was like another male's scent was on her, because he knew that fear was forcibly placed there. He hoped his presence brought her some comfort, but it was hard to tell through her tainted scent.

Colt stopped her just out of reach like a cruel joke. His fingernails scratched against stone while Colt put a knuckle under her chin, making her look at him. Phantom wanted to slice off his fingers one by one.

A delicate tear ran down her cheek. *Why wasn't she singing?*

"Have a seat, birdy. Entertain our guest for the night."

She swallowed thickly but obeyed. Some relief filled him when their skin made contact. She was alive. There was nothing he could do to save her without risking her life, but seeing her breathing and feeling her weight in his lap eased some tension inside him.

"Rose," he whispered, wrapping one arm around her waist and pulling her closer while his other hand grazed her cheek. He drew her face upward to see her eyes, and the duller shade of gold in them. "What have they done to you?"

More tears fell, but he kissed them away. "Don't let them see. They don't deserve to see you break."

Shaking her head, she moved her lips, but no sound came out, only a slight tremor.

"Love?" She stiffened in his lap.

Dante leaned against the throne, too bloody close. "You'll find her voice has been... locked away for the evening." Rose glared at the demon like she would cut his throat with her fingernails. "Fear not, she'll still be able to use it when the time comes, brother. Just couldn't have her enchanting my guests."

Phantom growled. "I am not your brother." Whatever lies they were telling her were taking effect. This little act was an attempt to create a rift between them. One he'd never allow.

Dante ignored him, walking away and leaving them alone.

The music shifted. The once cheerful drums and tambourines took on a sultry quality, slower, the beat low and steady, but Phantom paid it little mind. Not with his songbird in his lap.

He placed his forehead on hers. "I'm so sorry. I can't save you tonight, but I will." A dry sob heaved from her chest, but no sound left her. Drawing back, he guided her eyes to his with a hand on her cheek. "Are they keeping you in the palace?"

She shook her head subtly.

"I do hope you aren't spilling our secrets, birdy." She stiffened at Colt's teasing tone. "That's a punishable offense, unless you've grown to like your punishments."

Phantom held her closer, growling and shifting her away from the demon as much as possible. "If you touch her again, I will inflict much worse upon you."

Colt smiled. "I look forward to it." His arm spread out to the revelry before them. Only now did Phantom scent the salty sheen of sex in the air. Couples had withdrawn into darkened corners, on dining tables, some of them in the middle of the dance floor. It occurred to him the ease of which the clothing allowed for such things.

"I do hate to see, ah — *soulmates* parted for so long. I hear it leaves a nasty ache on that wretched soul of yours." There wasn't a bit of his tone that suggested he spoke the truth. "Join in the fun. After all, you may not see each other for some time."

With that, Colt descended into the revelry, picking a partner to enjoy, but Dante still sat ramrod straight on his throne. He was far enough away to not hear their conversation, but close enough to suspect what they spoke of. Or what Phantom spoke of.

"Do you trust me?"

She nodded without a moment's hesitation. He breathed a sigh of relief at that small mercy. Lifting her chained hands, he placed them behind his head. He smiled encouragingly as he did. Her arm came right around where his mouth was.

"To block our host from reading my lips, but I need you to play along, love." She stiffened again, and he wondered where he'd gone wrong, but after a breath and a nod he understood. It wasn't him; it was the eyes on her back. She needed a distraction.

His hand drifted to the exposed skin of her rib, just under the soft swell of her breast. Her breath caught.

"When this night is over, I will find you, but I need your help. I can't bear to know they're punishing you. If you allow me to touch you, you can pretend to take pleasure while giving me answers." His cock hardened at the idea, but he willed it to calm down. He'd have negotiations with his desires once he could get her very far away from here.

Her gaze rose to his, and her eyes glistened with unshed tears.

These didn't seem like the same kind of tears as before. Her eyes lowered to her own body, and a sob jerked her shoulders.

Finally, he understood.

"Rose, look at me." She obeyed. "Make no mistake, I am attracted to you more than any other woman in this world. You are my sole desire, and my complete focus. I will do anything for you."

A single tear fell from his own eye as he crashed his mouth over hers. He needed to prove to her that she was all he ever thought about. Or maybe he needed it himself, to feel her lips on his.

His finger brushed her rib again and her breath caught even though she refused to break the kiss, as if she could reveal all her secrets through their locked lips alone. Sadly, that wasn't the case, so he pulled away and found arousal written all over her face. In the parting of her lips and the rush of her breath, and the darkening of her gaze.

It made him want to take her on this throne, bloody audience be damned. But that thought died instantly. More than anything, he needed to free her.

As he caressed the skin of her side, his other hand parted the gauzy fabric to slip beneath it. He found the softness of her legs to be lacking in fullness, but no less smooth. Drawing circles around her sensitive inner thigh, he watched as she panted, the teasing bringing genuine pleasure to her features.

He made certain to keep away from the imaginary lines while also making it appear that he was ruining her. She would have to put on a good show for the eyes watching them if they were going to pull this off.

"You're doing such a good job. Keep making them believe our ruse." Her fingers dug into his hair pulling at the strands since she could do little else.

"Are they keeping you in the city?"

Rose subtly shook her head, making it appear more like ecstasy.

His brows rose. "Outside the city. In the desert?" She tugged sharply at his hair and the brief look she shared with him made him understand it to mean 'yes'.

"How far into the desert?" He was so eager to ask that he forgot to pose the question more easily for her. She tugged twice.

Two miles.

He smiled at his songbird. "You're absolutely brilliant." Naturally, his fingers drew closer, brushing the bottom swell of her breast. Her breath hitched, and he drew them away, not wanting to push her boundaries.

Then she twisted, his fingers returning to where they were.

He froze. More uncertain than he had ever been with a woman. "Are you certain?" She responded by tugging on his hair.

Yes.

Then her lips were moving. Though no sound came out, he could make out the word 'please' on her lips. Removing his hand from her thigh, he lifted it to her lips, wanting to feel her say the words. He pressed the pad of his thumb against her mouth as it moved.

'*Watching.*'

Over her shoulder, he could see Dante had his head turned to watch them from his peripheral vision. He was growing suspicious, and they needed to make a more convincing scene. Phantom didn't want to think about how she could sense him.

"Anything you want, love," he said loud enough for Dante to hear. There was no tension in her body, no indication of hesitance as he returned his hand to the skin of her thigh. Higher.

Phantom watched her mouth part, and her eyes roll back as he grazed her slick heat. He couldn't decide if she was a good actress or simply giving in to his touch.

"Does the scene we're painting arouse you?" She nodded, exaggerating her movements a bit more. "A crowded room, eyes taking in the pleasure on your face. Do you like them watching us?"

She tugged on his hair.

"Ah," he whispered across her ear, turning her until she could see the party and the dozens of eyes on them. "You're more depraved than I even guessed." His finger found the peak of her nipple beneath her dress, and he pinched softly, letting the motion tease her. She squirmed, attempting to gain more friction.

Phantom felt the temptation to believe his own act; to let the pretending become real, just for a moment. He didn't feel the unquenchable agony. There was dread and tension, but seeing her alive, feeling her warmth, gave him hope that he would find a way to free her soon.

Dipping his fingers into her heat, her head fell back, and he knew she would have moaned loudly if she were able. They'd only been intimate once, but he already felt like he knew every movement, every sound her body made in reaction to him. He dragged his fingers in and out while his thumb toyed with where she was most sensitive.

Her eyes were closed, but he was desperate for connection with her.

"Look at me, love," he whispered into her ear then drew back. She obeyed, her eyes hooded, but she strained to keep them open and locked on him. He wanted to tell her so much more, that he would kill every soul in this city to get to her, why he sat here on this throne, how miserable he had felt since she'd been gone.

None of it came forth. She wasn't safe. Not even close. With her in his lap this way, it was easy to pretend otherwise, but he couldn't. He'd say everything once he got her back.

Her inner walls tightened around his fingers, warning him of her impending release.

Keeping her distracted in this bubble with him for as long as possible, he drew his fingers out. Her brow furrowed, but she still didn't look away from him. As if she were trapped in his gaze more than the chains could ever cage her.

He took the fingers into his mouth, sucking them clean of her. He growled low. "You are delicious. I've spent my nights thinking of this taste on my tongue again."

Her breath sharpened again, rich desire gleaming in her eyes.

The rest of the room fell away, narrowing in on the pair of them. He began to believe the lie. That she was in no danger, and they would never be parted again. The soft burn of his palm reminded him of what his reality was, but she caught the slight wince in his eyes, and the flicker of the hand on her breast.

She began to raise her arms from his neck.

"No," he whispered. "This isn't over." Phantom let his gaze

wander to the onlookers, finding Dante with his head tilted, as if sensing their shift.

Panic began to seep into her eyes again, her breathing quickening for an entirely different reason. No, she wasn't allowed to let the world slip back in yet.

He kissed her again, not bothering to be soft about it. It was a claiming kiss, one she returned in full force. As the world melted away again, he devoured her like she was the very air he needed to breathe.

Finally, he pulled away, his forehead landing on hers. "While you are on my lap, you focus on me and only me. Is that understood?"

She nodded obediently, and he groaned. "Good girl."

He noted how she enjoyed the praise as his fingers slid beneath her dress again, but this time, when her head tossed back and she clenched around his fingers, he did not stop. She writhed on his lap, no longer caring who saw or what was coming next. All that mattered was their time together and the distraction he could give her.

Just as pleasure tore through her, pulsing on his fingers, he whispered, "I love you. More than the land loves the sea, and more than any space that could keep us part."

Her eyes grew drowsy. He pulled her close, wrapping her up in him as much as he could manage, taking care to lift her chained hands until they were in her own lap. Once he did, he felt the coolness of her fingers open his still slick hand. There she found his palm with that familiar rose symbol.

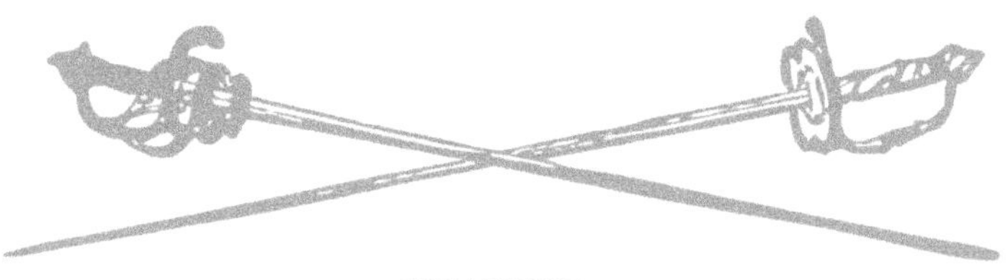

NEMAIN'S MARK

BLACK

"Smith! I need you. Get here, now!" Black shouted through the training yard as she came in search of the one person, she was certain could help.

Sophia was slumped in her arms, growing more lifeless by the minute. Her skin turned ashen in the moonlight. Her breathing was rapid and shallow.

Serena squawked at them as Black rushed to the doctor's chambers. The little dragon could sense the urgency, following after them to perch on the doctor's window.

Smith's wide eyes greeted them as he waved them into the room. Ramirez was already inside, cleaning the table in the middle of the room for her to be laid upon. Smith had the largest of chambers for such a purpose as this.

Sophia groaned as she was placed on the table. Black whispered, "It's okay. Smith is here. He'll help you."

The doctor already had two fingers on her pulse point, his brows furrowed, but he gave nothing more away.

"How did this happen?"

Black recounted everything Sophia did since she entered those doors. She didn't consume any drinks or food. She didn't get a chance to do much of anything, except —

"She was dancing with one of the *Imari*. Two minutes later she was falling to her knees."

Smith kept calm, easing Black's racing thoughts. "Check her over for any puncture wounds. It would be small if she didn't notice it, likely near a vein to cause damage so quickly."

Black looked over every inch of available skin, but the dress was blocking most of her. Modesty was not worth her life.

"I need to cut away your dress."

Black didn't expect her to answer. "Not precisely the circumstance I hoped to hear those words," Sophia huffed between pants like she wasn't struggling to intake air.

Black forced an easy smile to her face, hoping it would help settle Sophia's racing heart. She lifted a knife from her waistband, cutting away at Sophia's sleeve. "Survive and I'll participate in whatever circumstance you are referring to."

Sophia winced as the sleeve fell away from her right arm, exposing a handprint on her forearm, like someone dipped their hand in tar before seizing her. Little purple trails spider-webbed from the print, spreading the poison. Sophia growled when she saw it. "That conniving snake." She seemed angrier rather than concerned with her own well-being.

Black ignored it, turning to see Smith's face drain of all color.

"You've seen this before? What is it?"

Smith rarely spoke of his time in the Necromite War, but the shadows that haunted the man's eyes made it clear what it did to him. Some of those shadows grew darker as he watched the pulsating rhythm of the purple veins.

"It—" he started, clearing his throat when the word came out choked. "We called it Nemain's Mark. When the hand appeared on a soldier, it worked too quickly to stop." He took a step back. "No antidote, no amputation could halt the process. They say it was Nemain's hand herself, pulling the victim to the afterlife." The doctor's eyes were wide, his hands falling to his sides as if there was nothing left for him to do.

But that couldn't possibly be true.

"Are you telling me there is nothing you can do?"

Finally, Smith met her eyes. "I'm so sorry." It was not an apology. It sounded more like condolences.

"No," she whispered, looking to see what this was doing to Sophia. Her face gave away nothing. No fear. No acceptance, but no fight either. She grasped Sophia's cold hand, so starkly cold compared to the hot, dry air around them. "Don't give up on me. Don't you dare, Sophia Clare."

"I'm not going to die." Like it was as easy as just saying it.

Ramirez cleared his throat, gaining the room's attention. "If I may, Smith, this disease, would you say it's the marking of a soul? As if Davina herself has destined this ending?"

A shiver went down Black's spine at the thought. It was not Sophia's destiny to die here. She knew it. She wasn't sure how she did, but it was a feeling in her bones.

Smith's voice shook. "That's one way of putting it."

Ramirez's eyes centered on Black, a weight to them that she could feel resting on her shoulders. "Our dear captain may be the answer."

Black didn't question it, if there was a morsel of a chance, she had to take it. "Smith, how long does she have?"

"An hour at most."

Sophia sputtered at the idea, like it was laughable. Whether she was in denial or stubborn enough to believe she could stretch that time frame, Black didn't know. But she'd take whatever strength Sophia could give her.

She reached for Sophia's hand, giving it a firm squeeze. "Don't die on me. Not until I can try to save you."

Sophia's breath still came in fits and starts, but she nodded. "I won't die."

A tear fell down Black's cheek, but she didn't acknowledge it. There wasn't time. She tore herself away from the coolness of Sophia's body, a feeling she'd rather not think about. She took to her feet, hitting a sprint the moment she left the room, flying through the training yard. Serena squawked at her again, following behind.

She needed to get Phantom back as soon as possible. The

tunnels would take too long to navigate. A dragon was exactly what she needed to get through.

CHAPTER 41

PICKED LIKE A

ROSE

Rose knew this symbol like looking in the mirror at her own face.

It was the rose from her necklace, the one her mother gave her. The one Colt had taken from her. Now, it was imprinted on his skin with a shadow of ink. She wished she understood why it was on his hand, but she didn't have the voice to ask.

It was Davina-damned annoying to have her voice locked away. It was a weapon she had relied on, but in her pirate's lap, she'd found all she wanted to do was talk to him. Tell him exactly where they kept her and that there were monsters surrounding the building. Her heart broke at seeing all the concern and guilt on his face.

She'd even tried to sign, but with her wrists clasped together with iron and still painful from the burns, there was little accuracy she could manage. She could feel Dante in her mind, reminding her that this time was temporary.

Rose traced the lines of the new tattoo on his palm, that familiar rose. Guilt drowned his features, dragging his eyebrows together. She hated it. Then she noticed the shadows around him growing and curling, almost in comfort.

She had so many questions about *that*. She'd watched what

he'd done with them in the ballroom before he changed into the beast. Everything about that was wrong. All the pieces didn't quite fit together, but it had something to do with this symbol.

"My failure. I made a bet and lost," he breathed, pain so evident in his tone. His hand lifted, splaying across her chest, over her heart, the contact of his skin driving electric shocks through her. "This tattoo is connected to your heart. If I disobey them tonight, it's your life that will pay the consequence."

Her lips parted, wanting to speak again. The question of why they would be so reckless with her life, but she knew the answer. They were patient enough to wait for the next life. They didn't care about Rose, only their agenda.

Yellow flickered in her vision, reminding her that she was not powerless. Colt and Dante may not burn, but everyone else could. It was her bound hands that made that difficult without burning herself. That, and the need to hold onto her power with a vice grip. The little embers of magic she received from the bowl of soup could easily be extinguished.

James' head fell on hers again. "I'm sorry." His words brought her thoughts back to him. "I should have won the game. Then you would be safe."

She felt safe though. In his arms, right now, she felt like there was nothing that could touch her.

A high-pitched roar rattled the walls, causing sandstone to crumble and tapestries to sway. There was only one thing that made a sound like that.

Serena.

One look at James told her this wasn't part of the plan. His jaw was tense, his arms wrapping tighter around her.

The crowd grew quiet, moans and revelry ceasing in anticipation of what was coming for them. The clanking of swords outside the door caused them to gasp. Someone was trying to get in and it didn't take a scribe to discern who it was.

The party was over.

Rose turned her panicked gaze to James, shaking her head fervently. It wasn't enough time, but it could never be enough time. She needed to tell him about the necromites beyond her prison and the fact that the prison lay northeast of the city. She just hadn't figured out how to tell him.

Attempting to use hand language through her bound wrists, she made the sign for 'north' then 'east', but with their position and need for discretion it was hard to tell if she did it properly. James confirmed her failure with a short shake of his head.

Frustration ate at her as she frantically tried to look for another way.

She gripped his palm in her hand, drawing a circle with the symbol for 'north' at its peak. His brows scrunched together.

"Do you mean for this to be a compass, love?" She nodded her head, ignoring how the endearment made her shiver unpleasantly and hoping the eyes that were once on them were focused on the impending chaos instead.

She then drew the symbol for 'east' and pointed between them. His eyes lit with understanding, and he mouthed 'northeast'. She nodded her head, excitement tearing through her at being understood.

"Has our little birdy found a way to communicate?"

Mierda.

Colt shuffled up behind her, splaying his hand against her exposed back. Disgust rolled her stomach ruining what remained of the pleasure James brought. The man beneath her, growling like the beast he was, shoved Colt's hand off her. She was grateful for it but feared the consequences he'd face for disobedience.

"Ah ah ah," Colt cooed, wagging his finger. "She's a temporary gift, not a permanent offering. She still belongs to us." Dante slid up next to him as if marking the point with his presence. "And your time is up."

James' grip grew tighter as if he could absorb her body into his own to prevent them from taking her away. Shadows deepened, swirling around them.

"I could drag your people to Hell, effectively ending your rule." His voice was guttural, danger leaking from his tone. More shadows swarmed the exits, pushing panicked courtiers back. Screams and pleas rose up from them as they realized how trapped they were.

"Do it," Dante dared. "Their lives mean little to us. There are many in this city who would take their place."

Rose watched as James considered it, but she knew he wouldn't. The two demons were powerful with or without numbers.

"Don't forget who holds your leash, Maahes." Malice covered Colt's features, none of his usual smiles present. James flinched, clenching his fist, and she noted the red glow from beneath his palm. The symbol with her necklace. Then her flesh burned, singeing her like it did when she walked up the dais.

Looking down, she found the same symbol on her chest. That's how they were controlling him, with her life. He said it was for only one night. Praying that was true, she took the burning. It surprised her the first time, but now she knew how her pain was being used. She could take it. She'd endured worse.

Rose kept her face straight, yellow flickering in her gaze. Scarlett was there, taking most of the pain for her. They were not fireproof, but Scarlett had danced with flames more than anyone. This pain was an old friend.

The pain increased, and a silent growl crawled up Rose's throat.

"Careful, dear. You'll want to hang on to some of that power for later."

She refused to let fear take hold. She wouldn't let him see it.

Chaos erupted behind them as the doors caved inwards. Shadows scattered around Black's boots, knowing not to harm her. Her face and clothes were bloodied, her sword before her as she scanned the room. Serena flew in from behind her, lighting the tapestries on fire and drawing more screams from the guests.

"Birdy, I will ask you this once. Come back to your cage, or I will command him to kill himself. You will still belong to us, but you'll have to wait for him in the next life."

James bristled beneath her. "Don't do it, Rose. If it means your life, I will lay down my own." His hand came back to her cheek, cupping it gently and shutting away the rest of the world. "Just pray that our next lives are kinder."

Her lips parted to ask him what good his sacrifice would do if it changed nothing? But her damn voice still didn't work.

"*Now* birdy," Colt snapped. "I won't ask again."

She tore her gaze away as her feet hit the floor. He reached for her, but she gently shrugged him off. The pain in her chest eased as the distance between them grew.

One step was all it took before Colt had his hands on the chains of her manacles, pulling her to his chest like a rag doll. She winced, hating the contact more than the pain.

James growled again, and her gaze fell to his. His eyes were feral, his hands white-knuckled on the stone at his sides.

"You really are a pretty bird, aren't you?" Colt's knuckle grazed her chin. James growled again. "I can see why you want her to remain in this form."

"Damn you to the depths. Your cursed soul is mine to take," James spat out, but Colt laughed, repositioning himself to the edge of the dais.

"Release your shadows, Maahes." Pain hit her like a battering ram and she finally broke, a scream tearing from her throat. The pain faded with the sound of large doors opening and the scurry of footsteps, along with panicked shouts.

"That's better," Dante praised, and Rose nearly spat at him for it.

"See you on the flip side," Colt said before throwing a familiar bag to the ground. It was much like the one Jon had thrown to escape the ship. The same sickening feeling took her, rolling her stomach as the world around her went up in smoke. When it cleared, she made out the familiar walls of her prison cell.

Colt and Dante were nowhere in sight.

Rose glanced down at her clothing, having returned in the rags she wore before. Her chains were loosely linked to the wall, allowing her minimal movement. Everything was the same as she left it, like she never left.

Like she'd never seen her pirate.

The familiar ache in her core was her only proof, reminding her that he touched her.

Holding onto that, she sat on the sandy floor, curling her legs into herself and focusing on the memory of his skin on hers and wishing they'd had more time.

A cough drew her attention to the darkened corner ahead of her. There, Jon sat, bloodied and bruised. He was chained to the wall, same as her.

"*Goddess-damned* demons. I was hoping you'd escaped."

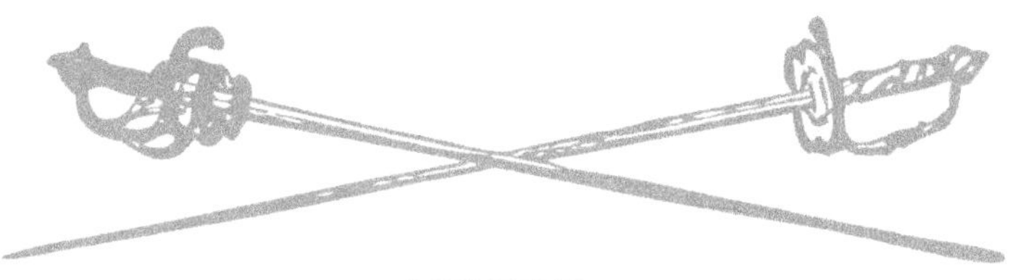

CHAPTER 42
HALF MOONSHINE
BLACK

Unfamiliar anger rose as Black made her way through the melee of panicked guests, most of them half-dressed and fumbling to right themselves before spilling out of the newly opened doors.

Disgust rolled her stomach, also unfamiliar since she couldn't quite place where that came from.

Black focused on her own emotions, blocking out the distracting ones. Sophia was dying, and they had run out of options. Seeing Rose disappear in a puff of smoke disoriented her enough to run into several escaping courtiers. With a growl of frustration, Black pulled a pistol from her holster then shot at the ceiling. Gasps and screams rang out, but she had their attention.

"Move!" She shouted, in no mood to waste time. The sea of people parted, staying out of her way as she ran to the dais where Phantom stood staring at his palm.

"Captain?"

He looked up, emotions rolling through his eyes and translating to her own. She could feel them at the edges of her mind.

Anger. Fear. Shame. Hopelessness.

She bristled at the intrusion and the array of colors accompanying them. She shook her head, banishing the onslaught and focused. His gaze shifted away, staring at the place where Rose had disappeared.

"Captain, Sophia is dying." No reaction. He just continued to stare. "Captain, I need you. Sophia needs you."

Nothing.

Serena screeched behind her. Could she feel what was going on with the captain, too?

Black jumped onto the dais, sheathing her sword and pistol. "We'll find Rose. I swear to you, but not tonight. Sophia is going to die unless you come with me."

More of that useless shame bubbled up inside of her. It's like he could feel everything, but he couldn't release himself from it all. A sharp, piercing ringing dominated her hearing, a painful, overwhelming sound that left her reeling. By the flickers of blue in her vision, it was coming from Phantom.

Because she could think of nothing else to do, she slapped him — directly across the cheek.

He reeled, cupping the side of his face. "What—"

"Sophia is dying, and you're the only one who can help her. So come on," she rushed out.

Concern softened his features as he rubbed at his face. A loud roar drew their attention to Serena blasting guards with blue flames.

"Is that why you brought the beastie?"

Serena's eyes found theirs, perking up at the attention and scrambling to follow them. The little dragon landed next to Phantom, nudging his hand for a pet and looking a little too pleased with herself for scaring away the guests and setting fire to the guards.

Phantom jumped off the dais, Black on his tail as they ran for the newly emptied hall. With a dragon flying above them, they found little resistance at the gate.

They ran through the streets of the citadel with Serena trilling above them.

Black's heart pumped in her chest, but it had little to do with the physical activity and more to do with each minute that ticked by bringing Sophia closer to death. It wasn't until they reached the training yard that Black realized how fast they had run.

Ramirez smoked a pipe outside Smith's room, tipping his head to Phantom, then returning his gaze to the heavens.

"Find it in your heart, Captain, to understand her."

Black couldn't make sense of the stargazer's words, but she couldn't read Phantom's blank stare for any clues either. His riddles could wait.

Smith's grim expression was not one she wanted to see as she entered the room, death already heavy in the air and Sophia's form unnaturally still on the bed.

"She's alive, but just so. She has but a few breaths left. The end is painful." He reached for his knife. "Say your goodbyes and I'll—"

Black's hand snapped out, wrapping around the doctor's wrist, begging him not to give up. "Not until he tries to save her." *What could the captain do?* The words that were in the back of her mind sprang to the surface. She had retrieved him, for what? Rose could heal, but she was out of reach. As far as she knew, none of Phantom's unworldly talents involved healing, or whatever Sophia needed.

"Release him."

Blue crashed over her vision, her hand falling to her side involuntarily. She opened her mouth to protest, but the words stopped short when she saw Phantom staring at the handprint on Sophia's arm. Did he recognize it?

"Leave."

At first, Black thought he meant the doctor, but her feet moved of their own accord, directing her out into the training yard. She huffed at the dismissal, finding a smiling old man at the entrance.

"Quite the commotion." A smile played on his lips, and she frowned. How could he joke at a time like this?

"Are you not concerned? The doctor is already preparing to—" Black's voice caught in her throat, choking her. She let her back hit the wall beside the door, her feet not allowing her further.

"She will not die." He said it so casually that it drew a hollow laugh from her.

"And how are you so confident?"

It was odd to see two old men who were veterans to the Necromite War, both who had lost everything, and yet one came out more optimistic than the other. If war did indeed change people, what did it make of Ramirez?

"Because," he said, pulling from his pipe again. "She said so herself."

As if that was enough to go on. Sophia didn't say it like she was going to fight for her life, she said it like she couldn't possibly die. It was only her denial in the face of death, nothing more.

But Black didn't say as much. Ramirez's confidence lent her the strength she severely needed.

More devils piled into the training yard, cheering as they went.

Hyne held a wrapped trinket above his head. "We got it!" Tick and Earhart followed close behind. She doubted Rose was wrapped up in that cloth, so they must have found Sitamun's scarab.

"Where's the captain?" Hyne asked, excitement brightening his features.

She wanted to answer, but her throat closed at the idea of explaining the situation.

"I'm afraid he's severely occupied," Ramirez offered. "Your spoils will have to wait."

She wasn't sure if it was written all over her face, but Earhart eyed her carefully before asking, "What's wrong?"

The curtain drew back, and Phantom exited the chambers, Sophia limp in his arms. Black leapt to his side, trying not to think about how still she was, but her chest still moved with shallow breaths.

The captain didn't spare her a glance as he placed Sophia on a table in the center of the yard, silver moonlight covering her completely.

Phantom's gaze fixed on the moon as a shout tore from his lips. "Is this what You want?" Black looked between the sky and her captain. "What is she to You?"

Nothing happened for a moment. Black thought perhaps Captain's voices were getting the better of him. That is until the silver moonlight glowed brighter. As if the Goddess of Fate herself answered.

Moonlight spilled like a waterfall from the heavens to the unconscious body on the table, blinding the surrounding devils. Black leapt to the huntress. She wasn't sure what she would do, but before she could solidify a plan, the light flared, an unnatural wind pushing away all who stood nearby.

Cries and groans followed as the devils were flung into the walls. Black rose to her feet, shielding her eyes from the light that blinded them. She approached again, but this time, the light faded, winking out of existence. Sophia lay lifeless on the stone table, as if in offering to the Goddess.

Panic seized Black's breath as she ran to Sophia's side, bending to place her hand on the huntress's cheek. "Sophia? Wake up!"

Sophia jolted forward, inhaling a gasp of air as she sat up into Black's arms. They embraced, Black's heart slowing at feeling Sophia's heavy breathing against her chest. She was alive.

Black pulled back to inspect her face, both hands roving over her. There were no marks, no sweating or paleness. Whatever ailed her was gone, but the handprint on her arm was still there, if a bit faded.

"What was that?"

Sophia's features gave away nothing.

Phantom's darkened form approached her side. "Davina offered aid to her *immortal* servant." The deep cadence of his tone was her only warning. "Seize her."

Strong arms wrapped around hers, dragging her away from Sophia. She struggled for a moment, but seeing the kind eyes of the first mate and the ship's drunkard disarmed her until she saw a glimpse of blue in them.

Phantom looked down at the huntress with an intensity that bordered on hatred.

"No," Black said, pulling at the devils' grips. "She's done nothing against you."

The captain didn't command her to be silent, but he ignored her just the same, instead studying Sophia as she stood from the table, no hint of the illness she'd suffered.

Phantom huffed like a beast in a cage, pacing before her. "How long have you been manipulating me?"

Confusion fogged her mind. Sophia wasn't a threat to them.

"Davina came to me as a child. She has commanded nothing of me except to join your crew. Every choice I have made has been mine alone."

"Liar!"

Phantom's jaw hardened, his anger boiling over until Black could feel it. She recognized it as his, but by the angry faces around her, the other devils were as convinced as the captain was.

"What does She want with me?" The question came out almost pained. "What purpose does She have for you?"

"She has not yet revealed that to me. I only know my fate is tied to yours."

His boot stopped before her. "You expect me to believe that?"

"Whether you believe it or not is your choice."

He growled, unsatisfied with her answer as he continued his pacing. He walked on, back and forth, the air thinning as he did. Black stared at her huntress, Sophia finally lending her gaze, but only hardened resolve remained there. Everything fell into place, their conversations, the meditating. All of it was because of Davina.

The slide of steel brought Black's attention back to the captain. She struggled, trying to break free of the two devils as Phantom's sword landed on the open skin of Sophia's chest.

"No, she's not a threat. I'll take her away. You'll never have to see her again."

Phantom's eyes slid to hers. "Would you betray me so soon then?" Her voice caught, not realizing she confessed her willingness to leave the devils to save Sophia. Then his gaze traveled to the gapping devils around them. "How many of you should I count as enemies?"

Silence answered him, no one knowing the right thing to say to curtail his anger.

"Only one," Sophia's voice came out soft, unassuming.

"What?" He pushed the sword further, dimpling her soft flesh. Black lunged, attempting to kick her away through the devils. She managed to free one arm, but Earhart's grasp was unbreakable.

"Yourself," she answered. "Turning on your crew now will bring you only strife."

He growled. "Are those your words or Hers?"

Her soft ebony hair flowed over her shoulder as she inspected him, no sign of fear in her gaze. "Mine." He seemed to relax at the answer. "But you should consider who the Mother of your love is. Davina wants you to save Her daughter. You have a common goal, a common enemy." She gestured to the palace dome that could be seen in the distance. "Is that not enough to create allies?"

His features hardened. "Allies? With the Goddess who cursed me?"

Sophia's head fell back then, and the devils flinched watching the unnatural, horrid angle of her neck. Black felt her stomach bottom out at the sight. Sophia's head snapped forward, silver light shining from her eyes.

The presence was unmistakable, charging the air with thick electric power.

Davina.

"Who would you be if I had not cursed you?" Her voice echoed as if filled with the voices of many.

Phantom stood his ground, glaring at the Goddess of Fate. How was he not trembling? Cowering in submission? Black felt her knees grow weak enough that she was glad for Earhart's vice grip.

"I would be free. I would have come for Your daughter anyway and I would have saved her—"

"You belonged to Nemain. *I freed you.*" Sophia's hair lifted as the air zapped with ethereal energy. "I would think you would understand the consequences of betrayal. My curse prevented your eternal punishment, and My daughter would not know you again. You should thank Me."

"Your gift?" The energy snapped and popped as the shadows deepened, their combined power causing the air to thin.

"You watch us find each other just to lose each other time and again and You call it a gift. Are You so cruel to the one You claim to love so dearly?"

"Silence," Davina demanded, the word so sharp it made Black's ears ring. "I did not come here to be scolded by a child. My daughter suffers. Find her before the sands of time run out."

The air shifted again, silver light winking out as the pressure released. Black was able to fill her lungs fully. Sophia's body fell to the sand, and no one was there to catch her.

"Ramirez." The old man shuffled next to the captain. "Lock her in the brig until I decide what to do with her." Ramirez's skeptical brow showed how much he doubted the confines of the brig could hold a Goddess vessel, but the captain was in no mood to listen to concerns.

"Yes, Captain."

Russet scooped up her limp body, as the two of them walked out of the barracks to visit the ship. Black wanted to follow, make sure Sophia was alright, then ask her — well, everything. There were a thousand questions burning in her mind.

Phantom's eyes focused on her. "You will stay with us, Black. If I find you have visited her before I permit it, I will consider you both traitors, is that understood?"

Black swallowed back her fear. "Sophia — will you?"

"She will not die by my hand."

Black nodded, willing her raging heart to slow.

Phantom nodded, and the devils released her.

CHAPTER 43

DESPERATE TIMES

SEBASTIAN

I f Indigo had expected Sebastian to sit in her hovel and wait for her to assemble their escape plan, she would be sorely mistaken. She had a better chance at gathering the Khelitians and readying everyone for departure, and Lord Casimir was already preparing the boats for the voyage to Kheli, but he couldn't sit around and do nothing.

Not when there was something only he could handle.

Afraid to draw attention on the streets, he pried a window open on the ground floor. It gave easily enough, letting him slip through to the shadowy room. There was very little moonlight escaping the haze hovering over the island tonight. It was the perfect weather for a mission of stealth.

It only took a few steps into the dark halls before Sebastian understood how much the orphanage had improved. The walls were reinforced and touched up. The floors were freshened, cleaned and ready for the next child-induced mess.

When he'd lived there, Mama Owen had demanded that they clean up after themselves with a list of chores they had to do every day to earn their keep. It taught him hard work and dedication, especially when work on the house needed to be done. Normally, he wouldn't condone the labor of a child, but if this house didn't operate, he didn't have a home. It was enough incentive.

If he were to hazard a guess, he'd say the same was happening now.

It was good to see health and brightness within the walls again, even if death was at their doorstep.

The floorboards creaked and Sebastian turned to the sound, but not fast enough.

Pain slammed into the back of his skull. Not enough to knock him out, but it still hurt. He turned to find Mama Owen in her nightgown, and a wooden toy sword in her hand. Apparently, she was using the pommel to bludgeon him.

He found himself grateful that it was not a real sword, and she was not particularly strong. But if he had been a real intruder, her toy sword would not have been enough.

"Mama!" He grabbed the sword from her hand, but it was too dark to read lips or recognize his features. Or perhaps she did, thinking he was no longer himself again.

Managing to take hold of her hands before she ran off, he laid them before himself, then signed into them.

It's okay. I won't hurt you.

A short gasp left her. "*Mio?*" She gripped his hands in hers as if holding them would keep him here indefinitely. She pulled him into a nearby room, the classroom, she would call it, with lines of chairs facing a board where she would teach. She really did everything she could for the children here.

After lighting a candle, she signed rapidly speaking along with her hands. "I was so worried." *You did not visit.* "*Pudo haber muerto, mio.* What was I to think?" He held back a nostalgic laugh at seeing her switch between Brettanian and Quencerian all while signing on and off furiously. It reminded him of a simpler time when all his concern was about staying in her good graces.

Her frantic pace and incoherent words made it impossible for him to grasp her meaning.

Mama, I need you to listen to me.

She blinked a few times, clearing her panic long enough to understand that he must have come for a reason if he had to come through the back window in the middle of the night.

Get the children ready and be quiet. Meet me at the eastern dock, I'm getting you out of here.

That's all he needed to say, so he began to turn when Mama Owen's hand landed on his arm, dragging him to face her again. He used to be punished for turning his back on her and the movement brought a shot of old anxiety, telling him he was in trouble.

And go where, mio?

She didn't speak any longer, understanding the urgency and discretion needed for this conversation. He hated the worry in her eyes, but he was doing what he could to lift that burden from her.

We're going to Kheli. It's not safe here.

"*Puta mare de los malnacidos, párate ahí!*"

Her words came so fast he barely had time to translate them, but he understood that a sailor would blush saying them.

He expected worry and fear, but he didn't expect her to be angry. What exactly had he done? Besides avoiding her until he broke into her house and asked her to pack up an entire orphanage in an hour. They wouldn't exactly be able to take much with them.

She paced before him, running fingers through her perfectly tied back hair. Finally, she went back to signing.

I cannot leave. It is no safer there than here. You would have me risk dozens of little lives by traipsing across the island to be smuggled across the sea on a ship.

It was a handful of fishing boats that had no business being on the open ocean, but he wasn't about to mention that while she was yelling at him. Even if she was managing to yell with her hands.

He shook his head, signing back, *you will all die on this island when the food runs out.*

Her features turned stony. It was that no nonsense look that he never managed to talk her out of. *I know what can happen. But if Kheli is no better. What chance do we have then?*

I will find us a place. You have my word.

Tears welled in her eyes, giving away how afraid she really was. Then she set her hand against his cheek. "You cannot protect us from everything, *mio*." She pulled away so she could sign again. *Go to Kheli. If it is safe, come back for us.*

I cannot leave you to die here.

More tears fell. *And I cannot risk them to the sea without the promise of safety. We will make do with what we have.*

He knew what that meant. A horrible drought when he was a child had forced the island to ration their resources. He and James had become thieves to survive that year.

Mama Owen wasn't above criminal activities if it meant her orphans lived longer.

Sebastian nodded then pinned her with his gaze. *Promise me you will survive.*

She gave him a withering look in return; one he didn't particularly like.

Promise, she signed.

He wished he believed that was enough to keep them safe.

CHAPTER 44
DESPERATE MEASURES

SEBASTIAN

Dark clouds continued to keep the land shadowed, as if Davina herself was hiding them from sight. The refugees clung to walls until they could get to the eastern docks.

Sebastian spotted Lord Casimir's silhouette before he could make out any others, but soon more and more figures appeared. As he approached, their faces became more and more familiar. Officers he had worked beside, the missing ones who had been freed.

He turned to Indigo to find her eyes wide beneath her deep purple hood. The color brought out the ethereal swirl of violet there.

Casimir clapped a hand on Sebastian's forearm. "They found me, but they have little trust for you. I assured them that you weren't under the priestess' sway and would in fact help them, but they remain unconvinced."

Sebastian hated his reputation, even though he understood how it got him this far. "And yet, they came?"

"Well, once they heard you were bringing refugees to Kheli, they wanted a chance to protect their island."

There were easily twenty men standing before him, stern distrust marring their faces. At this point, he was cursing his reputation.

"That's precisely what I need them for." Sebastian brushed past the Lord, facing the Khelitians. "I need you. All of you. Samsara is going to fall, and I don't know how long Kheli has." A few faces dropped at the revelation, but no one corrected him. "I know you don't trust me, but know I'm putting my life in your hands by boarding these ships."

Heads turn to the man standing to the right. He was slightly taller than the rest, with ebony hair he had tied in a bun at the top of his head and a jagged scar across his left eye. "We would not be here if we didn't understand the risks." He placed a hand on the pommel of his saber. "But if you get in our way, *Commodore*, I will not hesitate to strike you down."

Sebastian nodded. "Understood. What's your name?"

"Vincent, sir. Vincent Clare."

Sebastian grunted in approval. "Do you all remember your training?" They nodded cohesively. That meant they could sail these boats. "Good. Then divide yourselves amongst the ships, you will be operating them." He turned his head to the families behind him. "We need to go as soon as possible. Someone will notice us soon."

The Khelitian men hesitated, but after a nod from Vincent they ran to the fishing boat on the far end, the families following after him as they directed people onto each boat. There were far more than thirty refugees for him to get to Kheli safely. No doubt, there would be even more on his second trip.

"Casimir, how many can we fit on these boats?"

The lord's face fell, blanching a little as he watched the nearly unending stream of refugees load onto the boats. Running his fingers through his hair, he mumbled, "My biggest smuggling mission yet."

"My Lord," Sebastian snapped, and the lord returned his attention to Sebastian.

"The boats can carry sixty combined without sinking, but to keep everyone hidden — no more than forty."

There were far more than forty among them, the last of them being shuffled below decks while the officers remained on deck. Fishermen weren't known for uniforms, so their casual dress should do the trick. The swords and pistols at their sides could become a problem, but he didn't want to disarm them at a time like this. He'd had to rely on the cover of night to make them blend in.

It was a calculated risk.

The last of them shuffled on deck, and Casimir patted Sebastian on the back.

"Never thought I'd see the day I'd be smuggling *you*, old friend. I will continue my search and prepare the next batch for your return."

Sebastian put a fist on his chest, a habit he had obtained from working with the lord, who returned it.

"Survive this, and I'll see you again."

Nerves littered Sebastian's stomach. He couldn't decide if William was better off on Samsara or coming with them. "I could say the same to you. Watch out for the dead. They could come in the form of animals too."

He shot Sebastian with an egregious wink. "I will be vigilant. Perhaps, I will finally enlist my son's help."

Voices carried from low town, multiple lanterns growing closer by the second. They were out of time.

Lord Casimir slipped back into the tunnels while Sebastian directed his attention to the refugees. With a glance at the Khelitians, he ordered them to hide.

Get below. Stay quiet.

Indigo tried to slip past him to follow William, but Sebastian stopped her. Dragging her to the last ship by her hand, he hauled her out of sight. Then he realized how close she was. She warmed his side, peering over the top of the stairs, but he'd be lying if he said he didn't enjoy her closeness.

Vincent stood on his other side, and he had to wonder at the relation between him and the archer who had joined James' crew. Though, he suspected telling him Sophia was a pirate now would be a distracting conversation.

The lanterns grew brighter until the figures holding them came into view. Enchanted officers and those who chose to still serve in the navy. Felix at the helm.

They didn't stop to investigate, seeing that the dock was quiet and unattended, they continued their search southward. But Felix stopped, looking at the boats too closely for Sebastian's liking.

His corn-yellow hair was unmistakable in the light of the lantern he held up as he walked onto the dock. The air was still as anticipation buzzed through him. The refugees trembled with fear and trepidation.

After a moment, Felix spun on heels, ready to rejoin the hunt.

Until a babe's wail came from below deck.

Felix turned, and Sebastian jumped onto the deck of the boat, catching the man's attention. "I assume you are looking for me?"

Felix's smug grin was unmistakable in the darkness. "I should have known you would run." He raised his fingers to whistle, calling Ravana's officers to his side, but Sebastian put his hand out.

"Wait, challenge me."

Felix's brows rose. "What need is there for that? Once Ravana knows you've deceived her, she will tear you apart."

Sebastian offered him a mocking smile, hoping the refugees would seize the little time he'd stolen for them. "Then you'll never know if you truly deserve the title of commodore. Tell her you defeated me, single-handedly, and she won't be able to deny you the position." Darkness flickered in his face as Sebastian moved closer, locking in on his prey. Felix was too selfish and prideful to know what it would truly cost him. "To prove yourself not only loyal, but capable."

He stepped from the boat; boots firm against the dock as he raised his sword.

"But if you deliver me to her, she'll look right past you, focusing on my betrayal rather than your position."

Felix took a step forward, pointing his saber in accusation. "You only wish to defeat me in battle. I'm no fool."

"Then you are a coward."

He froze, inspecting Sebastian. The visceral hate crinkled his eyes. "I'm no coward."

"Then face me, and we shall see who is truly worthy of the title we share."

Felix needed no further encouragement, swinging for Sebastian's head with lethal efficiency. Sebastian blocked in time, along with the next four of his attacks. Perhaps he had goaded Felix too far with that feral glint of rage in his eyes. But the distraction was holding.

Sebastian maneuvered them until they were close enough that Felix couldn't see the boats. He was left unaware as they made their silent, gradual exit into the open ocean.

He felt no loss in knowing he had managed to save some of the people today, even if his own life was forfeit.

He blocked another blow, parrying and driving Felix back a step. He was more efficient with a blade than Sebastian had expected, but he could not defeat his superior. No, Sebastian knew his end would be at Ravana's hands, which would be a fate far worse, yet still, he could not find it within himself to regret his decision.

At least, until he noticed a lone figure at the end of the dock, hands glowing with shimmering lilac light.

Indigo.

Panic seized his chest at the sight of her. What the hell was she doing?

Felix's gaze landed on the little witch, and he laughed, cruel and loud. "You care for witches now?"

No, she was a means to an end, but even as he opened his mouth to say as much, he couldn't. Something about the assertion wasn't entirely true.

"What? Too proud to admit it? I wonder, if she births your heir, will you have to kill the abomination yourself?"

Rage. One he had never felt before boiled his blood, but before he could lunge at Felix to shut him up, the other man whistled, alerting the nearby officers to their presence.

Indigo struck, sending a stream of purple magic into the enemy. Felix blew past Sebastian and into the trees surrounding the shore. Sebastian considered racing after him and ending him.

"Have you become a statue? Come on," Indigo shouted at him, panic apparent in the way she waved at him.

He raced to her side, finding that she had held one of the boats back, a frowning Vincent holding the helm. They should not have stayed so long. He could already hear the distant footfalls of marching officers gaining on their location and Felix's shouts in the distance.

Climbing aboard, he put a hand out behind himself, beckoning for Indigo to take it, but she promptly swatted it away.

Frustration had him grinding his teeth and growling.

"You can't possibly think you can still stay here. Felix knows your face. He will hunt you down."

"He will not find me," she said, stepping further onto the dock and away from his outstretched hand.

"Indigo."

"I will not wait a moment longer," Vincent announced, and the Khelitians around him pushed off from the dock, wading further out to sea. But if they left, Indigo would die. Maybe not today, but he wouldn't get back in time to rescue her. And that's if Felix didn't think she would make good bait.

There was something so incredibly wrong about leaving her behind. It made his insides twist.

No.

He jumped, rolling onto the dock at the last possible second. Vincent and the other men called out to him, but he ignored them, reaching for Indigo.

She whispered under her breath, the unnatural violet in her eyes brightening.

"Whatever you are doing can wait. We must leave." She ignored him like he wasn't there at all, keeping up her chant even as pistols and muskets fired, hitting around them, but she didn't flinch.

Did she even plan on surviving or was this an attempt to give them a head start?

"Indigo, we have to go now."

Her head snapped back, the final words spilling from her. Everything went silent as her eyes refocused, widening when she saw him standing there.

"Sebastian, what—"

"What did you do?"

The water moved on either side of them, and he dared to

glance over. The waves shifted until shadowy figures emerged. Even from here he could smell how foul they were.

Bodies of the dead, human and sea creatures alike crawled onto the shore, breathing in shallow, wet gasps of air. They passed by the dock as if it didn't exist as they clamored to the firing officers.

"The dead's only enemy is the living," Indigo rushed out, pushing Sebastian to the edge of the water, which seemed like an entirely bad idea.

"Do you wish me dead then, *witch*?"

Her eyes hardened before she materialized a length of rope around his waist and hers, tightening until they were close together.

"Not this time, *Commodore*."

His body jerked from the dock. Instinctively, he wrapped his arms around Indigo, holding her close as her hand orchestrated the rope to land them where she wished. They flew upwards, gunshots firing around them as the officers noticed, then towards Vincent's boat.

Blessedly, their aim was poor, and they missed entirely.

Sebastian's back collided with the deck in a painful splat. Luckily for her, he managed to cushion Indigo's fall. He searched her face, checking her for injury.

But Indigo's body wasn't moving.

"Indigo?" His fingers dove into her hair as he examined her face. She couldn't be dead. "Indigo!"

She whimpered. "No need to shout."

Relief swarmed him. He pulled her into an embrace. "Don't you dare do that again." It wasn't until she relaxed with him that he understood what he was doing. And who he was holding.

With a grunt, he lifted her off himself and onto her own two feet. Her own shocked expression reflected how he felt even if he tried to convince himself it had more to do with being shot at and magically flung across undead-infested waters than with their embrace.

Screams of agony reached them, and he noticed Indigo was looking to the shore. Sebastian rose to his feet. The necromites were too numerous. The officers didn't have a chance to defend themselves. He felt sick watching them. Some of them hadn't been freed from their mental prisons yet. And now, they'd never have the chance to pick a side.

Indigo shook beside him. "I didn't mean to summon so many." The screams died as abruptly as they started, but the silence that followed was more deafening. "Did I make it worse?"

As he watched Samsara disappear behind them, he wondered if there would be anything left to save.

CHAPTER 45

WHAT DREAMS MAY COME

ROSE

Sleep. Rose desperately needed to sleep, but with the ex-devil across the room, she didn't dare close her eyes. It was one thing to let him carry her limp body through the halls of a foreign palace when she could hardly move. It was another thing entirely to share a cell with the man who stole her away from everything she knew.

When he fought the guards in the palace halls, she swore he wouldn't survive, yet here he was, in her damn cell.

It was no coincidence. Colt and Dante had a reason to keep him alive, and if they decided to keep him in her cell while there were dozens of other cells he could have been dumped in, there was a reason for that too. Maybe it had to do with the fact that he had tried to help her. A fact she hadn't quite been able to work out yet.

Her eyes drooped, and it took tremendous effort to widen them.

"You can sleep. I'll wake you if one of those bastards shows his face."

She didn't answer, only stared.

Maybe it was ridiculous to hold on to this animosity, but it was difficult to find forgiveness in her heart when she hadn't managed to crawl out of the mess he'd made.

Jon sighed heavily. "I don't blame you for not trusting me, but I don't want to hurt you, even if I could." He held up his shackled wrists, a testament to his imprisonment.

It was a trick. It was the only explanation she could think of.

He'd done as asked by the demons. Why was he even imprisoned? What was he doing in one of the cells before or wandering around the palace, for that matter? Nothing made sense, but one question stood out amongst the rest.

A question poured from her mouth, "Why?" He set his hands down, a grim expression painting his face. "Why betray them?"

Jon's lips pursed as he touched the swelling around his left eye. "I didn't want to." He put an arm over his propped-up knee, getting comfortable. "When I first accepted the captain's offer, it was to keep an eye out for you. They knew he would eventually find you and I needed to be close enough to witness it." He cleared his throat. "And to bring you in." Rose felt her skin crawl.

"When I left with Phantom, it was only about the money. But as the years went by, I found a family in the crew I was meant to betray." He cupped a fistful of sand, letting the granules slip through his fingers.

"The last time I was in Draiocht, the royal family still held the crown. Some Draion cities had fallen, but the capitol still held strong. I hadn't considered what the *Imari* was capable of until I heard the royal family was dead. The same day, a hawk passed over me, dropping a red bandana at my feet. As I touched the fabric, I got a vision of my benefactors and the threat I would face if I failed."

"Your sister." Rose recalled what he had said before she lost consciousness. "You said you did it to save your sister."

He nodded grimly. "She was thirteen and living with our mother when I left Draiocht. I haven't seen her in three years. In the vision, they killed our mother and took Iris." Hysterical laughter left him as he ran a hand through his dark hair. "The worst part was that they had no intention of letting her go. I only bought her time."

Rose's resolve softened. She wasn't so inclined to hate him

when he was only protecting his sister. She couldn't imagine seeing her mother die horribly in a vision, unable to save her. Her mother's death had been terrible in its own way, but she hadn't been killed. Her heart had simply given out.

"I tried to deny that you were Davina's daughter at first. It wasn't until your nightmare that I knew for certain."

She sucked in a breath, having forgotten that he had witnessed her loss of control. Usually, she could contain the nightmares to her own mind, but something about being in James' arms or the fear of returning to her father made her control slip. It was so intimate, knowing someone could see what nightmares tormented her. Especially knowing most were memories from past lives.

Rose curled up on herself, pressing her knees tight to her chest.

"I'm sorry, for what it's worth."

She ignored his apology, not ready to forgive him. "What changed? You tried to save me."

He tugged against his hair. "I was looking for Iris. I need to get her out too. I thought I could get you both out, but I couldn't find her." He raised his shackle again. "I can't even get myself out."

Rose's eyelids drooped again, her vision growing hazy in the darkness of night surrounding them.

"Sleep, Rose. You need as much strength as you can get."

He was right, of course. If she couldn't eat, she needed to sleep.

She let her aching body relax, giving in to her exhaustion. It was cold, but she was too tired to care. She slipped into a deep slumber.

Falling. Rose was falling, wind whipping her hair around and the ground growing ever closer. She screamed, the air sucking the sound away from her. There was no one to save her, no hero in the air to snatch her before she hit the ground, no one.

No one to stop Ravana from slicing into her again. It was one night. Only one night to lay with an officer before he was broken and bruised on the stone floor. She reached for him, but Ravana laughed, the sound mixing with the whipping winds. Weightless death surrounded her on all sides as the priestess tore into her skin, forcing scars that she shouldn't have.

Scars she could have healed, and she tried to sing the song of healing that her mother taught her. She sang to him too, patching up the bruises and scratches on his skin.

He shouldn't be bleeding for her. She'd made the mistake of telling him what she could do and the torture Ravana inflicted upon her because of it. He'd tried to save her and now, he was paying the price.

"No, that won't do," Ravana hissed, reopening every healed slice like the smoothed-over skin offended her somehow. "If you heal again, I will just have to start over." Rose screamed into the wind, but the sound too choked to go anywhere. There was so much blood that it covered her skin, staining her clothing.

Ravana sliced through the officer's throat, blood pouring down his neck. Horror slammed through her at the knowledge that she had done that. If she had never encouraged his attention, he wouldn't be here. The light left his eyes, and she screamed again.

Of their own accord, her lips started moving, singing through her screams and her tears. It was a song she didn't remember, but it was instinctual, filling the surrounding wind until her own voice wrapped around her. It was like there were five of her singing at different intervals to overlap one another.

She was still falling, the images shifting around her of the fast-approaching ground and Ravana's twisted smile.

A voice that was not her own bled into the wind, calling her name.

"Singing still?" Ravana asked, excitement clear in her eyes. She wanted Rose to disobey. "I can fix that." The priestess seized her chin, cutting off the song. She forced Rose's lips to part until she could get ahold of her tongue. She fought against Ravana's hold, unwilling to let this happen. Without her tongue, she couldn't sing. She'd be more help-less than ever. There would be no stopping the final descent to the ground.

Ravana held firm, the metallic taste of blood coating her tongue from her dirty hand. With the gleam of victory in her eyes, she sliced through the flesh—

"Rose! Wake up!"

She sucked in a lungful of air as she bolted forward. Moving her tongue, she melted with relief at the full feel of it in her mouth. Nightmare. It was a nightmare. Ravana wasn't there, and she wasn't falling.

The horrified look on Jon's face echoed on her own when she watched the last remnants of her blue ribbons fade from the air. She had projected her nightmare for him to see. She closed her trembling hands into fists. There were enough people in her mind, the last thing she wanted was for him to see what had happened to her.

"Rose," he whispered, pity plain to see on his face. It was made worse by the utter weakness she felt in her bones. Her body used magic reserves she did not have, taking more energy away from her body. So much for sleep being a good thing.

"Is that what you went through at the Fortress?" He choked out. She didn't need his damn pity. Not answering him, she curled herself into the smallest ball she could. "I'm so sorry."

She huffed a laugh, but she was too raw, and the nightmare was too real. Her next breath was a sob, tears following in streams.

"You're sorry? Great, just what I needed to hear." Sarcasm lamely dripped from her tone but still hit its mark. Jon's shoulders slumped and his gaze cast downward. He'd only tried to save her because he felt guilty, and he'd happened to find her while he was looking for his sister.

"It doesn't change anything, does it? Knowing what I've been through? You still would save your sister. You don't have to explain." If the roles had been reversed, and it was him or Lara, she would have done the same.

The door opened then. If it was possible for Rose to shrink inside herself any further, she would have. Dante and Colt charged into the cell like a wild storm, fire lighting their eyes.

She expected that fury to land on her, but instead they stared at Jon like their gazes alone would obliterate him. Dante straightened, regaining some sense of his usual mask.

"We have been more than kind to you. How many acts of defiance did you think we would tolerate?"

Colt narrowed his eyes on Rose. He smiled, but it was the smile that belonged to Phantom. The rest of him followed suit before he was crouched down before her. She could see the differences more keenly now. James' recent memory helped her understand when even a freckle was out of place.

"Did you enjoy our time together, birdy?"

Her hands trembled and her tears were still drying, but she stared at him like she could cut him open with a glare.

The crack of a whip drew her eye to Jon who didn't so much as flinch with the fresh slice tearing down his chest.

"Jon!" His name was out before she could stop it. She may not have forgiven him, but she wasn't beyond wanting to see him hurt.

"Come to care, little birdy? Why don't we show him how we play?"

A shiver ran down her skin. His brand of torture was the last thing she wanted anyone to witness but denying him only made things worse.

When she didn't move, Colt stood to pull the lever on the wall. She could hear gears turning behind her and shuddered. There would be nightmares with that sound and what followed. It forced the shackles to move upwards, dragging her off her feet. She cried out with the pain, her hands still recovering from the fire and her arms aching with familiar agony.

"No! Leave her alone. I'm the traitor. She's done nothing wrong." Jon's pleading only encouraged her tears to fall faster.

Colt's fingers brushed across her bare arm, feather light and painless. He was only teasing her, a twisted game he liked to play.

"That's where you're wrong." Jon's horrified expression confirmed that he too saw Phantom's face on Colt. "All she has to do to be free of us is reunite the voices in her head. Then my life will no longer be tied to hers."

She wasn't sure if he was speaking as Phantom or himself when he said as much, but Jon's brows lowered, his expression turning livid.

"This is what you've been doing to her?"

Colt shrugged. "That, and this." He whirled, lifting her shirt and splaying his free hand over the hollow plane of her stomach. Excruciating pain ripped through her like he had punched his entire fist through her skin. Screaming filled her head as every counterpart inside her felt it too.

Not once in her life had it ever been this painful before.

Colt removed his hand, and she slumped, too exhausted to do anything else.

"Stop this. You don't achieve anything by killing her!"

The whip cracked again, and Rose flinched as another line of red spread across his chest.

Colt drew her attention back with a finger below her chin. Her breath came in uneven pants. "Why do you make me hurt you, love?" Rose blinked a few times, her mind too addled to understand.

His finger traveled down her neck, making her skin pebble as small shocks sparked against her. It awakened her nerves, setting her on edge and using the last reserves of her energy.

Deep blue eyes, like the sea during a storm. She'd fallen in love with those eyes, with the man they belonged to. A hero who called himself a villain.

Pain shocked her senses as his fingers drifted across her collarbone. "I don't want to do this. I'd rather bring you pleasure than pain, but you won't listen. Give in to the voices, Rose. Then it will all be over. No more pain. We can finally be together." His head landed on hers, like it had on that throne where he'd held her.

Rose closed her eyes, soaking in his closeness and wondering why she was even resisting. It was Phantom. The man who freed her. She would do anything for him.

"Rose! It's not him!" The whip cracked. "Don't let them fool you!" Another crack followed by a pained wail. "It's not him, Rose! He would never hurt y—" The cracks grew more frequent, as did the screams.

Everything in her mind was quiet, but she could hear Jon. Hear him taking the lashes just to get through to her.

And—

He was right. James would never hurt her.

Pulling on her chains, she reared back before slamming her forehead into his nose. Colt jolted away, his facade melting away until the face she detested reemerged. The pain in her head was nothing compared to the satisfaction she felt at seeing him bleed. It gushed down his nose, dripping along his chest.

"Fine. You want to play dirty?" He charged up to her, seizing her chin. "Let's play."

Blinding pain blocked out anything else until she fell into darkness.

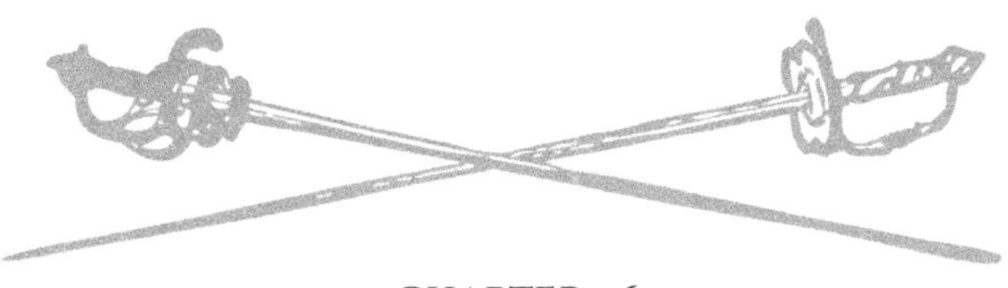

CHAPTER 46

PAINT IT

BLACK

Black tossed on her cot at the barracks. Sophia was in the ship's brig, and she was supposed to stay in the city. In some ways, it was a blessing. Betrayal ran hot in her blood when she thought of all the moments she'd shared with Sophia and not once was she privy to the most important aspect of Sophia's life.

A true immortal. Sophia was an actual immortal. Albeit a young one considering they're meant to have their lives extended for centuries but no less important.

Unless Sophia was a lot older than she'd admitted to.

Black rubbed at her face, then ran her fingers through her hair like she could expel the racing thoughts that way.

She had a lot of questions for her huntress. Mainly, what did that mean for them? Did immortals even have lovers? Was there some kind of rule she was missing?

Black growled low in her throat before tossing the scratchy blanket off of her. She couldn't sit there and stew in her thoughts any longer. She needed her feet moving. If she could clear her head, maybe she could wear herself out enough to sleep.

Grabbing her sword, pistol, and every other weapon she could stash on herself, she walked out into the silver moonlight. She glared up at the moon, not sure if she should be thanking the Goddess or cursing Her.

Instead, she stalked out into the thick darkness of night.

There was no plan or reason for where she was going, but some instinct told her that she needed to be in the tunnels. Trepidation electrified her blood, making her vigilant as she ducked into the familiar darkness of the tunnels. After lighting a torch, she walked through quietly.

Uncertain of what she was looking for, she followed the same path Dalilah and Aya showed her. Maybe she could check on them while she was down here. If she found any more slavers, disposing of them wouldn't hurt either.

Both kept her mind off—

Nope, not going to think about her.

It wasn't until she got to the entrance to the shelter that she realized there was no guard keeping watch. Odd, it seemed like there was always one who remained through all hours of the day.

A dark spot on the wall drew her attention, but when she moved her torch across the sandstone, it turned bright red.

Black's eyes widened before she drew her sword, ready for a fight. She moved the torch down to find the guard crumpled on the steps of the entrance, his eyes open and unseeing. Fear punched her gut as she stared at the corpse before her.

Aya. Dalilah.

Panic seized her breath as she jumped past the guard to the door. Having enough sense to not charge through, she put an ear to the door.

Nothing. Not a single sound.

She opened the door a fraction to peer inside, but it was too dark to see. It was unlikely someone knew to wait for her in the dark since she didn't even know she was coming here, so she pushed the door open.

Then she wished she had stayed in bed.

Bodies lay *everywhere*.

There had obviously been some battle that was heavily stacked against the women and children here. The only men present were too old to fight. This was a shelter, for goddess-sake. These weren't soldiers or fighters of any kind. There were people trying to crawl out of their misfortune.

Now, they were dead.

Black felt numb as she searched their faces, looking for two in particular. It wasn't long before she found Almu, her throat sliced open and her eyes glassy. Still, Black felt nothing. No, she held onto the nothingness with a death grip, willing this to all be some nightmare she had to endure.

Until she reached the back of the room, where small bodies were huddled in a pile of red. There, Aya and Dalilah lay with their little hands clasped together and their stomachs slashed open.

Her knees hit the sandy ground, followed by the soft clamor of her sword. A sob, raw and ragged, tore its way from the bottom of her throat. She'd never felt agony like she did at that moment. Everything she had ever felt came with every sob that forced itself through her carefully constructed walls.

This was unfair. Completely and utterly unfair. These were two little girls that did not deserve this. The world was cruel and unyielding to allow this. Davina was cruel.

She screamed her anguish to the unrepentant sky. There was no seeing it through the shelter's ceiling, but she knew Davina heard her.

It was then she noticed the words written in blood above her head.

BLACK SHADOWS SHOULD STAY IN DARKNESS WHERE THEY BELONG

Devastating, crushing, all-consuming guilt hit her in the chest harder than any bullet could manage.

Black Shadow was written. Not *Shuyet.* This was about more than two girls in a distant country. All the work she did as the Black Shadow in Samsara hadn't gone unnoticed. The slavers knew exactly who she was.

They were all dead because of her. She tried to save them, the two little girls she saw in the streets. But the slavers would have brought them suffering, not death. They came back and killed perfectly good able-bodied woman and children because she dared to stand up to them?

There was a message beneath the one written in Brettanian. At first, she thought it was a translation to Draion, but her eyes caught on a word. *Shuyet.*

Dante spoke with the slavers about the *Shuyet*, the Black Shadow, her. The slavers weren't acting alone. This was a political message. She didn't have to know Draion to understand it. Anyone who helps them will meet the same fate.

Anger solidified into resolve as her eyes fell back to the broken bodies of the little girls she met in the tunnels.

She had a message of her own to deliver.

The sun had risen by the time Black heard the telltale sound of metal against metal. The forge of a blacksmith lay beyond the door she opened. The slavers couldn't have gone far since the blood had not yet dried, so she followed the trail.

A little voice in the back of her head reminded her to ask questions, but she ignored it. That was the thinking that got her into this mess. There could be no acceptable explanation for killing those innocent girls.

"Everything ready?" The sniveling one asked.

The brute answered, "Oh yes, the ship is ready, and the cargo is secure."

"Good, I want to get out of here before *Shuyet* finds us."

His friend scoffed. "You don't believe the rumors, do ya? No spirit is after us."

"You heard the captain, legend might be wrong, but the Black Shadow took down dozens of men in Samsara."

Black closed her eyes briefly. She hoped it wasn't true, but if they knew who the Black Shadow was, those deaths were on her head.

"In *Samsara*," he stressed. "Here, she can't touch us. Let's get off this *goddess-forsaken* rock."

Over my dead body.

Not bothering with stealth or subtlety, she pushed open the door.

Regardless of bravado, they both turned sheet white when she entered the room. These were the men who'd slaughtered dozens of innocents to prove a damn point.

"Who else?"

"W-w-what?"

"I don't believe you two alone could have done it. So, who else?"

A bullet answered her question as it shot from across the forge, hitting the wall behind her. Apparently, they didn't have good enough aim. Slavers crawled out of the edges of the room, focusing their attention on her.

The two she met before relaxed when their friends arrived.

"Ha! That's right, *Shuyet*! You die now."

Five opponents. She'd had worse odds.

Before she could lift a weapon, two came from behind her, pinning her to the dusty worktable before the hearth. She grunted as they held her arms back.

One hollered behind her. "We got ourselves a catch, boys!" He shoved a hairy arm before her, showing off a slaver's brand that was burned into his skin. The angry red skin was raised with the symbol of a whip and a sword crossed over each other. "Like it? You'll be wearing one just like it, little lady."

She bucked and kicked, trying to get them off of her.

"Ah ah ah. Get the iron!" They moved around her, obeying the order. "Filthy pirate. Think you can impede on our territory?"

She fought them but failed to gain proper leverage with her hands behind her. The one to her right seized her arm, pulling the sleeve back before displaying her wrist.

"Captain wants his brand on you. You'll be one of us, he says."

The brute she met before had malice sparkling in his eyes as he approached her with a heated iron, the image on the end a mirror of the slaver's mark. As it pressed to her skin, she bit her tongue to keep from screaming as her flesh melted beneath it.

"Come on, girl. Give us a scream."

Her head snapped back, hitting one slaver in the nose and

making him lose his grip. She turned to the man who'd been talking, a dazed look painting his weathered features.

"Let's hear one from you!" Her knee came up between his legs hard enough to crush bone. He screamed in agony before she palmed her pistol.

Black shot one slaver between the eyes before he could fully unsheathe his sword. The remaining four pounced on her all at once. It made things complicated, but not impossible.

She let the anger boil her blood and focus her mind. It was that same emotion she had been blocking, the one that came from the captain. But now, it only fueled her own fury and strength.

Her movements were faster than ever, her strength unheard of as she flung a man across the room from the blade of her sword. She couldn't think about it past the raging in her head. She wanted them dead. Every one of them.

Soon, only two stood alone. She saved them for last.

She returned to the one who had pinned her down; he was still on his knees, clutching his crotch. He pleaded for his life, but she didn't hear any of it until he dared to taunt her.

"You're one of us now," he rasped. "That's right, little lady, you belong to–" She shot him through the skull before he could finish that sentence. She didn't care what he had to say. She belonged to no one.

Whirling on the last two, she backed them against a wall. The same two she first met. With a pistol against the head of one and a blade against the neck of the other, she took in their fear. They were trembling, and their whimpering pleas landed on deaf ears.

"One of you will live." Hope lit their eyes, then they looked at each other. "Take a message back to your captain and to the *Imari*. They have a debt to pay in blood. I will be the one to plunge my sword into their hearts and watch the light leave their eyes. Tell them the Black Shadow is coming for them."

When neither responded, she shot her pistol through the skull of the sniveling one. He screamed as he died, blood pouring from the wound. She pulled a bandana from his shirt pocket before he fell.

Usually, she would leave the weaker one alive, but the brute didn't believe she would come for them. Now he knew better.

"Do you believe in the *Shuyet* now?"

She didn't answer, but his pale face spoke volumes. She displayed unnatural speed and strength. To a small-minded slaver, she was a dark spirit.

He practically tripped over his own feet to get away from her.

As he left, she wrapped the navy blue bandana around her newly branded flesh.

CHAPTER 47

CROWNING SCARAB

PHANTOM

The next day, Phantom brought the devils beyond the citadel to search the dunes two miles northeast. Black had returned while they prepared to leave, her eyes were dark but not just from lack of sleep. He suspected his eyes looked much the same.

He tossed in his cot all night, keeping Serena awake. He wanted to scour the sands for his songbird, but with the tattoo still on his palm, it was too much of a risk. The bloody thing didn't fade from his skin until the sun rose high above the horizon line.

Black reported what had transpired after the rest of them had fallen asleep. Slavers were getting involved in their affairs now. They had overstayed their welcome. No more waiting for answers. No more delays.

It was time to get Rose and set sail.

They'd found a large stone building in the middle of the desert sands. Presumably, Rose was inside. It was the hundreds of necromites that surrounded it that posed a problem.

After a couple hours of cutting them down and hardly making a dent in the massive horde, he had made the decision that they needed more men. The devils might eventually be able to take out the horde, but at the progress they were making, it would take too long. He stepped back from the fight, pulling out the dark blue scarab and staring at its glistening quality.

He called to his first mate. "Earhart!"

Earhart jogged back to his captain, black blood covering his shirt and pants. His eyes flicked to the scarab. "It's time the princess got her country back. I'll bring back enough men to cut through the horde."

Earhart nodded before returning to the melee, cutting down the walking corpses one by one.

Phantom turned back to the city. He needed to pay a visit to a princess.

The priests attempted to stop Phantom at the door, likely sensing the restless energy he carried. They moved when the shadows thickened around them. Holy men of dead deities could hardly stop him.

He pushed the doors open to find Sitamun at the altar of Rán, bowing reverently. Her beastly guards stood in his path before he could take another step. These ones were less threatened by his darkness, but he could see how their eyes shifted as the shadows curled around them.

Phantom didn't let them feast, though. He needed men like this on the sands, plowing through necromites.

"I hear you've sworn fealty to my enemies." The princess continued to stare at the altar instead of looking at him. "It's a wonder you would even show your face here."

He balled his hand into a fist, a memory of last night's disaster flashing through his head.

"I have no loyalty to the *Imari*. They forced my hand."

She laughed under her breath before turning to face him. "Does your word mean nothing?"

He growled; a lion's growl that made the guards before him tense. "Not when the choice is taken from me. If I were a loyal to the *Imari*, you would already be dead." He used the shadows to mark his point, but her gaze didn't waver even if her guards closed in around her.

"What do you want, *Maahes*?"

He didn't need to prove himself to her. Not when what she wanted was sitting in his pocket. He closed his hand around it.

"I have a gift for the new *Queen*."

Phantom hurled the blue and violet scarab at Sitamun. One of her men caught it before it could find permanent residence in her face.

"What is the meaning of this?" Sita said, standing to her full height and stepping across the alabaster floors.

The guard opened his hand, presenting the glistening scarab to her. She sucked in a breath of delight, looking down at the little object that was meant to simultaneously change her life and save her people.

"I expect you will take the throne. My love is trapped in a building two miles northeast of here, surrounded by an army of the dead. I expect you to offer your men to help me get her."

She smiled as she reached for the scarab. "Only if that means you will leave with her immediately. I don't need the unrest you inspire." The moment her skin connected with the scarab, gold rippled across the metal. It glowed so brightly it mimicked the sun and the shrine to the sun god behind her. The beetle came to life, stretching its wings, and flying from the guard's hand.

It circled the air, cutting through his shadows and lingering before Phantom long enough to make the princess squirm. Like it was choosing its host and the next ruler. It never occurred to him that he would even be considered. Then it flew to Sitamun, driving into her chest and burrowing beneath her skin. The act looked painful, but it was only pure bliss upon her face.

Everyone watched, the priests around them chanting softly as they witnessing a divine crowning.

Gold swirls erupted across her skin, like an invisible hand was painting her. The image of the scarab appeared at the base of her neck, taking up enough of her chest that it could partially be seen at the top swells of her breasts. The beetle pulsated on her skin like the design was living on her chest.

It occurred to him that all her dresses were designed to show this work of art. He assumed it was to show her cleavage, but this was about power. It was a crown given to her by Rán himself, even if the god no longer existed.

She breathed heavily, sinking into her new position, but it wasn't quite true. She still needed to take her people back.

Her eyes opened with swirls of gold that reminded him of his songbird.

"Once the palace is secure, I will send my men."

It was then that he felt it. The shadows drew around him excitedly.

we seeeeee her

CHAPTER 48

THE SKY RAINS FIRE

ROSE

Rose awoke with an ache in her belly and a throbbing in her head.

Dante and Colt had bled her dry of all the energy she possessed. Every time she'd passed out from the pain, Dante would rouse her mind enough to feel the torment, even if her body could no longer move.

She was more surprised that she wasn't dead, but part of that she attributed to the man sharing her cell.

He was broken and bloody, but still breathing. Every time they woke her, she could hear him shouting at her to hold on.

"This is not the end!"

"He will come for you!"

"You're strong, Rose. You can survive this."

They were lies. Beautiful and wonderful but lies all the same.

Cain was allowed in to shut him up, but she let his words run in her head on repeat. *This is not the end. He will come for you. You're strong.* Over and over again, she repeated the phrases like they were the life threads holding her here on earth. She didn't hear Colt's taunting or Dante's frustration, or even Cain's maniacal laughter. She only heard Jon's voice.

Sobs tore from her throat even if her eyes were too dry to cry.

It roused Jon. He stirred with a pained moan before setting his sights on her.

"Rose, you're alive. Thank Davina."

Rose felt more like she was forsaken by the Goddess. Her real mother would never have allowed this.

"Please say something to me," Jon begged.

"This happens to me in every lifetime. I suffer and die." It was the only thing she could think to say, but it was to the sky that she asked, "When does it end?"

The unrelenting sun had no answer for her. There was no silver light to scream her frustration at. Maybe she should die, let them try again in the next life.

"Rose," Jon said, his tone showing that it was not the first time he'd said her name. "Listen to me." She turned her eyes to him, and he breathed a sigh of relief. "You will not die. Not here. You cannot let them win."

"If I die—"

"They. Win. Don't you see that? They are only tormenting you."

She sucked in a shallow breath. There was truth in his statement, even though he didn't understand. They had stopped trying to help her assimilate with Skye. Now, they were inflicting the most pain they could.

"They've given up," she whispered. They'd rather wait for the next reincarnation and try again. Then why not just kill her? In any case, death could not bring her peace, only delay them awhile.

"That's it," he said. "You can't let them win. We can get out of here, together."

Somewhere inside her, there was anger for what he did, even if it was in service to his sister, but she couldn't feel it now. He was the only thing keeping her from giving up entirely.

"We will," she whispered, not completely believing it but feeling a little better when he smiled at her words. She could tell it hurt him to do so, but he smiled for the same reason she'd agreed. Hope. They needed all the hope they could get.

The door swung open, and Rose flinched, knowing that pain would follow.

Jon stared up at their captors, scowling through his injuries.

For once, Colt and Dante paid no attention to her, only focusing their energy on Jon. "I'll have you know, you brought this upon yourself."

Rose's bones ached with fear, but for once, it wasn't for her.

"Leave him alone," she croaked out, her voice raspy when she tried to raise it.

They all ignored her.

Cain shuffled into the room, his hand seizing the arm of a girl no older than fifteen. She had dark skin and curly brown hair that bounced with her every step.

Iris.

She struggled against his hold, but a smile curved his face. He was enjoying this, the sick bastard.

"This could have been so easy for you, Jonny boy." Colt grinned widely. "All you had to do was wait patiently. Instead, here you are, messing with our calculated work."

"Don't hurt her. She has done nothing wrong."

"Come now." Colt grabbed a fistful of her hair before pulling it back. She cried out with his rough treatment. "You know that doesn't matter. She was only here to motivate you."

"Unfortunately, we no longer desire to motivate you."

Colt ran a blade beneath her chin, cutting deep.

"No!" Jon screamed as blood poured from Iris's wound. Rose snapped her eyes closed, but she would never forget the sounds. The gurgle and choking sounded more like she was drowning, followed by a thud as her body hit the ground. Jon continued screaming, cursing the demons who had taken his family from him.

She felt his pain, down to her bones. It made her want to scream.

"Monsters!" It was the only thing she could manage to say.

"Are we?" Dante's curious gaze landed on her, but then she noticed the simmering rage that lay just beneath his eyes. "Count yourself lucky that you must die to live again. That you don't have eternity to live while you lose everyone that ever mattered to you. That your loved one is reborn with you." She'd never seen him show such emotion before. Dante was always so stoic, so unaffected that she shivered at seeing this side of him. "Once you see true eternity, we'll see what kind of monster you become."

He turned away from her, refocusing on Jon. "Though, I suspect, we shall see much sooner than that."

Dante held his hand over the sobbing mess that used to be one of the Eleven Devils and Jon screamed.

It was a painful scream that was louder than she'd ever heard before, speaking of unimaginable pain. When Dante flipped through her mind like it was his personal reading material, it didn't hurt so much. Pain was Colt's specialty.

But this? This was something Colt's shocks could not produce.

Blood poured from his mouth, his nose, his ears and even eyes as he screamed. It lasted for what felt like hours as she screamed and cried, begging them to stop. No offer. No promise of obedience or success would make them stop. Dante had a point to prove and nothing could save Jon now.

He still screamed as his body was lifted into the air, Colt's chanting drawing his body up from the ground.

Jon's head moved abruptly, followed by silence as his screams cut off. Then he fell to the ground in a heap of flesh.

Rose stared at his body, too shocked to move. He was gone. Just like that.

"Perhaps now, you can understand."

Dante and Colt left with Cain snickering behind them. When that door closed, she was left alone with only silence and an aching heart.

***

The hunger pangs were so familiar that Rose found solace in their presence, reminding her that she was still alive and hadn't shriveled away into nothing.

Jon and Iris were left to rot in her cell. Night had not yet come, so she had to assume it was the same day. She could have fooled herself into believing that they were only sleeping, if not for the blood covering them both. Blood that had since dried and darkened on their skin.

It was because of her that they were dead. She knew that as starkly as she knew she was about to die. Death was in sight, and she wondered what would be so bad about taking death's hand in hers. She would see James again in the next life and her suffering here would be over.

Don't let them win.

But she thought of a way around that. She could sing one last time. Let the magic take too much from her body until she melted away into nothing. She already knew what song she would sing.

Rose rested a hand against her chest where the necklace usually sat. The song of peace that always calmed her anxiety and spirit. She could think of much worse ways to die.

She opened her mouth to sing when she noticed the shadows around her growing darker. There was no fear, no threat of death, only darkness reaching a hand out for her. As she listened, she could hear them speak, but it sounded no different from the whistling of the wind. She couldn't make sense of it.

Until—*rossssse*

She drew in a short gasp.

tresssssora

Tears of relief pricked her eyes. James. It was him. The real him. She could feel his presence.

ssssssurvive

I am clossssssse

pleassssssse rossssssse

It was the please that stopped her breath. He was begging her to survive. He didn't want to wait for the next life and the new horrors there. James wanted this life with her, and every broken shard left of her.

A new surge of energy zinged to life inside her, like it was waiting for this very moment to emerge. Finding the hidden nail she had stashed beneath the sand; she pried at her shackles.

The shadows curled around her in encouragement as James' distorted voice whispered to her.

I am coming sssssssoon

Her shackles opened and she let them drop to the sand.

"What's going on in there?" Cain poked his head up through

the window, his eyes widening when he saw her standing in the middle of the cell, free of restraints.

He opened the door, surprise lighting his features. "You're supposed to be chained up!" A glint of sadism flashed in his eyes as he smiled, pulling a knife from his belt. "Guess I'll have to get my hands dirty." Stalking close, he licked his lips. "I'm sure they wouldn't notice if I had a taste."

He lunged, and she dodged, but he didn't look at the shadows close enough. They pounced on him, pouring into his mouth and cutting off his air. They held him long enough for her to pry the knife from his chubby fingers and bury the blade in his chest.

He roared in pain. Regrettably, she missed his heart, but she was too weak to pull it free to try again, so she left him to crumple to the sand. He couldn't follow and the door was wide open for her.

"Don't you leave me here, bitch!"

She shut the door on him, sliding the lock in place. Hopefully, the world would forget about him, and he would die next to Jon and Iris.

Cain screamed at her as she walked down the halls, more profanities that fell on deaf ears. Her skin buzzed with anticipation, a part of her understanding that this was the end. There were no second chances. She either escaped or died trying, and she needed to fly.

A deep-rooted survival instinct surfaced, blocking out all other thoughts.

Skye was here, looking through her eyes. She'd never felt closer to the counterpart than she did right now.

Rose picked her bare feet up into a run, dashing to the exit, but as her feet hit stone and sand, she faced inward, searching for the girl who died too young. She followed the scent of saffron, honey, and cinnamon.

She wasn't certain who controlled her body, but someone was keeping her feet moving as she dug into her mind. Finally, she found a candle, singularly lit in the darkness.

Skye stood there, covered in bright red robes, silks draping and hugging her body, her brown wings spread out behind her. She put a hand to Rose's face.

"*It is time.*"

Cool metal laid against Rose's palm. It was the same dagger James had given her on his ship. Though only a mind's trick, she felt a pang of longing for her pirate.

Skye reached for the blade, placing the tip against her lower stomach, a plea in her eyes. "*End this. I can no longer take it.*" She pushed against Rose's hand, blood seeping from her. "*I'm begging you.*"

"*I'm sorry,*" Rose whispered before stabbing Skye deep in her gut. Her wings twitched behind her as her mouth fell open. Tears, unbidden, fell from Rose's cheeks as she felt a part of herself die with Skye. That childlike innocence. The belief that people should be given the benefit of the doubt. All that naivety died too.

As Skye fell to the ground at her feet, Rose mourned for the girl even as she became her.

She snapped her eyes open, her feet still running as fast as her frail legs could take her, but the entrance would come soon, and she couldn't afford to try this again. She could feel her energy draining already, too weak to do much more than a final push.

Her back burned as something clawed its way to the surface. Through fire and ash, her wings spread out behind her, the tips grazing the stone walls beside her.

Rose let them extend as far as they needed to catch the air she was rushing past, wincing at the scrapes caused by the stone. Sunlight signaled the end of the hall. Just as she reached the front room, she lifted from the ground, soaring over the door and through the hole above it.

Wind rushed around her face, making the loose strands of her hair whip around her, but she felt none of it. Not the heat on her back. Or the fear that should claim her from the half-dead beasts scrambling below her.

She was too low, their decaying hands reaching out to take hold of her and drag her to the ground. But she would not fall.

Though she had one foot in her next life, she refused to succumb to it. To not let death have her, but as she thought it, her eyelids grew heavy, exhaustion taking its toll. She was not free of the horde yet and she couldn't rest until she was safe. Otherwise, she would die, or those demons would find her again, and she'd prefer the snapping jaws below her before that.

The choice was slipping out of her hands as her limbs grew heavier, the muscles of her back straining to keep her wings unfurled. She couldn't do it. The end was too far away, and her strength was failing her.

Turn!

Green flickered in her vision. Isabeya was trying to speak to her, but her magic reserves were so dry and desolate that her voice came in sputters.

Shi — shift!

Hadn't she? She had wings. She finally killed Skye and ended her misery. Was there more than wings?

You — ar — phoenix — now rise!

Pain. Her flesh burned like she had dived into a flaming pit, the heat consuming her completely. It charred all her thoughts, her desires, and humanity, leaving only the baser instincts of an animal.

A bird.

A songbird.

We sang. A call only the Phoenix could make, drifting over sand dunes and walls to reach the ears of the only being in existence who would recognize it.

We were dying, but we sang, filling the sky with a call so potent, the world stopped spinning to listen.

And a roar answered.

CHAPTER 49
ALL'S FAIR IN LOVE & WAR
PHANTOM

Phantom was running onto the dunes when he heard her call.

It was a beautiful sound that carried through the winds like a siren's call, but he'd felt it more than heard it. He knew it was her, and that she needed him, more than ever. It was only after a few more minutes of running through the dunes when he spotted her flying form.

She was breathtaking. A large bird with red, brown, white, and orange feathers with flames flowing out behind her. The glint of firelight shone across her body, singeing those feathers like her own nature contradicted itself.

Flying directly over the horde, she veered right, towards an empty patch of sand.

She called again, and he picked up his pace, vaguely aware of the crew following him. A look back confirmed that Earhart had Smith on his back, running with the doctor faster than he could manage on his own.

Rose would need him. He felt the song in his bones. She was dying and calling out to him as a last resort. After he saw her on that dais, he feared what more they could have taken from her.

As he approached, one last call of desperation left her beak as she fell into the sands, the fire burning the rest of her wings.

He ran faster than he thought possible as he watched her return to her human form, rolling down a sand dune as the flames extinguished.

"Rose!"

Jumping down the dune, he shed his coat, catching her in it before she fell too far. He held her close to his body. She was warm, but his arms wrapped too easily around her frail frame. Pulling back, he inspected her. There wasn't a scrap of clothing left on her, baring all that was left of her.

She looked like a skeleton with a layer of skin. He could count every misshapen rib, her pronounced cheekbones, and even the outline of her eye-sockets. The joints of her shoulders were clearly visible along with her hip bones and knees. She looked closer to death than the necromites wandering the sands.

The breath in Phantom's lungs caught, coming in ragged pants as the panic took hold. She wasn't moving and her eyes were closed.

"Smith!" He commanded with so much fervor that the rest of the crew scrambled to get the doctor to him. In the meantime, Phantom felt for a pulse, just needing to feel the beat of her heart. It was there, but it was so very faint.

"I need Smith, *now!*"

Earhart dropped the doctor to Phantom's side, and he went straight to work, feeling the pulse that Phantom had found. The doctor closed his eyes reverently, but he didn't need to say it. He knew what someone who was dying looked like.

Smith put a heavy hand on Phantom's shoulder. "I'm sorry. She is halfway gone already." A tear fell down Phantom's face. He knew it. How could someone who had suffered so greatly come back? "I'd say it's only sheer force of will that she remains with us still."

Yellow that was reminiscent of the surrounding sunlight flared in his vision.

Force of will?

Phantom's brows furrowed, reminding him of another time her will had saved her. When she refused to believe that his beast would harm her. When she found the exact song that would relieve his soul.

"That's it," he whispered as he focused in on Rose, praying to any goddess who would listen that she could hear him. "Love, I need you to listen to me. I need you to sing."

"Captain," Smith interrupted. Phantom would have bitten his head off if Rose didn't need him. "Her magic is depleted. Any further push will send her into death's arms."

"I can see the state of her body, Smith, but leave the state of her magic to my judgement," he snapped. This was the only chance she had. If he did nothing, she would die, but there was a small chance this would work.

"Rose. Sing the song that takes my magic. Take as much as you can." When she didn't respond, he put a hand to her face, angling her head up. "Rose, listen to me. Don't leave me. Sing and I can save you." She didn't respond. "Sing, dammit!"

Another silent beat followed.

Then she took a breath.

MY SOUL SHALL TAKE WHAT IT CAN

Her soft voice filled the surrounding air even if her eyes never opened, as if the song was some instinct rather than a decision, taking what he had to offer. Blue ribbons swirled around him, then buried into his chest, stealing his magic and breath with a clawing desperation.

"That's it, love. Take it all."

I CONTROL THE HUNGER IN THE MAN

With a sickening twist to his gut, he realized how low his own power reserves were. He had been frugal when it came to taking life as of late, not wanting to give the *Imari* a reason to punish Rose for his insolence. Now, he wished he had. He would have enough to pay for her life.

FREE THE BEAST BY STEALING THE FEAST

She sucked the last of it away, but nothing changed. Her face was still sallow, and her chest still rose weakly.

"Rose? Please tell me that was enough. Rose?"

"Captain?" Russet called. "We got company." Phantom ignored him, focusing on every breath that filled her lungs.

Smith inspected her again. He shook his head. "No change. The power she gained from you was easily used by the song she sang to claim it. If you have no more to give—" He didn't see fit to finish that sentence, whatever he saw on his captain's face kept him silent.

Phantom cursed himself and his own powers. Here he was completely drained with no effect to himself other than powerlessness. Yet, when her power was drained, it affected her survival. How could he have allowed her to get this far?

"Captain! They are already upon us!"

Finally, he deigned to look at the new threat approaching them. Guards, ones from the palace. The *Imari* must have sent them out once they noticed Rose's escape. The princess wouldn't have taken the palace so soon. He'd only just left her, which meant these men had chosen the *Imari* over their own people.

And now, they would pay for it.

Phantom rose from the sand, pulling his pistol out first. He reached for his shadows, but they could not attack in such bright conditions. Not to mention is depleted power, a weakness he intended to destroy.

Earhart flinched beside him as a shot rang out, felling the first guard running at them. Phantom felt magic fill his veins as the shadows delivered the soul to Nemain.

"Rose, I need you to sing again," he called while refocusing his pistol on the next target. His crew stood dumbfounded, watching as their captain killed one guard after the other, nothing but determination driving him.

Rose's song started again, her voice breathy and unstable.

MY SOUL SHALL TAKE WHAT IT CAN

Six shots were taken before his pistol was empty, Rose's blue ribbons attaching to his chest again. He holstered the gun, and Earhart took his own pistol, aiming it at the next approaching guard.

"No," Phantom commanded with a hand on the top of his barrel. "The magic is diluted when any of you take the life. It needs to be me." He pulled the sword from its sheath, walking to meet the guards still running for them.

I CONTROL THE HUNGER IN THE MAN

Phantom slew the first, the guard dropping to his knees before falling face first into the sand. It was curious how death looked straight at them, and they did not cower. Some influence of the demons they follow, no doubt.

"Hold them," Phantom commanded, allowing a bit of his power to be used for this while the rest was funneled to Rose.

The devils responded, blue glinting in their eyes as they attacked the guards, taking two to one just so they could seize one without killing him. It was an unfair advantage, but Phantom cared little for the rules of combat.

Rose was dying. This was war. All was fair.

FREE THE BEAST BY STEALING THE FEAST

He heard her breathe in deeply behind him as his sword spilled the entrails of the next guard. Her song wavered, but he could feel the significant amount of power she had taken. It might have been enough to save her, but he wasn't taking any chances.

"Keep singing, songbird!"

She obeyed, a new verse emerging from her like it was buried inside her soul.

FILL MY LIFE WITH THE POWER OF LOVE YOU POSSESS

The new words filled him with fervor, feeling them in his heart and fueling his every move as he cut through the ranks of guards like weeds in a garden. Blood sprayed against his face, dousing his black shirt in the metallic smell.

"Captain? We got necromites on our flank." Smith's voice rang over the others, the only one Phantom did not want to aid in the fight. He had to be at Rose's side, but he couldn't hold a horde of necromites at bay.

UNTIL MY FLESH NO LONGER HOLDS THE SCENT OF DEATH

Phantom flinched at the new words to the song, feeling how they related to their situation. It was curious how her songs worked, but he didn't question it. His own magic scratched at him, seemingly frustrated at losing power as fast as it was acquired. Or, perhaps it was Nemain, simultaneously rejoicing in the fresh blood and loathing that it served to revive Her enemy's daughter.

HERE, THERE IS NO MORE FEAR.

Only five more guards approached, still no hesitance in their gazes. Phantom had lost count of how many had fallen. The blood on his hands felt too right for him to regret it. He slew them all. Every guard found their last breaths at the end of his blade. A rush of magic filled his veins, too much passing through him and not enough filling him, but he finally noticed that the ribbons were gone, and the songbird had ceased singing.

"Captain," Earhart said gently.

Phantom met the eyes of his first mate, who then looked at the woman in the sand. She was covered by the coat Phantom had given her, but the hollows of her cheeks had rounded slightly. Her eye-sockets were no longer visible. Even a touch of color had returned to her cheeks, but her eyes had not yet opened.

He wasn't sure why he'd expected her to wake up after everything. It would be some confirmation that she was alive and well.

When his gaze turned to the doctor, Smith's face held a tinge of fear. "She will live, but she needs rest and food."

Phantom nodded, walking back to his *tresora*. He picked her up in his arms, holding her sleeping form close to his chest.

"Prepare to return to the ship. We set sail when Davina's moon is high."

The devils collectively nodded, walking in the direction of the docks. He followed behind, staring down at Rose's face, disbelieving that he finally had her back and praying she would forgive him for what he had to do to save her life.

CHAPTER 50
THE GREAT LEVELER
PHANTOM

As the sun dipped below the horizon, the sky exploded with vibrant reds and pinks, casting a warm glow on the landscape. The clouds surrounding the dying light imitated a Nemain moon, reminding Phantom of the blood he'd just spilled.

"A bad omen," Ramirez supplied, smoking his pipe on the quarterdeck as Phantom tried not to think about the girl sleeping in his bed.

The devils were preparing the ship to leave. Sitamun's men finally arrived, but since they were too late, Phantom demanded provisions for the trip. He cared little about a deprived city when his songbird was starving.

"When the sun looks more like the death moon, blood will spill throughout the night," he continued to recite. An old Kalonite wise tale.

"Let's hope it's not blood of our own." It was all Phantom could think to say with the gnawing sense of worry eating away at him. Rose was not well. Not even close. He saw the evidence of it, but feeling the power still lingering in his veins rotted his stomach. A power that was essential to her, a vital necessity, but it remained firmly in his grasp.

She needed to sleep, not sing, but how could he stand here watching sunsets while she suffered?

"It's not your fault," Ramirez whispered, as if that somehow cured his paralyzing thoughts.

Phantom laughed, the sound hollow and breathy. He spread his arms. "Is it not?"

"Those demons found you. They sent their assassin to join your crew to locate her. Had you any knowledge of that, would you have asked Jon to join us?"

The sting of Jon's betrayal hit him all over again, especially after seeing the result of it.

"Perhaps, you should be asking Jon if he would have done the same, knowing what he does now?" The former devil had not been seen since they brought him into the palace. He would be halfway across the world if he knew what was good for him.

Phantom's left fist balled, his other raising a flask of rum to his lips. "Thinking of regrets does nothing to help us now."

Ramirez adopted a pointed look. "Precisely the point. Your guilt can't change the past."

Phantom took a step towards the stairs. He needed to see her. Even if she slept, just seeing her chest rise and fall would help his nerves.

"That's where you're wrong, old man. My guilt will prevent anything else from happening to her. I'd rather die than see her taken from me again."

He didn't bother letting Ramirez respond. There was nothing he could say that would help. With a final look at the reddening sky, he opened the door to his quarters.

Rose lay asleep in his bed, covered in his blankets, her hair spread across the pillow. With much of her body covered, he could almost pretend that nothing was wrong. That it was only his woman sleeping in from a long day. Not a month of consistent torture.

He sat on the bed next to her, watching her chest rise and fall. His hand drifted over the smooth skin of her face, pushing locks of hair from her forehead.

"I love you," he whispered, leaning forward, "my *tresora*." He kissed her forehead, feeling heat and sweat there. Likely a fever. Unsurprisingly with all the trauma she endured.

Wide golden eyes snapped open, and it struck him how dull they were. She jerked away from him, sitting up in bed and screaming.

Terror seized him. He froze as she screamed like he was about to hurt her.

The doors burst open, Smith hobbling into the room, followed by Lara and a couple of his devils. He couldn't be sure since all he could see was Rose's terrified face. He never thought he would see her afraid of *him*.

"Captain, I beg you to step back," Smith said with as much command as possible, pulling him from his stupor, Rose's screams still echoing in the room. It was Tick and Hyne who pulled him away. He could command them away, but this was for Rose's good. How could he argue that? He just never thought the removal of his presence would be required.

Lara had pulled Rose into her arms, his songbird folding into her friend easily enough. The small woman shot him a glare with a single gesture.

Go.

But he couldn't. He needed to fix this. It was all his fault. She was so much worse than he thought. She needed to sing, to take his power, all of it, and it would heal her.

Smith's hand on his arm finally drew his gaze away. "Captain, leave. I will take care of her, but I cannot do that if she can't calm herself."

Phantom brushed off the arms bracing him, giving Rose a final glance before exiting. He felt the door close behind him, taking a deep breath as his own panic reared its ugly head.

Green flashed in his vision. *She will heal. Give her time.*

But they'd already lost so much time. He could help her heal faster.

The small rush of power in his veins wasn't enough. She needed more if she was going to make it out of this. He'd gladly let her have it all, his soul included, but he feared it wasn't nearly enough.

He needed more power.

A trilling rumble drew his attention to the beastie. Serena sat on the railing of the ship; the city stretched out behind her. Her head twisted as she sensed the lethal intention coming off him.

Phantom's eyes turned to the sandstone city washed in the red light of sunset.

"*Sígueme.*" Follow me.

Don't do this.

Do you truly think she will forgive you?

Green vines and yellow flames twisted around each other so much in his head that he could hardly tell the voices apart. Draven didn't join in their concerns, but he stayed close, listening.

James. I know the power is tempting. I've used the shadows myself, but this is not what they are meant for.

Considering he was an agent of death, in every lifetime, he sincerely doubted that.

The shadows will take you too, then what will be left for her, boy?

Blue spread across his vision like an incoming tidal wave, the power all his own. Instinct guided him as he directed that mental wave. He willed it to wash over all that was green and yellow inside him, drowning the voices until they could no longer be heard. Draven remained there, the only one he needed for this.

Stepping foot back into the city, the walls darkened. The shadows swirled around him, sensing the destruction on the horizon. Phantom set his pace, walking through the streets where most had already retreated to their homes.

It wasn't him they hid from. Serena flew behind him, snarling into the street with her eyes glowing bright blue.

Shadows crawled across the walls, darkening the city, and blocking out the light of the moons and stars like there was no sky. Only darkness.

The first soul ripped from its shell with a deafening scream. A guard loyal to the *Imari* who was on the run. Phantom felt the essence travel through him, a man who was cruel to servants but loved his children. Now part of his soul fed Phantom's magic whilst the rest was sent to the arms of Nemain.

The shadows paused on a sleeping mother and babe, tenderly asking for orders.

Phantom spared them. The city didn't have to perish, but there were plenty of guilty souls to reap. He was their judgment now, with the power over who lived and who died, and he could see the worthiness of their souls.

A man attacked him with malice in his eyes and an axe above his head. Serena spat blue flames over him before he got within ten feet of Phantom. His screams died within seconds.

More guards fell. Someone who only wanted to be a cook, but greedily took coin from his neighbors. A man who relished his kills, no matter the state of the victim. Another who had fallen in love with a servant and killed her husband so he could have her.

On and on they fell, and Phantom's vision tunneled as he stalked the streets of Amal. He'd heard the screams of those attempting to kill him, but he paid them no mind. Serena incinerated each attacker, unwilling to let them touch her master.

Shouts peppered against the screams, different from that of Serena's victim. They were more akin to war cries as people poured out of their homes.

Citizens' faces twisted in rage and loathing, brandishing weapons of every kind. Some with pistols and swords picked off the fallen guards. Others had candlesticks and pitchforks, or anything else that could cause harm.

Men and women of all types followed him, cutting down anyone Serena missed. He was leading a riot. He didn't even have to say a word to them. A glint of blue in each of their eyes was enough to explain the revolution. He'd gained their loyalty simply by challenging their oppressors.

Phantom continued, feeling the smaller bouts of power fill him as the citizens took lives. Then stronger surges as the shadows claimed more.

As he drew closer to the palace and the wealthy squares, he witnessed rich men being dragged into the streets and slaughtered like dogs with their heads in the dirt. He had little sympathy for the aristocrats who attended the palace soirée. They'd benefitted off the slave trade and the struggles of the poor.

Phantom reached the entrance, the one that led him to the throne room of the palace. The one that began the rumors. The doors didn't open as easily as they did before, barricaded by the palace staff. Putting strength behind his next push, he broke the doors down. Chairs, furniture, and other blockades groaned against the floor as he moved the doors inward.

The rioters cheered, barreling in behind him. Blood sprayed the alabaster and gold floors and columns as necks were sliced open. He couldn't find it within himself to care for anything but vengeance.

All he wanted was to find the two bastards who'd orchestrated all of this. Who'd stolen Rose away from him and made her fear him. Maybe he couldn't use his shadows against them, but he'd like to see how they'd fair against dragon fire.

Serena landed on his shoulder, roaring so loud, it echoed against the walls.

Phantom spread his shadows through the palace, searching for the *Imari*, but they were nowhere to be found. The cowards abandoned ship the moment they lost their leverage.

He growled his frustration as the rioters swarmed into the empty throne room, splitting off into hallways, looting and destroying any signs of the current rulership. It wasn't long before curtains and tapestries were burning.

"What is the meaning of this?"

Sitamun stood at the entrance he had left open, staring at the blood coating the floor and the bodies lining the walls. Her face was stricken with horror and anger, her shiny new tattoo glinting in the firelight.

Then her eyes landed on him, finally seeing the monster she had aligned herself with. He scented no trace of fear on her, only determination that set her features into a stoney glare.

Letting her eyes leave him to look at the throne, he saw when she realized it was hers for the taking. The last thing he wanted to do was to challenge her for it.

Without glancing at him, she stalked through the rioters to the gleaming throne. Only one and far more golden than the ones the

Imari had sat in, as if the palace itself had recognized its rightful ruler coming home.

Rioters stopped, silencing their pillage to witness this event.

She turned, her golden tattoo gleaming as silver moonlight flooded the dome above their heads. The moment she sat on the throne, the palace shifted, gold spreading from the throne and throughout the palace like a tidal wave of power. He felt it shift the marble beneath his boots. Serena's tail swished back and forth in agitation. The foreign magic was old, far older than the demons who had held the palace.

Sitamun sat at the throne like she was born for it, her eyes glistening with that ethereal gold and her chin held high. The citizens, mouths gaping open, gravitated towards her.

They looked to Phantom, waiting for his challenge. He smirked at the opportunity. To be King. But he was never meant for a throne. Instead, he could offer the princess a parting gift.

"Bow, for your new Queen."

Blue flashed brightly across his vision, echoed in the eyes of the surrounding citizens. The riots stopped, silencing everything as they fell to their knees and bowed their heads.

Sita's gaze found him, but he did not bow. Not to anyone.

"Rise," she ordered, and they obeyed. He offered her a final nod before turning, ready to return to his ship and put this entire country behind him.

"Maahes," she called. He stopped to look back, Serena snarling. "My guards found this man trying to buy passage out to sea. Do you recognize him?"

"Get your filthy hands off me! I want to speak to the *Imari*!"

He knew who it was before two guards dragged him into the throne room. It was the guard who had brought Rose onto the dais with a chain and collar. The one who had threatened her in the cell. The shadows had plenty to report about him.

"I know him," Phantom growled, gaining the man's attention.

"Consider him a gift."

The man's eyes grew wide as he took in shadows swirling around Phantom and the lethal dragon on his shoulder. The man had enough preservation instincts to be afraid, as his scent turned potently tangy.

"No. No. Let me go. They'll kill you for this. I'm chosen by the *Imari*."

Phantom prowled towards him slowly as the guards backed away from the condemned man.

"Haven't you heard?" Sita asked in a sickly sweet tone. "The *Imari* have no power here. Not anymore."

Serena jumped off his shoulder, making the man jolt. "Pathetic," Phantom remarked, witnessing the man piss himself in fear as Serena inched closer. He backed up until his back pressed against a wall. "I'd prefer to take my time. Extend your suffering until you beg me for death." Phantom crouched closer. "However, you simply aren't worth the time."

A growl, raw and visceral, ripped from Serena's throat, the sound echoing deep within his soul.

Phantom stood, turning to the doors as he commanded to Serena, "*Que ardan.*"

Flames erupted from her breath and the man's screams echoed off the walls in a sound Phantom savored. He didn't look back at Draiocht's new Queen or the burning body he left behind. If the *Imari* were not here, he had no further business with Amal.

Serena followed close behind as he returned to the streets.

He pulled back the inky blackness to allow moonlight to shine across the bloody sandstone streets as he prowled back to his ship, back to Rose.

Part Two
ORANGE

LIGHT & DARKNESS

"Are you ready for another story?"

Kendall jumped onto the settee next to the raging hearth. "Yes, mother." She'd been reluctant to ask for another story, although some part of her understood that she needed to know them. But did they all have to have bad endings? "Can it be a good story this time?"

Her mother was dressed in a glistening silver and white gown. The woven beads glimmered in the flickering light from the fire. She was a rare beauty, something glowing in the soft smile on her face. Kendall hoped that one day she would be able to be as beautiful as her mother.

"In a manner of speaking, it will be. But you shall have to listen to know for certain."

Curiosity tugged at her. Just knowing that the ending would be different, it urged her to snuggle into her mother, ready with open ears.

"Let's see, what do you know of Nemain, my sweet?"

Kendall sucked in a breath. Every tutor she had warned against the darkness and trickery of the Goddess of Death. "She is evil. She lives in darkness." There was a fear Kendall never admitted to her mother. That one day, something would be in the shadows of her room, ready to take her away.

Her mother pulled her tighter to remind Kendall that she was safe.

"What if I told you there is nothing evil about darkness? Just like there is nothing good about light." She scrunched her nose, directing her confused expression to her mother, who chuckled in response. "People can use darkness and light for good or evil, but there was a group of people that believed the same as you. While others believed just the opposite."

She reached for the table before them where a map was laid out, pointing to land that sat on the furthest western reaches. If there was anything further, they were unaware of it. "This is where the tribes of Nemain reside, but centuries ago they weren't as harmonious as they are today. They disagreed about light and darkness. Half of them believed light represented the soul, and that Nemain governed the soul."

Kendall didn't know this word. "What's a soul?"

Her mother smiled. "The soul is the part inside you that represents you. This," she said, pinching Kendall's round cheek, "is only the body. The soul is like magic, containing your true self."

Kendall beamed at her mother, liking the idea of magic inside her. It made her feel special, even if everyone had one.

"These 'soul weavers' have called it upon themselves to care about being good, about kindness and honor. The better they were, the brighter and stronger their soul was. They had the ability to wield their own souls in battle, turning light into weapons or healing people."

It sounded wonderful, to use her own soul to affect the world around her. That brightness that Kendall could feel in her own chest, pulsating. She looked down, half-expecting her chest to glow, but all she saw was her soft nightgown. Disappointment dragged the edges of her mouth down.

"Oh, my darling, soul weaving takes a lot of training and practice."

"Can I have a tutor for that?"

Her mother chuckled, amused by her naïve daughter. "I could not find one for you, but perhaps one day, you will find a tutor all on your own."

Kendall was about to ask how she could do that on her own when her mother continued, moonlight bathing her silhouette from the window.

"The other half of the tribes believed that Nemain ruled over darkness since she governs the afterlife. They surrendered their work and their lives to the armies of Hell, performing rituals to allow spirits of the dead or demons to inhabit their bodies. They were called *shadow spinners*."

Kendall's eyes grew wide. "Why would they do that?"

"They thought it would be just as holy as the soul weavers believed goodness to be. This disagreement led them to a war over the land they both thought to be sacred until one day, a priestess, one of light, had a prophecy that changed everything."

Prophecy. She knew this word. Her tutors used it often. There were papers framed and lying in a special room in the temple. They studied the old parchment day and night, trying to understand the predictions from Davina.

It seemed too ridiculous to read the same paper repeatedly, expecting to find something that wasn't there the first time.

"The prophecy stated that the war of light and darkness would begin with the birth of the brightest soul weaver and the darkest shadow spinner. They would be born at the same time under the light of Nemain on the longest night of the year."

Kendall wondered what they were like. These two powerful magic users existed on opposite sides of the same war.

"Years later, in the *Aashaa* tribe, was born a baby girl with light gleaming from her so brightly, her powerful soul magic could not be mistaken, nor her orange glowing eyes that shone whenever light hit them. She was born during sunset, Nemain's moon only just appearing. Later that night, in the *Otshee* tribe, a baby boy was born after the sun disappeared from the sky. He was bathed in shadows that swaddled him like a blanket, and his eyes glowed with orange light whenever in darkness."

Kendall stared forward seeing the imagery as clearly as if she were there, witnessing the awe of the tribes-people.

"The people used the prophecy as an excuse to start a war, attacking each other in brutal ways most warriors avoid. But both sides believed they were righteously defeating the enemy. They raised the two to be the greatest in their respective practices, and they were.

"Sixteen years later, they were joining the war efforts, leading armies into nearby villages, trying to push the opposing side out of their precious valley." Kendall knew her mother was leaving things out, and normally, she would push for answers, but somehow, she knew she didn't want to know. Not yet.

Her mother drew her chin up to look into her eyes. "Where are the questions, my sweet?"

Curiosity encouraged her, but something at the back of her mind promised her answers later, when she was older, but not now.

"I — I don't think I should know."

A deep, weary sigh escaped her mother's lips. "You are wise for a child. Yes, the atrocities committed against these villages were more terrible than even these teenagers should have seen, but the great soul weaver, Lani, felt sorrow and compassion for the *Otshee* people who weren't warriors, yet they suffered. She decided to enter the shadow villages with her face painted beyond recognition, drawing shadows across her skin so they would think of her as one of them. She could even bend light to make it look like she could wield shadows."

Bending light? Soul weaving sounded increasingly fun. She hoped one day she could do it too.

"Lani would sneak into their village, healing the injured, providing food, and even fighting off her own soldiers who attacked out of line. You see, tensions were so high at this time that many would attack unprovoked and without permission. Because of this, a treaty could never be reached."

"Why didn't she stop the war?"

Her mama looked at the flames, sadness hardening her features. "She wished to, but the elders of her tribe would not listen with the *Otshee* attacks. Her own people called it holy, allowing death. That healing magic should never be used on the fatally wounded since Nemain had already claimed the soul. In fact, it was a punishable offense, yet it was a rule Lani broke nightly."

Kendall found that she liked Lani. Her goodness was unique; a selfless empathy that extended to strangers, unlike anyone else in the story. Kendall hoped to someday be so compassionate.

"One night, just as the sun was setting, Lani entered a village that had both *Otshee* shadow spinners and *Aashee* soul weavers. It was the only one of its kind, where the two people lived in harmony, but that made the attacks there even more devastating. Had Lani not shielded them, they would have been destroyed. She went to heal the wounded, but she ran into a man. A mask covered his features, but it was apparent by his ivory clothing and porcelain mask that he was a soul weaver. They had dinner together at his request, talking for a great deal of time, and she enjoyed the company of someone who had no idea who she was. Over the span of an hour, a connection began to form between the two. Even the touch of his hand on hers proved how much they belonged together. Until the sun set. Lani looked into his orange glowing eyes and knew she faced her greatest enemy, Draven."

Kendall gasped, hanging on the edge of her seat.

"You see, she had never seen his face before, he was always covered in ceremonial armor and robes, but his eyes could never be mistaken."

Those questions rose up in Kendall, but this time she didn't feel the same warning in her gut. "But why was he there? Dressed as a soul weaver? And didn't he recognize her?"

"He did. He knew exactly who she was when he invited her to dinner. As for why he was there, it was for the same reason she was. Before the sun set and the darkness would give him away, he would visit the *Aashaa* villages disguised as a soul weaver priest. He provided food, expelling the demons that hopped vessels during war, even fending off his own rogue warriors. Doesn't that sound familiar?"

Kendall blinked at the dancing flames before her, the story laying out in a way that didn't make sense.

"But, if both of their villages were suffering, why didn't they help their own people?"

"They would have." Her mother pulled her closer. "But once the two got over their differences to talk, they realized their leaders and elders were lying to them. Lani was told that her villages were soundly protected. She didn't even know a demon could leap from one vessel to another. And Draven? He was forbidden from interrupting the natural process of death, even with his own people. In the *Otshee* villages, the elders would know it was him, but when he found out about a woman who was saving his people, he tracked her down. Once he found out it was the very enemy he fought in battle, he decided to do the same for her people. That, and he fell in love with her."

A wave of warmth spread through Kendall, lifting her spirits and making her heart soar. "He did?"

"Oh yes, she took some time to come around, but eventually she fell for him as well. They met in the hour of sunset and sunrise; the one time of day their eyes could not give them away. And they were as lovers were..."

Kendall blinked a couple of times, that last part was not making any sense. She'd heard the term before, but no one ever really explained it.

"What are lovers?"

Her mother's eyes widened, then she fumbled with her words. She took a breath, regaining that regal composure that Kendall was more used to seeing. "I will explain when you are older." She opened her mouth to argue. "No, darling. The only thing you need to know is that it led to her belly swelling with a baby."

Kendall's brows rose. "A baby?" She loved babies. Their little grabby hands and laughter, especially when they giggled and fell over. Babies were her favorite. "Mother, can I have a baby?"

"No," her mother snapped, more harshly than she'd expected, making her flinch back. Noticing her daughter's reaction, her face softened, pulling her daughter back. "I'm sorry, my sweet. You are not nearly old enough for that, but I hope that someday you will have lots of babies." She seized Kendall by the armpits, tickling her in a way that made her burst into laughter.

It was such joyful torture.

Her mother didn't let it last too long, arranging Kendall on her lap to tell the rest of the story.

"When the soul weaving priests noticed her belly swelling, they asked her who the father was, but she refused to tell them, knowing they wouldn't possibly accept the truth. The priests had her followed and were shocked when they found her with the enemy."

The pounding of Kendall's heart could be felt in every one of her breaths as she stared at the twinkling stars beyond the window. "But they understood, right? They were in love."

After a beat of silence, Kendall turned her gaze to her mother. There was sorrow on her mother's face, genuine hurt.

"I'm afraid not, my sweet." A tear slid down her mother's face. "The priests poisoned Lani. Not to kill her since they dared not destroy their greatest weapon, but they thought themselves holy to rid the world of what they considered to be an abomination. Her screams could be heard in all corners of the valley as Nemain claimed her unborn child."

Kendall's breaths came in sharper. She did not like this story. It was like the last, but her mother said it ended well, so that could not be it.

"But the loss of the baby took a toll on her body. Too much. Draven stormed into an *Aashaa* village in the middle of the night when he heard her screams. He found her dying, Nemain already close by to take her life to the next, but Draven stopped it. Using every ounce of his power and going against everything he was ever taught to believe, he saved her life. She survived, but before she could recover enough to save him, the *Otshee* people executed him for breaking their most sacred rule. Even in the last moments of his life, he didn't regret saving her life at the cost of his own."

Hot tears spilled down Kendall's cheeks, leaving trails of salt in their wake.

"Lani continued to rule over the people, uniting them on the grounds of preventing further bloodshed. Eventually, they found common ground, learning from one another as Lani did with her shadow spinner. Although, there were a handful of *Otshee* who moved on from the land so they would be free to practice their own magic. We know them today as witches, spread to the four corners of the world."

That couldn't have been the end. Was Draven just gone?

"What happened to Lani?"

Her mama bowed her head. "The loss of her child and lover were enough to destroy her. She had just enough kindness and compassion left to govern them with a firm hand, but she never loved again. There was no one else who could compare."

The tears continued to stream down Kendall's face. "That's not a good ending, Mother."

"It was not a happy ending, but it was still good. Lani created a nation that holds strong in the west, even now. She brought them together and stopped the bloodshed. As a ruler, you cannot hope for more, my sweet."

Kendall couldn't imagine making those choices. After losing everything, she could still chose peace. It seemed impossible.

Her gut swirled with warmth, the voice from before telling her she was capable of it. That there was still kindness to be found when it seemed like all was lost.

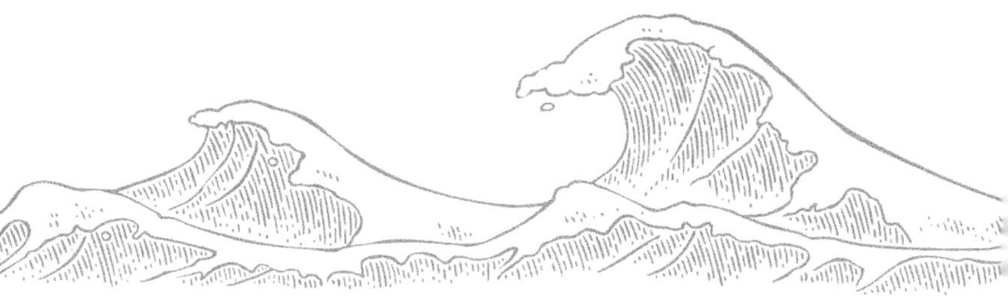

CHAPTER 51

THE GUARDIAN OF KHELI

SEBASTIAN

As it turns out, it takes two days to travel to Kheli by fishing boat. Provisions for the trip had been little to none with the state they left Samsara. Water was stored in barrels in the lower reaches of the boat, but that didn't help their appetites.

A heavy fog had descended across the surface of the water, making navigation difficult, but not impossible.

Sebastian held a compass out, one that led him to Kheli many times before, even though he had to admit this was a fog he could not predict.

"There is something you should know." Indigo stood beside him, looking into the cloud cover before them. Sebastian gave her a cursory glance before refocusing on the view ahead. He had little time to spot a stray boulder to correct their course. Or worse — the cliff side of the island itself.

"And what's that?"

There was a pause, then the words rolled out of her. "The witches have been sending their spelled sons to this island for some time. If the necromites have invaded Kheli like they have Samsara, the island will be crawling with them."

Sebastian faced the witch. He knew some sons resided there,

but not as many as she suggested. If what she was saying was true, the island would be in worse condition than Samsara without an army and natural cliff walls. Samsara was a highly fortified island, but Kheli? It wasn't meant to see battle.

"Eyes forward, Commodore."

He looked to the sea beyond to find a jagged rock in their path. With a quick jolt, he was able to sail past it.

But his mind was still on what Indigo had confessed.

"You didn't think this was important information to note when I came to you for help?"

"Commodore!" A sailor screamed, pointing at another incoming rock jutting out of the waters.

Indigo braced herself on the railing before the helm as Sebastian corrected them again.

"I was sworn to secrecy by my sisters. Should any of them find out I told you, they will seek me out. We needed to be far enough away."

Another rock followed the last, and he had to make a hard turn on the port-side, flinging refugees across the deck with yelps.

"And you speak freely now because what? Your own life lies in the balance?"

"No, as it turns out, I need Kheli to survive." A sharp turn on the starboard side. Indigo slammed into the railing before the helm. "You lot might be exactly what it needs to do that."

Sebastian didn't remember a field of rocks near Kheli at all. They must have gone off-course to be this hopelessly lost. He risked looking back to see the other boats following his movements. As long as they paid close attention, they would be fine.

"I couldn't risk you turning back, and tell me, Commodore, would it have changed anything?"

No, it wouldn't have, but he wasn't about to admit that now.

Screams bellowed from behind him as a fellow fishing boat crashed into a nasty rock. Wood splintered, and people jumped into the waves to escape the crumbling boat

"Take the helm," he ordered Indigo, reaching for her hands and placing them on the wooden wheel. His hand gripped over hers. "Hold tight and keep her near." She nodded. Thankfully, there was enough fear in her eyes to take direction. "Clare, with me."

Vincent understood him before Sebastian could bark orders, taking the shirt off his back. Sebastian descended the steps, shedding his own layers until he was only in a pair of trousers.

"Indigo," he called back. "We'll split the survivors among the remaining boats. Keep her close."

He could have sworn he saw a little salute from her. It brought a half smile to his face amidst the chaos.

With a nod to Vincent, they dove from the boat, swimming to its sinking comrade. Many refugees were still on the deck, but some were treading water.

Sebastian cupped his mouth to be heard over the waves. "If you can swim, make it to a boat." He pointed to the surrounding boats, including his own vessel, *The Dying Star*.

"Well, that inspires confidence," Vincent mumbled beside him.

The plan was effective. Many refugees swam to the boats with little hesitation while Vincent and Sebastian helped small children, a pregnant woman, and a man with no leg make it to a vessel.

Even with the sounds of chattering teeth and the damp chill of the crowded Dying Star, Sebastian was glad to have saved them all. Everything considered, it was the most he could ask for.

As the fog cleared and the rocks disappeared, the island came into view. Kheli's shores were a mile ahead of them, gleaming in the sunlight and completely unobstructed by the fog.

He could have sworn there were no rocks barring the way to Kheli before. Indigo stared back from where they came, a wall of fog and rocks looked like it was cut by some heavenly force.

"It's a magical barrier. Kheli is not as unprotected as we assumed."

With four fishing boats safely making it to the dock, Sebastian scouted the area with Indigo and Vincent.

Indigo, if the new magic surrounding Kheli posed a threat in the jungles.

Vincent, so the locals wouldn't kill him on sight. As Commodore, his popularity on the island had plummeted.

At the beginning of his career, he served the villagers as James did with his crew, but since their paths deviated and the Minister's influence grew, he was forced to oppress the people rather than help them.

His only consolation was Samsara. If he could take care of the island and allow the pirates to raid enough to bring back to Kheli, the Minister would be distracted enough not to pay attention to the slaves he freed. It was all a delicate balance, one that gave him no choice but cruelty when it came to the Khelitians.

But they had James.

Now, bigger problems awaited him.

Sebastian pushed through the jungle, cutting down overgrown vines and branches until he could find the village. Upon seeing the courtyard and surrounding buildings, he nearly dropped his sword.

"What happened here?" Vincent bit out.

The village was a ghost town; most buildings stood empty and decaying, while others were charred skeletons against the skyline. Supplies and belongings were scattered along the clearing. Even spilled grain and other foods were left behind.

But no bodies—

"I don't know. I haven't been here since the Minister's death."

Indigo mumbled beside him, chanting some kind of spell with her eyes closed. Years of training told him to shut her up, to force her away from using magic against him. Instinct told him not to disturb her. It was a disturbing mix of reactions he struggled to control.

Her eyes opened. "Death plagues this island. Keep your eyes open for the dead."

Sebastian reaffirmed the grip on his sword, using soft feet to enter the remains of the village. Vincent used his own sword to move curtains aside, peering in doors and windows.

Indigo poked through the remnants of supplies, including sacks of grain left on the side of a building.

"Do you think the food here is salvageable?"

Vincent focused on the spilled bags around them. "I wouldn't risk it. Dying from food poisoning is not a fate I wish to be served."

Sebastian pulled a hand down his face, not expecting a foul joke from the unsuspecting man, but his grin spoke volumes.

He needed to find them food. What did he rescue the refugees from if they only starved to death? Considering Kheli served to feed itself and most of Samsara for decades, there should be food close by.

"We venture into the jungle then. We'll find supplies and hope-fully the villagers." He didn't want to say what they must have been thinking. Just because the bodies of the villagers were miss-ing, it didn't mean they were alive.

Vincent nodded. "I know where the farms are kept. There would be food there and the villagers wouldn't stray far."

If they're still alive.

It took hours across the hard terrain of overgrown plant life, steep trails, and rain before they reached the southern part of the island. Necromites appeared in the form of monkeys, snakes, or other beasts, but none were human. Though the implications of the animated dead animals were heartbreaking enough.

Every time they came across one, he glared at Indigo. Until she finally replied, "Be grateful I told you."

He could strangle the woman.

The weather gradually worsened, showering them in a down-pour by the time they made it.

Sebastian could see silhouettes of apple trees when Vincent spoke again.

"Something is wrong."

The rain and foliage made it difficult to see far. "What do you mean?"

"There should be people manning this. We never left it unprotected."

The Khelitians had little in the way of people to man the fields and work them, but Sebastian thought better than to remind

Vincent of that. The remaining villagers had to make do with the hands they had when the men were taken to be a part of the Minister's Navy.

"Well, let's take a close—"

The air whipped beside him. Vincent cried out, an arrow sticking out from his shoulder, but the culprit was nowhere to be seen.

Indigo moved sharply, catching an arrow as it shot for her face, irritation sparking her features and violet swirling in her eyes.

The wind moved again, but Sebastian raised his sword in time to stop the arrow from colliding with him. They ducked behind a fallen log to avoid any more.

"Where are those coming from?" Vincent grunted as he pulled the arrow from his shoulder, making Sebastian wince. He really should have kept it in. There was hardly time to dress it now. "My sister is the only archer on this island."

"Apparently, not anymore," Indigo snapped.

Sebastian had a pistol out but didn't want to shoot at locals. If these were invaders that caused chaos in the village, then so be it. He rose, raising his hands, intent on surrender so he could witness the attacker's faces.

A hand pulled him back down. "Hold up, Mr. Righteous," Vincent drawled, clearly pleased with his own sarcasm that Sebastian was unimpressed by. "If these are invaders, they will shoot you. And if they are locals, they have an even better reason to shoot you."

Sebastian dragged a hand along his face, wiping the incessant rain along with it.

"What do you suggest then?"

"You could *all* surrender."

All three heads turned to the front. A figure stood before them hooded and drenched with a sword in each hand. They had good odds with three to one — until two archers stepped out from behind the figure, considerably shorter. It was hard to see every thing in the dark and rain, but he could have sworn they were children.

"It's been a long time, Commodore." The voice was decidedly

female but raised to be heard over the rain, so he failed to recognize it. "We no longer answer to the Minister." She didn't attack, only stood, waiting for his response, but she answered his question. They were locals, angry ones at that, but the last thing he wanted to do was harm them.

He raised his hands, standing before her, Indigo and Vincent following suit.

Lightning flashed behind them, and the rain grew heavier. He hadn't expected to have to deal with a Khelitian storm now of all times.

"I hear the caves are best suited to wait out a storm," the woman said, then she let her hood fall back. Lightning flashed close enough to reveal her features. Sebastian recognized her warm skin and dark eyes instantly.

"Angelica," he whispered, though he dared not share her last name, but that was more out of habit than anything. Her last name, former or current, spoken amongst the wrong company could cause an uproar.

"Who?" Vincent asked from beside him. He wouldn't recognize her since Angelica joined the village after his forced departure. After all, she wasn't native to the island like most of the locals.

Her eyes narrowed, as if inspecting Sebastian and ignoring his companions completely. "You never brought me in or revealed my identity. Why?"

Recognizing the test before him, Sebastian lifted his chin, a subtle shift in his posture signaling his readiness. There were several reasons he protected her for years as Commodore, but only one reason that kept his lips sealed above all else.

"You are Joseph's wife." He hadn't spoken his friend's first name in years. "I would never allow him to lose you."

A smile lifted the corners of her mouth, then she sheathed her swords, the archers behind her lowering their bows. She raised a hand he thought was intended for him to shake, instead, she lifted it towards the sky.

Finally, he noticed the tattoo of blue lightning spreading across the back of her hand. He could have sworn — indeed, it began to glow.

The skies above parted, the rain drawing to a slight drizzle, and the wind slowing. Two moons glistened in the now cloudless sky. He hadn't even realized they had been gone so long.

When he looked back to Angelica, her eyes were on Indigo, then sliding to Vincent.

"Sebastian, what have you brought me?"

CHAPTER 52

SHATTERED SUNLIGHT

ROSE

Exhaustion clung to Rose's bones, like weights dragging down her limbs so she could no longer use them. Her mind wasn't awake enough to be scared, especially with the softness of silk sheets around her and the most comfortable bed she'd ever slept in. It was like sleeping on a cloud.

Sea salt and oranges mixed with the soft smell of musty linens. It was so familiar she wanted to cry, but she wasn't exactly sure why. There was a reason, but it was too far away. It couldn't exist here at this moment.

There was something even softer beside her. The tips of her fingers tangled in the softness of — she couldn't think of the word, but it was warm and inviting. It moved, not heavily, only the rise and fall of breath that wasn't her own.

With significant effort, she raised her hand to drift it over the soft mound beside her. The gentle hum, a comforting vibration, lulled her back to sleep.

Rose sucked down a lungful of air as she snapped forward. The feeling of grating sand washed away from her, along with the pain and all those screams. Around her, blue faded, her ribbons of light fading into the natural sunlight streaming in through the foggy window.

She kept breathing in and out as she took in her surroundings. Around her were silken sheets and a comfortable bed, one she knew well from the dreams that were good. The ones she treasured and kept close to her heart.

Letting her heart slow to an acceptable rhythm, she realized she was not in that goddess-forsaken sandy cell in the middle of nowhere. The memories faded back to her. Running down a corridor, the aching soles of her feet remembered it better than her head. Then flying.

She had been *flying*.

Sweet Davina, she was dreaming.

Good morning. Orange like the first rays of sunlight filled her vision. She knew this voice, she'd heard it before, even rarely.

"Lani?" Rose whispered, her voice hoarse from screaming or disuse, she wasn't sure.

Yes, child. Skye is gone now. It's time for you to understand the light now.

"The light? What do you mean by that?" Rose rubbed at her throat, the skin there tender, though her entire body felt sore. She looked down to find that all that covered her was a leather coat, one long enough to cover her to her knees. James. She could smell him on it. Oranges and sea salt with a hint of cinnamon, like the tea her mother used to make.

What do you know of soul magic?

Rose threw her feet over the side of the bed, feeling very much like moving. After being manacled to a wall for Davina knows how long, she needed to move her legs. Preferably towards James' desk, where the warm, inviting smell of freshly baked bread and creamy porridge wafted in the air, waiting for her.

A glint brought her attention to the side. On the table beside her sat her mother's necklace. A wave of relief hit her hard at seeing it.

Rose reached for it but couldn't bring herself to touch it. Her thoughts had grown darker in that cell, like singing her mother's lullaby one last time—

But you didn't.

Her stomach growled violently, so she abandoned the necklace in favor of food. She reached for the bread, stuffing her face with it as she sat at the captain's desk. She could taste the extra spices and knew Wilson had made it. She'd missed his cooking, so much better than the filth she ate in the prison.

"I have no idea what soul magic is." Rose said around a mouthful of bread, not letting the conversation interrupt her meal. Instinct told her to eat it all before someone could take it away, half-expecting Colt to come through the doors and make it vanish.

Slow down, your stomach isn't ready yet.

Rose ignored the comment, reminding herself of who Lani was. "You were part of the tribes in the west, weren't you?"

The Aashaa *tribe, yes. I ruled over them for quite some time.*

Rose hadn't learned too much about the western tribes, other than the fact that they were part of the three goddess races. The *Aashaa* belonged to Nemain, but despite their affiliation with the Goddess of Death, they were a peaceful people.

"And soul magic?"

Soul weavers were common during my time, as were shadow spinners.

Rose froze at the mention of shadow spinners. Though she had never heard the term before, she remembered the command James had over darkness. The way they obeyed and killed for him.

Contrary to what people believe, soul and shadow magic are complimentary, not opposing. Though they can be abused, they were meant to be wielded in harmony.

The thought of her own power working in harmony with the ominous presence she witnessed seemed far-fetched and entirely intimidating. Her stomach rolled; the capacity shrunken enough to be full with only a handful of bites. In fact, she barely managed to restrain herself from heaving out her meal. She'd need to be able to eat more food than that if she wanted a swift recovery.

No need to worry. Your stomach will heal with the rest of you soon.

Awareness prickled at her neck, and she whipped her head to the door, finding no one there. No nightmare. No demons ready to take her to the next layer of Hell.

"I doubt that." It wasn't her stomach that filled her with dread. Her mind might be further gone than she could recover from. James' stricken face was evidence of that. He'd looked devastated, the memory still clear in her mind.

She'd thought it was Colt, his presence looming, ready to shatter her fragile peace. She'd nearly killed herself to escape her captors, and he'd found her again so easily. It wasn't until he left that she realized she was safe. Lara had rubbed her back and reminded her.

Looking away, she focused on the window behind the desk. With the rays of sunlight shining around her, Lani was in all her radiant beauty. She had warm brown skin, painted with swirls of shadows around her cheekbones and neck. A sheer orange dress swirled around her like it was made of newborn sunlight.

"You will heal," Lani said, her dark eyes promising the truth. Though Rose felt as though she must have gone insane. Again. Or, at least, it was some permanent damage from her time with the demons. "Now, stand."

She rose, unsteadily, but there was something more solid about the wood beneath her feet.

Lani placed a hand on her stomach. "This is where the soul resides. It's your essence that Nemain takes when your time has come. There is energy here that anyone can use if they know how. But yours — *ours* — is the strongest to ever exist."

Rose let out a sigh. "Of course it is." She didn't mean to let the words slip, but it was ironic how little that power supported her when the time came.

Lani smiled, though. "It is good to hear your humor again. I did miss it."

Rose blinked. Did she make a joke? A sad one at that, but she did. Did that mean she was healing already?

"Come, sit." Lani crouched, crossing her legs under her.

"You told me to stand, and now I should sit again?" She couldn't help it. The floodgates had opened and now everything felt like a joke. With a gently sharp look from Lani, Rose crouched, mirroring how Lani sat.

It was foreign to her. As a lady in Samsara, she was taught to keep her knees together, and even if the position wasn't sexual, her legs protested the idea of opening.

Lani was patient, waiting for her to convince her legs to obey. They didn't lay as neatly as Lani's did, but the *long-dead-voice-in-her-head* nodded her satisfaction.

"To first use your soul, you must meditate to find it." Lani closed her eyes, gracefully placing her hands on her knees, palms up, her clothing and hair floating around her and reminding Rose that she wasn't truly there. "Close your eyes and focus your mind. Find that energy within yourself."

Rose mimicked the pose, closing her eyes, but there were a few seconds of silence before memories pelted her. Some of her own horror that she survived, some fabricated by the demons who held her, some were Skye's. Her pulse rose, her heartbeat too loud to control, her hands shaking. She snapped her eyes open before the memories could drag her down completely.

"I can't do this."

Lani inspected the way her heart raced, her breaths coming in heavy pants.

"You can, but perhaps not today." Lani stood. "You must be at peace to meditate. Take the time to recover, Rose. We will try again."

Before Rose could ask her more questions, a flare of light made her form disappear. She was still in Rose's head, closer than ever, but not speaking.

The door opened and Rose flinched, expecting to find Colt laughing, telling her that she was never safe.

But it was Lara's face with pity and sympathy clearly written all over her features until relief washed over them. She lunged, tackling Rose in a crushing hug. Rose squeezed her back, grateful to see her friend, before pulling back to sign.

"What are you doing here? They were supposed to take you to Kheli."

Her brows furrowed as her hands began moving frantically. *"You expected me to wait on an island? I made them take me."*

Part of her wanted to chastise her friend for putting herself in danger, but most of her was grateful. She never considered Lara would come with them. Her presence was grounding.

"Phantom wants to see you. He asked me to make sure you were okay with that."

It softened her heart that he asked Lara to come in first, but considering the last time she saw him, it wasn't surprising that he would be cautious. She both dreaded seeing him and missed him violently. *"Yes, let him come in."* She stood, dragging Lara with her and straightening herself.

Lara's hands moved again. *"Do you want me to stay in the room? He told me not to, but I will if you ask me."*

Warmth spread across her chest at her friend's gesture, but she desperately needed the time with James.

"No, I need to see him alone."

Lara nodded, leaving her with a parting sentence. *"If you scream, Tick will let me know and I will come in here and—"* The final gesture she made was less of an official sign and looked more like she was wringing someone's neck.

Rose let a smile lift her face.

Lara parted, leaving the door open for James to walk through.

He was as handsome and alluring as ever, an aura around him that Colt could never quite replicate. Even as she thought it, she noticed how dull it was, tainted by his own torment.

Walking slowly, he went to close to the door behind him, but stopped, glancing at her for permission. He didn't have to verbally ask, his eyes conveyed as much.

She gave him a hesitant nod. The sounds of waves and seagulls beyond the door helped ground her, but she did not want him to think she couldn't be alone with him.

He closed the door, but didn't walk any closer, taking her in from where he stood.

She did the same, inspecting him from afar. Besides the shading below his eyes, there was little change. His black hair hung over his forehead but was still windswept from the salty sea air. The clothing he wore was all black, no hint of color as she occasionally witnessed, as if he had fully accepted his darkness. Those eyes, the ones that haunted her every moment, had not changed.

Memories of what his body looked like beneath it all and how his eyes filled with heat came to mind. That time felt like it was years ago.

"I am sorry," he said so softly, she barely heard.

Rose blinked, coming out of her reverie to hear his words. "What could you possibly feel sorry for?"

His brows slammed together, the darkened corners of the room growing thicker. "I put you in danger. Becau — because of me you were in that horrid place." He took a step forward, tentatively, the shadows followed him. "I can't imagine what you've been through, but I promise you, they will never touch you again."

She wanted to believe that, but just the mention of her demons had their faces flashing in her mind, mocking her, and telling her this was all a test, some trick to get what they wanted. That James wasn't there.

He took another step forward, his hand out to reach for her. "Rose, I love you so much. I was dying without you." She could barely hear him over the pounding of her own heart and the screams in her head. Not just her own, but Jon's and Iris'. Everyone was screaming.

Her hands snapped to her ears, holding them like that would stop everything.

"No, stop."

He did, halting in his tracks and letting his hand fall to his side. The look in his eyes, filled with guilt, made her stomach churn; she hated it.

"I'm sorry," she whispered between panted breaths.

"What could you possibly feel sorry for?" Her parroted words brought her back to the room she was in, to believe in her surroundings once again, but her breathing refused to even out.

She let her hands drop from her ears, hugging around her waist instead. Only then did she feel the tears streaking her face. She supposed she knew now if she could be alone with him. The wall between them had never felt more impenetrable.

Guilt consumed her when she looked into his eyes and saw the pain this brought him.

"If I could, I would wrap you in my arms right now. I'd let you cry until there were no more left, then I would kiss them away." Shivers ran down her spine, both in anticipation and dread. She couldn't have those things, not right now, but she'd also never needed them more.

"What else?" At his confused expression, she explained. "If you could touch me, what else would you do?" She didn't understand it, the heat that was pooling in her belly. Of course, she had felt it before, but never this strong, this demanding. Never had she felt this out of control with her own body. The torture of wanting more and not being able to have it at the same time.

His eyes darkened as he realized what she wanted. The shadows receded from him slightly.

"I would kiss you, more passionately than ever before, down your body until my lips have covered every inch of you." That heat pumped through her veins, causing her heart to hasten in an entirely different way. "Then when I have you soft and wet beneath me, I will pull you atop me so I can watch as you bring yourself pleasure on my cock."

Shivers racked her heated flesh, pebbling in a delicious way. But his eyes betrayed him, the hesitance in their depths contradicting the measured calm of his voice; she could almost taste the unspoken worry.

"Come now, *Captain*." The title brought back memories of her first days on *Nemain's Revenge*. "I know you've dreamt of filthier things than that," she challenged.

He growled, his fists balling at his sides. She wanted him to break, to beat down this insurmountable wall between them like it was nothing and take her in a way that didn't make her feel fragile.

James lifted his chin, a knowing smirk curving his mouth. "I think you underestimate how much I enjoy watching you ride my cock." She wanted to push him further, to let the heat between them grow, but that barrier was still there, and she could see his jaw tense from how badly he was grinding his teeth.

"I didn't come to arouse you, love," he said, grunting through his resistance. Still, she flinched from the word. Colt used it often when he was impersonating James. The reminder was like a bucket of seawater over her head.

James paused for a moment, noting the reaction, but saying nothing of it.

"I came to have you sing." Her arms pressed tighter around herself remembering why she sang the last time. He saved her goddess-damned life. "You are in desperate need of more power. Take it from me."

"James, I can't—"

"Yes, you can."

She shot him an incredulous look, her eyebrows raised high. "I can't take all this power from you. What happens to you if you get too low?"

"I won't."

"James—"

"I won't. I have enough power for the both of us, and you need it more than I do."

His eyes flashed, and those shadows crept in on him.

"No," he snapped, but not at her, his hand reached for the shadows, wisps of darkness wrapping around his fingers. "Not with her so close."

She watched the darkness recede from his grasp. "You control shadows now?" She asked incredulously, reaching for them. He moved to stop her, but the shadows curled around her fingers just the same. She doubted she could control them as he did, but she could feel them now, like a cat nuzzling against her palm.

"What are they?"

"They are more abundant than the stars in the sky. Agents of Nemain, like me. We speak of Nemain's Carriage as the passage into the afterlife. That is their job, to take souls to the location of their deserved sentence."

She felt them brush against her skin, feeling very affectionate.

"And they listen to you?"

James' head twisted a bit. "Mostly. If they are so inclined." She stared at them longer. If she understood what she saw at the palace, these creatures could snatch living souls from their bodies, leaving behind empty shells.

"Rose, I need you to sing."

She opened her mouth to protest, letting the shadows fade.

"Before you argue, this is something I can do to help you heal. I need you to let me."

She didn't like it, but she couldn't say no to him when he looked at her like that. Like he would do absolutely anything for her.

She nodded her head. The song poured from her easily, her ribbons attaching to his chest. It didn't escape her that this was the only way they could touch, through magic. At least, for now.

When it was over, his eyes drooped.

"Take more. I have enough to spare."

He might have, but she couldn't take more. It was like eating. Her magic reserves had to process the power before she could take more. "I can't. Not right now."

He nodded, understanding flashing over his features then something turned she'd never seen before. His eyes cast down to the floor while he pulled at his sleeves. Was he... sheepish?

"I found a canvas while we were in Amal. I thought—" His words cut off as he cleared his throat. "I thought you might want it, along with paints and brushes."

She hadn't seen a canvas, but turning to where he pointed, in the darkened corner of the room near his wardrobe, there it stood, on a stand, ready to turn into a masterpiece.

Orange spread across her vision at the mere thought of using it. No inspiration came like it had once; instead, she was left with hollowness, but the gesture warmed her heart. He gave her a gift. Just because he wanted to. Gratitude and love filled her senses.

She smiled. "Thank you."

For a moment, he just looked at her, a half-smile tipping his features, but just as quickly, it was gone.

"It was the least I could do."

She was about to argue that it meant more than she could ever express when cold salty air swept in. He left without another word.

CHAPTER 53

ALL IN YOUR HEAD

Let. Me. See. Her.

Draven had been commanding him to go back to Rose for hours. He could sense Lani's presence beneath Rose's skin. It could also have been the way she was glowing.

Phantom gripped the railing on the quarterdeck, his frustration growing. "She needs time to rest without your interruption." They'd been arguing for hours, his crew pointedly ignoring the mumbling.

Tell her to let Lani out. Then leave us be.

Draven had become insufferable without Sam or Kayden also taking up space in his mind. Draven was all that was required to go mad. The other two culprits hadn't arisen since Draiocht. That was two days ago.

Two days of bloody torture.

Rose had slept too long. He'd been sleeping next to her at night, but only in his beast form. He couldn't witness the terror in her eyes a second time if she woke to his true face again. As an overgrown cat, he'd been able to protect her and rest peacefully. She even curled into him on occasion.

"I'm not leaving the both of you alone. I can feel your lust fueling my own, and if Rose wakes in the middle of whatever you two will be doing—" Her face flashed in his mind again, the terror of seeing him beside her. A wave of nausea swept over him. "I will not risk that."

Seeing her for the time he had was agony enough. He wanted to kiss all her sorrows away, make her feel pleasure so profound that she wouldn't remember what her troubles were.

The lust you feel does not come from me.

He could not believe that. How could he want the things he does from her when she was still recovering? How could he take care of her and want to take everything from her all at once? No, this was only Draven's lust for Lani.

"Rose has much to learn before Lani can take her leave. You have time to be reunited. You best pray she's ready before I rid myself of *you*."

Phantom sent a wave crashing over Draven's essence and he floated away with the current, down to the depths of Phantom's soul with the others. He'd expected the shadows to recede too. To find that their master wasn't present and retreat to their corners.

Instead, they inched on him like minnows surrounding a shark, nipping at his fresh guilt for denying Draven to see his lover. It hadn't escaped him that one day he would be in a similar situation with the next bastard born with their shared soul. So, he sympathized.

The release felt freeing as the shadows took away that gnawing ache, but what replaced it was far worse. The shadows soaked into him, burrowing into his very being. How long would it take before they took over completely?

"They've really taken to you." Ramirez's gravelly voice rose over him, skittering the shadows back to their corners, but that didn't stop the ones burrowing their way into his skin.

"You're familiar with the shadows?"

Ramirez's face twisted, his lips pinching. "I am. Samuel struggled with them. They did not like having two masters."

Phantom took a steadying breath. He wanted to ask more or deny that he was anything like Sam, but losing control of them might be precisely what worried him.

Two masters?

"You know what helped?" Ramirez lit one of his cigars, having restocked in Draiocht; the smoke on these was darker, more pungent. "Isabeya." Tension racked Phantom's body at the mention of her, because for him, that was Rose. And what more could possibly be asked of her? "Whenever the shadows grew too demanding, too thick in his own mind, she was there to shed light. She cleansed his soul. I think that's precisely what you need now."

Phantom followed his gaze to the wisp of smoky shadow that disappeared into his hand at the thought of asking Rose for help. He felt guilty over something he hadn't even done and gave it over to shadows without even thinking about it.

He pulled his hand away from sight.

"You see too much, Ramirez."

"Or I see just enough. My boy, letting the shadows fester too long will destroy you and everyone around you."

"But not Rose," he countered, looking into those grey eyes, concern lines framing the edges. "She would survive it because of her light. And what happens if I ask her to use her power too soon? Would she survive that? What do the stars say?"

Ramirez's eyes shifted to the night sky beyond, to the Star of Nemain. It had been sitting there, waiting for him to come to Her. She didn't forget the summons She had given him while he was in Her realm.

Next to the Star of Nemain, two stars hung precariously close, already rivaling Her in brightness.

"I don't know of survival, but I know you are both meant to shine the brightest together. I imagine you must be alive to do so." Ramirez placed a steadying hand on Phantom's shoulder, the shadows pushing against his skin, asking if they should drag his soul to the depths. Phantom held them off. "I'm sorry for the weight of your decisions. Sam may not have known of the responsibility over one's own people, but I did." Phantom turned to see his friend again, a heaviness in his eyes. "And so did Isabeya."

Phantom averted his eyes, the shadows growing too impatient with him, but he shoved them away, forcing them back to the darkness to which they belonged.

"Tell Rose of your plight, and she will let you know when she is ready. Trust her to do that much."

The coolness on his shoulder and retreating footsteps let Phantom know that he was alone again. Shadows crept back to him, attaching themselves to his limbs like armor. He needed to find a way to take care of them, but he had no intention of taking from Rose.

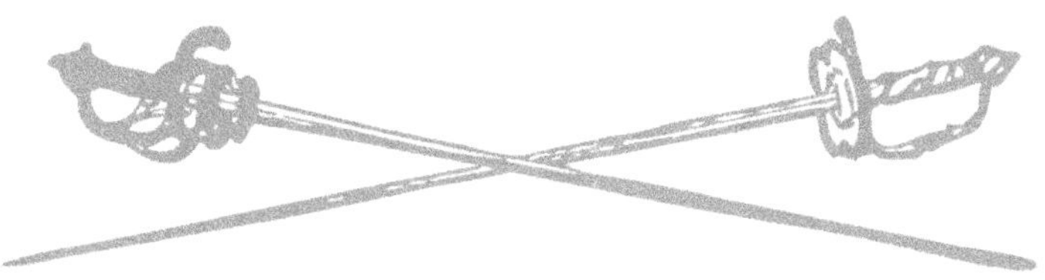

CHAPTER 54

THE SIDE OF THE LIVING

BLACK

The captain had permitted Black access to Sophia's cell.

She knew it was a test. If she were truly a devil, she would let her rot in a cell until the captain decided she was no longer a threat. If Black disobeyed, they were both traitors.

So why was it that sitting on the steps of the brig watching Sophia's chest rise and fall as she slept with the bloody key in her hands the hardest thing she had to do?

It was the middle of the night. They could be on a longboat, sailing back to Draiocht, or some other unclaimed land that they could build a life on, even if it was only the two of them.

Once Sophia woke up, she would make her decision, but in truth, she knew Sophia wouldn't abandon her goddess-given mission. Not even for her. Before finding out that she was a damn immortal, Black knew her to be responsible and wise. Someone like that would never forsake her own goddess.

The room was too dark, no moonlight cresting the singular porthole on the starboard wall. It felt lonely here. The silence gave her time to think about more than Sophia. The faces of those girls flashed in her mind every so often, reminding her what her attempt at kindness brought her. She should have killed the slavers before they could have spread their rumors.

379

She should have killed the last one, but there was no one left for them to target. As she thought it, she saw Sophia open her eyes.

"You have questions, I'm certain."

Black's eyes focused on the huntress before her, Sophia rolling off her pallet without a sound. Had she been asleep or did she just get tired of waiting for Black to speak?

"What does She want with you?"

Sophia's gaze snapped to the porthole, finding it dark, her shoulders relaxed slightly.

"I spoke the truth to your captain, She has yet to reveal that to me."

Black tossed the key between her hands, feeling the iron weight of it. "Is he not your captain as well?"

"He cannot be. Loyalty to him would compromise my purpose."

Anger bubbled up in her throat, spilling over. "A purpose you do not know," she snapped, not caring if Sophia flinched at her tone. She had every opportunity to explain this before.

The huntress let out a pained sigh. "Is my arrangement so different from yours?"

Anger simmered beneath the surface. There was a difference, aside from Phantom being mortal, but she didn't feel much like explaining when it was *her* who was owed the explanation.

At her silence, Sophia continued, "At least I knew the monster to which I was committing. What choice did you have?"

Black stood from the steps, closing the distance between her and the bars. "I had every choice. I didn't choose a goddess. I chose a family. That is what the captain offered me. Acceptance. Love. Freedom. There isn't one of us who regrets what it cost because of what he provided for us. What has She offered you?"

Sophia's face grew stoic, unyielding. If Black could use witchcraft to pull the thoughts from her head, she would do it now. At Sophia's heavy silence, Black turned, running her fingers through her hair, wanting to pull the short strands from her scalp.

"I may not know what is in store for me, but I know it is important."

Black focused back on the huntress, the vague responses were really grating on her nerves.

"The kind of importance that could tip the scales of who wins this war."

Black groaned, hating every word. "What war?"

"The living against the dead." Emotion finally registered in Sophia's watery eyes. It was fear, possibly panic. "It's been raging for thirty years, and it will not stop until a winner can be named." That weighty silence between them grew taut. Black's chest ached with her heaving heart. "I fight for the side of the living, what side do you fight for, Gwen?"

Blood filled her memories, flashing behind her eyes. All those civilians who were killed because of her. Her skin itched, specifically on her right wrist where she had a navy bandana wrapped around the healing burn marks. She shook off the memories. That had nothing to do with goddesses and their plans. It had everything to do with the greed and cruelty of men. For that, she would kill.

She turned away from Sophia, calling back, "Not all of us are soldiers in a holy war."

With that, Black stomped up the steps, leaving Sophia behind.

CHAPTER 55
WITCHCRAFT

SEBASTIAN

"We've made a mistake."

Sebastian's head snapped to the recruit and the pirate girl clutching at his arm. They were watching their enemies sail away before the navy could properly dispose of them. Captain Pike and his crew had committed atrocities across the Sumerian Sea, pillaging and raiding every port they came to.

They'd only just managed to scare him back to his ship without his precious grimoire. The magic in that book was twisted beyond measure, as proven by the pirate it belonged to.

Now, they stood on a cliff side, watching as the pirates fled.

"I know." James's eyes were so cold, Sebastian hardly recognized his brother.

"They'll be back," the girl answered, worry clouding her eyes. She was the daughter of Pike himself, but she helped them instead. Joseph still needed to explain that anomaly.

"I know," James parroted.

"They'll be ready." Concern laced Joseph's tone, he cared for this girl, immensely, it would seem.

"I know."

Sebastian looked down at the fleeing pirates. They would be back, if for nothing else but the woman clutching the recruit's arm. The most notorious pirate would not allow his daughter to defy him without punishment. He'd take the whole island in payment.

Sebastian would not let that happen. Once he spoke to the Commodore, to the Minister if he had to, they would see that protection over Kheli had to become a priority.

"They'll take me," she breathed.

"No, no. That's not going to happen." Joseph looked down at her like he would personally see to it, but he couldn't promise her that. Not until they could talk to the Minister.

"It's too late now," Sebastian offered. "They're gone."

Silence followed his words as fear and dread choked the surrounding air, but it was James who spoke next.

"No, it's not." Opening the grimoire, he flipped through the pages of the god-forsaken book. He didn't think he could use the book, did he?

"What are you doing?"

"Making this island safe."

Shivers tore down Sebastian's spine as he stopped on a page, one with a giant illustrated monster. It had eight tentacles and a bulbous head. It was pictured with its arms wrapped around a ship, dragging it to the depths of the sea.

"Earhart, if you please," James prompted, and Earhart somehow understood. In a second, he pulled a knife and ran it over James' awaiting palm, blood pooling and dripping through his fingers. He slammed his hand onto the page.

"James, no, you can't do this." Sebastian reached for the book. He wasn't going to let this evil magic take root in his friend. The price was eternal punishment, how could he let that happen? A phantom force knocked him back, like the wind itself was protesting his interruption.

Goddess-damned witchcraft.

"Listen to me, James. It is not worth your soul!"

James turned a pair of darkened eyes on him, something inexplicably corrupt lurking there. "That ship has already sailed, brother." Sebastian's eyes furrowed as he tried to understand.

James looked at Joseph, who nodded. "Do it."

Sebastian's heart jumped into his throat. It felt like the ground was shifting beneath him. It was wrong. Everything was wrong.

"Hafgufa, conjuro te aeternum de profundo maris. Hafgufa, inicios tuos occidere."

The air stilled around them; the sounds of the jungle silent for once as the world waited for what came next.

Sebastian watched the ship, where legendary lilac sails carried pirates out to sea. But it was the wave rolling towards them that he focused on; a wave that was going the wrong direction.

It slammed into Macha's Demise *making the ship jolt and rock. The pirates scrambled around the deck, searching for an explanation. They were answered when tentacles the size of tree trunks climbed up the sides of the ship. It went so slowly that Sebastian could barely tell it was moving.*

Once the tentacles reached the deck, the crew was frantic, screaming loud enough for Sebastian to hear. He closed his eyes, willing the nightmare to be over. He didn't care that they died, only that it was done so horrifically. Against the officers, they would have had a chance to defend themselves. This was a slaughter.

Gunfire and cannonballs popped into the distant air as the pirates fought for their lives. It was to no avail though. There was no walking away from this, for any of them.

Not being able to resist looking, he opened his eyes to find that the sea around them had become crowded with fins. Creatures of a predatory nature had gathered, waiting for the monster to provide them with an easy meal.

They couldn't even abandon ship without death awaiting them.

A loud crack that Sebastian would never forget signaled the failure of the main mast. The wood and sail tumbled to the sea as the tentacles dragged the pirates to the waters, their screams fuel for his future nightmares.

Sebastian wanted no part of this. He wanted to join the navy to protect people and though he wasn't above killing a pirate, this was not the way.

Two heavy tentacles fell over the middle of the deck, splitting it in half and effectively destroying the ship. There was no chance of salvaging it now.

Sebastian fell to his knees on the grass, just at the edge of the cliff side. He'd never seen anything more horrific in his life than the image of a monstrous beast dragging a ship to the seabed below. Even worse was the silence that followed. Not a soul was left behind.

James cried out as he landed on the grass a few feet behind Sebastian, a hand going to his throat. He moved, running to his friend. Had Nemain already named her price? Was She taking him in payment?

"What's happening?" Sebastian pinned his eyes on the pirate among them. The only one who could answer.

She swallowed at his stare. "The grimoire demands a price." Her words were so soft, not panicked as they ought to be while a man writhed on the ground before her. "This is Nemain's way of keeping track of your debts."

James recoiled, his hand flying away, and Sebastian sucked in a sharp, pained breath. A tattoo now covered his neck in inky art. Tentacles climbed up his skin like they did the hull of that ship. He stared in shock as James managed to catch his breath.

Then his brother was kneeling before him, his deep blue eyes locking with his own. Sebastian searched for a modicum of regret but found none. He could shake his brother for being so reckless with his own life. With his own soul.

"What have you done?"

Sebastian sucked in a breath as he woke, panic still ripe in his chest. He sat up on his pallet, the faint smell of mildew filling his nostrils. He rubbed his face, trying to remember where he was. Kheli, of course. He only had *that* nightmare while he was on this blasted island.

Angelica had taken him, Indigo, and Vincent back to the caves they were using as cover. It was a clever idea considering the amount of protection they afforded from the half-dead animals crawling about the island, but they didn't allow for much privacy.

He hadn't managed to wrap his head around the fact that Angelica had a magical tattoo. This one was nothing like the tentacles around James' neck, but it made him uneasy, especially considering her lineage.

Of all the moons in the sky, Sebastian never once considered that one day he would have been a refugee on Kheli while guarded by the strangest display of witchcraft he had ever borne witness to.

Well, except that of Angelica's father, but he was at the bottom of the ocean with the rest of his crew.

Female voices drew Sebastian's attention to the cave's entrance where a fire burned. He couldn't quite make them out, but he could see Indigo's shadow against the side of the cave.

Rising from his pallet, he put his naval jacket back on before joining them. Angelica gave him a quick smile that didn't reach her eyes but told him she didn't mind him there. Indigo, however, seemed wary. He half expected her to shoo him away, but she refocused on Angelica.

"Close your eyes," Indigo's lulling voice sounded even more ethereal in the darkness of the cave. Sebastian stood a few feet away, crossing his arms as he tried to work out what they were doing.

Angelica sat perched on a boulder. With reluctance, she obeyed.

Indigo smeared cream across her eyelids, which he cringed at the idea of. The amount of trust Angelica showed for a near stranger was unthinkable. The substance was spread across her cheeks and neck, transforming into a brilliant, azure blue.

"What do you see?"

Angelica's features softened, serenity relaxing her brow. "Clouds, like I'm flying."

Witchcraft was becoming an entirely too common appearance, but he found that he was warming up to it.

"Flying how?" Indigo asked, her eyes narrowing.

Angelica smiled faintly, in some kind of trance. "On wings, like an eagle."

Indigo snapped her fingers and Angelica's eyes popped open. "Your powerful blood does you credit, but it is not the source of your magic. Now, let me see the mark."

Sebastian stared blankly at Angelica. *Powerful blood?* Had she told the witch that her father was the infamous Captain Pike? The secret he'd taken great pains to protect.

Angelica's jaw clenched, her hands fidgeting with the hem of her shirt. She lifted her wrist, displaying the intricate lines of blue lightning decorating her dark skin.

"I know what a tattoo means when I didn't have it inked into my flesh." Panic and anger laced her tone, but her eyes landed on Sebastian. "You know too. You witnessed what happened to Phantom." He did, all those years ago when they were only lieutenants trying to protect an island by themselves. The nightmare was still too fresh in his mind. "I don't intend to live with debts."

Indigo inspected the mark closely, taking in its intricate detail and small lines.

"You are not bound to Nemain as your father was, otherwise, your lightning would be black, not blue. Color tells much about patronage." Indigo sat back on her own boulder, reaching her hands out, palms up. "Lay your hands up, palms to the sky."

Reluctantly, and with one brow raised, Angelica obeyed. "If not Nemain, who has bound me?"

"I believe it to be unintentional, and quite new. It may resemble your father's magic, your lineage likely playing a part in its similarities, but I don't think the world has seen this before. Now, take deep breaths and focus inward." Indigo closed her eyes, her breathing coming in sweeping motions. Angelica followed her example. "I want you to feel the magic, trace it within your own heart, right down to the moment it touched you."

Sebastian half expected to see the wind pick up around them, or the air to thicken, an indication that magic was present and being sought after.

Angelica peeked one eye open, her gaze traveling to Sebastian with an incredulous look. He shrugged in response.

"Focus," Indigo commanded. Angelica shut her eyes again. "Think of the truth in your life and sift through any lies."

Well, that was incredibly vague. He breathed his relief at not being the object of Indigo's current instruction.

Angelica winced. "I feel something."

"Good, pull it forward, let it fall into your hands."

With the way Angelica's face was contorting, the task was difficult and unpleasant. Sparks filled the air like the crackling of fire, charging the surrounding air.

"Focus it, Angelica. In your hands."

Panting, she narrowed the energy hovering over their palms

until rivulets of miniature lightning split the air. Blue light erupted from Angelica's palms, intertwining with the lightning until they created shapes together, like a painting, but moving.

There was something familiar about the color.

Sebastian shifted until he was behind Indigo, seeing the image fully.

"Sweet Davina," Sebastian said, rousing the women from their focus. Angelica's eyes widened as she took in the blue light before her, and the images moved.

It was her, badly hurt and bleeding to death on a bed. They were viewing the scene from above, like a reaper about to take her soul.

Sebastian recognized the devils tending to her, their doctor and Earhart at the side of her bed, kissing her hands like she would slip away at any moment.

Through the door came James and — Rose. The image didn't allow for any sound, but there seemed to be conversing between James and his first mate, hope shining in his eyes.

James and Rose approached the opposite side of the bed, James pulling the infamous Stone from his pocket. It glistened, even in the faded image before them. He deposited it in Rose's awaiting palm, and she exploded. There was no better way to describe how she lit up from within. Her eyes glowed, ribbons like the ones creating the image floated over the still body of Angelica. Rose's lips moved, singing a song they could not hear.

Like he had heard her do so many times. Binding him to the will of her father. His stomach soured at the image. Even if he was immune to manipulation now, he'd never forget what it was like to lose himself.

After a couple minutes of watching her sing and the ribbons moved around them both, the glow faded, and Rose fell into James' arms. The image was cut off as he lifted her limp body.

All traces of blue and lightning faded from around them, leaving nothing but the sound of crinkling rain and crackling fire.

"What was that?" Sebastian asked since no one else spoke.

"She saved my life," Angelica mumbled as if speaking the

words was what made them true. "I thought they had only overestimated my wound. I didn't — Joseph didn't say—"

"It appears that you are not bound to a goddess at all." There was a hint of wonder in Indigo's tone.

"But, how? And why now? Why not then, when she used magic to save me? And what do I owe her?"

"There is only one who can answer that."

Sebastian prayed, not for the first time, for the safety of those aboard *Nemain's Revenge.*

CHAPTER 56

CANVAS

ROSE

Rose stared at the pristine, white canvas, her eyes blinking at the smooth, unblemished fabric, the vibrant new paints a stark contrast to the untouched surface, practically begging to be used.

A glare of sunlight crossed her vision.

Using your creative talents is an effective way to access your soul.

Lani remained in her head instead of taking her projected form, though Rose had to wonder if their apparitions were truly a gift, or if it was just a mark of her dwindling sanity. She'd question it later.

It had been three days since she'd woken up and Lani trained her as often as possible. Lara had come in on occasion, bringing food and company, but James only came to have her sing. He wouldn't linger, finding an excuse to leave. Yesterday, she nearly ran after him, but she wasn't ready to face the rest of the crew just yet.

"I thought you said I had to conquer my fear first before I could access the soul."

The kimiya for your physical body and survival has been opened, your ability to fly is proof of that. Any remaining fear is a burden you must release, but I can see that time can do the healing for you. Instead, you will work on your soul weaving.

Rose didn't understand it. Why must she learn to soul weave, anyway? But seeing the paints before her drew her away from the questions. She wanted her hands busy, and her mind focused anywhere else but in her own head.

She let a finger drift over the coarseness of the canvas, her heart melting with thoughts of James. Amidst the chaos, he'd found a way to bring well-needed joy into her life.

Reaching for the paints, she halted, uncertain where to start.

"What exactly am I to paint?"

Lani stayed silent awhile before answering. *Paint your soul. Whatever comes to mind when I say that. Perhaps a memory of when you were small or the dream you have for your future. Whatever you suppose lives in the depths of your being.*

Rose thought for a moment, closing her eyes to look inwards, even going as far as to place a hand over her lower stomach. She took a deep breath before picking up a brush and her favorite color.

Blue.

Is it a tree?

Rose tilted her head, finding that her bird was most definitely looking more like a tree.

She sighed, ripping the fabric off the easel and throwing it to the floor. Luckily, there were still two pieces left she could work with as opposed to the six failures crumpled on the floor.

Lani stayed silent in her head, not offering creative advice like she had done numerous times before. It was clear this was Rose's creative block, not hers. The warring emotions inside her couldn't decide what they wanted to do.

There was chaos and peace, pain and pleasure, expression and repression, everything filling her head, but not wanting to come out properly on the canvas before her.

Growling, she pushed the easel away, letting it crash to the floor.

Patience, let your creativity flow like a river inside you.

"Yes, immensely helpful. Thank you," she bit out, not meaning the sentiment at all.

Pacing, she let her feet guide her while her hands could not.

Straight out in the blinding midday light.

She blinked rapidly in the sunlight, realizing she had seen little of it recently.

Before registering shapes around her, a pair of arms engulfed her. She recognized Lara's lithe frame in a second, hugging her friend back. Hyne and Tick followed her with bright smiles on their faces like they were... pleased to see her...

The concept was entirely foreign. Only Lara smiled like that at her.

Her friend leaned back far enough to free her hands to speak.

"You're out. You look so much better."

She had not meant to leave the safety of the captain's quarters, and she very much doubted she looked anything but terrible. If this was better, she didn't want to imagine how she looked before.

Rose signed as she spoke, not leaving out present company. "I feel better, but I needed fresh air." She hoped that sounded convincing. It was too late to retreat now. She signed without speaking the next part. *"Which one?"* Her eyes flicked to the two men behind her. The sunshiny jester and the quiet, mysterious one. Both were more attractive than was fair.

Lara turned as red as the sea during the solstice.

Rose had several questions for her friend, but Tick chuckled, possibly the first sound she'd ever heard him make.

"I've been teaching them the hand language." Her hands moved a bit too frantically to be a calm response.

Rose's mouth gaped, realizing her mistake. Now, she was considering a hasty retreat, and to drag Lara with her.

A magnetic laugh left Hyne as he slapped a hand on Rose's shoulder. "It's good to see you. Captain's been insufferable without you." That worried her more than anything. Was he that bad off? "I would still offer my bed, but I'd like all appendages to remain attached to my frame."

Tick pushed at his friend, Hyne breaking out a crowd-winning smile. He had received a haircut since Rose saw him last, his blonde curls falling over his bandana. Was that to gain Lara's attention?

The silent one tapped her arm to get her attention and signed fluidly. *"We missed you here. Welcome back."* Though he didn't speak a word, he felt the sincerest. It was the first words he'd ever offered her.

Rose smiled sweetly to him, then Lara led her further onto the deck. She watched as devils turned their attention to her one by one. Warm smiles and greetings came for her. They either really did miss her, or they had nothing better to do. She chose to believe the former.

"I would dance in delight at seeing you on your feet if my knees didn't prevent it." Ramirez's whitened hair and grey eyes drew her attention. Her arms fell around him, happiness radiating from her. Outside of James, Ramirez was the first to make her feel welcomed on the ship. That, and the excitement she could feel from Isabeya at his proximity. She had missed him dearly.

It wasn't until this moment that she realized she needed to see them all. She may not have known them very well or for exceptionally long, but they felt like family. Hers just as much as they belonged to James.

A hand on her shoulder pulled her away from Ramirez.

The first mate stood with a solemn expression on his face. "Forgive me," he stopped and started a couple of times. "If I had been faster, or more observant, I might have ended your capture sooner." His shoulders slumped with the burden he must have been carrying since the soiree. It was sobering to witness his undeserved guilt.

It wasn't James alone who searched for her, who had traveled to Draiocht to find her. They *cared* about her.

She reached out, placing a hand against his arm in comfort. "You are not to blame." Pain split through her heart like a knife wound, tearing her apart.

Jon. He might have betrayed them, but what he did for her kept her alive even if he didn't survive it himself. Tears threatened to spill from her eyes, but she looked to the sky to banish them.

They deserved to know what happened to him, but she hadn't told James yet. She needed to tell him first.

Beyond the crowd, she witnessed Wilson leaning against the

mast, a drink in his hand as he raised it to her. Just beside him, Russet batted the air around him like a pestering insect wouldn't leave him alone.

"Blasted beetles are following me," he complained, and Wilson dropped his head into his free hand.

She laughed softly, before the air left her lungs entirely as Robin filled her field of vision, hanging from a rope like he was born a primate. "Hyne made a new song. You should sing it with us."

Rose raised her hands as the boy dropped to the deck. Singing a new song without understanding what effect it could have wasn't how she wanted to show her gratitude. They did save her, after all. They wouldn't want that to cost them their lives as her song lulled them over the edge of the ship.

Yes, that was a dramatic example, but she couldn't be too careful.

Most songs worked as subtle emotional manipulation, even if it wasn't her singing them. It was the beautiful art of song while her gifts enhanced the effect. They worked like spells with a more powerful response. It all depended on the song.

"I'm afraid that's not a good idea."

There was a disappointed frown in Robin's face before he hid it with a smile, then rushed over to Hyne.

"At least, give it a listen," Hyne started. "I think you'll like it."

CHAPTER 57
MAKE ME YOURS
PHANTOM

"Aside from continuing to gain weight, she's recovering quite remarkably. Her body has amazing healing properties. I assume the magic you supplied has something to do with that."

Voices floated from the main deck along with the strum of a bandolim and the buzz of a harmonica. The crew was finally settling from the experiences of Draiocht.

Smith went on about the parts of Rose's body that mended beyond her normal capabilities. At least, if she were human.

"Her ribs reassembled themselves, and her hair is already regrowing. A month from now, she may not have a trace of her capture remaining."

Phantom let out a strained breath. She shouldn't have had to endure it at all. "Some scars aren't left on the body." It was becoming clearer that Rose's mind would not heal as quickly as her flesh, even if all he wanted was for her to feel happy and safe again.

Every night, he snuck into the room, but he feared waking her, so he curled into a ball at the side of her bed as the beast. It was enough to hear her breathing and know she was safe.

Smith's hand landed on his arm. "In time, those will heal too. Have patience, Captain."

Phantom gave him a curt nod, turning over the fish and barley

Wilson had provided. It was musty below deck, making Phantom's skin itch to return to the open air, the open sea. Or it was only an excuse to watch her door, waiting for her to finally emerge.

Magic pulsed in his veins, more concentrated than he'd ever felt before. It was difficult to breathe through the overwhelming presence of the power, but he wouldn't use it. Not if that power could help Rose, but she couldn't take it fast enough. That was clear every time he came to the room to have her sing, but he couldn't linger. The shadows got louder when she took from his power, as if rebelling against the loss of it.

They whispered to him constantly now, singing of truths he could do nothing with and filling his mind.

sssnakesss in the ssssea

The words etched across his nerves, making his skin feel tighter, constricting—

"Sophia shows almost as remarkable a recovery as Rose. There are several bruises that will heal naturally, but nothing to be concerned over. The mark on her arm has faded to a pink spot. Truly, I've never seen someone survive Nemain's Mark."

Phantom cleared his throat, banishing the remaining strain from the consuming presence of the shadows. "That's what happens when one has a goddess's protection."

Smith's brow furrowed, noticing his captain's bitter tone. Phantom knew Sophia could break out of her cell at any given moment, and she proved that she was not a threat by remaining.

"Do you know what happened to Jon?"

Flaming anger responded to the thought of that traitor, but it dissipated just as quickly.

Jon was dead.

He didn't know how or why, but there was a tether between them that was severed the day he'd found Rose. Despite all he had done, Phantom hoped that meant he found a way to break their connection, but instinct told him that wasn't the truth.

He thought to ask Rose, but he didn't want her thinking of her time in Draiocht, much less of the traitor who put her there.

"I don't know," Phantom lied.

Smith nodded solemnly. He could feel it too. The absence of his comrade.

"It's strange to think of us as the Ten Devils." He offered a small snort. "After all those years losing soldiers in the war, you'd have thought I would have grown used to comrades. There was something about this ship that made me believe we would never lose each other."

Phantom lifted his tin of rum to Smith, who inclined his in return. They didn't say anything before drinking. They didn't need to. It was an understanding and an acknowledgment of what was lost.

OH, BE MERRY
GOOD MEN OF THE BARGE
BE MERRY AND SING
OH AYE DITTLE DEE

The crew's shanty grew loudly over the sounds of crashing waves, enough devils joining into the melody for the words to be clear.

WE FIGHT AND WE SING
FOR THE MOUTHS THAT WE FEED AND COIN WE ACHIEVE

The tone was too light, the music was so joyful that it stirred Phantom's mood. It was too much to expect his crew to remain melancholy as long as he did, yet still happiness grated against his soul, unable to penetrate his cold, dead heart. He could command them to be sad, let his magic take the joy out of *Nemain's Revenge* until his songbird could also feel it.

That's a bit dramatic, don't you think?

Draven's skeptical tone brought him out of his drowning thoughts.

His devils were his family. If they could find any happiness during this time, what right did he have to take it away? He promised them freedom, but he never expected that the biggest threat to that promise would be himself.

The shadows closed in on him, begging him to feed on the guilt souring his soul. He wanted to give it to them, let them have every traitorous thought until he could only feel emptiness.

He nearly let them have it.

COME MERRY MEN, HAVE A DRINK WITH ME

That was her voice, Rose's undeniable sweet voice that he would recognize matched his own soul no matter what life he lived.

FOR THE SEAS CAN WAIT AND THE RUM IS FREE

Her potent spell wafted down to him, deflecting off the natural shields of his mind. Though the shadows still begged him for access to his sorrow, he couldn't help but mourn the presence of her song. He'd never experienced it like others had.

One look at Smith's resigned smile, and he knew this was precisely what the crew needed. Happiness, even if not truly made, lightening the hardened features around his eyes, ones that had been there as long as Phantom had known him. Even that trodden dismay from his time at war seemed more bearable.

Yellow flares split across his vision.

Don't do it. Don't let her in.

But Kayden didn't understand; he had already let her in. Rose had ownership over him. That much had been clear when he'd sailed in the opposite direction of salvation to get her back.

OH, BE MERRY
GOOD MEN OF THE BARGE
BE MERRY AND SING
OH AYE DITTLE DITTLE DEE

"Pardon me," Phantom said before abandoning Smith to his food. He needed to see the evidence of her survival and recovery with his own eyes, watch her sing in merriment.

Sunlight hit his face as he breached the main deck, setting eyes on the magnificent creature before him. She was ethereal, wearing the clothes he had saved for her, the airy white shirt and brown trousers that made her look like she belonged on the ship. Her smile was bright, and her posture relaxed.

Pride swelled in his chest at seeing her smiling so soon. He thought it was too much to hope for, but there she was, singing with the crew, a certain glow around her. Was she glowing?

It wasn't the blue of her siren magic. This was a glow like sunlight reflecting off her skin and glistening, as if she were the surface of the sea.

WE FOUGHT AND WE SANG
FOR THOUGHTS OF LOVE AND THE PROMISE WE MADE

With a deep breath, he let it in, the promise of peace her voice would bring. It came in subtly, like an approaching tide, lapping at his mind with serenity and joy. The shadows receded, his guilt disappearing enough for them to grow uninterested.

The receding shadows brought a wave of tranquility, relaxing his tense muscles, a feeling akin to Rose's soothing touch, relieving him of his burden.

OH AYE DITTLE DEE
OH AYE DITTLE DITTLE DEE
COME MAKE ME YOURS BEFORE YOU LEAVE ME

Opening his eyes, he found her staring directly at him, that softness and peace washing over him, but there was something else to her stare. Heat. An invitation in the form of heart-melting need.

Their first time had been intense and passionate, but he was too overcome to appreciate the beauty before him in the way she deserved. There wasn't enough time in the world to worship her the way he wanted to, but he was willing to try. To take her lovingly, slowly, to torture her with pleasure, his touch, his tongue—

He wanted to take her more brutally than before, bent across his desk, on her knees, over the railing of the ship—

Phantom wanted everything from her, every ounce of pleasure he could wring from her flesh. His heart seized in his chest, even as his cock grew uncomfortable in his trousers.

He couldn't cross that boundary too soon, her recovery vastly more important, but perhaps she needed him as much as he needed her.

yesssss take from sssssshe

That guilt still clawed at him. He was asking too much. He was taking back the magic he gave in the form of peace and now he wanted to do unspeakable things to her body.

The song continued, the rest of the crew joining back in, but Rose was no longer singing, her spell had already taken effect within the crew. No one noticed when she stood and strode over to him, that glint of heat in her eyes.

Phantom's jaw tensed as he otherwise stood perfectly still, watching her approach. She walked like she was pleasure incarnate. Her skin radiated a soft, inner light, and the intensity of her gaze made him feel as if he might fall to his knees.

She stopped only a foot away from him and he felt like he could die.

All he wanted to do was drag her into his arms and kiss her until they could no longer breathe.

"Captain," she addressed, a hint of sultry seduction to her tone. He needed a drink, a strong one.

With a hopeful look, he extended his hand, the gesture a silent invitation, wanting nothing more than her acceptance.

She stared down at his hand, unblinking. Indecision and weariness were clear in the way her brows drew together.

Lifting a shaky hand, he moved to take her hand but stopped. He witnessed a flash of fear on her face before she drew her hand away.

"I'm sorry," she whispered before retreating a step. She turned, running to his quarters.

His heart cracked open watching her leave.

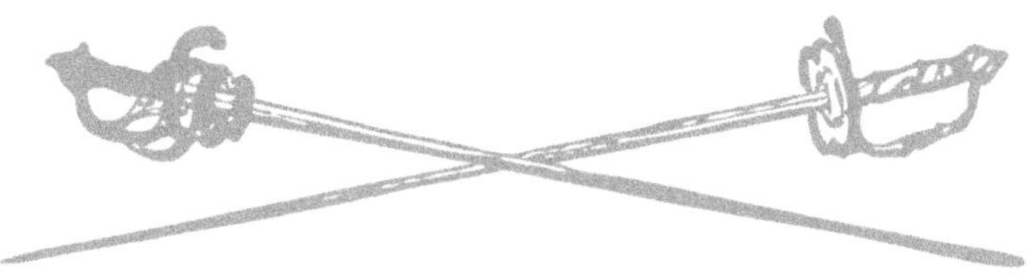

CHAPTER 58

PERKS OF THE JOB

BLACK

Black tossed a coin around in her palm, a habit she'd picked up in the last week.

Russet stumbled near the stairs to the quarterdeck, unsurprisingly drunk and whispering to himself. He even swatted at the air like those insects from Draiocht had followed him.

Across the ship from Black's barrel perch, Hyne, Tick, and Lara conversed. It was odd to see someone besides Hyne talking, but Tick was moving his hands, and Lara was translating. Though Hyne looked to be trying to learn the hand language as well.

It amazed her that all Tick needed was a new form of communication. He'd never tried to write his words, so she assumed that he didn't have anything to say.

Or it was Lara that brought out his desire to communicate.

It was likely the latter. She wasn't certain what the three of them were, but she hoped it wasn't anything that would tear Hyne and Tick apart. They were too inseparable to be torn apart by a woman.

Black tossed the coin again. They'd been at sea for over a week, and it was rotting her brain. She needed something to do, something to hit.

Letting the coin go, she went to sharpen her sword instead, pulling out the stone she used for it. Davina knows the sword was sharp enough, she'd already taken the stone to it nine times in the last week. She'd need a new sword by the month's end.

But it kept her hands busy.

Metal sang as another sword hit hers. She tracked the blade to the man holding it. The first mate was growing out his beard, keeping it more maintained than most sailors would bother with.

"Spar with me. It's been ages."

Black let a false smirk paint her face. If she'd learned anything from the captain it was to appear as if nothing is wrong, even if everything is wrong.

She stood slowly, controlled. "I'll just put you on your back again."

Earhart spread his arms. "You're not the only one needing something to distract yourself with." Black felt a pang of guilt for forgetting. This was the longest time they had spent away from Kheli.

Instantly, Black wanted to apologize. She may not know what to think of Sophia now, but at least she knew the huntress was safe behind bars below deck. Earhart had a wife and two daughters that he didn't know were alive or dead. How was he not going completely insane?

"Don't look at me like that." His brows rose up his face. "This is to forget our problems for a time, not invite them to join us."

She nodded; he needed this more than she did.

Keeping her sword low, she circled the first mate, as he returned in kind, their eyes focused and unwavering. The other devils began to accumulate, already trading bets, most in Black's favor.

He heard their exchanges, biting the inside of his cheek. "The confidence of the crew is astounding."

Black smirked, before taking a bow, never letting her eyes drop. Earhart lunged before she could fully rise, giving her little time to parry.

She blocked, pushing him off her in the next breath, though it took more effort than it normally did. Rotting on this deck was taking more than her mind.

"You know what I'd like to know?" Earhart started, a teasing glimmer in his eyes. "Did people refer to you as Lady Lockness?"

She lunged, her blade a silver flash, but he met her attack, the clang of steel echoing through the wind as he forced her back. She raised him a devilish smile.

"What did they call you? Blacksmith? Or was it deserter?"

A slight smile played on Earhart's lips as he brushed off the taunts, unfazed by the woman's attempts to goad him. This is how they spared. It was not all steel and strength. Sometimes it was words. Today, it appeared they both needed to be sufficiently distracted.

When he didn't strike at her, she took the opportunity, driving him backwards towards the ship railing, every blow to his blade like hitting a solid wall.

His eyes glinted right before he put his weight into the next blow. It blew her backwards, onto her back.

"Looks like you beat me to the ground." He lunged for her, but she was fast, dodging his blow not a second too soon. The devils grew silent as they watched Earhart's sword split straight through the floorboards, buried to the hilt.

Black breathed heavily, looking at the spot where she could have died.

It wasn't like Earhart went easy on her before, but he usually didn't use enough force to split open the deck.

The first mate blinked, and a blue glint faded. He backed away from the sword like it had burned him.

Silence overwhelmed them as the devils stared at the sword. Panic shook more than one of them, but none more than the first mate as he looked down at his hands.

Ramirez stepped up to the sword, inspecting it with a critical eye. "It appears we will have to be careful with our talents from now on."

She remembered chasing after Jon in the city. How she ran faster and for longer than she thought was possible. Could it have been more than the thrill of battle making her swift?

Movement in the corner of her eye brought her gaze to the drunkard leaning on the stairs to the quarterdeck. Russet kept swatting at the air, that invisible insect tormenting him. It took a couple of focused seconds for Black to see the shadows swirling around his hands.

"I—" Russet started, staring at the shadows, as big as fish, flying around him. "I thought I'd imagined them. I blamed the rum, but I haven't a drop in five days."

Wilson's eyes narrowed on Russet's hands. "*Tashin.*" Didn't that mean demon? Before Black could ask him what he meant, Wilson disappeared into the main cabin.

Russet kept his eyes on his hands as Black turned her focus to Ramirez, who was currently scrutinizing him.

"Do you know what's happening to us?"

"I have a theory, though I suspect this hasn't truly happened before."

Black felt her heart race in her chest. "What's your theory?" Ramirez was hesitant, keeping his hands close to his face. "Please, we need to know what this is."

He let out a defeated breath. "I believe we are sharing in the captain's power."

CHAPTER 59
TO THE DRINK
PHANTOM

Phantom had been hiding in the treasure room of his own ship.

It had been weeks since he had been here, but it felt like the only place of peace he could find. A bottle of red moonshine sat to his side. He didn't usually turn to the bottle for a casual drink, especially whilst still at sea, but it was the only thing currently blocking out the shadow's whispers.

Even now they swirled around his fingers, wanting him to use them or let them consume him completely.

If you cannot manage their presence, then command them to leave or allow Lani to relieve them.

A hysterical laugh bubbled up his throat, though he wasn't certain which part of Draven's words held more weight. If he commanded them away, would he lose the tentative trust he'd built with the little creatures? Would they even listen?

Rose ran away from him. He knew it would take time for her to recover, but he could only withstand her fear for so long.

"She can take however long she needs."

Guilt soured his stomach, breaching past the haze of alcohol. The shadows curled in further, asking to relieve the pressure in his gut. He couldn't allow it, taking another swig of the burning drink.

Yellow flames burned his eyes. *Get up, you idiot. The last thing she needs from you is to turn into a bleeding mess.*

"Oh, that's a right cheeky claim coming from you." Phantom pointed at his reflection in a gold-framed mirror as if Kayden were standing there instead. "Aren't you always telling me not to let her in?"

Yes, and see what's become of you now.

Phantom rolled his eyes. The last counterpart's advice he was willing to take was the one who rejected the only perfect thing in his life.

The flames flared again. *Do not pretend to know. You do not.*

He ignored the man, focusing on the bottle in his hands instead.

ssssomeone isss coming

He'd learned to differentiate between the shadow voices and his own counterparts. The shadows sounded more inhuman, unnatural, like a whispering in the wind rather than an errant thought in his head.

it issss the old one

Phantom turned, expecting to face Ramirez or even Smith, but seeing Wilson's face was a surprise. The Yokan man looked to be no older than forty-five, so why did the shadows consider him to be old?

The last thing Phantom wanted was to see Wilson.

"What have you done to them?"

A wave of hysterical laughter swept over Phantom as he struggled to his feet, his legs shaking before he found his balance. Wilson glared at the state of him. He doubted his drunkenness would last long; ever since assimilating with Maahes, it never did.

"You'll have to be more specific, to which of my sins are you referring? Could it be the Draion filth I purged from the city? Or perhaps the Samsarans I left in the care of a mad woman? I know, it's the Khelitians I abandoned who could all be rotting away on their precious island. All in the name of a woman I have failed spectacularly."

Wilson's face was stony and impassive to the point that

Phantom laughed again, the liquid in his stomach making everything feel like a joke.

He picked his half-drunk bottle from the floor, lifting it to his mouth. "Perhaps, I should just end it all and hope the next life is more merciful."

The bottle flew from his hand, crashing to the floor, the moonshine spilling across the floorboards. The culprit stood with his staff outstretched, completely unamused.

"That bottle was bloody expensi—"

His head whipped to the side with the force of Wilson's palm flat to his cheek. Phantom felt a bit of his drunk haze parting as he turned his eyes back to the cook.

"Will everyone stop *slapping me*?"

First Black had slapped the sense into him at the palace, now Wilson was what? Slapping the drunk out of him? Even as he thought it, his vision was becoming clearer.

"Damn the countries you never promised to protect! The people you *did* promise are standing on that deck, waiting for you." Phantom blinked rapidly, clearing the rest of the haze. Wilson thrust a skin of water towards him. He eyed it wearily before lifting it to his lips and taking greedy gulps of crisp water, letting it sober him.

"What's happening?"

"Your devils are scared. Earhart is stronger than he should be, Black is faster, and Russet—" Wilson's eyes darkened. "You must see."

Wilson turned to the door, but Phantom stopped him with a hand on his arm. There had always been something more to Wilson's story that he had not shared, but that darkness in his eyes told Phantom it had something to do with this.

"What are you not telling me?"

Instead of answering, Wilson's gaze landed on shadows curling around Phantom's arm. "Careful with those. Death was not meant to be commanded."

Wilson shrugged off his hand before continuing up to the main deck.

With Wilson's words still repeating in his head, the sun lit Phantom's face, nothing but blue skies and ocean beyond the vessel. Expectant eyes fell on him as every devil waited to hear what he would say.

Searching for that spot of green within himself, he pulled until Sam was awake and present in his mind.

What's going on?

"Listen," Phantom whispered. The devils had wide panicked eyes, all except one. Taking a deep breath, he looked at Ramirez. "Explain."

The old man nodded.

"We were hoping you could provide the answer. You see, our swordsman and first mate engaged in a sparring match that ended with Earhart's sword embedded into the deck of the ship."

Indeed, there was a broad blade cutlass half impaled into the wood; the devils were spread around it like it was diseased.

Phantom approached the blade, pulling it out with significant effort. It was a precious piece to the first mate, one he had once done a great deal to retrieve, but now Earhart stared at it like it might bite him.

Ramirez continued his explanation. "During the match, Black displayed significant swiftness while Earhart showed exceptional strength. It begs the question of how, Captain." Phantom inspected the two in question, but aside from being shaken, they didn't seem any different.

But there was another Wilson mentioned...

"Where is Russet?"

Eyes turned beyond him to the shadowy stairs by the quarter-deck, where the darkness was too thick for the midday sun to penetrate.

friendssss

Adjusting to the light, Phantom finally saw his massive red beard and scared eyes.

"Captain, how do you... make them... stop?"

Shadows swirled around the devil, weaving through his fingers and winding around his limbs like snakes. Unlike the evasive way they treated Phantom at first, they *gravitated* to Russet.

He must have possessed truly horrific sins if this was only done with his guilt.

"What are you feeding them?"

"Captain?"

Phantom made it to the man, taking a fistful of his shirt and pulling him into the light. The shadows skittered into the corners they had come from.

Russet took a shaky breath. "Oh, thank you. That was a right sticky situation, wasn't it Cap?"

Phantom's head turned, inspecting the drunkard closely for the first time in years. What had he missed? There must have been a reason he drank so much, but Phantom hadn't thought to ask before.

But now was hardly the time.

He turned to his devils, whispering under his breath to the voices listening, "Any ideas?"

Draven answered first. *They're taking on your traits. It never happened to me, but I couldn't command an army against their will.*

Green and orange, vines and shadow filled his periphery.

Not in my lifetime either. James, I don't believe this has happened before, not in this way.

Ramirez placed a hand on Phantom's shoulder. "The *Imari* mentioned a shared power between us and you. Something that grows stronger with the more souls we provide for you. Did he not mention that a portion of that power then remains in us?"

Phantom had paid little attention to Colt's ramblings at the time, but he searched his memory.

"It's like shares of treasure."

He watched the rest of the crew remember too; the explanation offered up to them weeks ago.

Ramirez lit a cigar next to him, and Phantom was tempted to ask for one. "It would seem this is an ability exclusive to you, Captain. At least, not since your true form roamed the world." He chuckled. "That would be a sight to see."

"Hold on," Black spoke, one hand firmly on the hilt of her

sheathed sword. "If I kill someone, not only do I provide you with power, but I earn some for myself as well?"

"And apparently, for Nemain too. Powerful little things, these souls." Ramirez puffed his cigar before leaning against the railing of the ship.

"What a share of power that is," Hyne commented, staring at his own hands like he'd never noticed them before.

"Will we all eventually control shadows?" Black looked back to Russet who had a small shadow resting on his shoulder like a parrot.

"*Shindemo sasenai,*" Wilson spat, angrier than Phantom had ever seen. Roughly, it translated to *over my dead body*.

"The shadows take a great deal of concentration and even then, they are more like pets. They only obey you when they trust you." Phantom scrutinized the wide smile on Russet's face. How did this man control the shadows so quickly? Wilson stood a step behind him with a disapproving frown.

There were a great many things Phantom still needed to learn about his devils.

"And the beast? Will we turn?"

Phantom refocused on Black. "The speed and strength, that is from Maahes, but I doubt any of you will turn." He'd been wrong before, but the beast only belonged to him. He could feel that truth in his bones, but he couldn't explain it.

The devils all seemed skeptical still, so he looked at each of them. "We will figure this out together. It can only make us stronger. And we need it more than ever." He pointed to the sea behind them. "Those demons are likely after us, since we have the most precious treasure aboard." He pointed beyond the horizon. "Kheli lay waiting for us with perhaps new horrors that we must navigate." Then he pointed west. "Beyond Samsara and all the places we know lies the next adventure. I have not forgotten where we were meant to go."

He turned back to them. "But now, we are stronger, faster, more powerful than we were before. We needed this, so we could have the strength to survive what comes next."

CHAPTER 60

ANY FORM YOU TAKE

ROSE

Lost in contemplation, Rose gazed at her unfinished painting, the brush still clutched in her hand, but the image of James' face kept flashing before her eyes.

He'd looked so devastated when she ran from him on the deck, but she couldn't stay when the fear was paralyzing her. A part of her couldn't believe she was truly safe, even if she was drawn to James like a moth to a flame, she couldn't trust herself. Not when Colt and Dante could be faking all of this.

Letting out a frustrated breath of air, she dropped her brush and climbed to the bed. The sun had set hours ago, and all she had was a candle to see by as she climbed into a bed that felt too cold. She told herself she would warm up soon, but there was a bone-deep chill that told her it would never go away.

Rose blew out the candle but didn't fully sink into the blankets. She didn't feel tired, only that she had nothing else to do. Staring into the darkness, she let her mind wander, Lani's memories of battle with light and darkness playing in her mind.

The door clicked open, and she stayed perfectly still as James walked in, silently shutting the door behind him. She could just see his silhouette in the darkness as he shed his clothes, lilac and silver moonlight highlighting the outline of his shoulders and head.

Once his clothes were gone, he shifted, his smooth skin becoming thick fur as he dropped to all fours, a low chuff rumbling in his chest.

She'd seen his beast form twice now. Once while he was chasing her through a rose hedge maze and the other on that dais in Draiocht. This time seemed more peaceful than those, like the transition came easier for him.

Mesmerized by his movements, she watched him stalk closer, disappearing behind the edge of the bed. As silently as she could manage, she leaned over. He had curled up into a ball on the floor beside her, unaware of how she watched him. It was so reminiscent of that night after their game of Kazeboon. He had won his right to sleep in his own bed, yet still he'd chosen to sleep on the floor because she was scared.

Reaching out, she stroked along his soft fur. He was so warm, it made her want to curl up with him on the floor. A soft, contented purr filled the air an instant before his body stiffened.

She pulled her hand back, and he jumped to his feet, taking several steps away from her. She didn't want him to leave, so when he turned to the door, she reached out her hand.

"Wait, please."

He stopped, turning those red eyes on her. It was odd seeing a feline with such depth and expression.

"Stay with me." It was an echo of the words she had said to him months ago, even if it felt like years had gone by since. The night before she'd returned to her father, and she wanted him to hold her.

He couldn't speak, but she could see the response in those eyes of his.

Always.

Slowly. Ever so slowly, he walked back to her, jumping onto the bed. It creaked a bit with his weight but held firm as he laid next to her feet. She wanted to insist on him lying next to her, but she wasn't sure if she was ready for that.

She raised an eyebrow at him, usually his move. "Did you shift into a lion just so I wouldn't be scared?" She laughed to herself. "It's an ironic idea, that I would be less scared of a lion."

He chuffed in a way that she took as agreement, but there was something far more serious in his eyes and she understood. If this was the only way he could be near her, so be it.

"Oh James," she whispered before placing a hand on his massive paw. He tensed but didn't draw away. She stroked further, inching closer so she could pet his soft mane. "You're so soft this way."

He chuffed again, dipping his head to nuzzle into her neck. His whiskers tickled her cheek, and a laugh escaped her. He drew back until he saw the smile on her face. He pounced on her, dragging his whiskers around her neck and drawing more laughter. It was torture, but smiles were so rare that she didn't mind it.

Eventually, she struggled enough that he moved to lie beside her instead, somehow looking entirely too proud of himself.

She leaned up on her elbows. "That wasn't fair," she complained half-heartedly. "I didn't even have a chance."

He lifted his head as if to say, *that's not my problem.*

She laughed softly, and she swore she saw a smile. There was so much to tell him. Every awful thing that happened to her, but it was hard to put them all into words.

"Jon is dead." She didn't know what surprise looked like on a beast like him, but he only lowered his head in a *go on* gesture. "Before I saw you on the throne, he tried to help me escape. He fought the guards to buy me time, but I was too weak to get past them. Still, I couldn't get free. I couldn't find you."

He growled, but she continued, stroking his back to soothe him.

"Then they brought him back to my cell. I was skeptical at first, but then—" She didn't want to speak of the things Dante and Colt did to her. Not now, but she wanted to talk about Jon. "Then he talked to me. When I needed it most, he was there, grounding me and making sure I didn't give up."

His eyes were intense, but he didn't try to interrupt.

"I know there are no excuses in the world for what he did to me, but he was doing it to protect his sister. That, I can understand."

Desperate for his radiating warmth, she inched closer to James.

"They both died before me. His sister, then him, like they both meant nothing." She snuggled into him as tears began to fall. "I'm so sorry. I couldn't save them."

She cried into his fur until she drifted into sleep, warmer and more comfortable than she had been in a long time.

"Today, we talk about soul ties."

Lani sat cross-legged before Rose in a patch of sun.

James was gone when she woke up, and it felt entirely too wrong. She wanted to wake up with him every morning, but it would take time. She should be patient.

"Soul ties?" Her mother had spoken of such things before, but she knew extraordinarily little about them.

With a wave of her hand, cords appeared all around Rose, all in distinct colors.

One stood out bright and shimmering, leading to the deck beyond. Lani pointed to it.

"This is your bond to James." She touched it delicately. "It is also my connection to Draven. The same two souls, meeting again and again. It's as strong as a diamond and cannot be broken, even by death." Her eyes darkened. "Though it hurts inexplicably when one side is missing."

Rose thought of Lani's story. Lani had been saved by Draven's act of love, only for him to be ripped away. She had lived on. They had so little time together.

"I do hope you never know what that is like."

Lani and Draven needed time together, she could feel it, but she wasn't sure it was a good idea.

Another brilliant cord of blue stretched out through the window, and she tugged at it. "What is this one?"

Lani smiled softly. "You will see soon that the acts of kindness you perform do not go unappreciated."

Rose drew her brows together, ready to ask a million more questions when a knock shattered the silence. Lani's gaze locked onto the door when they both noticed the diamond cord stretched to the door. She knew who was behind it.

Scrambling to get to the door, she opened it to find James there, but there was something darker in his eyes. It wasn't her James looking through his eyes. He dipped his head.

"I apologize for the intrusion, but I would like to speak to Lani." Draven, it had to be, she could feel Lani's excitement to see him. He didn't look to the side where Lani stood, and Rose had to remind herself that he couldn't see her.

"Come in," Rose offered, knowing what she wanted to do the moment he stepped through. Lani and Draven had truly little time and she would want the same thing if given the chance to see James again.

Once the door closed, she turned to Lani. "I can give you today." Her eyes lit with so much hope that Rose knew she had made the right decision. Draven's eyes narrowed, looking to where Lani was without seeing her. "Go ahead, it's alright."

Lani stepped into her, even if it was only an illusion. She could feel Lani take over her body. Rose was still partially present when she witnessed Draven realize who was there.

"Lani?"

"Draven," she whispered with such love and heartache that Rose chose to disappear into their mind. The world around her disappeared just as they collided.

CHAPTER 61

KEEP AN EYE ON THE TREES

SEBASTIAN

There were forty-seven caves on the cliff side of the volcano, though he suspected more had been here before the last volcanic eruption. An event Sebastian hoped Angelica's new magic would not trigger.

In those existing caves, Angelica had set up a fortress with the archers at higher caves and walls built of cut trees lining the ground level ones.

Roger and his family were in the largest cave, the man in question still recovering from the loss of his leg.

When he asked Angelica what happened, she had replied, "Necromites washed ashore, bringing death with them. We would have been able to manage them, but they started infecting the animals here. Some died from the venom, others turned into necromites themselves. They attacked in a swarm one night and we had to abandon the village." She had wiped the dampness from her cheeks. "Not everyone made it out alive."

"And Roger?" He had asked.

"He was the reason we made it this far, but — I had to cut off his leg to keep him in the world of the living. He won't be the same, but he's alive and with his family."

Even now, as Roger struggled to stand on his left leg, Darla aided him, hoisting him to stand and lean on a heavy stick. They smiled at each other, grateful to have one another.

The reunion of the long-lost men of Kheli with their families was bittersweet, filled with joyful cries and quiet tears. For the ones who hadn't returned and the ones who had nothing to return to, including Vincent.

"Where is my sister?" The man in question approached him from the side, a line of worry etching his face. "I've asked everyone, but they told me you would know." It didn't take long to put together his concern. The commodore being the last person who had seen her wasn't a good omen.

"Who is your sister?"

He suspected it but needed to be sure.

"Sophia Clare."

Sebastian winced at the name. The truth was that he didn't know if she was alive, dead, stranded, all of it unknown without a way to communicate.

"You do know her."

Sebastian nodded, and a flicker of panic, like a spark in dry grass, ignited in Vincent's dark eyes before being consumed by a blazing rage.

"Did you kill her?" His hand was on his weapon, ready to punish Sebastian for a crime that was not his. But there were so many others, did it matter if this one was false?

"I don't know where she is. All I know is who she left with and where they were going, but I've long since lost contact with them." Vincent's eyes narrowed with his irritation, but he suspected this brother would not like the answer. "She left on *Nemain's Revenge* heading for Draiocht."

Vincent's face flushed scarlet, and he swore. He grabbed a fistful of Sebastian's shirt, his other fist raised high. "You mean to tell me my baby sister left with the crew of pirates who raid Samsara and worship the Goddess of Death?"

Darla was beside them in seconds. "I will not be having this brawlin' shenanigans. We cannot be turnin' on one another now." She placed a hand on his arm. "Vincent, set him down."

"He's one of them. Their leader even, how can all of you be okay with having him here at all?"

"Sebastian be doin' more for us than I can put to words. Now, set him down, we be needin' him just as much as we be needin' you."

Vincent dropped him, sending him one last glaring look before walking away.

"Pay him no mind," Darla supplied. "He be mad at the world, more likely his sister than you. You see, neither of them knew their father, Mahya came to us with one hand on her rounded belly and the other in her son's hand. Vincent always be feelin' responsible for his sister."

"What happened to her?"

Sadness crept over her face. "The Minister's Navy. Not all officers are as kind as you."

He knew well what the officers were capable of. It was a wonder Vincent lasted this long without lashing out at him.

"Why did you defend me? I've done nothing—"

Her hand came up to silence him. "I've not been forgettin'. You helped scare away Captain Pike when his guns be ablazin' on our shores." The old pirate met a crueler fate than that, but he wasn't about to bring that up. "That, and there be many secrets you be keepin' for us. I know you found those hidden barrels of grain beneath the bar."

He had, choosing to ignore Darla's attempt to hold onto a portion of their own food stores. It wasn't fair, the amounts they took from Kheli, but Samsara was too close to starving. Every day they drew closer to that line.

Sebastian caught the edge of dusty purple fabric slipping into the woods. What was Indigo doing out in the jungle late at night? It wasn't safe, not even for her.

"If you'll excuse me."

"Oh, how gentlemanlike." Darla gave him a crooked curtsy he assumed meant she accepted his departure, but not before calling out. "Keep an eye on the trees."

He kept one eye on the surrounding trees, and another on the fabric disappearing ahead.

Indigo slipped through the woods effortlessly, shifting through trees like a stream of water. The further he followed the more the jungle came alive, little fireflies blinking. The calls of birds and monkeys echoed as the sun set and darkness crept in.

In the tree beside him, he spotted a monkey with matted fur, white clouded eyes, and enough battle scars to secure blood loss as the cause of death. But the beast breathed heavily, clearly not dead.

Sebastian smacked into a body, nearly toppling over the witch if he had not seized her waist before she took a tumble.

"Watch where you're going, Commodore."

"You can no longer taunt me with that term, witch."

She scoffed, but curiously, did not push him away. Even curiouser, he found he did not want to let her go.

In the fresh moonlight, her skin glowed and her eyes sparkled, even though they glowed that unnatural shade of violet that reminded him of what she was, he was enraptured within their depths.

Her mouth parted slightly, drawing attention to her plump lips. Without conscious thought, his free hand moved to brush them gently, his thumb dragging her lower lip down.

Did he want to kiss her? Perhaps there was another unseemly act she could perform with those lips—

He cleared his throat, releasing her and stepping away. What was wrong with him? She was a witch. She couldn't be trusted. He wouldn't let himself get entangled with such a woman.

"What are you doing out here, Indigo?" His tone came out harsher than he meant. Her eyebrow raised at the shift in his mood.

"Are we going by first names now?" He finally noticed the scrying bones she had in her hand, but he didn't get the chance to question her about it.

A long howl that ended in a growl echoed in the distance.

"There are no wolves in Kheli," he whispered, his skin crawling with warning.

Indigo threw bones in the air before catching them and looking at how they landed in her hand. "Natively, no. But not all witches cared for subtly when changing their baby boys. Some preferred strength." When her attention shifted back to him, worry lines crinkled her eyes, dimming their brightness. "Kheli has more secrets than any of us could predict, and I fear there are far more witch sons here than there should be."

"Are they all turning?"

"Eventually, yes."

Sebastian turned to the sky and the trees. How was he supposed to defend against an attack from everywhere? How were the villagers keeping them at bay?

"Mothers sent their sons here as a refuge, and when Nemain came calling, it meant nothing."

Sebastian remembered his conversation with Ravana, hating himself for understanding what she was trying to do. Her entrapment was meant to save them. They would have remained caged, unable to join the wilds as animals, unable to join society as children. Why was that their only choice?

A boar snorted nearby. He couldn't think of it. He could do nothing to help them now. Reaching out to her, he whispered, "We need to get back to the caves. It's not safe here."

"They're out there. The ones who haven't turned, but they won't survive."

A parrot flew down from the sky, landing on a branch before them, one eye lost, his feathers rotting off. He wouldn't be able to fly much longer. With its good eye, it inspected them.

"Indigo—"

She reached out to the bird, the creature squawking in a pitch so unnatural it grated against his ears. Violet light shimmered in Indigo's hand as she whispered beneath her breath, but her magic swerved around the bird, like there was an impenetrable barrier around it.

"I can't help them." Tears slipped down her face, but she kept trying to heal the creature.

The bird snapped at her, its beak a flash of sharp ivory, a warning that it could do far more damage than just a bite. He pulled her away from it. If that bird was truly a necromite, why did it wait until she approached to bite?

"Why isn't it attacking?"

Indigo wiped tears away as she pulled from his grasp. "Animals weren't meant to be necromites. Their instincts are at war with one another. Only creatures with an aggressive nature toward humans will attack unprovoked."

A low growl sent shivers down his spine.

Indigo reached for the bird again, but he snatched her hand away. "We must go. I swear to Davina, I will carry you out of here if you do not run."

His words finally snapped her to reality as her gaze flew to the opposing side of the jungle, where animals stalked towards them. Wolves with matted, bloody fur. A jaguar with bald patches and sunken eyes. A boar with sharp tusks and an open bloodless wound. Monkeys swung from trees with missing appendages.

He couldn't have conjured an image so horrifying, even in his nightmares.

"Run," he shouted at her. Finally, she listened, sprinting in the opposite direction. He followed closely after her. The high-pitched sounds of monkey calls, followed by unnaturally low roars and growls filled the surrounding space.

"We can't lead them back!" Sebastian shouted over the amplified sounds of the jungle.

Indigo turned her head back to shout. "I'm not!" Her eyes widened with whatever was behind him.

"Eyes forward!"

Her gaze snapped back, her pace increasing. He picked up his too.

They were going downhill towards the coastline. Getting trapped by the sea wasn't a particularly agreeable idea, but he wouldn't risk Indigo having to turn her head again. He was trusting her with at least wanting to live and being smart enough to pull it off.

They raced through the abandoned village, avoiding fallen barrels and buildings.

There were loud cracks behind him, informing him of the damage the stampede was causing.

It wasn't long before Indigo's boots pounded against the dock, but there wasn't a single boat tied to it.

"What are you doing?"

"Saving our lives!"

If not for the ravenous animals on his heels, he would have objected. At this point, he was prepared to swim out to sea to avoid them. Though he doubted that would stop them all.

Indigo halted before the end of the dock, turning to face the threat. She lifted her hands, purple sparks crackling from her palms as she whispered under her breath. Alright, trust it was. He pivoted at her side, drawing his sword to face—death.

Their numbers increased during the chase. They were working as a unit, when their live versions would have torn each other apart for a chance at a fresh meal. These creatures moved as a horde, snarling and running straight for them.

"Please tell me if your plan is any good." Sebastian wondered if praying to Nemain was appropriate, given the situation.

"We're about to find out," Indigo said, pushing her hands forward with a scream. Two balls of light lunged forward, rattling the dock as they exploded, separating the end of the dock from the onslaught of creatures, taking the first row down with it. The unstable slabs of wood they stood on pushed further out to sea.

Sebastian's mouth dropped open as the ocean began to separate them from death.

A pained moan left Indigo's lips, and he noticed in time to catch her as she fell, blood trickling from her nose. He may not know much about magic, but he knew that wasn't supposed to happen.

"Indigo?" Her eyes were closed, but her chest still rose and fell, regaining air after their run. She was alive, but she could do no more to help them.

The roars and howls echoed into the night, followed by splashing water. The creatures were getting into the water, swimming after them.

That was it. This was how they died. Of all the ways, this wasn't what he'd had in mind.

Indigo's eyes blinked open, watching the creatures come after them.

"I only delayed them," she said, her tone morose. They had minutes at best. Her gaze took him in, and he found himself lost in that violet sea of her eyes.

He placed a hand on her cheek. "You're not so bad, for a witch."

She smiled, and he swore she'd never looked so beautiful. Had he never seen her smile before? "You're still insufferable."

The corners of his mouth lifted because she wasn't convincing at all when she said it. He couldn't help but think he had grown to rely on her, even if he had denied it. They could have meant more to one another if Davina had been kinder.

"Maybe I'll see you in another life," he mused, unsure if he would get another one or the chances that she would be there.

"Make certain you make a better first impression next time."

He smiled again, letting himself imagine meeting her, flirting with her, and all the other ways two people were supposed to fall in—

Blue lightning struck the ground on the shore, storm clouds rolling in above them so fast, it blocked out the light of the moons. A cerulean mist grew over the shore and sea, engulfing all the animals that swam towards them. The necromites seized, falling into the waves like the dead animals they were. They floated on the surface, the smell of burned and rotting flesh reaching his nose.

The mist drew closer, and Sebastian feared it would finish them, but it drifted over his skin as if it couldn't touch them at all. He looked down to see Indigo had fallen asleep in his lap, but the mist had traveled over her too. He checked her pulse to find a heavy beat. She was drained from the run and magic, but she was unharmed.

With no way to paddle back, he waited, holding her close, not allowing himself to take his eyes off the floating bodies around them for a second. Just in case any of them survived.

Twenty minutes later, Angelica appeared on a longboat with Hiln helping her row.

"I reckon you could use some help," Angelica teased.

Sebastian didn't want to wrap his mind around what Angelica had done, but he gladly accepted the help.

He passed Indigo's limp frame to Hiln, who placed her in the longboat, Sebastian following soon after.

They rowed back to the shore, but Sebastian was lost in his own head; it had nothing to do with the necromites, or Angelica's magic. It had everything to do with the witch next to him and what he'd nearly admitted to himself.

No. He'd take *anything* over falling for a witch.

CHAPTER 62

ONE STOLEN NIGHT

ROSE

Sunlight drifted through the fogged windows of the cabin, lighting up the bedroom. Silky sheets met no resistance against Rose's skin, sliding easily around her as she stirred awake.

Beneath her hand, she felt the rise and fall of a chest, her fingertips drifting over coarse hair. A hand laid across her back, cupping her bare backside. Her senses came back to her slowly as she blinked rapidly. Something about this was different, but she wasn't certain how, until the body beneath her stiffened.

"I'm so sorry." James' raspy morning voice had everything rushing back. Not just the sorrowful tinge to it, but the fear that gave it a slight tremble.

It was Draven and Lani who'd fallen asleep last night, and by the looks of things, they had gotten carried away.

She didn't want to move, fearful that if she looked up and saw his face, she wouldn't see her pirate. Only the monster who'd tormented her with his face. Instead, she thought of how far Lani had gone with a body that wasn't hers. In a way, she had consented, and would do so for them again, but it was unnerving to know her body had been used without her present in it.

James growled, as if realizing the same thing. He cleared his throat. "If it's any comfort to know, my trousers remain on. Draven expressed *some* restraint."

There was a warmth of satisfaction tingling across her skin, but she wasn't deliciously sore like she was after their last tryst.

He let out a long sigh. "Draven is trying to tell me that you consented to their time together. Even when *I did not!*" He shouted the last words to the ceiling like he could yell at Draven. "Please tell me that they did not hurt you, Rose. If they did, mark my words, I will find a way to make his posterior corporeal so I can kill him."

A breathy laugh left her, followed by warmth in her stomach. "I am fine. No need to hurt yourself over it." She barely held in her laughter as she waited for his reaction, which came in the form of a heavy sigh.

"If I had known you had awful humor like that, I might have thought twice about falling in love with you."

She giggled in response before her heart warmed. Feeling light and unburdened, she turned to see his face. James was smirking down at her, looking happier than he had in some time.

"Not that you had much choice in the matter." She'd meant it as a small joke, but the fear she'd been avoiding rose up in her. This was James. She knew that in her heart, she could believe it now. But Colt had left her with another fear, what if James didn't truly love her?

A flicker of worry clouded his eyes, their usual brightness dimming. "Rose? Do you really believe that? That I had no choice?"

"What if—" The words caught in her throat, unwilling to voice themselves. "What if you don't really feel what you think you do?"

He squeezed her ass before releasing it in favor of caressing her back. "In love with you, you mean."

Rose nodded, fear souring her stomach. She couldn't bear the thought that everything he felt for her was only an illusion.

His other hand reached for her face, wiping away an errant tear. "I am in love with you, Rose. I know it's not some manipulation. I know it like I know the sky is blue like the color your eyes turn when you sing. I know it like I know the sea will see the sun again."

Doubts rattled in her head. "That could all be false emotion."

An eyebrow lifted on his devastatingly handsome face, and she couldn't resist melting further into him. "Answer this for me, love. Do you love me?"

"Yes, deeply." She did not need to think about it. Every beat of her heart echoed the sentiment. If he had been the one taken, she would have torn the city apart looking for him.

He smiled at her immediate response. "You have no doubts that someone could replicate that emotion inside you?" No, it felt too right for that.

She shook her head.

"I feel the same. What I feel for you is too passionate, too all-consuming, too dangerous to possibly be conjured by anyone but you." She gasped at the thought. "And I wouldn't have it any other way."

Look at your soul tie, Lani supplied.

Rose closed her eyes, reaching deep within herself as she looked for that glittering diamond cord that stretched between them. But she couldn't find it.

Open your soul. Let him see it.

Relaxing into his touch and the feel of his warm body beneath hers, she succumbed to it, letting the light inside her spread. His caressing stopped and his chest fell.

"Bloody hell."

She opened her eyes to find him slack-jawed, staring at the glittering cord that tied them together. It connected her bare chest to his, sparkling in a way that reflected in his eyes.

"You can see it?"

"I can. It's brilliant and beautiful. This is us?"

This is your soul tie connection. A soulmate, some would say, but it cannot be replicated. Not by any living goddess. It can only manifest once love blooms, not before.

Rose nodded enthusiastically, feeling happier than she had in months, maybe years. "Lani says it cannot form until we fall in love with each other."

His fingers drifted over the glistening refracted light spitting across the room. He seemed more relaxed than he did before, like seeing the light himself alleviated some of the burdens he carried.

"You are absolutely breathtaking."

They locked eyes, and she was extremely aware of her state of undress. Completely, that is. The blanket covered up to her waist, but her bare chest was pressed against him. Her skin grew hot at the desperate look in his eyes as they traveled over her exposed flesh.

But her body wasn't the same as when he'd fallen in love with her.

Crimson flooded her cheeks as embarrassment washed over her, making her instinctively curl inward and shield her body.

He lifted her chin to return her eyes to his. "Where did you go?"

"I—" She sniffed, hating that this bothered her so much, but what if he no longer liked what he saw? "I don't look the same." It was all she could manage to get out, but his arm shifted over her waist, hauling her over him.

She yelped in response, bracing herself on his chest as the blankets and sheets fell off her. Exposed completely to him, she squirmed to get away, but he held her hips firmly.

"Stay still," he commanded, and she froze. The command was almost an afterthought; it was the intense, feral need blazing in his eyes that held her captive.

His eyes took in every detail, roaming over her skin like he was a painter, studying his muse before the creation of a masterpiece. His hands followed, drifting over the flat plane of her stomach, over her hips and legs, certain not to miss an inch of skin. Caressing upwards, his hands drew circles around her breasts, and she realized she wasn't only the muse, she was the canvas as well.

Gently, he pinched her nipples. Pleasure skittered through her, causing her to lean into the touch. He smiled at her response to him before sitting up in bed. He shifted until his back was against the headboard, adjusting her easily atop him.

Then they were eye level, and his hand drove into her hair, keeping her eyes on him.

"You could never be anything except the most ravishingly, devastatingly, unimaginably gorgeous woman I have ever seen. I am beyond infuriated that you were taken from me, but nothing can ever change the way I feel about you." He thrust his hips into hers and she gasped at the feeling of his hard cock straining against his trousers. "And I mean, every way."

He dragged her lips to his, devouring her with a ferocity bordering on insanity. She gave back in full force, meeting his intensity as her hands roamed his chest and arms. She couldn't get him close enough.

The moment her mouth opened, his tongue entered as his touch grew firmer against her skin, pulling her against himself so there was not an ounce of space left between them.

The desire was overwhelming as she rocked against him, her breath catching in her throat. He groaned in response, his hands snapping to her hips to stop her.

James pulled away from the kiss, his eyes darkened with desire and a growl rumbling from his throat. She blinked a few times, trying to understand what was happening.

"What is it? Do you not want this?"

He laughed incredulously, like that was the furthest thing from his mind. "You have no idea how much I do."

Heat rumbled in her core, and she feared she was making a mess of his trousers. "I have some idea," she said breathlessly, which only made him growl deeper. The sound curled her toes as she rocked against him again.

He pinned her hips so they couldn't move anymore, but it created a teasing pleasure instead.

"Bloody hell, woman. I can't continue without telling yo—"

"Sail ho!"

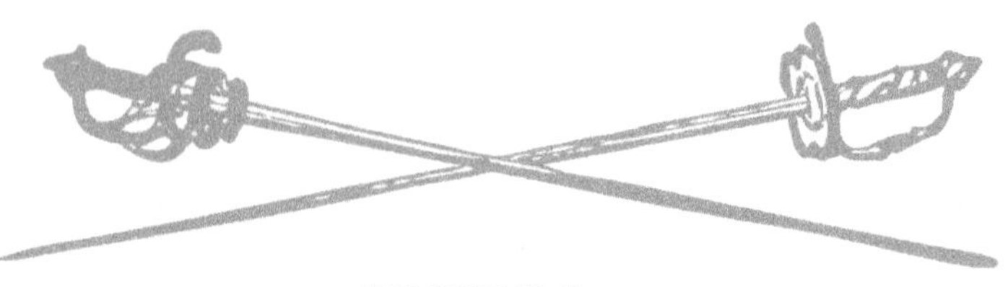

CHAPTER 63

SMOKE ON THE WATER

BLACK

A thick, smoke-like fog, heavy with the scent of molten earth, clung to them, swallowing the sunlight. *Nemain's Revenge* drifted lazily, so still that Black thought the currents, like the wind, had completely ceased, a strange stillness settling over the water.

Never had she felt the world around her calm so absolutely. It was almost like the moments before a great storm.

Even the devils had gone silent, weapons and positions at the ready. Black held her cutlass before her as she looked up and around. Something wasn't right. The entire crew could feel it.

"Sail ho!" Robin shouted from his perch in the crow's nest. He pointed out to the sea, but not before them. Behind them.

Black knew then. This wasn't some coincidence. The two *Imari* demons had caught up to them and slowed them down for good measure. She should have known this was bloody witchcraft.

"Stations!" Earhart shouted, earning the attention of the crew as they scrambled to their battlements. "Black, get the captain. He'll need to see this."

"Aye!" Black shouted back before charging into the captain's quarters. To be quite honest, perhaps she should have knocked. She put a hand up to shield her eyes from the naked flesh on the bed.

"What the bloody hell?"

"We need you on deck, Captain. A ship's been spotted."

"What are the colors?" A rustling of sheets, then other fabrics, told her they were getting dressed.

"They fly none, but there is a fog blocking our sight, and the ship has stalled completely."

"No wind?"

"No winds. No currents. Nothing. We're dead in the water."

Deafening quiet followed. They didn't need to see colors. There was only one enemy with that kind of power who would find them here. Find Rose here.

"I'll see for myself." The captain's tone had grown darker, more lethal, as he came into view, fully dressed and armed. "Let's go."

Black didn't question him when he closed the door after him or when his shadows filled the spaces around the door, darkening it until the wood could no longer be seen.

Phantom ran towards his first mate, taking the scope offered.

"They found us," he whispered as he lowered the spectacle. The crew waited, hearts pounding, for his next command, each word hanging heavy in the air. "Come now, devils. We knew they would catch up. Are you cowards shaking in your boots or are you devils?" He pointed to the ship that was rapidly gaining distance. "They will not defeat us!"

"Aye!" The crew agreed, but Black's eyes remained on where white sails had disappeared into the fog. There were men on that ship that ordered the deaths of little girls. They would pay for their crimes.

The sound of rigging sprung free, followed by something flying.

"Hit the deck!" Phantom commanded. Black saw a flash of blue before she forcibly fell, narrowly missing her own sword.

A crashing impact and whining wood followed. Two cannon-balls connected by a chain had wrapped around the main mast, not completely breaking it, but the damage would be enough to ruin the integrity. One more hit and they'd be down a vital piece of the ship.

And they still couldn't see the damn enemy, but they knew what direction it came from.

"Starboard side! Fire!" Phantom shouted, and the cannons below deck exploded in a deafening roar, the sound echoing through the ship and shaking the very planks beneath her feet. Black jumped to her feet, expecting to hear breaking wood or screams, but instead, it was only the sound of water splashing with the impact of a cannonball.

What the—

Grappling hooks flew from the port-side, redirecting their attention.

Black was the first to the lines, cutting down as many as possible before the enemy could step on the ship, but there were too many and the devils weren't fast enough. One jumped over the railing before her. He was dark-skinned, but not tall. His skin was ruddy, and his teeth were yellow and rotten as he smiled at her like she would be easy prey.

He wouldn't be smiling for long.

She struck hard, he deflected, but she pushed him back to the edge. He wasn't strong enough to keep her at bay. He screamed as he fell into the water between the ships. The siege continued, men swarming the ship in droves. She took on the next set of slavers, certain that's what they were by the brands on their arms. The same one on her wrist under the bandana. It itched with the healing skin, a sensation that was more obvious now that she was thinking about it.

Blocking a blow from above, she pivoted on her heel to catch him off balance. The slaver fell backwards, looking dazed as she reached for his dropped cutlass. She had forgotten her strength but was thankful for the boost.

He sneered at her from the deck. "Filthy pirate."

It reminded her of the man she'd slain at the forge. A man who killed children to make a point.

She ran him through, blood seeping through his cream shirt from his chest. Whatever mercy she had for a man like this died with those little girls.

I fight for the side of the living, what side do you fight for, Gwen?

She swung at the next attacker, trying to put Sophia's words out of her mind. Black pushed the next one over the railing, letting Davina decide his fate. Her eyes turned to the main cabin.

Sophia. She was still in her cell.

Black watched as slavers kicked open the cabin doors, heading down. Panic surged in her chest. Sophia had no weapon. Maybe they wouldn't kill a captured, unarmed woman, but she wasn't about to take chances.

Surging towards the main cabin, Black cut down anyone in her way. They could burn in Hell for all she cared.

She tore down the steps, turning to the brig. Sophia stood with her back against the wall, as far as she could get from the leering slavers. One knelt before the lock, picking it open.

"Pretty one, aren't ya? Want a ride?" The slaver made a vulgar gesture with his hand near his crotch. Black swore right there to relieve him of that appendage.

Sophia rolled her eyes, the epitome of calm even if Black could see how tense her shoulders were. "I'm afraid I don't partake with your kind."

"What? Draion?" He scrunched his nose as if her rejection was confusing.

"Men, you dead-minded cretin," she spat out.

Her insult drew a smile to Black's lips, and she stalked them. She could easily take them out, but she didn't want to give either of them time to pull a pistol on Sophia.

At the first one's silence, the one kneeling supplied, "She's calling you stupid, mate."

"She what?" His hand went to the pistol at his hip. "I'll teach you who's stupid when I blow your brains out."

Black lifted her sword to his neck, pressing it in and blocking his escape with her body. "You won't get the chance." She sliced his neck open, blood spurting onto the floorboards as he sank to the floor.

The second one abandoned his work to reach for his pistol, but Black had her own barrel to his head before he could reach it. His eyes went to the bandana on her wrist. He smiled like a cat.

"Got something to hide, *pirate*?"

She shot him through the temple, his body falling on its side and life leaving his eyes. Should she feel guilty for that one? She didn't. The feeling of eyes against the side of her face told her she should.

Instead of addressing the surrounding bodies, Black pinned her with a stare.

"You'll stay by my side." It wasn't a question. Black needed to let her out if she was going to rejoin the fight, but Sophia needed to be close enough to protect.

Sophia bit her cheek. "Will you leave me in here if I say no?"

"Damn it, Sophia! This isn't up for discussion. I need to know you're going to be careful."

She watched the huntress contemplate the order. They were under siege, there was no safe place. Not even by her side was enough, but it was all she had. The clashing of swords, cries of pain, and stomping from above deck made her impatient.

"Fine," was all Sophia offered, but it would have to be enough.

Black reached for her keys, unlocking it as swiftly as possible. The iron bars swung open, and Sophia wasted no time acquiring her weapons left on the opposite wall, including her bow and quiver still full of arrows.

Their conversation played on repeat in her head.

"I hope you're ready to use those."

Sophia gave her a grim nod. "I will do what I must."

Together, they climbed the steps to join the fray, but not before witnessing a sight that stole their breaths.

Jon climbed onto the ship deck, his face bruised and bloody and his eyes clouded over.

CHAPTER 64

WHY MUST YOU FIGHT?

ROSE

Rose banged against the door after trying the handle at least a hundred times. The bloody thing locked from the inside, so how was he keeping it shut? Thickening shadows curled around the edges of the door, filling the gaps.

"Damn it, James! Let me out," she shouted, hearing swords crashing and people screaming just beyond her door. She'd already tried to open the door with her voice, but the opening song didn't work on bloody shadows, did it?

It was like being in that cell all over again.

Except she didn't feel scared and helpless. She was angry, like she was going to rip him apart for leaving her out of the fight. Yes, she'd have to use her magic sparingly, but she could handle herself without magic.

With what muscle mass exactly?

Isabeya's irritating commentary made her groan. She looked at her stick of an arm. She was so worried about the loss of her curves earlier that she didn't even think about if she was strong enough to pick up a sword.

"I'll use my knife," she supplied.

Against swords and pistols? I'd lock you in here too.

Rose groaned, pacing around to the desk. She sat on the chair, staring at the door as if it would open at any moment. She doubted the shadows were meant to hold a door or how much power it was taking from him to do so. He had to let them go, eventually.

She leaned back into the chair with her arms crossed, feeling very much like a petulant child.

"Could I burn it down?"

Yellow flared in her vision at the call. *Not without burning the ship down.*

"What about soul-weaving? It repels shadows, right?"

With what power reserves? Shadows are strong, especially these. You'd only encourage them to fortify the door further.

Grinding her teeth together, she searched her mind for the solution. There had to be something.

Half-gloved hands landed on the table, snagging her attention. Following the black sleeves, she found Isabeya glaring at her.

"Why do you want to escape so badly?"

"I want to help," she said immediately.

"That's not it. Try again."

Movement drew Rose's eye to the side. A woman with fiery red hair leaned against the bookcase trailing a finger over the binding of a nearby book. The trail her finger left behind was ashen.

Scarlett.

A flicker of light drew her attention to the window. Lani appeared in a glare of sunlight, one that was quickly swept away by the dull darkness outside.

"Eyes on me," Isabeya demanded, snapping her fingers. "Why join a fight when you have little to offer it?"

Rose considered why her skin was crawling with anticipation. Staring at a door, just waiting for it to open and reveal her enemies had her body shuddering.

"I don't want to just sit in this room waiting for someone to come after me."

"Nope. Try again." Isabeya's eyes were hard and unforgiving. If there was a right answer, how was it that she didn't know what it was?

"Then I don't know." She raised her arms, done with the pointless conversation. She needed to figure out a way out of there.

"Yes, you do!"

Lani and Scarlett strode to Isabeya's side, staring at her. It suddenly felt like the world depended on this realization.

Lani asked the question. "Why must you fight?" When Lani asked, it felt more intimate, like the answer was something deeper. Rose thought about the fight happening beyond those doors. Of all the people whose lives were in danger.

"They came for me," Rose spoke aloud, not looking at the apparitions of her past lives anymore. "They won't stop until they have me."

Isabeya nodded, "Yes, why does that matter?"

The devils came all this way to find her, to save her. They put their lives and their mission on hold to save her. Was she truly worth all of that?

"I don't want them to die for me."

Isabeya finally smiled, the sight looking almost sinister rather than proud. "And what are you going to do about it?"

"Apparently, sit in this room and do nothing. Great revelations don't help me open a damned door." She was right back where she started.

Looking at the door again, she noticed there was mist slipping under the wood past the shadows and seeping into the room. It was darker than fog, but not as deep as shadow.

"Or you can open the door," Isabeya supplied.

When Rose was about to test if she could land a punch to her counterpart's projection, she caught the swing of Isabeya's eyes. She looked down at where a desk drawer had opened, shadows receding from it. Inside the drawer was a small onyx velvet pouch she was all too familiar with.

The mist increased, filling the room. When it passed over her counterparts, it washed them away. Rose's head was filled with silence as they were stripped away from her, but she didn't pay them much attention.

Rose plucked up the pouch, emptying the contents into her other hand. A rush of magic filled her veins the moment her fingers brushed the smooth surface of the Stone.

It pulsed with lilac and silver light as the voices whispered to her. They weren't coherent, not until she asked a question. They sounded like a room of excited patrons all speaking at once until she asked, "How do I disperse the shadows?"

CHAPTER 65
HELL HATH NO FURY
PHANTOM

Phantom's blade sliced through his nearest victim, cutting down the slavers as fast as his arms would allow, even if his focus was shared with the shadows at the door, but he could feel his control on them slipping away. His lips twisted in a smile as he felt the brush of Rose's magic against his own.

His counterparts faded as that blasted fog grew thicker around them. It was bloody poison, like what Lockness had used on him.

That left him with his strength and speed from the beast and his ability to command his own people. A lot of good that did him against his enemy now. He was counting on having his shadows. To wipe them out the moment they were in range, but the ones he could still feel were occupied keeping Rose locked away.

She would be furious with him when she got out. And she would. It was only a matter of time.

Bloody hell.

Shouting a war cry, he dragged his cutlass through the belly of the next attacker. A glance told him that Serena was in the sky, setting fire to the men around them. Smith was a step behind her, pushing men into the water to prevent the ship from catching fire. Serena might have to be locked away too if she couldn't control the flames well enough.

A horrible screeching noise filled the surrounding space just before a dark mass slammed into the beastie. It had wings of charcoal grey and eyes of beaded black. It screeched again, as if from a nightmare. Serena shot her fire at it, but it dodged. Soon, the two were in a battle, flying out to sea to battle in the sky.

He'd dwell on that if not for the brute who caught his eye.

Jon stood at the far side of the ship, knocking devils back as a new onslaught of attackers filled the ship. There was something foreign and sluggish about the way he moved. His eyes turned and Phantom saw the truth.

That wasn't Jon. His friend was dead, and this was a shell left behind.

Phantom moved to jump ahead to slay the monster when a flash of light drew his attention to the cabin under the helm.

Rose's furious eyes blazed blue as the door to the captain's quarters crashed open, the sound echoing through the ship.

"*Mierda!*"

He really hoped it would take her longer to escape. Of course, she would have, but he was hoping to have control over the battle before she did. Instead, they were overrun.

"James," she yelled, a knife in hand as she marched towards him. The attackers shifted their attention, their eyes gleaming with malice, all homing in on her.

"*Me cago en tus muertos!*"

Swinging his sword through the neck of the nearest attacker, he downed every soul in his path, eating up the distance between them. Rose defended herself with efficiency, using her knife to slice through anyone who came too close. Luckily, she was small and quick enough to maneuver around their strikes.

She stopped, attempting to pick up a fallen sword, but when she pulled, the heavy metal hardly budged. Another attacker came from behind her, raising his sword to her neck.

"Lost, little birdy? Your keeper is calling you home," he taunted as she glared up at him. "Such a pretty litt—"

Phantom ran him through until the point of his sword ripped out through his belly. "I'm sorry," he mocked. "Did I interrupt?" He pulled his blade out, allowing the man to bleed to death on the deck.

He put a gentle hand on the back of her neck, inspecting her for even a single scratch. There was none aside from the nick on her throat. "Are you alright?"

She nodded, fury still lining her eyes as she pressed her lips together. It was so adorable that he smiled. "Don't be cross with me, *tresora*. I knew you'd get out. Can you blame me for wanting to protect you for as long as I could?"

"Yes," was her sharp answer. "What if I couldn't get out and you died out here?" Emotion choked her words, barely allowing her to say them.

A sword swung for her head, so he batted it away with his own, letting his free hand clasp hers as he slit the throat of the man brave enough to interrupt them.

Dropping her hand for a moment, he freed his pistol, handing it to her. "Here, shoot them before they have a chance to hurt you. It will serve you better than a knife."

"James," she snapped, cocking the pistol back before shooting the next attacker. It was incredibly attractive and unfortunately, the battle was distracting him from her.

"You cannot just lock me away whenever you think I can't handle a battle."

Phantom put his free hand on her waist, wanting to keep contact with her as much as possible. "You are low on power, love." Reaching over her, he ran through the next attacker, spilling his guts along the deck. "And these goons would like nothing more than to get their hands on you. Do you realize how vulnerable that makes you?"

Using both hands, she shot a particularly wild-eyed man. "I am more than capable of taking care of myself. With or without magic."

"Is it so hard to believe that I wouldn't be willing to risk that?"

Her silence was as cold and hard as the granite features of her face. Apparently, she was going to remain stubborn.

"Captain?"

"*What?*" They answered in unison, turning to Russet who flinched away from their glares right before he pointed to the ship beside them. A plank had been laid across the railing, allowing men to walk over.

Colt and Dante sauntered across the plank as if they had already won, the unnatural fog swirling around Dante's coat as it swept by. Jon took to their sides like a bodyguard the moment they stepped aboard. Not a mindless necromite then, but not entirely himself either.

If it wasn't for this bloody fog, he'd try his luck with an attack.

Phantom pulled Rose's arm until they were behind the steps to the quarterdeck. She started squirming as if he would lock her back up.

"Rose, listen to me," he started, grabbing her attention by turning her chin towards him. "I have a plan."

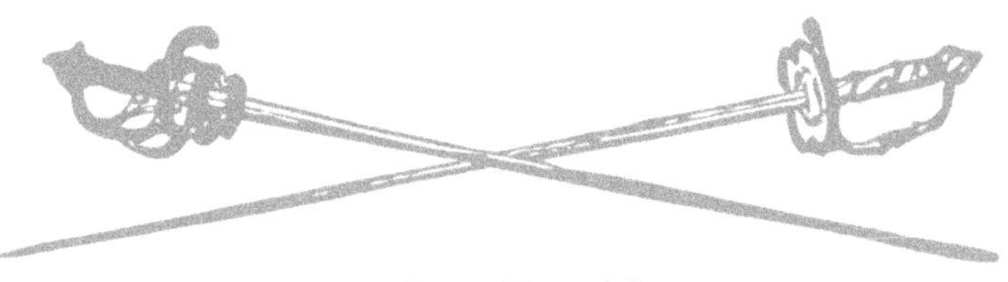

CHAPTER 66
ONE OF US

BLACK

Sophia was missing. Either something had happened to her, or she had run off on her own. Knowing Sophia, it was likely the latter. Still, worry clawed at her insides.

Black sifted through the fury of attackers.

She pushed a man overboard with a kick to his chest, letting him career over the railing with a shriek. Finally, she spotted Sophia on the far side of the ship, sending arrows into the formless fog mass that was entwined with Serena. The dragon roared in pain as the creature sank sharp jagged teeth into it.

What exactly did she think arrows were going to do to the bloody thing?

Black stepped towards her, ready to reprimand her to stay close when a barge of five men stood in her path.

"Hello boys," she drawled, smirking at them. The malice in their eyes made it clear they knew exactly who she was.

"We know who you are, *Shuyet*." One sneered at her with a patch over his missing eye and crooked teeth.

"Yeah, got yourself a reputation on *our* hunting grounds, did ya?"

"Then left us with a little message, huh?"

Black studied each of them. They were incredibly average. They varied in nationalities from the fair-skinned Brettanian to dark

Draion, but none of them were exceptionally large or impressive. Those men at the forge were likely considered some of their best men.

Pity.

"Which disappoints you more, I wonder?" She dared a step forward. "That your finest men lost to little old me or that I didn't say goodbye?"

In the corner of her left eye, she saw a man step forward. She flinched towards him, raising her sword. Before she could, her knees were knocked out from behind her, forcing her to the ground.

There was a sixth man, who kicked her sword away then ripped the bandana off her wrist. The burned skin beneath showing a reddened mark matching the ones on the surrounding men.

"You're one of us."

Black stared up at him, refusing to stare at the mark that meant nothing on her flesh.

The man looking down on her had a larger presence than the rest. He was older by a couple of decades and his full beard was silver. A large hat rested on his head with jewels and rings decorating his neck and hands. This was their leader. There was a glint in his eyes like he knew something she didn't.

Until she recognized him.

Black's mouth fell open as two of the slavers came behind her to restrain her arms.

"Captain Finn?" Her heart pounded in her chest as she stared at the man she'd known since she was a child. The one who'd been working with her father.

He smiled like that was the exact confirmation he needed. He tsked. "Your father will not be pleased. Killing useful men. Fighting for a rogue band of pirates. And your new appearance—" He reached out to her shortened hair, flipping a strand near her nape before she pulled away. "Very undignified for a lady."

Black spit in his face. He paused for a moment, reining in visible rage before taming it enough to wipe his face clean.

"I also hear you call yourself *The Black Shadow* or *Shuyet* to the locals. They actually believed you were a spirit," he mocked, his men laughing with him. "I'm eager to tell your father that the vigilante who's been disrupting his trade deals is his very own daughter." He lifted a finger in the air. "Or are those days behind you now that you are a pirate?"

"You just have me all sorted, don't you?"

"I believe I do, you see," he started, seizing her singed hand and raising it. "I already said it; you're *one of us*."

"I'll never be one of you." Black tried to pull away, but he grabbed her elbow to keep her arm up.

"Oh, but you are. Slaving is in your blood." He leaned down to whisper in her ear. "Your entire life was built off the backs of slaves. If they didn't need saving, would you have found this life you have?"

A shiver ran down her spine. His words punched deep into her gut. Had she really benefitted from slavery so much? Even if she was working against it, everything she had was because of them.

He moved right before her, and she struggled against the hands that clamped against her arms and shoulders. If she could just get free, she could cut down the man who'd been responsible for hardships of thousands. End the slaver's route once and for all.

That was a death worth taking.

She lunged, managing to part from a set of hands, freeing her arm enough to punch him straight in the nose.

Finn screamed, blood gushing down his face as the men reaffirmed their grips, pushing her down. There were four sets of hands keeping her on her knees.

When Finn turned his eyes on her, his nose crooked and broken, there was fury tensing his jaw. "Your father was about to marry you to me before you disappeared. You would have been a lady I would have treated well." He smiled, spreading blood across his blackened teeth. "Now you are the filth we fight against, but you're still mine."

Black's blood ran cold.

"I'll take you back to Samsara myself, marry you like the lady you should have been, then lock you away like the criminal you are. Your father will sign his empire over to me, and you'll give me a son." Ice slid across her veins while the fury boiled in her core.

"Los murertos de haras!" Like the dead you will.

"Children," a familiar voice chastised. Black struggled against the slavers, but they pushed her down further, forcing her to bow to the demon. "Such a mortal concern."

Dante arrived, his coat fanning out around him, kicking up the fog.

Black glanced at the crew. The devils were all in similar positions, restrained, but they weren't being killed. At least, not yet.

The captain was missing.

Just over Finn's shoulder, Black spotted Sophia ducked behind the helm. They would search there soon, but they hadn't caught her yet. The quarterdeck was mostly cleared due to the ongoing battle of beasts taking place there. Serena screeched as the fog creature pinned her to the deck by her neck.

They were all failing. Everyone was about to die.

Where was the captain?

Sophia's concerned eyes connected with her. She looked like she wanted to help, but there was nothing she could do.

No no no, stay there. Stay hidden.

"Captain Finn tells me you've been quite the troublemaker," Dante said in that cool, detached voice of his.

Then, Black understood. It never made sense why slavers would destroy their own merchandise. Why would they kill an entire community underground when they could capitalize on it? Because it wasn't them—Dante turned his head, as if he could see the wheels turning in her head. "It had to be done, you see." The breath seized in her lungs. "They had to be made an example of. There are consequences when someone commits treason."

Treason?

"Allowing pirates into the palace would qualify for a guilty party. There was no way around it. Men. Women. Children. It made no difference. They betrayed their country."

"Plus, it was personal." Captain Finn's gaze narrowed on her.

Black pulled against the hands, trying to find the strength

inside her, that powerful magic gifted to her by being a devil, but it wasn't there.

She was just — Black.

"Go to hell!"

Dante didn't even blink when he said, "I have, I don't intend to return." He took a deep breath before facing the rest of the ship. "We have decided you are all guilty, punishable by death."

"No," Finn rushed out. The demon's eyes turned to him in an instant, and he crumpled like a coward. "I mean, she is valuable, your eminences." He gestured down to Black. "I can use her to gain a powerful foothold in Samsara."

Dante blinked once. "Samsara is marked. They will not last the year."

Colt took over for him, a splitting grin overtaking his face. "Power there is meaningless."

Finn visibly paled.

Colt turned his eyes to the devils, taking the time to look over each one. "Come out, *brother*, unless you'd rather watch them all die."

CHAPTER 67
BATTLE OF WILLS
PHANTOM

"Here I am!"

The sound of Phantom's boots against the deck was louder with the sudden silence of the tense battlefield. He checked over the faces of every devil he could see. They were being gagged, their hands restrained behind their backs as they were filed into a line and forced to their knees.

All except Black, who they kept at Dante's feet as if she would be the first victim.

A couple of men pulled Tick by the hair, followed by Ramirez. "What do we have here? You two will fetch a fine price in Brettania."

Rage and anticipation boiled his blood. As long as he was breathing, he refused to let that happen. He had a promise to see through.

He opened his arms wide, knowing full well that he wasn't a threat to them with this blasted fog.

"Are you wanting to negotiate? I'm not certain I want what you're selling." His eyes shifted to Jon and his predatory stillness, wondering if he could manage to command him in his condition.

Colt threw the blunt side of his cutlass over his shoulder before following Phantom's gaze. "Oh, you are welcome to try, but I'm afraid Jon isn't home anymore." He took a few steps towards

Phantom. "As for negotiations, how about your life and the lives of your men in exchange for the little birdy? How does that sound?"

Even while a raging fire of fury threatened to tear apart his very soul, he kept his face neutral, unaffected.

"I know what she's worth to you. You think I'd bargain for such a low price." He sneered at the demon, letting him believe that this was nothing more than good business. Not his family in exchange for the love of his life.

Colt shook a finger at him. "You're bluffing." He dropped his hand, circling around Phantom instead. "I could mention the fact that I have the men and the firepower to send you and your crew to the depths of the Sumerian Sea, but I don't have to. I know there is no amount of negotiation that could convince you to peacefully hand her over."

"Then why are we having this conversation at all?"

Colt smiled faintly before disappearing behind him like a shifting ghost, too unnatural to track. "Why aren't you putting up a fight?" He kicked the backs of Phantom's knees, forcing him to the deck, same as his devils. "You have full control of Maahes. The beast could be trying to tear my head off at this exact moment. You'd at least get a bite in. What are you waiting for?"

Phantom grunted, lifting his head. A soft breeze lifted the hair from his forehead. "Maybe I don't like to risk my own people."

"Nah," Colt scoffed. "You have control now. No risk in putting a bit of teeth into the mix." He pointed his sword at Jon. "Put this one out of his misery, at least. But no, you choose to give us the least amount of fight you have." Colt placed the tip of his blade under Phantom's chin. "To what end, *Captain*?"

Phantom smiled. "To my own end."

Colt laughed, seeing only a helpless man on his knees. "Cute," he chastised before turning to Jon. "It seems we have to show him how serious we are. Kill the bitch."

Jon groaned in that strangled way only a necromite could. He looked and sounded like the undead creatures, but necromites didn't follow commands.

Somehow, he understood the unspoken command, drawing a

giant scythe from his back. Colt's sword on Phantom's neck pressed in harder, sending a trail of blood rolling down his chest.

"Ah ah ah. This is for you to watch."

Jon set his clouded, vacant eyes on Black as she faced her death.

"No!" Phantom shouted. This was not part of the plan. He was supposed to distract them long enough, keep their attention off the devils.

Come on, Rose.

Jon stopped next to Black who didn't even bother to struggle, glaring at her killer like she would haunt his soul in the afterlife.

As he neared, the men behind her pushed her down until her neck was parallel to the deck. It was an execution. One intended to relieve her head from her shoulders.

"No! Colt, listen to me. We can negotiate."

Colt laughed again. "Now, *that's* what I like to hear! But I did warn you. I have to make an example now. Just remember, you made us do this." Guilt slammed into him at his failure. Perhaps he *should* have changed into the beast.

He slammed his eyes closed, looking for that ancient creature inside him. A growl rolled up his throat as it easily came into his grasp. It had become easier with his visits to Rose's bed.

Dante's hand shot out from his robe, flexing in the air like he was holding something. Phantom grunted at the feel of that hand on his throat. It felt like long, fat fingers, or snakes constricting his airflow. The tattoo. Kraken tentacles squeezed the life out of him.

Phantom couldn't hold onto his beast form, his control slipping.

"I'm afraid it's too late for that." He pushed against the hold Dante had on him, but this magic was like a cork in a bottle, blocking any chance of escape. His breath grew painful as his air was cut off.

Jon stood over Black, his sword primed at her neck before he lifted it. Panic shot through his veins as he felt entirely helpless.

A tortured yell, raw with agony, sliced through the air above the pirates and slavers.

"No!"

Phantom turned to see Sophia Clare before the helm with a bow in her hand. She had freed Serena from the dark creature, if only for a moment. Serena screamed with her, spitting an arc of blazing blue fire. Sophia had her arrow stretched out before Serena's maw, the flames licking around the arrowhead.

Sophia screamed in utter agony as the skin of her hand melted. A rush of men climbed the steps, heading straight for her.

"Sophia, no!" Black shouted, watching men descended on the huntress.

Jon swung the sword down, the trajectory heading straight for Black's head.

Sophia screamed before letting her arrow loose, blue burning the end of it.

It plunged into Dante's chest, directly into his heart.

Jon screamed with the effort it took to stop the blade from falling on Black's neck. He dropped the sword, the blade burying itself between the planks of wood before Black's face. She reared back, the men loosening their grip enough to let her straighten.

"Sophia!" The huntress had fallen on the quarterdeck, the men dragging an unconscious body down the stairs.

Dante looked down at the arrow sticking out from his chest, his eyes wide.

"Dante?" Colt asked, fear lacing his tone.

The demon fell to his knees, clutching where the arrow had shot him through the chest. His skin darkened with decay even as his chest still rose and fell with his breaths.

His magic faded, releasing the tentacles back into Phantom's skin. Four men were on him before he could stand, restraining him with chains. He desperately begged Rose to be ready.

Colt scooped up Dante just as he was about to fall to the deck, panic written over his features. "Come on, you're stronger than this."

The demon coughed, black blood flowing from his mouth. "It's time we go back home, don't you think?" Dante said as the arrow in his chest began to glow. "It's been a few centuries, maybe She isn't mad anymore."

"I wouldn't count on it."

Cerulean flames licked up the arrow, spreading across his chest. "I am being called home, regardless." He looked down at the flames like he didn't feel them at all. He put a tender hand on Colt's cheek. "I'll see you soon."

The flames burst out, causing Colt to jerk back as they consumed Dante's body. Only the faint shape of a man could be seen in the fire. He did not scream as he burned alive, nor was there the smell of burning flesh. This was no ordinary pyre. In a matter of seconds, the flames disappeared along with every trace of the *Imari*.

Then there was one; and they'd just found out he could be killed.

Colt stood in the wake of his friend's ashes. His fists clenched at his sides as he stared down at the empty spot on the deck.

He sniffed before turning to Phantom, a lethal promise in his darkened eyes.

"Little birdy, it's time to come out now," he called, turning his body to try to spot her. "Or I just might *squeeze* too hard!"

The tentacles tightened around Phantom's neck again, pressing down on his windpipe with brutal force. Any more pressure and he wouldn't be able to breathe at all. By the wicked gleam in his eyes, Colt was hoping he'd get the chance.

He felt it then, the wind picking up speed, encircling around them. Streaks of blue swirled with the wind, pushing it along. The sails filled, and the rigging groaned with new life. The devils all looked to the sky to see the fog parting, letting the light of day in. He watched the wariness wash over Colt's features, bleeding into his scent.

Jame — What — is that —

Phantom's counterparts were blinking in and out of existence as the fog cleared, but he didn't have a handle on them yet. It was taking too long as Colt squeezed further.

A bluish glow drew their attention to the quarterdeck where swirls of blue could be seen. Phantom let a prideful smile brandish his features. One of genuine warmth.

"It seems our little birdy got a little power back. Well, that simply won't do."

In horror, Phantom watched as Colt's features morphed and shaped, his hair turning black and curling at his nape. His build turned taller and stronger. Even his clothes changed until they were identical to the long leather coat and accessories Phantom wore. They looked exactly alike, even down to the deep blue eyes.

"No," he breathed just before a gag was secured around his mouth. He struggled against his chains, but without his added strength, it was useless.

Colt swaggered towards him, crouching to his level to seize his face. "Let's see just how long it takes her to realize I'm not you." A low sinister chuckle escaped him as Phantom struggled against the chains, screaming through the gag.

Looking around, he found his devils were gagged as well. Not a single person aboard could warn her.

Colt rose before turning his sights on the quarterdeck.

CHAPTER 68

HELLO, LOVE

ROSE

"*Damn it*," Rose swore as she continued to attempt a song. The fog had interfered with the control she had over her magic, the cerulean blue streaks fizzling out. She had managed to get a small breeze going, but her control had been flickering.

Serena screeched at her from where she was pinned to the deck. She was too weak to destroy the smoke creature. Those big reptilian eyes pleaded with her, but she couldn't help, not yet—

She just needed the fog to clear.

Rose hummed again, but the sound got stuck in her throat. Growling, she nearly threw the Stone for how useless it had become. Instead, she buried her head in her knees where she sat, hiding on the quarterdeck.

"Hello, love."

Her head snapped up to find James watching her from the stairs, stepping out of the fog like a vision clad in black leather.

"It's okay now. You don't need to sing anymore."

The panic subsided in her chest at the sight of him unharmed. He was alive, not a single scratch on him. She hadn't been able to see what was happening on the main deck with the blasted fog, but she was able to hear the commotion after Sophia had shot the arrow.

The fog had hidden her from sight as the men came to collect the huntress. She almost gave away her position, but she managed to stay hidden a little longer.

But now, James was here. Was it over?

"Are they gone?"

Instead of answering, he held out his hand. She accepted it, rising to her feet. "We've come to an arrangement."

Chills shot down her spine so violently that she took a step back. "What sort of arrangement?"

Pinning her with his gaze, he walked into her until her back pressed against the ship railing. Ever so slowly, he lifted his hand, caressing the apple of her cheek and down to her chin.

"It's simple, really. You don't want to be cursed anymore, am I correct?" Something was wrong, his eyes were too cold, too unfeeling. "I want to know if these... *stirrings* I have for you are real. There is only one way to find out."

Her hackles rose as something screamed at her. This was wrong. All of it. It went against everything he'd said.

His hand came up, encircling her waist. He was so cold. It was a stark contrast to the warmth he normally brought her. "You let them break the curse."

Silence washed over her. "What?"

"Go with them. Do everything they tell you and they've agreed to return you to me. Then we can truly start our lives together, knowing what we have is true."

Serena bucked then, screeching as she tried to escape the creature above her. It wrapped ropes of smoke around her snout, shutting her up.

He crowded Rose, only inches from her face now, his other hand snaking up to tangle in her hair. It didn't feel like tenderness and affection. It felt like control.

"Can you do that for me, *birdy*?"

Birdy. Not love. Not songbird. Not *tresora*.

Colt.

Bile rose up her throat, knowing whose hands were surrounding her, but she didn't let it show. Now that she knew this was a game, she had to play it.

Looking back at those false blue eyes and seeing only emptiness, she whispered, "I trust you." It went against every fiber of her being not to pull away, but she needed him to let his guard down.

He smiled and Rose wondered how she ever thought he looked like James. This was the smile he used on his enemies. Not her. Never her.

"Come then," he started, stepping back to give her space. "I'll take you aboard."

A weight on her back reminded her of the weapon she had hidden there.

She stepped alongside him, passing by the struggling dragon.

"Let her be, she'll be released soon."

Rose's skin itched watching Serena. She doubted the world's last dragon was meant to survive this siege. There was despair in her eyes as she watched them pass. Rose shared a look with the creature, one of understanding. They were the same. An ancient creature in a young body, too powerful to be left alive.

Trouble was, Rose wasn't about to let either of them die.

As fast as she could manage, Rose bent, using her knife to slice through the smokey bonds, feeling very much like a real rope. The monster screeched in her face just as Serena pushed the creature back. Using her fire, the dragon drowned the smoke monster in blue flames.

Colt reached for her, but she slipped out of his grip, thrusting her blade into the onslaught of flames. Pain sliced through her hand, heating it to an unimaginable degree.

"You bitch!" Colt lunged for her, but not before she moved, screaming through the pain. Her hand was covered in blue flames as she plunged it into his chest.

Pulling her hand away, the flames dispersed, leaving her flesh charred. It was painful beyond belief, but it was worth it as Colt's eyes lit with fear. He stepped back, his illusion melting away as the flames began to spread over him. Only belatedly did she notice that she had missed his heart.

He stepped far enough away that his foot caught on a plank of wood. His eyes widened right before he pitched over the railing to the main deck below.

She jumped to the edge, that breeze growing stronger around them as the fog dissolved. Behind her, the smoke monster had disappeared, leaving an exhausted dragon slumped against the deck.

Rose raced along the steps, careening herself forward just as she heard her counterparts returning.

Green crawled up the edges of her vision first. *What happened?*

Yellow followed. *Did we win?*

She ignored them in favor of finding James. She couldn't shake the sight of him, the awful things he'd said. Her James would never agree to that.

CHAPTER 69
DIVINE SOULS
PHANTOM

Orange painted his vision brilliantly, like a sunset exploding across the canvas of his mind.

I'm here.

The fog cleared enough for Phantom to see where each of the slavers were. He could see the blackness of their souls now, the shadows all too eager to take their fill. They dove into the slavers, feasting on them like a pack of piranhas.

sssssupper

Their screams tore through the wind, echoing in his mind. He hadn't told the shadows to attack, but they did, bodies falling like logs to the deck.

Phantom pulled at his chains, but they were still firmly in place with his gag. Luckily the devils were spared, but he had little assurance that they wouldn't be next.

You've had too much.

A groan drew his attention to the form that had fallen from the quarterdeck. Colt was back to his own face, cerulean flames licking around the base of a dagger that was rooted in his chest. He recognized the knife.

He smiled at the thought of his songbird stabbing the man who'd tormented her. But there was something different about him than when his companion had fallen. The flames weren't consuming him.

Colt rose to his hands and knees, spitting out black blood. "You think this is enough to kill me?" He laughed, the sound chilling Phantom's veins.

Strength returned to him in droves, and he pried apart the chains in an instant. His beast rushed to the surface just as Rose rounded the stairs.

For a moment, he considered holding it back for her sake, but if anyone could handle the beast, it was her.

He shed coat before shifting, his nails extending to claws, his skin growing dark fur, and his jaw opening and filling until he was the image of Maahes. They were one and the same even if they had lived different lives. He was the dark lion of Draiocht. A powerful force that could bring a kingdom to its knees.

Phantom stalked forward on soft paws, his black fur shifting in the wind. The shadows joined him, creating an illusion of darkness around him like an aura.

Colt raised a hand to control Phantom's tattoo again. Only it didn't work this time. Phantom felt nothing except the consuming rage. The fire had cleansed him. The demon had become a man. The evidence of that was in the way his black blood flowed bright red now. The color of humanity.

The demon wiped at the blood flowing from his mouth, examining his sodden fingers and laughing. It was deeper and darker than he had laughed before.

"Oh, how many times I wished for this moment." He blinked up at Phantom as he struggled to his feet, one hand on where the dagger was lodged in his chest.

Phantom advanced, growling low.

Colt shrunk back, his head hitting the door to the captain's quarters as he cowered on the ground.

There was nowhere left to go.

"This isn't the end. You can kill me, but I'll come back for you. Perhaps I'll bring back all those souls you've feasted on."

Phantom felt the presence of his songbird before he saw her.

Rose joined his side, perhaps wanting to see her tormentor destroyed for herself.

A half-smirk touched Colt's cheek before he zeroed in on her. "Do you know what he did? The number of souls he had to consume to become this powerful?" His eyes shifted to Phantom. "I bet they tasted divine." Then he set his eyes back on her and Phantom wanted to rip his face apart for looking at her, but this was Rose's life to take.

"Your precious pirate is a murderer."

Rose approached him, her face giving nothing away. She pulled the hilt of her dagger, dragging it out of him. The blade itself was covered in his blood, but just under that was blue steel, flames still dancing around it. He growled when he noticed the fresh burns on her hand, but she ignored the pain.

"I know what he did." She plunged the dagger back into his chest, aiming more to the right this time and piercing his heart. "He told me just before you got here." She twisted the hilt, earning a piercing scream from his lips. "I told him I would have burned it all to the ground for him."

Warmth flooded Phantom's chest at her vile words. She looked so beautiful and strong as she destroyed her enemy. It made him want to drag her back to bed and show her what her words had done to him.

She stepped back to let the flames consume him completely. They grew around his chest, covering his body and up his neck.

He laughed again. "Then I'll be seeing you both in Hell." The flames swallowed him up, leaving only ash behind.

Rose's eyes found him the moment her tormentor was gone, those gold coin eyes looking directly into his soul.

Releasing his beast form, he let the change take him until he stood before her as a man. A very naked one, but a man, nonetheless. Hands dropped his coat over his shoulders, but he didn't care to see who it was because he was mesmerized by the tears in her eyes. They lined the corners, dripping just as his callused hand drifted to her cheek. He wiped them away, recognizing them for what they were, relief.

"They're gone," he whispered. "And they will never hurt you again."

A sob tore from her throat. She collided with his chest, and he bundled her in his arms as she cried into him. It was over. He nearly thanked Davina for Her timing of when he told Rose of the shadow riots on Draiocht before the demons came aboard.

When he finally gathered the courage to tell her, she proved that they were made for one another with her unrelenting understanding. How could he have found a woman so perfect?

He put his head on hers, a hand tangling in her blonde locks as he remembered her words.

Her eyes darkened, taking in all he laid bare before her. Of the guilt that was tormenting him, not only for killing as he did but for losing her in the first place. All of it, he laid at her feet, waiting for her to tell him what a monster he was. That she could never love a man so vile and cruel. That he would always be the villain.

Instead, she seized his chin, making him look up at her, at the intensity in her eyes.

"I love you, James Hawkins. If they had taken you, instead of me, I would have burned their city to the ground to get you back."

He breathed in her scent, of burning flowers that was so deeply a part of her, no amount of time in a cell could change that.

"Sir," Earhart's concerned tone drew Phantom's attention elsewhere. Jon sat at the ship's railing, shivering as he pressed against the hull. Phantom straightened his coat, buttoning up for modesty, but he kept his hand intertwined with Rose's, unwilling to be parted from her.

They stepped up to Jon and Phantom curled Rose into his chest, as he looked over the former devil. He was still half dead, even if he looked more like himself now. Gone were the clouded eyes and paling skin, but black blood still dribbled from his chin. The shadows closed in on him like they were ready to take him away.

His time was near.

The brute's eyes didn't land on the captain though, they traveled to the songbird in his arms who sniffled before she fell to her knees. Her tears flowed freely as she scooped up his hand, cradling it in her own.

Despite everything he had done, regardless of his intentions, he had been there to help Rose when she needed it most. For that, he would be grateful.

"I'm so glad to see you better."

Jon raised his other hand over hers and Phantom growled. He would only allow so much leniency. Jon let his other hand drop, heeding the warning.

"I can still save you." She pulled out the Stone. "I can–"

"No." His hand covered the Stone, lowering it until her hand rested on her knees. "It's time for me to go. I will not risk you using power on me when you need it for yourself." More tears flowed down her cheeks. "No more of that for me." He tipped his head to Phantom. "And take care of that one for me, will ya?" She nodded her head furiously.

"Thank you." She didn't need to say for what, and Phantom wished again that he would have saved her sooner.

He pulled away from her before accepting her thank you. After all, he did put her there in the first place, a sin Phantom would not soon forget.

Jon's eyes found Robin whose cheeks were stained with tears, and winked at the boy, before turning to his captain.

"I'm ready."

Phantom could sense his soul waning, a light that was flickering out. This had nothing to do with his physical condition and everything to do with the sorcery inflicted on him by the demons. Rose couldn't save him now, no one could. Phantom understood that sacrifice, as small as it was. His soul would aid in making Rose stronger. It was a sacrifice Phantom could honor.

"May you have smooth waters, old friend," Phantom recited, letting the devil say it one last time.

"And open seas for all days." No sooner did the words pass his lips that Phantom let the shadows in. Peacefully, Jon's eyes closed for the very last time, his breathing ceasing completely.

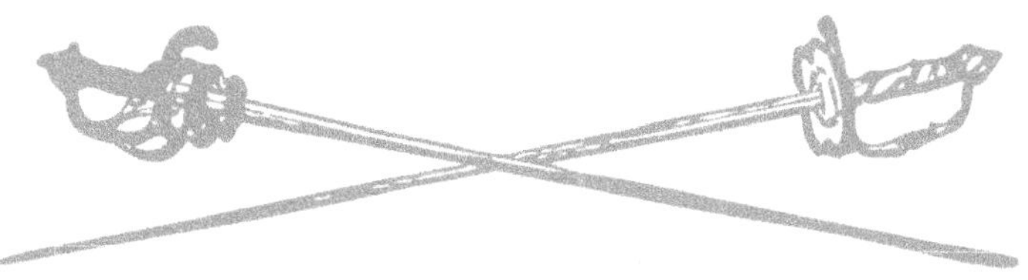

CHAPTER 70

THINGS HAVE CHANGED

BLACK

"All hands!"

His voice hoarse, the captain roared his commands on the creaking deck, desperately wrestling the helm to avoid the jagged teeth of the rocks surrounding their island home. The rocks hadn't been there before, and now the wind picked up, whipping them into the stone again.

The surrounding mist showed no signs of clearing, sticking to the rocks as if instructed to remain there.

They hadn't seen the rocks coming as the remaining slavers sailed in the opposite direction. The mist was different from the dark fog that had entrapped them. For starters, it didn't block out the sun, only hid sharp rocks from view as the devils navigated around them.

Black pulled on the sail, fighting the winds to roll back the mast. It was a hefty task that took four of them on only one sail. The winds were unearthly, certainly not natural with the way they seemed to understand the correct moment to strike and unfurl the sails again.

"Bloody hell!" She shouted over the turbulence.

Ramirez clung to the railing as he climbed the steps of the quarterdeck, addressing the captain with words she could not hear.

Earhart huffed next to Black, the sail continuing to slip from his grasp and his face growing redder.

"Hold on, devil, we'll make it." It was a common thing they said to one another when the seas grew fierce, but the first mate's glare showed her the words did not hit their mark.

"I don't give a damn about me, or this ship, or even the rest of this goddess-forsaken crew. My wife and two daughters are on that island."

Just before the fog rolled away, and they were faced with the mists, Robin had spotted the tip of Kheli's volcano. It was hard to tell what was happening, but with what that last weather anomaly had done, the mist was not a good sign.

The sail ripped in two, straight down the middle, like a ghost had drawn a blade through it. The good news was that the wind couldn't catch them so easily anymore.

A jostle proved her wrong a moment later, knocking the ship into a tall rock. The sound of splitting wood filled her ears.

"Move, devils!" Earhart shouted to Tick and Hyne who were helping roll up the impossible sail. The impact was the more urgent problem. They each made their way down to the deck, Tick and Hyne crawled down the mast. Earhart fell like a cannonball, bracing his knees, but Black took a nearby rope, swinging down with swift ease.

She could get used to the extra boost of power being a devil provided.

They rushed down below deck to find the hull intact, for now, the impact only brushing off a few of their porthole flaps.

"Back on deck!"

They ran back to the main deck to find that there was little more they could do. All the sails that could be secured were and everything else depended on which way the captain steered the ship. By the looks of it, he had no intention of giving up on Kheli.

There was a beat of silence, as if the waves anticipated something new.

Then notes drifted through the air. The song of a siren calling sailors to drown in the seas. With the rush of the river and wind whipping through her hair, a sense of peace settled over her—everything was perfect.

The notes floated around them, blue light mixing with the wind and swirling, breathing tranquility into the very air around them.

Black turned to see Rose standing at the edge of the ship, the Stone in her hand and her eyes glowing like the very sea had possessed her. There were no lyrics to her melody, only the rise and fall of music like a steady heartbeat.

Resplendent, Rose stood among the men, her eyes blazing blue, a radiant glow illuminating her and the Stone, making her appear as a goddess among men.

The wind gradually subsided, the mist slowly lifting, as if nature itself responded to her command.

Rose's song ended and her eyelids grew heavy. The captain sprung from his spot on the helm, rushing to her. Beyond placing a hand to the railing of the ship, she was fine.

Earhart took up the helm, sailing the ship around the sharp rocks until Robin shouted for an opening ahead.

Once docked, a glance back confirmed the mist rolling back over the new rock formations, but the cover didn't extend into the island at all. The sun beat down on Black's back, the air clear.

Nothing about it was natural, like a protective ring was surrounding the island in a shroud.

She took a deep breath after the vessel was secured and the devils began to depart. Earhart ran off the dock, Phantom following him, heading straight for the village, but Black's eyes snagged on the fishing boats on the opposing side of the dock.

Sophia stepped up beside her. "I didn't think those boats could make it this far."

"They're not meant to, but it seems a lot of things have changed."

Black eyed the huntress with her usual red barmaid dress hiked on one side for easier movement, and a bow and quiver strapped to her back. There was still so much between them, a bit of trust still lost. They needed time alone to talk.

A group of people shifted down the hill and onto the dock. Some of them Black recognized as villagers, such as the chief's wife, Darla, but there were more men among them than she remembered.

One took off in a sprint when he saw who was standing on the dock. The closer he got, the more his intense features became visible.

Black had her sword unsheathed, blocking Sophia as best she could before the man stopped a few paces before them with his hands raised. "I'm looking for my sister."

Though she didn't recognize his face, something about his dark, intense eyes, the subtle curve of his nose, or the perpetual frown etched into his features felt unnervingly familiar.

"Vincent?" Sophia rounded Black, blinking at the man before her. Sister?

"Soph!" He wrapped his arms around her, spinning her around on the dock with a grin lifting his whiskers. He dropped her, then cradled her face like she was a precious child. "I thought you were dead. I cannot begin to tell you how deeply sorry I was to leave you on your own."

An endearing smile lifted her face next. "You don't need to protect me, brother. I did alright. How did you get here?"

Before he could answer, Robin raced onto the dock next to them heading for the trees, Russet followed, stopping beside Black, concern wrinkling his forehead.

"He's looking for those right friends of his. Ya know, the furry ones."

Vincent focused his attention on Russet. "He's looking for the animals?" Russet nodded. "The creatures of the island have gone mad, most of them are walking corpses."

Panic seized Black's heart. She hadn't considered what could become of the island. She ran after Robin, hearing footsteps behind her, but she outpaced them easily, leaning on her abilities. Robin was swift in his own right, but she caught up to him, her heart threatening to beat out of her chest as she witnessed Robin only paces away from a large, slow-moving ape.

Vincent was right, it appeared to be half-dead, its orange fur matted with blood stains both red and black. Some of its fur had fallen off, creating patches that looked like raw wounds.

It snapped its jaws but couldn't move very quickly, even if its clouded eyes were locked on Robin.

"Miss Coral, please, it's me. It's Robin."

Black's heart ached at the sight of Robin's tears. Although denial urged him to reach for his friend, he knew there was nothing they could do for her now. Coral was no longer in there.

Black needed to slay the creature before she bit and infected anyone, but she didn't want to do it in front of the boy. She pulled on his clothes. "Come on, Robin. I need you to go back to the ship. I'll take care of Coral." His eyes snapped to her, and he understood too much.

"No," he whispered, almost imperceptibly. "You can't kill her." Tears sprang from his eyes, but he ignored them. "I won't let you." Black closed her eyes, already regretting what she had to do. Robin lunged for the half-dead ape, but Russet's arms bracketed his body before he could get further.

Robin wiggled and screamed in his arms. "No! You can't! She didn't do anything!"

Black ignored the boy, finding Russet's sad eyes instead. "Take him back to the ship. I don't want him to see this."

"No!" Robin screamed, doing everything he could to break Russet's hold, but the former drunkard held too much love in his heart for the boy. They would not risk his life.

Black focused on the beast before her. Coral inched closer and closer with heavy breaths and vacant, clouded eyes, much like Jon's had been. Flashes of his last moments were still fresh in her mind. In the end, he wasn't a necromite like Coral. She still didn't understand how that worked.

"Wait! Tie her to a tree! Please, don't kill her. Let me try to save her!"

The words stopped her. Robin needed to try. Maybe if he could have time to see that this rotting body of orange fur was no longer his friend, he could accept it. The world was changing, they couldn't protect him from the horrors of it forever. She'd seen worse things as a thirteen-year-old.

"Wait."

Russet stopped in his tracks, inspecting Black with a confused expression.

She sheathed her sword, nodding towards the ship.

"We're going to need rope."

CHAPTER 71

A FAMILY REUNION

PHANTOM

The first mate raced through the jungle after seeing the disrepair of the village. Luckily, there were enough villagers around to explain that they had been overrun by necromites with a warning of the dangers in the jungle.

As Phantom suspected, the witches' sons who lived there had changed too.

"Papa!" Little Maria sprouted from the ground once they neared the cave, running to her father's arms. Earhart scooped her up, kissing her cheek repeatedly as a fraction of tension left his shoulders.

He pulled her back so he could see her smiling face. "Where is your sister and mother?"

"I here!" A smaller body escaped Phantom's notice until she was clinging to her father's pant leg. Anna was such a small creature. Earhart scooped her up next, holding each daughter in an arm as he kissed their cheeks repeatedly.

They laughed and smiled at their father's affection.

Phantom watched the display with bitter jealousy. He'd never wanted what Earhart had before, but the woman he'd traveled the sea and battled death to retrieve had made all that change. He could see little versions of her running around them, laughing.

Davina forbid they would be *anything* like him. No, they would have to take after their mother.

After seeing Jon pass a second time, Rose needed a moment alone. She'd made it clear, after his intense interrogation, that this was something she needed to do on her own. Last he saw her; she was picking up a paint brush.

"Where is your mother?" That last bit of tension in his shoulders released as a figure stood before them, but she didn't run to him. Angelica had tears in her eyes as she stopped ten paces from her husband.

There was something very different about her.

Her appearance was mostly the same, same dark eyes, same curly black hair and sepia skin, but there were additions like the blue circling her eyes and lightning cracking across her wrist. Worry wrinkled her brow as she looked at her husband. Something had changed.

Earhart's expression was unreadable as he let the girls down to the ground.

After a moment of silence, Angelica spoke first.

"You must be angry. You must think I finally followed in my father's footsteps. That I let magic tarnish me, but you must understand, I had to protect this island." Earhart took a step towards her. "There was no one else here, and we needed a miracle." Another step and Phantom planned to run off with Maria and Anna if their parents had a marital spat that turned violent. Though he couldn't imagine Earhart ever hurting his wife.

Angelica took a single step back as he approached, clearly not entirely comfortable with the way he walked up to her.

"I don't like it either, but I can protect them. I can keep them alive, and I never needed a grimoire to make it so."

How was that possible? What exactly was she capable of? He assumed part of it was the new obstacle on the horizon. Phantom would be peppering her with questions had he been willing to interrupt—whatever was happening.

Earhart was only two steps away now.

"Say something, damn you." Sparks sprang from her arms and her white-knuckled fists as her power reacted to her panic.

One more step and his hand was on her cheek, her widened eyes staring into his. "You're more beautiful than even my dreams could recreate. I missed you, *tresora*." He wiped away an errant tear on her cheek before they crashed together, lips locked in a kiss so passionate it spoke of the endless weeks they spent apart.

They could use a private moment.

"Uncle Phantom!" Maria shouted, pawing at his leather coat.

"Come on, you two." Phantom picked up the two girls, feigning exaggerated effort that made them laugh before perching them on each arm. "Let's give your parents a moment alone." The girls looked at each other conspiratorially.

"Where the 'izard?" That was Anna's way of asking about Serena, but the last thing the little dragon wanted was a pair of small hands grabbing at her. And with the dragon's new ability, they would need to be more careful around her. Not to mention, she was exhausted and currently hiding in the main cabin.

Phantom walked around the still kissing couple, continuing to the caves the villagers spoke of. He needed to see everyone was alright and speak with Roger.

"Serena is sleeping, but why don't you show me where you've been staying?"

"Mama says the animals are mean now," Maria complained, half chewing on the sleeve of her dress. "All we see is the caves."

"They *are* mean now, and you're too small to fight them."

"I is not small!" Anna protested, puffing up her chest with a scowl written across her tiny features. He had to bite his tongue to keep from laughing at the sight, since the twenty-pound little girl in his right arm would not take kindly to it.

Upon seeing the caves, he set the girls down, holding their arms loosely so they could look at him. "You two are very brave, a trait you no doubt got from your mother, but I need you to listen to me. The world is more dangerous now. Even this island isn't safe. We cannot risk a single hair on your heads, so you won't wander, and you'll listen, sì?"

When did he start sounding like Mama Owen?

They both nodded their heads.

"Okay, I promise to play with you two in a moment, but I need to talk to the chief. Can you tell me where he is?"

Maria pointed back to a small cave to the left, but when Phantom's eyes followed, he saw the last person he expected to.

"Brother." Sebastian wrapped him in a bear hug before he understood what was happening. A blink later, he embraced him back, letting a bit more of his worry drip from his conscience, his guilt easing a bit. Sebastian was here.

As they pulled back, Phantom inspected his friend's face. "What happened? How did you get out?"

Shame passed over Sebastian's features. "I tried to help them, but Ravana was close to the truth, and I couldn't let her kill me before I did something."

Phantom remembered the fishing boats at the dock, and the number of men who weren't here before.

"You brought the Khelitians home."

A haunted expression passed over Sebastian's features. "Not all of them."

Phantom craned his neck to look around the massive man before him to see the other villagers, looking for a face in the crowds. "Mama Owen?"

Sebastian's head dropped. "I could not convince her to come. I had to transfer the orphans back to her when the Fortress fell to Lockness' criminals. She won't abandon them. I need to retrieve them soon."

As he spoke, Phantom tracked movement from the corner of his eye. A small crocodile inched into the clearing before the caves, stalking the nearest villager, a woman who was busy kneading dough.

The creature didn't move like a normal crocodile though, its movements languid, but choppy. It appeared half-dead, with scales flaking off its rotting body.

Phantom reached for his weapon, but before he could draw it, an arrow snapped through the creature's skull. It slumped instantly.

One of Sophia's apprentices stood on the cliff side above the caves. She lowered her bow once she saw she'd hit her mark.

Phantom sighed away the nerves. "Is this island any safer for them?"

Sebastian's jaw tightened. "They, at least, have food here. That's more than I can say for Samsara."

He remembered the signs, the rotting earth and sand he'd seen before they departed from the main island.

Before he could ask about the state of Samsara, Roger hobbled towards him using a heavy branch to walk. Apparently, he had lost a limb since they last met.

"My boy!" Roger wrapped Phantom in his arms, going so far as to lift him off the ground and squeeze the air from his lungs. "We be prayin' for your swift return."

By the time Roger set him down, he rasped, "Good to see you too, old friend." His eyes wandered down to the bandaged stump where his leg once was. "At least, most of you."

Roger let out a barking laugh. "There's that good humor. We be missin' it from the former Commodore here." With a firm grip on Sebastian's shoulder, he winked, a mischievous glint in his eye. "I'll be needin' to hear of ye great adventures and hero-in', but first we all be needin' a drink."

Sebastian's hand on his shoulder stopped Phantom before he could follow. "You still plan on visiting a Goddess?"

He offered a sharp nod. "Plans haven't changed, only delayed awhile."

"Then, I'll be needing a word before you leave." Sebastian didn't offer anything more before he followed Roger, Phantom a step behind.

It didn't take long for a couple drinks to turn into festivities, and as the sun set over the misty horizon, Phantom found himself looking back to the trail that led him there.

He wanted Rose by his side; there was an ache in his chest with her absence. Before he could think better of it, he was on his feet, making his way back to the ship.

CHAPTER 72

FINISHED MASTERPIECE

ROSE

"Done."

Rose dropped her paintbrush, looking at the painting that was finally satisfactory.

Is that a spider?

Lani's skeptical tone was to be expected.

Technically, she painted Jon. Not in his last moments, broken and fading, but how she remembered him on the ship. He was so full of life then with his meaty shoulders and wide stance. Even if he looked at her with a raised eyebrow on more than one occasion.

But in those last moments, while his soul was at its dimmest, she saw it for what it really was. She had a strong sense that it reflected his character. He was patient, observant, resourceful, skillful at trapping others, and secretive. Not all those things were good in the end, but they still made up who he was.

The *cerbalus*. Her new knowledge of Draiocht from Skye told her that many knew a *cerbalus* was a bounty hunter, but the true meaning of the word was spider.

It was intricately fitting.

In the middle of Jon's image was a glare of sunlight, like a ring around his soul and the spider who lived inside him.

It made her wonder if everyone had some type of animal or insect that represented their personality.

Hers would be her phoenix.

James was that giant lion. One day she planned to paint his lion with him.

Perhaps that's what the witch sons really were, a manifestation of who they were at their core. Or they took on that role after being transformed. She had so many questions.

I'd never thought to test the theory myself.

"Pity. It would be nice to know."

Feeling a weight lift from her shoulders as she stared at the painting, she stretched out her tired limbs before snagging James' long brown coat.

This painting was the goodbye she needed. Now, she was ready to face the island.

When did it become so dark?

That's what happens when you spend hours staring at paints and cloth.

Isabeya didn't quite understand the practice. The creativity she expressed usually found an outlet in battle strategy.

Or in bedding a lover. She added with no small amount of pride.

We don't need the reminder. Scarlet snapped at her.

Rose giggled a bit, feeling too elated to care if the voices in her head got along. Her tormentors were dead, and she'd finally painted. And she had a devilishly handsome pirate to return to.

As she strolled down the dock, she checked in with Lani.

"Am I almost aligned? Can I soul weave?" She snagged an apple from a basket one of the villagers was carrying to the ship with a polite smile. The girl frowned, no doubt noticing that Rose was indeed talking to herself. If only she knew—

That answer is not so simple. But for the process to be complete, a coupling will be in order.

Ha! Isabeya shouted loud enough to make Rose flinch. *Sorry.*

Rose felt her cheeks heat at the prospect of getting James to herself again. They hadn't had time in the cabin before Colt and Dante showed up, or since.

It had been a long day. Honestly, she should have felt more tired, but the buzz of everything that had happened kept her feet moving. She wanted to see her pirate.

Her burned hand ached, but Smith had applied some ointment and wrap to help it heal. She thought of singing to heal it but using magic felt too frivolous.

She slowed at a group sitting around a fire. Black and Russet manned the fire with grim expressions, but Robin was staring at a tree. A few more steps and she witnessed an orange ape tied to the tree like a hostage, but its fur was dark and matted, its eyes clouded with decay.

There were questions she wanted to ask, but Lani's voice cut through.

Look closer.

After closing her eyes for a moment, searching for that cord that connected her to Lani, she opened her eyes. Their souls were illuminated. Black blazed the brightest and if she looked closely, there was a panther, licking its paws. Russet's light was darkened by shadowy fingers but at his core was a bear sleeping soundly. It was no surprise to find a monkey in Robin's soul, but when she looked closely at the beast they had tied up, she swore she could see a tiny glimmer—

"There you are."

Rose's attention was stolen by her less-than-subtle pirate who scooped up her uninjured hand to kiss the back of it. But it was his brilliant, sapphire eyes that looked up at her, and the intensity of his gaze made her knees weak.

"I couldn't wait any longer. If you had still been in front of your painting, I would have had no choice but to use my power of seduction over you." He used her hand to pull her to him, nuzzling kisses into the crook of her neck.

She melted into his arms almost instantly. As much as she wanted to make fun of his 'power of seduction' comment, she knew it would have worked. He had the kind of face that let him get away with everything. Davina forbid them to have a child with *his* face.

Her eyes bloomed at the thought of children. She hadn't exactly been able to get a witch's tonic lately.

One eyebrow rose on his face. "Where exactly has your mind gone, love?"

It was too soon. She couldn't tell him that she was imagining what their children would look like. She struggled to get out of his arms, he was too inclined to get answers if she stayed.

"Ah ah, not until you answer me."

Forgetting the struggle, she got lost in those deep ocean eyes and words came pouring out. "I was thinking about what our children would look like."

"Were you now?"

She expected him to pull back. This wasn't exactly the time for this. Thinking of children while the islands struggled to survive?

Instead, he pulled her closer until their bodies were flush to one another. Self-conscious thoughts made her concerned with the devils still sitting around a fire, only to find a wall of shadow blocking their view.

With her head turned, he took the opportunity to whisper in her ear. "What if I told you, I want nothing more than to see what you look like carrying our child?"

A blurry haze of emotions hit her all at once. Worry. Excitement. Hope. The most surprising one being arousal.

"Oh, you like that thought."

She smirked at him. "Unless you've decided to carry a pistol *inside* your trousers, I would say the same about you." The telltale sign of his arousal was currently pressed against her stomach.

"Oh love, I need only to be in your presence for that to happen."

"Captain," Black said warily. "We may not be able to see you, but we *can* hear you."

Rose's cheeks flushed with humiliation and James had the nerve to look amused at that fact.

"Children are present," Russet shouted, unnecessarily loud.

"I'm not a child," Robin protested.

"I meant the half-dead orange beast."

The two continued to argue, but their bickering faded into the background as James' eyes heated. "It appears our conversation will have to wait."

Seizing her hand before stepping away, James disintegrated the wall of shadow to reveal Russet and Robin in a heated argument while Black stared at the fire like her life depended upon it.

"Come with us, mate," James offered. Black was more than willing to slip away with them as they climbed their way through the jungle.

CHAPTER 73

DRINK WITH US

SEBASTIAN

Sebastian had refused three drinks, all offered to him by some pretty villagers, an interested gleam in their eyes.

He had one drink that was stronger than Roger let on, but he knew he couldn't have more without risking his vigilance. Though there were plenty of men and women who had chosen to abstain in favor of protecting the families, he couldn't shake a restless feeling in his gut.

It felt like danger was waiting for them around the corner. Though with all the threats, he couldn't tell which one was more pressing. Even if James told him it was only nerves and that more drinks would cure him.

With most of the Khelitians back where they belonged and the devils back on shore, many of the villagers were more relaxed, and excited, having more than one reason to celebrate now.

Sebastian took a walk around the camp, observing everyone he could.

James and Rose had become inseparable, cuddling into one another on a log near the fire. He understood why James had chosen her over both islands, and he was glad to see them both find happiness in one another.

Leaning close, James whispered to her, his words eliciting a smile, then a blush as she playfully pushed him away.

Sebastian had to ignore the pang of jealousy that came with seeing them. He wasn't sure how to decipher it, though. There was no connection between him and Rose to speak fondly of, but he wasn't sure if he wanted the attention of his best friend back or the happiness they so easily shared.

The red-bearded one spoke in whispered tones to Arita. Sebastian had met her briefly upon arrival, but whilst she looked at him with suspicion and disdain, she looked at the devil like he hung the very moons in the night sky. They sat very close to one another, a fact that had another devil scowling. The one with a staff in his hand glared at the couple like he was moments away from shoving them apart.

Sebastian wished he had known them. They were the friends he could have had if Davina had been kinder. Instead, he had to rot on Samsara; though he'd helped many, he could hardly resent that fact.

Robin eyed him from across the bonfire between them.

There was a brief time when Sebastian had known Robin as a boy, and he was a few years younger then. A few similarities in their appearances had led him to believe they could be related, but there was little chance of that.

Maybe he did need another drink, his mind was wandering too much.

His eyes landed on Indigo as she hoisted part of her dress up to better crouch next to one of Earhart's daughters, but she nearly exposed her entire leg. It was indecent to say the least, so why couldn't he look away from her olive skin? And why did it look so mouth-wateringly soft?

He *definitely* needed another drink.

Shaking his head from thoughts of her, he moved to Roger's side.

"Ah, ready to be joinin' the real fun, ya?"

He gave the chief a sharp nod. "I'll take whatever you got."

Roger handed him an unmarked bottle that was likely full of something homemade. Those were usually the most potent, but with the smirk the chief was currently trying to hide, he suspected the liquid would drive him straight on his ass.

The recent memory of Indigo's exposed thigh had him downing half the bottle in one swig, the unholy mixture tasting like drinking metal.

"Whoa there, siren bait, don't be throwin' them inhibitions to the wind quite yet."

Sebastian ignored him, plopping onto the log beside the chief. Unfortunately, the log was in perfect view of where Indigo was currently helping the girl into a pair of shoes, her breasts nearly spilling out of her cinched top as she bent over.

He glanced at the bottle. Was the bloody concoction making him worse?

She's a Davina-damned witch. You have no business thinking of her in such a way.

"Ah, I see. Your eye be catchin' on the bonnie lass. No wonder ya be turnin' to the drink for courage."

Sebastian's head turned sharply to the chief, the images around him spinning a bit. What on Macha's blessed earth had he drunk?

"Don't be lookin' at me like that." Roger smirked, clearly enjoying this. "I be keepin' ya secret." He took another swig of his own drink while Sebastian considered calling it a night.

A heavy hand landed on Sebastian's shoulder. "It's good to see you, old friend." He had to blink some of the fog away, but that was Joseph Earhart sitting on his other side.

"At long last!" Roger bellowed. "Ya be back from ya conoodlin'. I thought I'd have to be sendin' out a troop to look for the both of ya."

Earhart gave a crooked smile to the chief. "When you haven't seen your wife in over a month, I think you can understand."

"Aye!" Roger tipped his head before offering Earhart a bottle. The beast of a man took a swig without even flinching, but he supposed as a pirate, he had more practice.

"Speakin' of," Roger started, his lips already loosening. Sebastian shot him a glare promising death. Unfortunately, it only served to encourage him. "It be seemin' our former Commodore be havin' eyes for his own warm bed to be returnin' to."

Sebastian prayed that gibberish would not be understood by

the first mate, but with a glance as his old friend, those hopes drowned.

Earhart had a smirk and a gleam of mischief in his eyes. "Is that so? Who's the unfortunate target?"

Roger offered a not-so-subtle nod to where Indigo was enjoying her own meal, biting into a bright red apple.

Earhart feigned a gasp. "Commodore! A witch? I thought you too self-righteous for that."

"In fact," Roger offered. "He swallowed half a bottle of red moonshine just to gain the confidence to be talkin' to her."

"No, I drank—"

Before he denied it, Earhart patted his back. "Good on you, mate. After all you've been through, you deserve a good woman. Though I never thought you were a man to need a drink to talk to one."

This was ridiculous. He didn't need the liquid to talk to her. He needed it to forget her. A task that was growing increasingly more difficult.

Tension strained his shoulders and jaw as he let his gaze wander to her again. Indigo had finished her apple, tossing the core into the fire between them, then she licked the sweet juices still running down her fingers.

Davina above.

"Mate, what enchantment did she place on you?"

That must be it. An enchantment.

But Earhart didn't mean it in earnest, it was only in jest. Yet it was the only explanation. Why else would he be falling in love with a bloody witch?

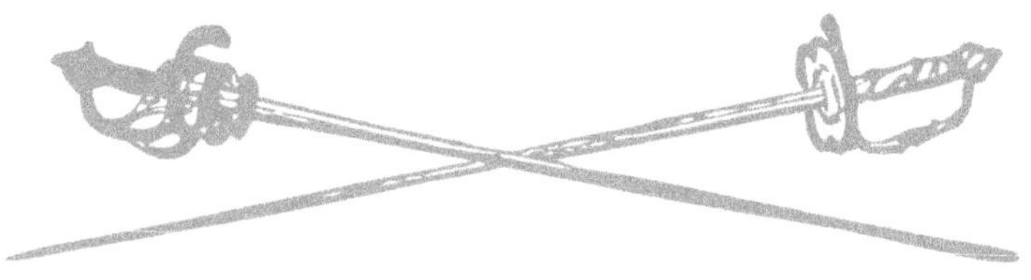

CHAPTER 74
IN ANOTHER LIFE
BLACK

As the festivities continued and the people around Black became merry, she painted a smile on her face. She hadn't felt like drinking; her mind was too occupied to enjoy the songs and company. Especially when Sophia refused to look at her.

The huntress in question had spent hours catching up with her brother. It was understandable, they hadn't seen each other in years. But it didn't help the unease in her stomach.

She was beginning to believe the kiss they shared on a rooftop in Amal really was a mistake. She hadn't been able to get it out of her head, even if Sophia had.

As if her thoughts summoned her attention, the huntress turned her eyes to Black. The entire world melted away as she drifted into those dark eyes. Their stolen moment, a glimpse of true connection, vanished when Sophia smiled at something her brother said.

"I'll be right back," she whispered to Ramirez who handed a lit cigar to her. She'd only indulged a couple times, but she craved the calming effect the smoke provided. She thanked him with a nod before shuffling away to find an empty cave.

It was half a mile away. She puffed on the cigar, eventually finding a cave far enough away to breathe. She leaned against the cave wall, inhaling smoke to watch it stream before her.

The darkness of night was intensified by the clouds that hovered over Davina's silver light. She wanted to curse the goddess, though she wasn't sure for which transgression. For those girls she lost in Draiocht, for Her sovereignty over Sophia, or for Her existence at all.

The cigar burned out, so she tossed it into the nearest puddle.

Black ran her hands over her dirty face. Her foul mood was doing her no favors. She needed to let Sophia go, accept that one kiss was all she would get and move on. It was never meant to be.

Just as she was about to walk back to camp, a shadow darkened the entrance. Silver light spilled around her as Sophia stepped into the cave.

She didn't say anything as she walked in, those stoic features giving nothing away.

Emotion made Black's throat tighten, but she cleared her throat to shift past it. "I know why you're here." Sophia said nothing, only stepped further into the cave. "You don't need to worry about me. I'm sure your purpose is very important. I understand you have no room in your life for me." Another thought punched her in the gut. "We'll have to leave here soon. But you'll stay here. Protect your people. It's what I..." She choked on the words, unwilling to let them slip past, but Sophia had stopped, waiting for the end of that sentence. "It's what you're meant to do," she said instead.

She blinked away tears so they wouldn't fall, then she offered Sophia a sad smile.

Still, the huntress said nothing.

Black's mind wandered, thinking of sleepy mornings and clasped hands. Of laughter and sweet kisses. The passionate ones too. All the things they might have had together.

"In another life, perhaps?"

It was the little hope she dared to grasp.

"No." Sophia said with relentless authority.

"No?"

The last bit of hope died in her chest. Maybe none of it mattered to Sophia.

"That's all you have to say? No? You won't even tell me why we can't be together. Does Davina command your unhappiness or perhaps, it is I who cannot make you happy?" Sophia stood there like a statue with the only sign of life being her rapid breathing. "Is it because I'm just a pirate?"

Sophia's eyes blazed through her as the clouds moved from the sky, allowing silver light to bathe the tips of her dress. Black watched as she tensed.

"Tell me," she pleaded, willing Sophia to listen. To say anything. "For once in your life Sophia, tell me what's going on."

Silence rang out between them, the world slowing and waiting for the answer.

Instead of speaking, Sophia drifted further into the cave, walking past Black but never once breaking eye contact. Black followed like a moth to a flame, deeper into cave until no moonlight touched them.

"Davina cannot see me if Her silver light cannot touch me."

The words are so beyond what Black expected that her mind stuttered. "What?"

Sophia took a step towards her, reaching for where her sword was strapped to her hip. "I was six when I found a bear in the jungle." Completely lost, Black's brows furrowed, but she listened as Sophia unbuckled her sheath and set her weapons on the cave floor. "There aren't supposed to be bears on Kheli, but there it was, reaching its claws for me like it might tear me apart." She pulled at the hemline of her dress, lifting it over the leg she covered. "It tore me apart." Deep scars lined Sophia's right leg, wrapping over her thigh and extending up her hip.

Mesmerized by the story, Black reached a hand down to trace the nearest scar. Sophia's sharp inhale encouraged her to continue. The scars were so faded, they were difficult to see in the darkness, but she felt how deep they ran. This happened when she was six?

"How did you survive?"

"I wouldn't have, but Davina saved me. Her light washed over me, healing the broken skin and replenishing my blood." Sophia lightly pushed her coat from her shoulders until it fell to the cave floor, all while Black caressed her scars. "She whispered of this great purpose I would have. One day, an opportunity would come for me to board a ship, and my true destiny would follow." The ties of her corset came next. Black licked her lips as the material loosened, then fell to the rocks below. "She never told me what it would be, only that I would understand when the time came."

Tension heated the space between them as Black lifted Sophia's skirt to her hip, gaining access to more of her skin. She didn't understand what this dance was between them, but she was too helpless to stop it. She studied Sophia's parted lips, wanting to taste them again.

"Then She saw us together and told me I am forbidden to have you."

Black's caresses stopped. Was this some twisted game to play on her heart?

"Sophia."

"Sh sh," Sophia put a finger to the seam of Black's lips, returning that heated tension between them. "I tried to resist. I tried to remember the destiny that awaits me, but then I see you laugh. I see peace on your face when you hold a sword. I watch how much you care. Even for lost little girls."

Black's shoulders slumped thinking about the little girls she failed. "You knew?"

"Davina saw. Gwenivere, I am so sorry."

She let her head fall on Sophia's, their foreheads pressing together. "I am too."

They stayed that way, in the silence of the cave until Sophia whispered. "I go where you go, and I don't want you in another lifetime." Black pulled away, gazing into Sophia's eyes, they were like molten lava. "I want you in *this* one."

Black's breaths grew heavier as she watched Sophia's gaze shift. Black followed, watching as silver moonlight reached for them like the tide coming in.

Davina cannot see me if Her silver light cannot touch me.

"The moonlight." Black turned to her huntress, finally understanding. "Davina only knows what we are doing if we are in Her moonlight."

A small smile lifted the corner of Sophia's mouth. "Yes."

Though the moonlight crept closer, she watched it without alarm, its distance still reassuring.

Black moved quickly, her hands finding Sophia's waist and drawing her close until they were pressed together. Her hand paused, lightly touching her huntress' soft cheek. "I think I'm finally understanding."

A spark ignited as their lips met, a searing heat that consumed them both. It traveled through her like a blaze, uncontrolled and unstoppable. Sophia's lips parted and Black explored her mouth, wanting more of her. Black pressed her to the cave wall, drawing her scarred leg up while they fell into their passionate embrace.

Black's hand traveled up her leg until it reached Sophia's soft, round ass. So much of her was soft; her skin, the way her flesh bent under pressure, her hair. All of her, even her delicate vanilla scent.

Sophia's hands explored too, lifting under her shirt to feel the skin beneath, then higher until she was cupping Black's small breasts. Pleasure soared through her like lightning, heating her blood to an unbearable degree.

Black tore her lips away to descend upon her neck, nipping and sucking at her elegant skin until Sophia pulled on her hair.

"Gwen, baby, please." She lifted her head to see Sophia's eyes heavy and wanting. "We've been here too long. Davina will notice."

They panted together as Black ached for more, and yet, she didn't want their time together to be rushed.

She leaned forward for one more kiss. "It's just as well because when I have you, I want to wake up beside you."

Sophia smiled in a way that she'd never seen before. One that brightened the darkness of the cave. Was she… happy? Uncontrollably, Black returned the smile.

They fixed their clothing, buckling her sheath and tying Sophia's corset.

Before they walked back out into the moonlight, Sophia laid a hand on her chest to stop her, right over where the 'v' of her neckline opened.

"If you'd like to pick up where we left off—"

Sophia's gaze traveled to where her hands were, clearly

debating the offer before she cleared her throat. "We can't tell anyone about us. Davina sees and hears everything Her moonlight touches. If they speak of us at the wrong moment..."

"We are found out."

"Precisely."

Just how long would they have to keep this up? But with the world on the verge of ending and their journey to Hell's Gate, there was little time to worry about that. For now, she would live each moment to its fullest and consider the consequences later.

Black pulled the hand off her chest, giving Sophia's wrist a slow kiss before releasing her. "Our secret."

Sophia's gaze heated again, and Black loved how she reacted. She gave Sophia's ass a firm squeeze before sending her off. "Go first, I'll follow in a while. Make sure you watch the trees."

She watched Sophia leave, warmth blooming in her chest.

CHAPTER 75
AMONG FRIENDS
PHANTOM

"You're serious?"

Phantom's grin was wide, feeling content with Rose sitting between his legs, his arms draped over her shoulders.

He put a hand to his chest. "Have you ever known me to be a liar?"

"Infamously, actually," she retorted.

"Well... not about this. Our resident huntress is in fact chosen by Davina." He, of course, failed to mention that he had locked her in the brig when he found out. Though it didn't escape his notice that Black had let her out, it was the reason he gave her the key. It was Black's decision to let her go, not his. He trusted his devil, and that was that.

"Where is she? I don't see Sophia."

Phantom's eyes scanned the revelers, searching each face. "Black is missing as well."

"I'd bet they'd found an empty cave, ya know," Hyne remarked, leaning over to wink at her. Anger flared in Phantom's chest that anyone would *dare.* His growl was cut off by Rose giving him a light shove.

Lara sat below him, her back leaned against the log Hyne sat on, Tick on her other side.

Tick signed, "*I'll take that bet.*"

"Will you now?" Hyne attempted to sign back, though it was amateur at best. The three sat awfully close together without fully touching beyond a few brushes. Hyne nudged Lara so she could read his lips. "Will I get a kiss if I win?"

Phantom had tried this method of flirting before. It usually didn't end with a kiss, but getting her picturing the action was the point of it.

Tick blushed, his cheeks turning bright red as he realized what he would get if he won, or maybe what he would lose.

Lara looked between them rapidly before putting her hands up. The common gesture for 'leave me out of this.'

Rose giggled in his arms, the sound melting his heart. He leaned in, burying his face in her hair and inhaling her scent. The smell of burning flowers smoothing his very soul.

"It appears your coin will have to do, my friend," a deep feminine voice interrupted them. Angelica appeared before them, reminding him more of when he first met her. Back when she was the daughter of a ruthless pirate captain. He knew the pirate never left her blood. She wore a puffy brown shirt with black pants below her belt and boots. A hat sat atop her head, making her appear taller than she was, even if she already rivaled her own husband's height.

Angelica's gaze locked on Rose before her knees fell to the ground.

"I know it's late to say but thank you for saving my life."

Rose leaned forward, away from his arms as she looked into Angelica's eyes, seeing blue rings around the pools of brown. "Wha—what did I do to you?"

With a heavy sigh, Angelica raised the sleeve of her shirt to expose the new tattoo there. Blue lightning spread across her forearm like it was sentient. Rose reached for it. Phantom had the urge to pull her away, scared something irrevocable would happen, but he steadied his nerves.

When her fingertips brushed the lightning, it flared, glowing brighter for a moment in answer to her touch.

"Thank you for giving me the strength to protect this island."

He didn't see Rose's expression, but he sensed her apprehension as she pulled her hand back. "You're not the only one I've healed. How did this happen?"

Footsteps drew Phantom's attention to the witch approaching them. Last he saw Indigo, she was using her magic to trap him. It set his nerves alight yet again. He pulled Rose close, shielding her from potential harm.

Orange painted his vision. Draven said nothing, but the shadows spoke instead.

sssssssend her to usssssss

Their collective presence darkened the surrounding space.

"You've never healed someone with this much potential before." The witch's eyes tracked Rose in a way that made Phantom growl. This time Rose didn't stop him. "Angelica's bloodline is strong. Your magic sparked her own and tethered her to you."

He wanted to ask if it was like his connection to his devils, but he didn't dare reveal that information to Indigo.

Rose closed her eyes, breathing in and out a couple times before a cord appeared. It glowed lighter than the cord connecting Phantom to his *tresora,* but this one tied Angelica to her.

Angelica's eyes were wide as she took in the physical manifestation of their connection. Rose opened her eyes. "I saw it before, but I didn't know what it was. What can you do with it?"

"Thunder and lightning mostly, but I also managed to summon the rocks and shroud around the island, so I'm not certain I know what I'm capable of yet." Angelica laid her hand on Rose's, gentle as a falling leaf, her voice like a delicate breeze. "I'm sorry for what you've endured. I laid awake at night, listening to your screams."

Rose pulled away from her hand, burrowing into Phantom. Angelica accepted the distance, standing. "I cannot thank you enough for what you have given me. Let me know if there is anything I can do for you."

Then, she walked away, but the witch remained, staring at them. Something burned in her gaze that Phantom didn't like, the shadows reacted, slithering towards her.

we feasssssssst

Just before they brushed her shoes, Phantom pulled them back, regaining enough sense to know this wouldn't help. He couldn't kill everyone who made him wary, but Indigo's glowing violet eyes made him uneasy. She knew something.

"Excuse me," she whispered before departing from them.

It took him too long, absorbed by the pull of the shadows, to notice Rose was shaking.

"I need a moment," she said, breaking from Phantom's hold to run off into the jungle by herself.

"Rose, wait!"

The shadows pounced, reaching out to all sides, snuffing out the light. The fire continued to burn, but the light of it no longer reached the people.

The villagers gasped, backing away from the rising darkness, but this was night, when darkness ruled. Right now, he blended in with the night, molded to it like it was exactly where he belonged.

sssshe ssssssscreamsssssss

The shadows echoed Angelica's words. He worked hard not to think of the torment Rose survived. She wasn't recovered, he understood that, but if he thought of it too long, he'd let the shadows take over like they had in Amal.

Guilt slammed into him, shaking his very being. The shadows licked at the residual energy, begging him to give up his weakness to them.

give it to ussssssss

He held onto his guilt, letting himself soak in the utter despair or the crushing idea that she was there because of him.

A scream focused him back on the shadows, on taming them. He pulled on them, but they didn't budge, powerful enough to ignore his wishes.

"Bloody hell," he cursed, then did the only thing he thought would help.

He ran into the jungle, hoping the shadows would follow him there.

CHAPTER 76

WHAT IS LIGHT

ROSE

Rose followed her feet until they led her to the lake. The same one she'd found James in months ago. It seemed like years with everything that had passed between them since. Davina's waning moon was the only one in the sky, bathing the lake in silver with its reflection rippling in the calm water.

She stared at that glowing orb in the sky, wondering what Davina thought of her. Was She proud of Her daughter?

A groan rumbled in her throat. Her mother was Josephine Davenport, not Davina. Her mother made her tea when she was sad and stroked her hair when she was falling asleep. She surprised her with new paint and posed in absurd positions for hours so Rose would practice.

What had Davina done?

James. She gave you James. Lani's soft tone softened her raging heart. She took her mind off Davina and focused on Angelica. What fate had she created for a woman she respected so much? Would she no longer age like the immortals of ancient times? Would she have to watch her husband die?

The Khelitian men came to mind. She recognized every single one of them. They had all been taken to her father's dungeon and stripped of their humanity, by her.

She sighed heavily, wiping angry tears from her cheeks before marching to the water's edge. She needed something to calm her down, make her thoughts clearer. James would swim in this very pool to calm himself.

It might work for her, too.

Following her instincts, she stripped her clothes, letting them fall on a nearby rock. Even the knife she had clung to since arriving back was laid across the stones. Only her locket remained on her chest, just above the slight swells of her breasts.

She didn't much care if anyone saw her, yet she hoped James would.

But that's not why she dipped her toes into the freezing water. She'd wondered why it was so cold as she let the coolness roll over her skin. No hesitation plagued her as she kept moving until she was waist deep in the water.

She took a long breath, letting her soul hum with contentment. It soothed her from the inside out, warming her cool skin like a morning sunrise. Looking down, she saw light form from the water, spilling forward until it formed a figure before her. Lani's translucent body projected from the light.

"Why did you come out this way? Leaving the man you only just returned to?"

A wave of terrible memories washed over her, each one as sharp and cold as a winter's wind. Her mother's final breath. Angelica's upturned life. An entire squadron of ex-naval officers. Lara bleeding from her ears.

"Yes, you have much to feel guilty for. Though some of it is shame. Scarlett will work with you on those next."

Numbness swept over her. She recognized the sensation as her natural defense against the emotion. It helped her look at those instances with a clear eye and she had to wonder if Lani provided the reprieve somehow.

"How do I know which is guilt?"

"Close your eyes," Lani instructed, and Rose obeyed. "Think about these times carefully." Rose focused, seeing the events from afar to examine them. "Think of the action you did to earn these feelings. What did you do to the officers?"

Screams. Blood-curdling screams echoed in her memory. All the men she enthralled. "I took their lives from them."

"You did this to survive. Would any of them done differently?"

Be useful, child. Get him to tell me the truth.

Rose gritted her teeth, the guilt wearing down the block on her mind. "Not at first. I did it to please my father. I only—" her words choked her breath. "I only wanted him to be proud of me. He only threatened and tortured me when I stopped needing that from him."

Tears fell silently down her cheeks.

"Look what became of them. Most of the Khelitians are home, they are free to live their lives because you defied your father. It is a heavy burden to decide the fate of so many, but it is done. Let your guilt go."

The dam broke, letting in all that raw emotion swirl inside her. She latched onto the guilt, understanding it, how it shaped her and accepting it. All the things she had done could not be undone.

"Good, now think of all your regrets. All the moments that prevent you from enjoying your life."

The water swished around her, dripping as if Lani had cupped it in her hands. She poured the cool water over Rose's head, letting the droplets rain down her hair, face, shoulders, and chest, until they returned to the lake.

"Let the water take all you see. All that guilt you've harbored, give it to the water and let it roll off your skin. That's what your guilt is from now on. It can linger in your hair or flesh for a moment to teach you a lesson, but it ultimately does not belong to you. It belongs to the lake. Let it return to its source."

Rose took one last breath, letting the water run down her skin.

She felt the shackles of guilt fall away, lifting a burden she'd carried for years. The air around her felt lighter, crisper somehow.

"Open your eyes."

Lani's kind brown eyes met hers as she opened her own. An orange halo, almost a shimmering light, surrounded her breathtakingly beautiful form.

Lani smiled softly. "I am proud of you for achieving what I failed to. But you still have much to learn."

Rose blinked away tears as she thought of ending Skye. "Do I have to kill you?"

Lani sighed heavily. "Yes, child, but not yet. Once you understand how to wield your soul, I can rest." Another tear fell from Rose's eye. Lani inspected her face with a crinkled brow. "It wasn't meant to be like this. The alignments were to happen when we deemed you ready. Our passing would have been much subtler, but the demons disrupted the process, unknowingly teaching you to hold onto us. Now, your mind won't release us without a fight. I am sorry."

Rose hugged her arms around her body, feeling entirely too cold. She could use one of her mother's infamous hugs. Thinking of her mother, she recalled words she didn't understand at the time.

"Some wounds cannot heal completely." It was something Josephine would say when she referred to the loss of her sister, even if Isabeya watched from her daughter's eyes.

Silence descended upon the lake as the darkness deepened, swirls of inky shadow curling around them. Even Davina's moonlight dimmed.

Lani smiled at the darkness like it was an old friend. "It's about time we helped with these. Are you ready?"

CHAPTER 77

WITHOUT DARKNESS

PHANTOM

Phantom dragged the shadows into the depths of the jungle. They whispered promises of death and destruction all the while, goading him into action.

sssssswallow them kill them dessssssstroy

They were loud enough that Draven's calls were harder to hear.

Listen to — find Rose — Lani will know — to do.

He pulled the shadows back, tugging on their straining leashes. With a yank, he ran deeper into the jungle, until he reached the only place he knew there was peace.

Stepping up the lake, he scanned its glittering surface, landing on a figure.

His mouth dried up when he saw *her*, completely naked and staring at an apparition of light before her. Draven's tugging told him exactly who that light was, orange flaring brightly.

A sharp tug in his gut told him to run to her.

He continued walking, witnessing the moment when the apparition faded into the night.

Rose was a vision he greedily drank in. The way her skin glistened in the moonlight and the sharp points of her nipples. He wanted to put each one in his mouth, taking his time to pleasure her thoroughly. *Mierda*, he was thickening in his trousers already.

"No." He balled his fists at his side, straining, no, aching to join her in that water. To taste every inch of her. But he couldn't. He couldn't come too close, not with the hungry way the shadows swirled around him.

He was too occupied with his own thoughts; he almost didn't notice the way his skin deepened. He pulled apart the buttons of his shirt to find the shadows had taken him from the inside, swirling beneath his flesh.

"James?" Rose's voice drifted to him with the sound of moving water. She was getting out.

"No, stop." He couldn't look at her, the shadows whispering to him.

we take good care of her sssssssoul

"Don't come any closer." He didn't dare look, but the sound of moving water stopped. A sharp pang of guilt hit him at the thought she might have been hurt by his words. The shadows crept in on him, thicker than ever and whispering still.

give it to usssss let us feasssst

They wanted his guilt, but if he gave them any more of it, they would grow more powerful.

He fought against the darkness, trying to think of a way to banish them, but he couldn't hold them much longer.

Finally, he looked up to see them reaching for her light. That light blue essence was so much brighter than his own. They wanted her soul; he could sense it. He latched onto them, holding them with all the strength he possessed.

"Rose! Run!"

The shadows pulled away from him, slipping from his grasp. They no longer listened to him. They were bolder, more defiant, as if they collectively decided Phantom was not their master.

"No," he breathed, mentally pulling on the bloody things, but they ran through his fingers like sand. "Stop. Don't touch her." They ignored him, rushing to claim the bright soul before them.

And she wasn't running. She wasn't even trying to move away.

come with ussssssss ssssssssuch a pretty sssssssssoul

They reached her in the lake just as her light exploded outwards, a brilliant, dazzling light that filled the air with warmth and a resonant hum, like the dawn of a new day.

But it wasn't Rose.

Lani stood in the lake before her, shielding the songbird from the intensity of the darkness. Her half-faded hands flickered as she bent her own soul around the shadows, shaping them. Lani moved like it was a dance, her hands spun and swayed, golden light following each gesture. The darkness bent with the light like the currents of the ocean, guiding a ship's path.

Captivated by the ballet of light and darkness, Phantom gravitated closer, the water lapping at his trousers.

The shadows curved and condensed until a figure stood before Lani. Muscular shoulders blocked Lani from view, so Phantom drew close enough to see Draven's pensive features. He was made entirely of shadow, and his gaze was focused on Lani.

"Why do you remain? You know the shadows will not accept two masters. You must let him go."

Two masters? Was that why he lost control?

"I go when you go. If you stay, I stay." He said it with such finality, echoing in Phantom. He would have done the same.

Lani's near translucent hand came up to touch his shadowed cheek. The heavy contrast of light and darkness mimicking actual touch. With longing evident, Draven shut his eyes. Could he feel the touch of his lover despite their lack of flesh?

"I need to stay, but you cannot," Lani said, her voice trembling, a catch in her throat. "You must pass on."

Light spread from her hand, drifting through the shadows like rippling water.

"No," he said, panic lacing his tone. "Don't do this. I promise, I'll do better." She might have been made of light, but Phantom could have sworn, there were tears glistening on her cheeks.

"He cannot complete his alignment if you remain." The shadows lit, fading in Lani's light. "I'm sorry, my love."

Draven's face twisted in pain as he fought against her hold. He shot forwards, his hands cupped her face as they crashed together. Lost in the heat of the moment, they remained locked together, their passion consuming them.

Could they truly feel each other or was it a mind's trick?

Seconds later, Draven's shadowy silhouette faded, replaced by moonlight until he was gone completely.

Phantom looked inwards, still feeling gripped by the weight of shadows even if it was lessened, but Draven was gone.

When he turned to Lani, she was already staring at him, her eyes filled with grief. "He is at peace." She drew closer, floating like a leaf in the wind. "Now, let's lighten your load." His chest felt the weightless touch of her hand, like butterfly wings.

She transformed into blinding light, consuming his vision to the point of pain.

Phantom drew a hand over his eyes to prevent blindness as every scrap of darkness around him burned away. The light penetrated his soul, cleansing it from the hold the shadows had over him. He even heard their shrieks of pain as they evaporated into the air the way they were meant to.

He sucked in air, no longer weighed down by their heavy presence.

The light faded and Phantom lowered his arm, finding only the night surrounding him. No light aside from the moon above them. No unnatural darkness that grew too restless.

Even Lani was gone, and he could see Rose.

Having walked far enough that her hips brushed the water's surface, the gentle lapping of the waves against her skin only enhanced her already stunning beauty. There was a glow left behind on her skin, like she was heaven sent.

How many times must he fail before he understood? She was never meant to be his, even with the screaming need inside him telling him otherwise.

"I'm sorry. For so many things. For putting you in danger. The shadows," he stopped, swallowing his pride as he explained. "They offered to take away my guilt and I let them, but it made them more powerful." He looked at his own hands, wondering how much pain he would cause her.

She extended a hand in offering to him. "Come to me."

Like a sailor being lured to the water by a siren, he obeyed, wading through the water until he stood before her. He didn't question for one second what would happen. If she intended to drown him there, he would let her.

Yellow flared in his vision. *No, you would fight her.*

He ignored his angry counterpart in favor of giving Rose his undivided attention.

Rose's right hand, cool and gentle, came up, roaming over the exposed skin of his chest, lingering on the rapid beat of his heart, just like it had been when she'd woken screaming from that nightmare.

She lifted his hand with her left, placing it over her exposed chest where her own heart thundered. He felt the steady beat of it, fast, but strong. She was alright. She wasn't dying in some hole in Draiocht or rotting in her room in Samsara or harmed by his shadows. She was here, and she was alive.

He hadn't accepted that fully — until now.

"I forgive you. For everything you regret or carry guilt for whether you believe you deserve it or not. I forgive you."

He circled his thumbs along her ribs as he lowered his forehead to hers. "Thank you, love." The weight on his chest vanished, the world suddenly vibrant and full of sound as if her forgiveness had cleansed him.

She nodded furiously then moved both her hands to his chest, tugging at his clothing. "Let me show you just how much you're forgiven."

He stopped her hands, his own calloused and rough against her softer skin, holding them close to his chest, afraid she wasn't ready for intimacy again. Until he noticed the way heat blazed in her eyes, like a beacon calling for him. Need swirled there, waiting for him to act.

"James," she whispered, so much want in that one word. His name. He wanted to hear her moan it. Scream it for the entire island to hear.

Releasing one hand, she drove it through his hair near his ear, demanding his eyes.

Her eyes glistened with gold, as bright as any treasure he'd ever stolen.

"My *tresora*," he whispered, surrendering to the way her hand felt in his hair, bending to her will and leaning on her strength.

Rose took the hand still clutching hers, pulling it down until she placed it on her breast, his thumb drifting over her pert nipple. She sucked in a breath, and it broke any restraint he had left.

Driving his hands into her hair, he tilted her face up, the sodden strands tangling in his fingers as their lips met in a desperate, needy kiss. She pulled at his shirt until she reached his chest, and he could feel her bare skin on his. Groaning at the feeling of her hands exploring the planes of his chest, he rushed to rid himself of the rest of his clothes.

Never separating their lips, she helped him strip his coat and shirt, letting them drift across the surface of the lake. However, it proved to be more difficult to rid himself of his trousers and boots in the middle of a lake.

His hands drifted down her back until he palmed the flesh of her ass and lifted her out of the water. Her legs wrapped around his waist, their lips and tongues still locked, as if breathing each other in was the only suitable air they'd had in days.

Cold fingers tugged at his hair, messing it up to complete disarray. He chuckled into her mouth.

She pulled back, looking at him with heated eyes and panting breaths. "What's funny?"

He regretted laughing if it meant losing her lips, but he smirked just the same. "I think you fancy me for my hair, love." He walked towards the nearest rock, sitting on it with her straddling him, his bloody trousers still separating their skin.

She didn't join his laughter though, instead those cold fingers drifted over the lines of his face and neck. "Yes," she said between labored breaths. "Only your hair." Though her tone gave away her lie. A tremor ran through him as he met the pure, unwavering adoration in her gaze.

His cock twitched against his trousers. Groaning at how uncomfortable his wet pants were, he shifted her on his lap. There was something about seeing her completely bare before him that made him feel reverent. He wanted to worship every inch of her body.

Rose moved off his lap, and he nearly dragged her back until he saw her kneel in the shallow water before him. Keeping her eyes on him, she unlaced and pulled off each boot, tossing them to the shore behind him. He felt a primal urge to pounce, a raw need that warred with an equally strong desire to remain perfectly still. If letting her control this was what she needed, he'd gladly submit to her every whim.

Inching closer, she unlatched his belt and trousers, tugging them down his soaked legs until she tossed those behind him as well.

Finally, they were both bare beneath the moonlight, and he watched as her heated gaze moved from his face to the cock between his legs. As she licked her lips, a low growl escaped him, imagining the sensation of her lips on him.

"You don't have to—"

Her hands wrapped around his girth, stroking him in a wave that was more teasing than satisfying. "What happened to my foul-mouthed pirate?"

Phantom groaned, spying a mischievous glint in her eyes. This woman was made for him, though the opposite was also true. He released his inhibitions, surrendering to the woman who held his heart, her touch sending shivers down his spine.

"Then stop teasing and show me how much you want this."

Tightening his hold on her hair, he pulled her forward until her lips grazed his tip and he shuddered at the contact. He wanted to shove his cock deep into her mouth, and with the hungry look in her eyes, he could tell she wanted that too.

There would be time for them to live out their deepest, more depraved desires, but tonight wasn't for that. This act was meant to be savored.

Pulling her forward slowly, she opened her mouth wide enough to take him and moaned around him. She flattened her tongue on his shaft, and he growled at the mesmerizing feel of it. His hips bucked, thrusting into her mouth a little farther. She could take more, so much more, he was certain of it.

Rose got bolder, licking and sucking, driving him to madness.

He groaned deeply, feeling the heat of her desire radiating from her, a palpable wave of want that made his own need ache.

He needed to be inside her again. Not just her mouth.

Phantom pulled her off him and she whimpered so sweetly that he wanted to thrust into her mouth again. "Another time I'll fill your pretty mouth, but tonight I need to feel you find your pleasure on my cock."

With eagerness, she leaped onto his lap, and he gently guided her onto him until she was crying out. She was so warm and wet for him, proving how she'd enjoyed putting her mouth on him.

"You're so bloody beautiful, Rose. The most brilliant thing I've even been allowed to witness." He leaned his forehead against hers. "You're so bloody perfect. Being inside you is the closest I will ever be to heaven."

Part of him wanted to lean back and watch her ride him to her heart's content, using his body to find ecstasy. But he couldn't stop touching her. Letting his hands roam over her back, he traced the scars on her stomach and thighs like she was treasured artwork.

She rolled her hips, earning a pained growl from him.

"Please, James, I need more."

"Happy to oblige, love."

He thrust his hips upward, drawing a moan from her lips right before he swallowed the sound. One hand gripped her waist, keeping her still while his hips worked to bring them to the brink of bliss. It wasn't enough, the position not granting him enough leverage to properly claim her.

Releasing her lips, he kissed along her jaw until he reached her ear. "Hold on tight, love."

Her legs wrapped around his waist just as he stood, lifting her ass so he remained fully sheathed inside her. Adorably, her eyes widened at his ability to lift her in such a way. Though some of his strength came from his abilities as the beast.

Licking and sucking at her exposed neck, she whimpered and wriggled in his arms, trying to find fiction. He chuckled darkly into her skin. "Impatient, love?"

In answer, she grabbed hold of his shoulders, using them to gain the movement she needed, and *goddess above* did it feel good.

Only managing a few steps into the jungle, he fell to his knees between the trees and brilliant green foliage of Kheli.

Then, like a penitent man before an altar, he laid his forearm against her back, gently laying her in the grass, dirt, and leaves.

She reached up to touch his hair again, but he seized her wrists, pinning them above her head with his left hand.

"Not so fast. I'd like to have a bit of fun first."

He didn't mistake the desire filling her gaze at his words. He smiled devilishly.

Phantom let his other hand drift down the side of her face, grazing his fingertips along her jaw, her neck, her breasts and down her waist. Leaning down, he took one hard nipple into his mouth, drawing a cry of pleasure from her. He teased, using only light touches and flicks to drive her to madness.

Her hips rolled in rebellion, seeking that much-needed friction where they were still joined.

Snapping his hand to her hip, he halted her movements.

"Naughty, naughty. Are you getting greedy, love?" His hand continued down until it reached that sweet spot that had her breath catching. "Do I need to give you some relief before I continue?"

She nodded vigorously.

"No, I want to hear that perfect voice of yours."

"Yes, James, please."

That was all he needed.

His thumb found the perfect spot, and he studied her every breath and cry, seeking out every way he could make her tremble. All the while, his cock remained deep inside her and only jerked every so often. That small movement was enough to make her gasp. She was so sensitive to him. He could watch her bend to his touch all night, never finding his own relief because he just wanted to watch her.

His cock twitched, reminding him that he wouldn't have this control for much longer.

With each breath becoming more labored, she called out his name in the darkness of the night, clutching his cock tightly until she found release.

He pulled out enough to drive back in, adopting a slow rhythm that had her writhing beneath him. He wanted to take every drop of her pleasure until she had nothing left to give, then do it all over again.

Pulling back, he put his weight on his knees and lifted her legs forward until he could get deeper. Her eyes widened at the new sensation, at the feel of how deep he could reach.

"*Mierda!*"

He chuckled at her language before thrusting in again, this time taking on a fast rhythm, one that saw her covered in dirt and grime.

"Keep your legs up for me. That's a good girl. You're so beautiful taking all of me."

Her eyes lit up with the praise. She was so bloody perfect. He couldn't believe she'd fallen for a bastard like him.

"Say you love me."

He needed to hear it. He needed to hear her shout it from a mountain top.

"I love you," she gasped. "Desperately."

"Bloody hell, love." He found his release, sinking into her as far as he could before spilling inside her. Losing his strength, he caught himself with his arms on either side of her head. "I love you too. With everything I am, I love you."

Only then did he notice the soft glow on her skin, in stark contrast to the shadowy depth of his. He panicked, rearing back to get away from her, afraid the shadows would reach for her again, but she stopped him with two gentle hands to his face.

"It's alright. See."

She drew a hand back, and he witnessed the shadows dancing in her light, weaving between her fingers. He no longer heard their whispers.

"Lani?" He asked.

"She's still here, just not present currently."

He thought of Draven and memories rushed to him, the life he once led. It was different from the beast's life, which felt empty and alone aside from Skye's kindness.

Draven's life was complicated, full of love and loss, protecting a misunderstood group of people while also protecting others from them. Phantom expected to feel the memories as his own, but they didn't. Draven's life felt like a story, separate from his own.

"Draven?"

"Gone."

Phantom fell to her side, dragging Rose into his arms and delaying their trip back to the caves for as long as possible. With his love beside him, he wanted to drink in the beauty of the moment, letting happiness wash over him like a wave. He pulled Rose against his chest, nestling his head into her neck and breathing in her perfect scent. Lilacs and jasmine with a faint hint of smoke.

CHAPTER 78

LILAC

SEBASTIAN

Sebastian had made the decision to confront the witch.

He wasn't certain if he had made that decision before he finished the bottle in his hand or after. Why was he holding an empty bottle?

Staring at the dark glass as if it would answer his thoughts he tossed the useless thing behind him. It hit a tree, shattering on impact.

"My apologies," he told the dead bottle, as if that would help.

Indigo ran into the jungle again, and he ran after her, Earhart and Roger cheering him on. But they didn't understand. He wasn't trying to get the woman beneath him. He needed to break her spell, not bloody encourage it.

Leaning on several trees on the way, he caught up to her. Indigo had stopped on a cliff side, overlooking the sea. Without a word, he took to her side, thankful for the solid tree beside him to lean against, patting it softly in gratitude.

Indigo didn't bother to acknowledge him, her face pensive.

He looked out across the glistening water. Davina's light waned, creating a picture across the waves. Just beside the silver moon, a hint of lilac suggested the rising of Macha's moon.

Glancing back to Indigo, he admired the way the silver moonlight softened her beautiful skin. Her lips were so full, he longed to kiss them. Had he ever wanted to kiss a woman so much in his life or was that the moonshine talking?

Why had he followed her out here? To kiss her?

Yes, that must be it.

However, with the bile coating his throat, he thought better of that plan. He lowered his head, willing the feeling to pass before he spilled his guts on the grass.

With a closer inspection of the grass beneath his feet, he recognized the spot. When had he been here before?

Flashes of a memory reminded him.

A bloodied hand. An old book. Tentacles.

His blood froze to ice.

"I've been thinking about what Angelica said before, about the tattoo." Indigo's voice was so soft he had to inch closer to hear it. It absolutely was not because he wanted to brush her hand with his own. "Not her own, but how she witnessed Phantom earn one. I'd felt it myself, the tentacles on his neck, there's an energy there that can only belong to Nemain. I've always thought that it was the way he earned his ship and crew."

Sebastian didn't like thinking of it, the weight of Phantom's decision, how he begged for his friend not to damn his own soul.

"It wasn't until Angelica claimed she had seen it happen that I questioned my assumptions. She was not present when *Nemain's Revenge* was commandeered."

Indigo put together too much, revealing the secrets that he'd kept so closely guarded for so long. He blinked as if that would clear the fog in his mind. Then maybe he could say something, stop her from putting the pieces together.

"There is great energy in this spot." Indigo didn't look back, her voice softer than usual. "As if Davina herself has declared a moment here as fate altering." Indigo's eyes found him in the dark, fear widening them. Had he ever seen her afraid before? "What happened?"

He blinked more, wishing desperately he hadn't drunk at all. "I—"

"Don't deny that you know. Your approach made the energy

here sing louder." There was something urgent in her violet glowing eyes, begging him to listen.

He bowed his head, letting her see how much the memory pained him.

"Captain Pike tried to take the island long before James became a pirate. We scared him and his crew off, but we knew the moment he left that he would be back."

"For his daughter?"

Sebastian nodded, wincing as he put a hand to his head to stop the spinning. "I begged him not to use the book, but it forced me away like it wanted him to use it."

"The grimoire?"

Sebastian nodded again, swallowing the bile caught in his throat. "Pike's ship went down, and that tattoo appeared on James' skin." The horrifying image came back to him, of lilac sails, giant tentacles, and a crew screaming for their lives.

Indigo's eyes focused back to the horizon, terror lacing her eyes.

"Why do you ask? What difference does it make?"

Indigo didn't look at him, instead she kept staring at the sea. "Macha's moon isn't meant to reappear for another night. So, what is that?"

Sebastian focused on the horizon with her, finding that speck of lilac, but if it wasn't the moon—

His heart stopped in his chest.

Captain Phantom
WILL RETURN

Also by McKenzie A Hatton

Nemain's Revenge Series

Prequel: The First Mate of Nemain's Revenge

Book 1: The Captain of Nemain's Revenge

Book 2: The Siren of Samsara

Book 3: The Demons of Draiocht

Book 4: TBA

ACKNOWLEDGMENTS

Phew...

This book was a challenge for me as an author. It required a lot of rewrites and edits that the lovely Rachel helped me get through. The darker themes weighed on me more even if I really enjoy how it turned out.

I'm going to let you in on a little secret. My chapter titles are easter eggs. Some are obvious Shakespeare, Odyssey, or Taylor Swift references but some are more subtle. I always loved fore-shadowing in my stories and I'd love to hear some of your theories of what will come.

I want to shoutout to my alpha reader, Ana, who is also co-writing another project with me. You've helped a lot with the story and shaping it into what it has become.

Also to my husband, Brenton, for all the love and support. And for being patient.

My cover artist, Maria Spada, for doing it again and creating a beautiful cover that my readers are already obsessed with.

To @azurityart for bringing my characters to life!

To @sovana.art for bringing my scenes to life!

To Rachel, who goes above and beyond what an editor would normally do. You've truly made all of this possible for me and I'm extremely grateful.

Last, but not least, my readers. I love how positive and wonderful you guys are. All of you have been so patient and supportive waiting for this book. I can't thank you enough!

ABOUT THE AUTHOR

McKenzie A Hatton's ideal night is a glass of wine and a good book. She grew up in the rolling hills of Oregon, spending time with family at the beach, and petting every animal who would let her.

McKenzie is a world traveler with a town in Ireland, Killarney, being her favorite. She is lucky to have the chance to travel and to write, the two things that make up her passions.

www.ingramcontent.com/pod-product-compliance
Lightning Source LLC
Chambersburg PA
CBHW070300310726

48976CB00005B/1501